SHELBY FOOTE

Jordan County

Although he now makes his home in Memphis, Tennessee, Shelby Foote comes from a long line of Mississippians. He was born in Greenville, Mississippi, and attended school there until he entered the University of North Carolina. During World War II he served in the European theater as a captain of field artillery. He has written six novels: *Tournament*, *Follow Me Down*, *Love in a Dry Season*, *Shiloh*, *Jordan County*, and *September September*. He was awarded three Guggenheim fellowships during the course of writing his monumental three-volume history, *The Civil War: A Narrative*.

ALSO BY
SHELBY FOOTE

Tournament
Follow Me Down
Love in a Dry Season
Shiloh
September September

The Civil War: A Narrative
VOLUME I. *Fort Sumter to Perryville*
VOLUME II. *Fredericksburg to Meridian*
VOLUME III. *Red River to Appomattox*

JORDAN COUNTY

COUNTY

A Landscape in Narrative

by SHELBY FOOTE

VINTAGE BOOKS
A DIVISION OF RANDOM HOUSE, INC.
NEW YORK

First Vintage Books Edition, June 1992

Library of Congress Cataloging-in-Publication Data
Foote, Shelby.
Jordan County : a landscape in narrative / Shelby Foote. — 1st Vintage Books ed.
p.   cm.
ISBN 0-679-73616-6
1. Mississippi—History—Fiction.   I. Title.
PS3511.0348J67   1992
813'.54—dc20   91-50723
CIP

Manufactured in the United States of America
10 9 8 7 6 5 4 3 2 1

CONTENTS

JORDAN COUNTY

RAIN DOWN HOME

Dawn broke somewhere up the line, pearly under a drizzle of rain, but presently the rain left off and the flat eastern rim of earth was tinted rose. The sun came up fast, dark red while still half hidden, the color of blood, then fiery as it bounced clear of the landline, shining on the picked-over cotton that hung in bluing skeins on dead brown stalks. Ahead the engine was rounding a curve and suddenly a plume of steam was balanced on the whistle; it screamed, much as a hound will bay once in full course for no reason at all; then the plume disappeared and it hushed. The rain returned but the sun still shone, pale yellow through the mizzle. "I ought to watch," the young man told himself. He spoke aloud. But that was the last he remembered. He slid back into drowsiness and slumber, taking with him only the present sensations of dusty plush and cinders and vibration.

"Dont," he said. The hand nudged at his shoulder again and the voice came back, as if from a long way off.

"Bristol," it said. "All out."

He saw the hand, the black cuff with its gold-thread stars and bars of longterm service toward retirement, and looking up he saw the conductor himself, the face with its halo of white hair, the broken veins of the nose, the jowls and dewlap. "Hey?"

"End of the line. All out for Bristol."

Then he woke. It was there, outside the window, in broad open daylight. He had stayed awake all night, riding south out of Memphis through the hundred-odd miles of blackness, with only the soft gold gleam of cabin lanterns scattered at random across the fields and the infrequent sudden garish burst of streetlights announcing towns, and then had slept through the arrival. "Thanks," he said.

Rising — he was about twenty-five, rumpled and unshaven after the all-night trainride — he took his suitcase from the overhead rack and carried it down the aisle of the empty coach. At the door onto the rear platform he turned suddenly, looking back, and saw what he had known he would see. The conductor stood there, watching him, the ticket punch in his left hand glinting highlight. He narrowed his eyes and pulled his chin down. "Whats the matter?" he said. "You think I'm drunk or something?" The conductor shrugged and turned away. He smiled, swung the door ajar, and stepped onto the platform.

Brilliant early morning sunlight struck him across the eyes as he came down the iron steps to where the flagman stood on the concrete quay, the brass buttons on his coat as bright as the sun itself. "Mississippi, hey?" the young man cried. He smiled as he spoke.

"Thats right," the flagman said. "Home again."

"Jordan County. You think itll rain?"

"Oh sure. Cotton's all in: why not?"

"Why not," he said, waving his hand, and went into the depot.

He intended to leave his bag with the ticket agent, but the agent was busy at his window with three Negroes. Grave-faced, they wore funeral clothes, dark suits with heavy watch chains and boiled collars. The agent was scratching his head, grave-faced too. They had accompanied a dead friend to the station; they wanted to ship him to Vicksburg in his coffin. That was easy enough. The problem was they wanted him

sent back two days later for a second funeral. He had lived
both in Vicksburg and in Bristol, with lodge brothers and relatives in each, and since the widow insisted on burial here, they
figured it would be cheaper, more convenient all around, that
is, to send him to Vicksburg so his friends could see him there,
laid out in style, than it would be for all those people to leave
their jobs and buy railroad tickets to come up here and see him.
Then they would ship him back to Bristol for the second
funeral and the burial. That made sense; the trouble lay in the
question of fares. First-class was the normal rate, but the agent
was not so sure about the propriety of selling a round-trip
ticket to a corpse. His friends maintained he was entitled to it,
but the agent was doubtful; he was not even sure but what it
might be sacrilegious. "I'll call the office and get a ruling," he
was saying, still scratching his head, as the young man left with
the suitcase.

Again in brilliant sunlight he walked westward down the
main street of the town. Cars went past or paused at intersec-
tions, obedient to the traffic lights suspended between poles,
the lidless glare of red and green, the momentary blink of
amber, relaying the orders of some central brain, peremptory,
electric, and unthinking. The young man frowned. When he
had gone two blocks he stopped and gazed across the street at
a department store with a new façade of imitation marble that
was mottled like a pinto; *Goodblood's* it said in a flowing script
across the pony-colored front. He shook his head. Then as he
stood looking down the line of bright new parking meters,
each with its clockwork entrails ticking off the time between
now and the red flag of violation, he saw a man coming toward
him. The man walked with his head tipped forward, a worried
expression on his face. He stopped, patting his pockets, preoccupied, and the young man spoke.

"They changed it," he said to the man. "They changed it
on me while my back was turned."

"How's that?" The worried look did not leave the man's face.

"The town. They changed it. It's all new."

"Yes; it's growing," the man said. He nodded once and hurried on, preoccupied, patting his pockets.

"Hey!" The man did not glance back; he was already out of earshot. "You didnt know me, did you?" the young man said, standing at the curb with the suitcase held against his leg. "You didnt know little Pauly Green that used to deliver your paper. Did you, Mr Nowell?"

Just then a cloud blew past the sun. The glitter left the rain-washed streets but then came back as bright as ever; the cloud was gone and the parking meters twinkled in steady metallic progression along the curb. He turned to go, swinging the suitcase clear of his leg, and as he turned he saw an envelope lying face-down on the sidewalk. Something was written on the flap. Bending forward Pauly read the almost childish script. *Write soon!!* PS. *I am seventeen now. My birthday was Fri 13, I hope not bad luck.* He picked it up. When he turned it over he saw that the stamp had not been canceled and the address, damp from contact with the sidewalk, was written in the same adolescent scrawl. *Miss Norma Jean Purdy, Box 221 Route 7, Indemnity, Miss.* He turned it over again. The flap had come unglued, so he opened it and took out a sheet of blue-lined paper with three loose-leaf holes down the left margin. Another cloud blew past the sun while he read. The paper went from dazzling white to gray, then back to dazzling.

> *Dear Norma Jean:*
>
> *I was glad to get your letter. I am sorry I havent written you before now. I guess my letter got pretty dull, no exciting news. But I will try to write more intresting letters so you wont mind writing.*
>
> *I had a grand time at Ole Miss. If you had been there it would have been complete.*
>
> *We went Fri morning, got there about 10:00. We rehersed so much I cant hardly talk now. There was a party at the gym Friday night. I had a good time. I met a boy from Isstabula I think you spell it. He*

asked me to walk back to the dormitory but I refused because I do not like to go with just anybody. Saturday I had a real good time but made my self so tired walking and seeing everything on the campus. The boys were so nice, college boys. Sometimes we would be walking down the side walk and they would whistle at us.

I wish you could come see me sometimes, I sure would enjoy your visit. It wont be long until Xmas. I hope you can come and stay with me some. We could go on a shopping spree or something, so please come to see me when you can.

Hope you have good luck with your new boy friend. Hope you will get or got to go on the hay ride with him. Write me real soon. Love,

ALICE

Please write soon!! I am trying to make my letters more intresting.

Love & xxxx.

PS. *Went to the revile last night. That sure is a good preacher that is holding it. His name in Juny Lynch. He is a Methodist.*

Pauly smiled. The post office was one block farther; as he went past the mailbox he sealed the sticky flap again and dropped the letter into the slot. "Go where you belong, where youre not wanted," he told it as it fell from sight. As always, when he turned it loose there was the sense of having done something irretrievable. Another cloud went over the sun, but this time it did not pass. Rain began to fall and he hurried to the door of a café in the middle of the block. Inside, he sat on a stool at the counter, the suitcase up-ended on the floor beside him. "What will it be?" the waitress said.

"Whats good?"

"You want breakfast?"

"Breakfast." He nodded and the waitress watched him across

the glass of water she had brought. "Whats good?" He smiled but she did not smile back. Her nails were coral; they looked detachable, like earrings bought in a shop. She was no longer young and crow's feet were etched at the outward corners of her eyes.

"It's all good."

"Is the bacon good?"

"It's all good," she said mournfully.

"O.K. Give me ham and eggs. Coffee now."

"How you want the eggs?"

"What?"

"How you want them fixed?"

"Mm — I dont care. Looking at me, I reckon."

"Two!" she cried over her shoulder, in the direction of the order window. "Straight up, with ham!"

"Yao," a voice said from the kitchen.

When she returned from the coffee urn and set the thick white cup and saucer on the counter, he was waiting. He leaned forward and asked her, stiff-lipped with the steam from the coffee rising about his face: "Why doesnt everybody love each other?"

"Do what?"

"Love each other. Why dont they love each other?"

"Say, what are you anyhow? Some kind of a nut?"

"No — really. Why not?" He was not discouraged. He spoke stiff-lipped, his face wreathed with steam. "Were you ever wrapped in wet sheets, wrapped up tight? Thats what they need, and then theyd love each other. I'm telling you. Wrap them up, good and tight, leave them there for a while like that, then turn them loose, and believe me theyd love each other."

"Look," she said. "I'm busy."

She went on down the counter and did not come near him again until she brought the ham and eggs. Then she only set them down in passing; she kept moving, out of reach. He ate hungrily, all of it, including three slices of toast, and when he had finished he took up the suitcase and started for the door.

The Greek proprietor stood at the cash register. He had the drawer open, looking at his money. Pauly paid for the meal and turned to leave. Then he turned back. He was blond and short, with wide shoulders, small gray eyes, and an aggressive chin. "Say," he said. The Greek looked up from the cash drawer. "Could I leave this here for a while?" He raised the suitcase and lowered it again.

"All right," the Greek said. "Put back here. But not responsible, unnerstand?"

"Sure. I'll be right back."

"Ho K."

When he had put the suitcase behind the plywood partition he went to the front door and stood looking through the glass. A fine rain was still falling but there were pale gray shadows on the sidewalk. Pauly opened the door and saw the sun through the mizzling rain. "What do you know," he cried over his shoulder. "The devil is beating his wife."

He turned up the collar of his coat and went out into the rain, going west still, toward the river. The levee was a block and a half away, with the veterans' sign in front of it, blue and white except for the red stars and stripes on the flag in the middle. He walked fast and soon he stood in front of it, holding his collar with both hands at his throat. The sign had words in big letters on both sides of the flag. To the left it said: IN MEMORY OF THOSE WHO SERVED IN WORLD WAR TWO, and on the opposite side, in balance: MAY THE SPIRIT OF OUR BOYS WHO FELL IN BATTLE LIVE FOREVER. He had heard about that. Originally it was intended to put the names of the war dead on the signboard, the whites down one side and the Negroes down the other, with the American flag between. But the notion of having them all on one board caused so much ugly feeling — there was even some talk of dynamite, for example — that the service club whose project it was took a vote and decided that it would be better just to say something fitting about the spirit of our boys. That was what they did, and already it had begun to look a bit weathered around the edges. Pauly stood in the

rain, looking at it and holding his collar close at the throat. His
hair was all the way wet by now and the rain ran in trickles
down his face.

Presently he walked around the sign and climbed the levee,
no easy job for the grass was slippery and under it there was
mud. When he reached the crest the rain stopped as if by
signal; his shadow darkened on the grass, and below him lay
the river, the Mississippi. Tawny, wide, dimpled and swirled
by eddies, it sparkled in the sunlight as it swept along to the
south. Pauly was alone up here and a cold wind blew against
his face. Behind him Bristol thrust its steeples through the
overarching trees. "Hello, big river," he said. He felt better
now. He came down, slipping and smiling. "Thats one big
river," he said.

He did not stop at the base of the levee; he kept going east,
back past the café where he had left his suitcase, past the depot
— wondering if the corpse had got its round-trip ticket — past
the courthouse where the Confederate soldier watched from
his marble shaft, past the ramped tracks of the C&B, and on
out that same street, until finally he came to a park: WINGATE
PARK it was called on a wrought-iron arch above the entrance.
Sunlight glittered on the rain-washed gravel paths; the grass
was still green after the first cold snap of late November. He
entered the park and sat on a circular bench that was built
around the trunk of a big oak. Despite the coolness he took off
his damp coat and sat with it folded across his lap. The stubble
of beard was more obvious now, with a coppery glint in the
sunshine. His clothes were even more rumpled. The whites of
his eyes were threaded with red and each lid showed the edge
of its red lining. He leaned back against the tree, and almost
immediately he was asleep.

Singing woke him. At first he did not know where he was,
nor then how long he had been there. The singer was a little
girl who was playing with two dolls about five yards from
the bench. She wore a short wool skirt, a beret, and a corduroy
jacket. "Hello," Pauly said. She did not hear him. He leaned
forward, hands on his knees, and said it again. "Hel-lo."

Turning her head she looked at him and her eyes were large and dark. She was very pretty. "Hello," she said.

"What are you playing?"

"Dolls."

"Oh. Have they got names?"

"Yes."

"Tell me, are they nice names?"

"Nice," she said.

"What, for instance?"

"I'm sorry. Mummy says I mustnt talk to strangers."

"Well, you just tell your mummy I said she's wrong. Some of the nicest people I ever knew were strangers."

She smiled at this and he smiled back. Then: "Sal Ann," they heard a flat voice say, and Pauly saw a young Negress sitting on a nearby bench, holding a multicolored booklet in both hands. She wore loafers with new pennies in the flaps and bright green socks. "Come play over here," she said. Her voice was expressionless; she did not look at Pauly. Sally Ann took up her dolls.

"I have to go."

"You do?"

"Oh yes. She's my nurse."

"I know," he said. "Ive had them myself. Goodbye."

"Goodbye."

He watched her go, and suddenly feeling the chill he put his coat on. Presently, when the nurse had finished her comic book — *Bat Man* was its title; she seemed to have derived small pleasure from it — she rose and beckoned to the little girl. "Time for your nap," she said. Leaving by way of the arch they passed a man who walked bent forward, leaning on a cane. As he drew closer Pauly saw that he was old and there was pain in his face. Then he saw Pauly and turned aside, taking the bench where the nurse had read through *Bat Man*. He sat with the cane planted stiffly between his shoes, both hands on the crook, and his face was empty except for the lines of pain.

The sun was past the overhead. Pauly rose abruptly and

went to the old man's bench. From closer he saw that he was poor as well as old. His shoes were broken and there were holes in the ankles of his cotton socks. The cuffs of his shirt were badly frayed, as was the collar, and where the button was missing the points bunched forward, overlapping the knot of his tie, which had been tied and re-tied so often in the same place that the knot looked as tight and hard as a little piece of gravel. His coat, loose-fitting and almost as rumpled as Pauly's own, gave him a scarecrow aspect. When he turned his head Pauly saw that the pain was old, like the rest of him; he had lived with it for years. "How do," he said.

"Hello. Could I sit down and talk?"

"All right."

Pauly sat beside him on the bench, and again that stiff-lipped expression came onto his face. "Ive been trying to figure," he said. He paused and the old man watched him, unsurprised. "I came back from the war and all, back here where I was born and raised, and people dont even know me on the street. I see things all around me and it tears me up inside. A letter on the sidewalk, say, from a teen-age girl reaching out for love and already knowing she wont find it . . . Sad things, terrible things happen to people! Do you realize that right this minute there are people all over the world crying, weeping, lying awake in their beds at night, smoking cigarettes till their gums are sore, and looking up at the ceiling like they thought theyd find the answer written there? Kicked in the teeth, insulted, full of misery the way a glass can get so full it bulges at the brim with surface tension — what does it mean? What does it mean? It's got to mean something, all that suffering."

"It's just people, the way they are," the old man said. For a moment he was quiet. Then he added: "They got away from God."

"God? Whats God got to do with it? What does He care?"

"Maybe they just werent meant to be happy, then."

"No! Thats not true!" Pauly jerked his hands as he spoke,

clenching and unclenching his fists. "I want to live in the world but I dont understand, and until I can understand I cant live. Why wont people be happy? Not cant: *wont*."

"I dont know," the old man said. He looked away, across the park. "Ive been here going on eighty-seven years and I dont know. My wife died of a cancer until finally all that was left was teeth and eyes and yelling, like some animal. I asked myself all those things: 'What does it mean? What does it mean?' Then she died. She'd been a beautiful woman in her day, and she wound up like a run-over cat. I asked myself, again and again: 'What does it mean? What does it mean?' And you know, I finally found the answer; one answer, anyhow. It dont mean a thing. Nothing. Why should it mean anything? I stopped thinking about it is what I finally did. It's what you better do, too. Dont think about it. Theyll lock you up, you keep at it too long. They wanted to lock me up, down at Whitfield, but I quit thinking about it and they let me alone. Now they say I'm harmless. And I am."

The stiff-lipped expression had turned to horror; Pauly jumped up. He was about to speak, but then instead he turned and walked away. Near the entrance he looked back. The old man was just sitting there, his hands on the crook of the cane; he looked out across the park, the graveled paths glittering in the sunlight; he sat there, empty-eyed, and the young man might never have spoken to him at all. Pauly went under the wrought-iron arch. He walked three blocks fast, then three blocks slow, and by that time he was back in front of the courthouse, looking up at the Confederate, the blank stone eyeballs under the wide-brimmed hat. Within the next three blocks he passed the depot and was within sight of the post office. He went past it, walking fast again, and re-entered the café.

He took a booth this time, one in back. The same waitress came with a glass of water as before, still wearing the detachable-looking nails and the crow's feet at the corners of her eyes. "Hello," he said.

"What will it be?"

"Look: I'm sorry about all that other. I meant it, but I'm sorry I bothered you with it's what I mean. I was lonesome."

"I'm real busy. What will it be?"

This was not true. There were only a few people in the place, three men drinking beer in a booth across the way and three others seated singly on the stools along the counter. It was two oclock, the postlunch lull. "O.K. Whats good?" he asked. She was about to speak but he held up one hand, pontifical. "It's *all* good," he said mournfully. "Bring me liver and onions. Coffee. Apple pie. Can you do that?"

"All right," she said.

He went back to the men's room, the walls of which were penciled with obscenities so crowded that the later entries had had to be squeezed into the margins and even between the lines of the earlier ones. Pauly tried to close his eyes to them, pictures and text, just as he tried to close his nostrils against the stench of creosote and urine, but the two attempts were equally unsuccessful. *Kilroy was here* was scrawled in several places, opposite one of which someone had written: *A good place for him.*

When Pauly returned to the booth he saw through the front window that the rain had come on again, no drizzle now, but true rain, big drops pattering hard against the glass. Outside, the street was darkened and the buildings were hidden across the way.

"Say, thats *rain*," he said to the waitress as she set the food in front of him.

"Yes," she said, and left.

While he ate he heard one of the beer drinkers in the adjoining booth tell the other two a story. He was a young businessman but he broadened his accent, pretending to be more country than he was. "There was this scratch farmer, a white man working about sixty acres. But it was a wet year and the weeds began to get out of control, so he brought in some help, a dozen hoe-hands, and went down to the field to work alongside them. One of the women was brown-skinned, not yet middle aged, and he took him a notion. So he called her aside where the cotton was high, and the two of them lay down between the rows. Well, his wife came to the field about this time, bringing a pail of water, and she walked right up on them in the act. When he saw her he jumped up and began to run. She yelled after him: 'You, Ephraim! It aint no use to run. You know I caught you!' 'Yessum,' he said, 'I know you did. But I believe I'll run a little ways anyhow.' "

There was laughter, including the laughter of the man who told the story, and when it died down, one of the other beer drinkers said, "I can see how that might help." They laughed again.

Pauly frowned. He motioned to the waitress and she came over, still with the mistrustful look. "Bring me another cup of coffee with that," he told her, pointing at the pie. She brought it, and as she set it down in front of him he said, "I was wrong, baby, wrong and never wronger. It's not love they need. I know what they need. And I'm the one can give it to them, too. Wait till I drink this." He put three big spoonfuls of sugar into the coffee and stirred in the jug of cream. The waitress went away but he did not notice. His face was not stiff-lipped now. He looked happy, with a peculiar glint to his eyes.

When he had finished the coffee he rose from the booth and went up front, where the Greek stood looking into the register. "Hand me my suitcase, will you, bud?"

"Here," the Greek said, and held the swing door ajar.

"Thanks." Pauly leaned inside and took up the suitcase.

He came back to the booth with it. The waitress was still there, removing the dishes, all except the uneaten pie, but he did not look at her. He set the suitcase on the floor and opened it. From the jumbled disorder of faded khaki and books and shaving gear he took out an Army .45 and four loaded clips. He set them on the table, then turned back to close the bag. "Wait," he said. "Lets do this right." He rooted in the suit-

case until he found what he was looking for — an Expert
marksmanship badge, the maltese cross inclosed in a silver
wreath, with three bars suspended beneath it like a ladder;
Pistol, Pistol, Pistol, it said on the rungs. He pinned the badge
to the rumpled lapel of his coat, and took up the pistol, drawing
back the slide. It went back with a dry, thick, deadly sound,
then forward with a snick, the hammer cocked. "Now," he
said. He was talking to himself by then, for the waitress was
nowhere in sight.

The first shot hit the coffee urn dead center and a half-inch
amber stream came spouting from the hole the bullet made.
He swung on to the right where the Greek stood round-eyed,
his hands on the open drawer, looking toward the sound of
the explosion. "You and your goddam money," Pauly said.
"You wouldnt even hand a man a suitcase." He took careful
aim and shot him in the head. As the Greek went down he
pushed with both hands, closing the cash drawer. So Pauly
took two shots at the register. The second hit something vital
and the drawer ran out again, ringing a bell. "Cigar!" he cried,
and turned to look for other targets.

He found plenty of them — the light fixtures, the mirror
behind the counter, the glasses racked along the wall, even
the little cream jugs arranged on a tray beside a spigot. Each
gave off its particular brand of fireworks when hit. The cream
jugs were especially amusing, for they flew in all directions.
He had thirty-five shots and he took his time, replacing the
empty clips methodically. "This is doing me a lot of good,"
he said at one point, and indeed it seemed to be true; he appeared to enjoy the whole display, from start to finish. The
beer drinkers had disappeared, along with the three men who
had sat at the counter. He had the place to himself. It was
very quiet between shots. Between the sharp, popping explosions of cartridges he heard the rain murmur against the plate
glass window and the low moans of the Greek proprietor from
somewhere down behind the open register.

Though it seemed considerably longer to those who crouched

beneath the tables and behind the counter, the whole affair took less than five minutes by the clock. The thing that frightened them most, they said when they told about it later, was the way the shooter kept laughing between shots. He was sitting there eating the pie, quite happy, with the empty pistol and the four empty clips on the table in front of him, when the police arrived. He even smiled when they shook him, roughed him up. "Do your duty, men," he said, "just like I did mine."

Next day it was in all the papers, how he shot up the place for no reason at all. The Greek proprietor, whose injury had been more bloody than serious — all he lost was the lobe from one of his ears — used that day to date things from, the way old people once spoke of falling stars. The waitress was quoted too: "I knew it was something wrong with that one from the minute I laid eyes on him." DERANGED VETERAN the headlines called him, and the stories gave a list of the various institutions he had been in and out of since the war. Everyone agreed that that was what he was, all right, deranged.

RIDE OUT

The state executioner had set up the portable electric chair in a cell on the lower floor; now he was testing his circuits. Whenever the switch clicked there was a pulsing hum and an odor of heated copper. The turnkey, who had helped with the installation, watched the rubber-insulated cable that ran like a long dusty blacksnake from a connection at the back, through the window bars, to the generator in a truck parked in the cool predawn darkness of the jailyard. He watched as if he expected it to writhe like a pressure hose with every surge of current — as if any force with that much power must have body, too — but it lay in loose coils without motion. Low and wide, with heavy arms and legs, the chair had an unfinished look; the workman, a clumsy copyist of Louis Seize pieces, might have dropped his tools, dissatisfied, and walked away. It had been invented and built six months before, on order from the Mississippi legislature, by a New Orleans electrician who stipulated that he was to receive no profit from the job. Luke Jeffcoat, the executioner, was not so squeamish. He called it "my old shocking chair."

Deep creases extended from the wings of his nose to the corners of his mouth. Under the glare from the unshaded bulb, they appeared to have been carved there, exaggerated like the lines on a tragedy mask. Tall and thin, about forty, he worked in a sleeveless undershirt. Tattooed snakes ran down his arms and spread their heads on the backs of his hands. Other, more intimate designs were hidden under his clothes — a three-bladed marine propeller on each cheek of his fundament, for instance, and a bee in a particular place, which he called "my old stingaree." He hummed as he worked. It was low and within a narrow range, curiously like the hum of the generator.

Presently three men came into the cell. The first two, the sheriff and myself — I am county physician — were required by law to be there. But the third, the district attorney, came of his own accord: "to see this thing I'll be sending them to," he had said that afternoon, for he was young and recently elected; this had been his first death-penalty conviction. Entering, the sheriff jerked his thumb toward the window. "Who's that out there?" he asked the turnkey. We had seen them as we came in, a man and a woman on the seat of a wagon under a bug-swirled arc light fifty yards down the alley, both of them hunched with waiting. Two mules dozed in the traces, knees locked, ears slanted forward, and a long box of unpainted pine lay like a pale six-sided shadow in the bed of the wagon.

"It's his mamma," the turnkey said. His name was Jeffcoat too; he and the executioner were cousins. "She rented a dray and bought herself a box to carry him home in. I told her the county would furnish him one, but she said she wanted her own. Yair. They been there since before midnight, sitting like that; theyve got so they dont even slap at the bugs. Just after they got here I went up and took the horn away from him."

"How is he?"

"I think he's sleeping. Anyhow he's quiet. Hoskins is up there with him."

The sheriff took out his watch, a big one in a silver hunting case. He opened it, then snapped it shut with a sound like a pistol shot. "Three thirty," he said morosely. "Where's Doc Benson?"

I said, "He told me he'd be here by three fifteen. But it dont really matter, does it?"

"The law says two doctors, we'll have two doctors." He shook his head, red-faced, with bulging eyes. This was Jordan County's first electrocution and he didnt like it. "Damn these new-fangled inventions anyhow. The old rope and trapdoor method suited me fine."

We heard the sudden tearing sound of tires on gravel, an automobile door being slammed; then Dr Benson came in. He was rubbing his palms and his spectacles glinted fiery in the glare. "Sorry I'm late," he said. "I got held up."

"We arent ready anyhow," I told him.

Just then, however, Jeffcoat threw the switch for the final test, and again there was that pulsing hum, almost a throb, and the faint odor of heated copper. He smiled, then went to the washstand in the corner, soaped his hands, rinsed them under the tap, and dried them carefully on his undershirt.

"All right, sheriff," he said: "I'm ready if he is."

It may be I had seen him before. It seems likely, even. But so far as I know — since, with his shaved head and slit trousers and the fear and sickness in his face, he probably did not resemble himself much anyhow — my first sight of him was when they brought him into the cell a few minutes later. During the past twelve years I have learned his story and I intend to set it down, from beginning to end. I saw only the closing scene, as I said, but four people who knew him well have given me particulars. These were his mother, Nora Conway, a cook here in Bristol; Oscar Bailey, called Blind Bailey, a pianist in a local Negro dancehall; Pearly Jefferson, the New Orleans jazz musician, and Harry Van, the New England composer. In many cases I have merely transcribed notes of conversations with these four, or letters from them, and I want to state my obligations at the outset. There was also a young woman, Julia Kinship, but I have been unable to find her; I understand she went North. At any rate, if ever this gets printed I hope she sees it.

He was born in a time of high water, the stormy May of 1913, in a Red Cross tent on the levee at the foot of the main street of Bristol, Mississippi. His mother was fifteen the month before. The birth was not due until six weeks later, but in the excitement of being herded, along with three or four hundred other Negroes, onto the only high ground within seventy miles, Nora became alarmed and the pains came on her. In a steady drizzle of rain, while water purled up the slope toward where she lay on a strip of salvaged awning, she moaned and bellered through five hours of labor. Between whiles she heard the rain murmur against the canvas, a spooky sound. When the flood reached the level of the river on the opposite side, and therefore ceased its advance up the levee, the child was born. Someone among the white refugee families in the adjoining camp sent her a paper sack of candy. The midwife swaddled the child and placed it beside her. She was content, holding her son against her breast and dissolving a lemon drop in her cheek; but she wished the father was there.

His name was Boola Durfee; originally he was from the lower delta, down around Nitta Yuma, son of a freedwoman and a halfbreed Choctaw blacksmith. Nora was with him less than two weeks, in September of the year before, when the big warm moon of late summer glazed the fields and gilded the corrugated metal roofs of the churches and barrelhouses where he played engagements while she waited outside, too young to enter. A gaunt, high-cheekboned man, he had no home; he roamed the country, tall and flat-chested, with his guitar and his songs. He had warned her at the outset.

"I got a itchy heel," he said. "Some morning, doll baby, youll wake up and find me gone."

That was the way it turned out. The following week she woke with the sun in her eyes and found herself alone on the

pallet bed. She had expected this; she had not needed the warning, but at the time she told herself it was worth it. Later she
was not so sure. For the next ten years she would hear people
mention having seen him, sometimes in far places, Arkansas
and Alabama and up in Tennessee, sometimes nearby, Moorhead and Holly Knowe and Midnight, still playing for what
he called sukey jumps. But Nora never saw him again. She
made it a point never to ask about him or even show an interest when his name came up. At first this indifference was a
pretense. Later it was a habit, and quite real. Then she heard
that he had been killed in a cutting fight, over near Itta Bena,
when some man got jealous.

She gave the child its father's name, Durfee, for a first name,
and attached her family name, Conway, for a surname. By
pronunciation, Durfee became Duffy, which later was shortened to Duff, and that was how he came to be called Duff
Conway.

After the water went down she got a job as maid in a cotton
factor's house, and when the cook left three years later Nora
took her place. She lived alone with her child in a two-room
cabin in a section of Bristol known as Lick Skillet. When she
had saved twelve dollars out of her weekly salary of three-
fifty, she bought herself a mailorder pistol, a big one, nickel
plated, which she kept in a bureau drawer in the front room,
near her bed, so that she could turn to it in a time of trouble,
as other women would turn to a man.

Aborted thus into a flooded world, Duff was undersized and
sickly, cocoa-colored and solemn as a papoose. The red in
his skin was like a warning sign to Nora. If the boy could
inherit the Choctaw pigment and the pointed cheekbones, she
reasoned that he might also inherit the guitar-calloused thumb
and the itchy heel. So she kept him by her, in her cabin, at
church, and at the cotton factor's house, where at first she
put him in a crib on the back porch and later propped him
on a chair in one corner of the kitchen. Perched on the tall
straight-back chair he passed the waking hours of early child-

hood amid a clatter of pots and pans in an atmosphere of flour and frying food, his feet suspended ten inches clear of the floor, then six inches, then two inches, then touching it; then he was six and his mother enrolled him in school. Young enough herself to be mistaken for one of the girls in the upper grades, she would take him there every morning and call for him every afternoon.

"You going to mount to something," she told him. "Study hard and stay away from riffraff."

That was how it went; she sought to come between him and whatever shocks might be in store. Then on an April afternoon when Duff was in the fifth grade she missed him among the children trooping out of school. She went by the cabin, thinking perhaps he would get there before her, but he was not there. When she had waited as long as she could, muttering alternate imprecations and prayers, she went back to the cotton factor's house to fix supper, and when she came home that night Duff was in bed, asleep. She stood over him for a moment, watching. Then she shook him. "Where you been?" she shouted while he rubbed his eyes with his fists.

"Lemmy lone."

"Where you been all day?"

"Lemmy lone, mamma. I'm sleepy."

"Sleepy!" She shook him further awake. "Where you been, boy, till all hours of the night? Answer me when I'm talking to you!"

She whipped him. But he cried himself back to sleep without telling her anything, and four days later it happened again.

This time she went looking for him. On Bantam Street, in Bristol's redlight district, she found a crowd gathered around something on the sidewalk. Mostly silk-shirted bucks and their bright-dressed women, they were standing so closely packed that Nora could not see what they were watching but she heard strange music. She elbowed her way toward the center. There she saw four small boys performing on four outlandish instruments, including a jug, a banjo made from a cigar box and a length of lath, a jew's harp, and a set of drums invented from a battered suitcase top and a sawhorse with three stove lids suspended from the crosspiece.

Duff was the drummer. He sat on an upended cracker box, drumming steadily with a pair of chair rungs. Oblivious, he was entering a solo break, a caricature of a real full-sized drummer — head turned sideways down near one shoulder, eyes tight shut, lower lip sucked between his teeth — when Nora caught him by the arm, hauled him off the box, and snatched him through the crowd.

"Wait up, mamma," he wailed, straining back and waving the chair rungs; "I got to get my drums!"

Nora shook him until his teeth rattled above the laughter of the crowd. "Wait till I get you home," she said. "I'll drum you."

He was twelve the following month. For nearly two years after the Bantam Street incident it was a contest between mother and son, she trying in the only way she knew to keep him from becoming what his father had been, and he revolting against being tied to her apron strings. The four-piece band had been organized at school by the boy who played the cigarbox banjo. At first they had practiced only during the noon recess, but after a while that was not enough. They began to cut school, and then they went professional, playing on street corners for nickels and dimes and an occasional quarter. Thus Duff had already come closer to being a part of what Nora hated than she had even allowed herself to fear. He had received not only money but also applause, and from an audience of strangers. Nor was that all. Late at night, after his mother was asleep, he would slip away to Bantam Street, drawn there because something in the music answered something in himself.

At the largest of the places, a two-story frame building called the Mansion House, there was music every night by a blind pianist famous all over the delta. His name was Bailey — Oscar Bailey, called Blind Bailey — an enormous old man built

on the lines of a hippo; he had played on showboats until
vaudeville and the motion pictures drove them off the river.
Duff liked him best, but in time he came to know them all.
He would sit under barrelhouse windows, listening to ragtime
piano and rare three- and four-man groups, and next day he
would teach the songs to the other members of the sidewalk
band, drumming the rhythm, humming or whistling the melody, perhaps even singing snatches of the words, if any:

> *Blow your whistle, freight train,*
> *Care me on down the line!*

In this way he developed a sizable repertory of the songs
which remained his favorites always, the old riverboat and
New Orleans classics, Eagle Rock Rag and Creole Belles and
Ostrich Walk, Hilarity Rag and San and High Society. Just
before dawn he would slip back into the cabin and creep into
bed without waking Nora.

The contest between mother and son ended with an event
that took him beyond her control. He was indicted by the
grand jury for burglary and larceny, arraigned by the district
attorney, and tried by the circuit court. On a plea of guilty,
while Nora wept into her handkerchief and sometimes into
the hem of her petticoat, he was sentenced to be placed in
reform school for an indefinite period, to be released at the
discretion of the authorities. It really happened that suddenly,
and here was how it came about.

His three sidewalk-performing partners spent their share of
the coins as fast as they made them, but Duff had been saving
his fourth ever since the day he saw a set of drums in the window of an uptown music shop. When he had accumulated
almost four dollars in loose change, which he carried in a
Bull Durham sack worn on a string around his neck, he felt
qualified to price the drums. He did not believe that it was
enough but at least he felt financial.

He chose a quiet time; there was only the proprietor in the
store. When Duff said abruptly, "Captain, how much you aks

for them drums in the window?" the proprietor looked up from his newspaper, startled. He had been sitting with his feet on the desk, reading the comics, and had not heard Duff come in.

"Dont sneak up on me like that, boy," he said, loose-jointed, with gold-rim spectacles and a receding chin. His eyes, watching Duff over the edge of the paper, seemed to bulge and spin behind the heavy lenses. "Thats a fine set of drums," he added.

"Yes sir. Sho is."

"You want to buy them, or are you just looking and asking?"

"I want to buy them," Duff said. He unbuttoned his shirt and took out the tobacco sack, beginning to pluck at the knot with his teeth, the way he did every night when he added the day's receipts and counted the total.

"They are seventy-eight dollars and fifty cents," the proprietor said, still watching over the edge of the newspaper.

"Thank you sir." Duff returned the sack, still knotted, and buttoned his shirt. "I be back."

He was seventy-four dollars and thirty-two cents short. Using what little arithmetic he had managed to absorb in class while looking forward to the noon rehearsals, he computed that at the present rate he would require six years to earn that much. But three nights later he got what he believed was a chance to do something about it, a chance to increase his earning power in another direction. At the Mansion House — he had graduated from crouching under the side windows; now he came onto the porch to listen — he encountered a boy about four years older than himself. Duff had never seen him before. The boy asked if he wanted to make some easy money.

"How?" Duff said.

"Take it."

"Take it how?"

"Through a window, man. How you reckon?"

It would be easy, the boy told him. All Duff had to do was

stand outside the house and whistle if anyone happened along, particularly the law. They would split the take. "Fifty fifty," the stranger said.

"Will it come to seventy-five dollars?"

"Ought to, easy."

"Then I'm game," Duff said.

"Come on —"

But when he turned and saw the policeman walking toward him, his mouth went dry and all he could manage was a faint low moan. It was enough, however; the stranger got away through a window on the opposite side of the house. A neighbor had seen them and telephoned the police.

At the arraignment the district attorney gave Duff what he called "every chance," but all Duff could do was repeat what he had told the police. He did not know who the stranger was; he had seen him only in the gloom and could not even give them a description. "Dark, I think, and taller than me," was the best he could do. They did not believe him.

"All right, boy," the district attorney said. He was fair and pink cheeked, with hard eyes. "If thats the way you want it."

In circuit court he recommended that Duff be placed in the state reform school until such time as the warden and the parole board would declare it safe to return him to society. The judge so ordered.

Traveling in the custody of a white deputy, Duff and four other Negro youths rode across the dark flat delta and into the brown loam and loess hills where scrub pine grew and knee-high cotton stalks stood bare in the rain. This was his first ride on a train, his first sight of hills. He enjoyed it, up to a point. When they arrived at the reform school that afternoon, standing in the bed of the open truck which had met them at the depot, it was still raining, a slow steady drizzle that ran down their faces like tears. The school was an all-Negro institution, visited yearly by a group of white politicians on an inspection tour for the legislature. It was a low,

gray building of weathered clapboard — a short dogrun with
a narrow gallery connecting two deep ells: one the prisoners'
dormitory, with swinging oil lamps and three-decked bunks
along the walls, so that it resembled the fo'c'sle of an oldtime
sailing ship; the other the prisoners' mess and an apartment
for the warden and his family, the kitchen being shared — set
back from a gray, hard-packed, grassless yard like a surface
of zinc, and surrounded by a high wire fence which in the
dull light of the rainy afternoon had the flat, deadly glint of
gunmetal. All this combined to give it the look of an enormous
torture machine.

The boys stood in the truck bed, looking, and said nothing.
"Well, here you are," the deputy told them, turning on the
seat to look at them through the rear window of the cab as
the truck pulled up to the gate. "You can call it home for a
while. Hey?" None of the boys said anything. They stood
looking and the rain ran down their faces.

Then gradually, after the nightmare introduction, they discovered that their fears had been largely of their own inven-
tion. It was not as they had supposed from that early look.
They were left in the dormitory their first full day, but the
following morning they went to the field. Duff learned to run
a straight furrow behind the straining crupper of his mule,
to wear the lines looped around his neck like a long necklace
as he walked, and to reverse the plow with a quick, lifting
motion at the end of the row. The hours were long—from
dawn to dark during the busy season; "kin til kaint" the in-
mates called it — but he enjoyed the work and the queer,
trembly feeling of fatigue which came when he lay in his
bunk after lights-out. He had never known it before.

Sundays were best, however. Five of the prisoners had
formed an orchestra. They had real instruments, and every
Sunday afternoon they would play a gallery concert from two
oclock till sundown. Duff became friendly with the drummer,
a light-skinned boy from the piney hills, and was allowed to
sit in on an occasional number, reviving the technique of his

Bristol sidewalk performances. It involved a good deal more motion than sound, for he flailed his arms and rolled his head, hunching his shoulders like a victim of Saint Vitus.

"You pretty good," the drummer told him; "yair. But you dont hold the sticks right. Look at here." He tore off a long, pulsing snare passage. "Try it." Duff tried it. "Yair," the drummer said. He nodded approval. "Thats more like it, sure enough. But looky. Keep your wrists up. Like this here." He rolled another passage that rose quickly to crescendo, then died to a whisper, as if a mouse had scurried across the drum.

"Something must be wrong with me," Duff said. "I get it, all right, but it dont seem to come out right on the skin. I keep wanting something I can pick up on."

It was six months before he got what he wanted. Then the cornetist died of tuberculosis, a sad-eyed boy who had not been required to work in the field. Apparently he had no people in the outside world; all he ever cared about was music. He was not quite right in the head, and while the others were out working he would lounge around the dormitory, breathing sad, almost tuneless songs into the silver horn. He was sick a long time. Toward the end, though he could no longer play the instrument, he kept it with him in the bed, holding on to it even while unconscious. Then he died. There was no one to claim his effects, so the warden divided them among the prisoners as far as they went, which wasnt far.

"Ive seen you watching him," he said to Duff. "Here" — handing him the dead boy's cornet " — see can you learn to blow it."

Duff took it with both hands. It was heavier than he had expected, the dull gray of old silver, pewter-colored, nicked and battered along the column and at the bell. He held it close to his chest, walking back to the dormitory. This was Sunday and he sat sideways on his bunk all afternoon, learning to blow it. He found that he could control the sound by pushing down on the valves, but this made it doubly difficult because they would stick and he also had to learn to pull them

up again. He was still there, and he was still trying, when
the others came in for supper and began to undress for lights-
out. "Give it a rest, man," someone said from down the line.
So he lay quiet in the dark, lips pursed, imagining he was
practicing.

Two Sundays later he joined the musicians on the gallery.
At first he merely blared the horn, backing up the other players
as if the cornet were a rhythm instrument, more or less like
a trombone. They gave him strange looks, turning in their
chairs, but the drummer said, "Let him blare. Everbody got
to learn."

Soon he was able to follow the musical line. By the end of
the month he was beginning to lead the way, the horn riding
rough and loud above the other instruments, gravelly, sclerotic,
and by the end of the year there would be large groups in
the reform-school yard, their faces lifted toward the gallery
and the five musicians. They came from miles around, their
wagons and dusty automobiles parked hub to hub in a field
across the road, and sat or stood from soon after the midday
meal until well past sundown and into the gathering dusk,
when the supper bell would clang, strident and insistent, and
the breakup would follow, the boy prisoners going into the
low, rambling building and the visitors dispersing to their
wagons and cars across the road. They spoke in admiration of
the music, their voices floating back through the fading light:

"That was *playing*, warnt it now?"

"It sho was. How about that horn?"

"That boy mortally plays that thing!"

"*He* sho does."

The warden arranged Saturday night engagements for them,
loading them into the truck, drums and all, to drive to Jackson
and nearby communities for dances and barbecues; whatever
money they received went into a recreation fund administered
by themselves though with considerable cross-checking to dis-
courage peculation. Within a year of the time Duff was committed, the reform school band had become well known

throughout the central portion of the state. On Catfish Row and down Ramcat Alley, wherever people collected who were followers of such music, Duff's cornet began to be talked about. "I heard me a *horn* last week," a voice would say at a fishfry. He was beginning to amount to something in a way his mother never intended when she told him to study hard and stay away from riffraff.

Soon they were being offered more engagements than they could fill. The drummer was nominal leader of the group — they called themselves the Noxubee High Hat Rhythm Kings in memory of the dead cornetist, who had been sentenced from Noxubee County — but Duff was leader once the music got underway. There was no doubt about that; it had been true almost from the outset. The others followed his loud, blary horn on every number. They had no other style; apparently it had never occurred to them that any other style existed. They played the things Duff had learned while crouching under Bantam Street windows, the old songs that had been great before some of the boys were born, things never set down on paper but kept alive in places and in memories such as these. Thump: the drum would beat once and the others would go immediately into it. If anyone got left behind he caught up on his own. There was no vamping, no announcement of theme, no quiet introduction to set a mood. It came out full and uninhibited, the cornet riding high and wide, the other instruments falling in behind its lead like leaves sucked into the rearward vacuum of a speeding truck.

"Man, man," the drummer said once between pieces. "Wherebouts you get all that power?"

Duff looked down at the horn in his lap. He seemed not to have thought of it before. "I dont know," he said. "In my thoat, I reckon."

When he came home to Bristol in the early fall, nearly two years after the trainride with the deputy, there were chocolate bands on houses and trees from the great flood of 1927. In some of the cabins in Lick Skillet, which was in a sort of shallow natural basin, there was powdery soft yellow silt on the rafters, left when the water went down. An abandoned skiff bleached in the adjoining yard, derelict, its painter still tied to an upright. Two children sat in it, a boy and a girl, their faces grave with pretense, playing Steamboat. It was late afternoon, the sun three-quarters down the southwest sky. Waiting for Nora to come home, Duff sat on the steps with a paper-wrapped parcel in his lap. When he lay back on the porch floor the children's voices faded, as if the skiff were indeed bearing them away. Then they passed completely out of hearing, and when he opened his eyes the sun was gone and bullbats were flying. He was looking up into his mother's face.

"Hello, mamma," he said. "I fell to sleep waiting here on you."

"Get up, boy, before you catch your death of cold." She watched him quietly; he had not written to let her know he was coming home. "You had your supper?"

"Noam. I aint eat since I left Moorhead this morning."

He rose, carrying the parcel, and as he limped across the porch toward the door Nora saw that the fronts had been cut out of his shoes. "Whats the matter with your feet?"

"Corns," he said. "I got them plowing."

"Plowing. Well." She followed, watching him walk gingerly through the front room. "Maybe that place done you some good after all."

"Yessum."

"Leastways you aint apt to go breaking into people's houses again real soon, are you?" Duff said nothing. She said, "Are you?"

"Noam," he said.

He sat at the kitchen table, the parcel again in his lap. Nora went to the cupboard and began putting biscuits and cold sidemeat on a plate. Over her shoulder she asked, "What you got in the package?"

"My horn," he said. "The warden give it to me."

"Horn? What kind of horn?"

"A *horn*, mamma, that you blow in to make music. A cornet, they call it. Like in a band."

Nora halted, the plate in her hand. Then she came forward and put the food on the table in front of him. "I'll shake up the stove and perc you some coffee," she said.

△

He was fifteen that spring, five feet eight inches tall and weighing a hundred and thirty pounds—within half an inch and five pounds of all the height and weight he would ever have, though in later years the wedged shoes and padded suits would raise and broaden him and the perfumed grease would straighten the kinky hair which now fitted his head like a wooly skullcap. His eyes were black, the whites somewhat yellowed as if by jaundice, and his mouth was broad, with regular, white teeth and bluish lips and gums. Though his arms and legs were thin and gangling, his hands and feet were small. His voice was habitually low and he spoke so softly that people often had to ask him to repeat what he had said.

When he went out that evening after supper he took the horn with him, still in its newspaper wrapping. Nora watched him go. Again there was that impulse to restrain him, then to follow and bring him home. But she resisted it now; he was too big. Instead she waited, counting the hours by the courthouse clock, and at midnight when he still had not returned she went to bed. Finally she even went to sleep. At four in the morning — the clock was striking — she heard footsteps on the porch and then a hand fumbling at the door. Rising on one elbow out of sleep she reached automatically for the bureau drawer where she kept her pistol. Then the door came open; it was Duff. She lay and watched him, and as he passed her bed on the way to his cot in the kitchen, she saw that he still carried the horn. Unwrapped, it glinted silver where light struck it from a street lamp down the block.

"You act like that thing was part of you," she said suddenly out of the darkness. Duff turned in the kitchen doorway. "Where you been, boy, till all hours of the night?"

"I got me a job, mamma."

"What doing?"

"Playing this." He did not raise the cornet or glance down at it or indicate it in any way; he did not need to, for he knew she would know what he meant and he also knew how she felt about it. "At the Mansion House, seven nights a week," he said. "They give me a dollar a night."

This time the contest had been brief, was over, indeed, before she had time to plan; he had outgeneraled her so quickly that before she even became aware that an engagement was in progress it had ended in her defeat. The fourth stroke of the courthouse clock vibrated in the room; it was that darkest final hour before dawn. Nora lay back and pulled the covers over her face. Presently, as he stood waiting, she spoke from under the quilt, her voice muffled. "Go on to bed," she told him.

So now at last it was Duff who was on the inside, screened by whirling dancers and curtained by swirling smoke, making the wild Mansion House music while other boys, his age and younger, crouched outside under the windows where he had crouched two years before, to hear the music they were too young to approach. It was a new world to him, with a new population. Blind Bailey was there every night, but the other musicians were transients. Guitar or clarinet, saxophone or banjo, they seldom stayed longer than a week and there were never two of them together. Like Boola Durfee they traveled alone and they never stayed anywhere long; they were independent-minded men, troubadors who thought as highly of their freedom as they did of their music; they played for money and then spent it and moved on, and none of them had the least thought for tomorrow.

Usually Duff and the enormous old pianist were alone, a study in contrast. Blind Bailey was gray-haired and wore bluelensed spectacles and a boxback blue serge coat, double-breasted but always left ajar; he said it gave him "room to move around in." He affected a high celluloid collar and a narrow tie like a preacher, but he kept a flat pint of corn whiskey on the upright. Weighing just under three hundred pounds, with skin so black it glistened with purple highlights, he sat straight-backed, punching the keyboard with big hands whose fingers were dark and apparently boneless. He was said to be older than God. Duff, by contrast, was years younger than anyone else in the house. He wore denim trousers, an open neck shirt, and shoes with the fronts cut away to accommodate his corns. Sitting with his legs crossed and his body hunched over the silver horn, he kept his eyes tightly closed against the hard yellow glare of the lightbulb suspended on a cord from the ceiling. His manner was mild and gentle, incongruous with what came out of the horn, which was wild and blary and would almost deafen anyone who nudged up too close to the bandstand.

When the whiskey was good and the music went to suit him, Blind Bailey would sing. Then the dancers would stop and watch, for it was well worth seeing. Except by suggestion the songs were meaningless, without connected thought and sometimes even without words. He would begin bouncing on the oversized bench which had been especially constructed for his weight, cross-braced with two-by-fours and baling wire, then throw back his head and holler from down deep in his throat:

> *Shake it up, break it up,*
> *Throw it on the wall!*
> *Hug it up, lug it up,*
> *Dont let it fall!*

and then go off into a language all his own, composed mostly of shouts and moans, punctuated with growls and hisses, like an enraged sea lion — which, indeed, he managed to resemble at such a time. Duff learned to conform to these voice improvisations, obbligato, and they were the basis for much of the spectacular art of his later years.

He played at the Mansion House for nearly three years, by the end of which time he had learned all it had to offer him. He was not restless; he was never restless about his work; but he knew that it was nearing the time for him to be moving on. Then one cold February morning, a little after two oclock, a group of young Negroes, bandsmen off an excursion steamer that had stopped at the Bristol wharf for a moonlight dance, came in wearing unseasonal white flannel trousers, blue and white striped blazers with big pearl buttons, and two-tone shoes. The steamer was lying over until morning because of ice and debris on the river, and the musicians had come ashore to make the rounds on Bantam Street. They danced with the girls and listened to the music for an hour — both with an air of conscious superiority, bringing as they did into the dance room a cosmopolitan atmosphere of the wide outside world — then moved on, taking half a dozen of the best girls with them. They had been gone about twenty minutes when Blind Bailey began to strum the Farewell Blues, winding up with a few fast bars of Home Sweet Home; that was how he finished off each evening. Duff held the spit valve open and blew out the cornet, and Blind Bailey rapped with the piano lid to waken the boy who slept in the corner behind the upright every night until time to take the old man by the coat sleeve and guide him home to the Chinaman's store, Joe Toy's, where he had a room in the back.

The moon had risen late. As Duff came down the Mansion House steps he saw it shining bright and cold on the bell-bottom flannel trousers and gaudy jacket of one of the steamer bandsmen. "How do," the stranger said. He stood on the sidewalk, holding out his hand. "Ive been waiting to catch you, see you. I'd have seen you inside there but I make it a practice never to talk business with regards to hiring a musician while he is actually engaged in performing for someone else, for pay I mean. Excuse my glove."

"How do," Duff said. He had never heard such a speech before; it was like hearing a foreign language, one that required no breathing pauses. He felt soft, cold suede against his palm. Suddenly it was withdrawn.

"The name is Jefferson," the bandsman said. "Pearly, they call me in the trade." He paused.

"Glad to meet you," Duff said, like a prompted actor.

"Likewise. Would you join me in a drink somewhere where we can talk?"

"I generally get me a cup of coffee at the All Nite Café. It's just up the street a piece."

"That will be congenial," Jefferson said.

Over the coffee, and employing the same highflown garrulity with which he had performed the greeting outside the Mansion House, he explained that his orchestra — he was the leader — had lost a horn man on Beale, two nights ago in Memphis. "A woman," he said sadly. He paused; he shook his head. Then suddenly he returned to the business at hand. "I like your tone," he said. "With a little polish I think youll fit right in."

There were barely two hours before the steamer would take in her stageplank. When Duff woke Nora and told her he was leaving, she sat up clutching the edge of the quilt under her chin.

"I declare, boy, *I* cant make you out." She shook her head. "How come you want to be running off with strangers? Last time you got mixed up with a stranger you wound up in reform school for two years. Is that what you want, some more of that? Because this time itll be Parchman and lots longer."

Duff kept his eyes down, hearing her through. "I want to make something out of myself, mamma."

"Hump. You want to make that wild scandalous music: thats all you want. Why cant you stay here and play it? I aint stopping you."

"They going to pay me twenty dollars a week, mamma."

"A week?"

"Yessum."

This was impressive; Nora paused. But having paused she hurried on. "And whats the good in that?" she said. "Youll just spend it on riotous living — canned peaches, cigars, sardines, and suchlike."

"I got to go."

"You aint got to nothing."

"Yessum I have; I got to."

She waited perhaps five seconds, watching him. It seemed long, and she knew she was defeated again. Then she said quietly, "All right. If you got to, you got to. I aint holding you. When did I ever, once you took a notion?"

The stageplank was taken in on schedule. The paddle blades thrashed water, backing the steamer away from the wharf; the whistle screamed and rumbled, precipitating steam, and the paddles reversed, driving the boat ahead on the forward slope of a churning wave. From the rail Duff watched Bristol shrink and fade in the pale light of the winter dawn. When he was a mile downriver the sun rose big and scarlet, and as the steamboat rounded the lower bend he looked back and saw the town gleam blood-red for an instant, house roofs and church spires, smoke stacks and water towers burgeoning in flame. Then, apparitionlike, as the trees along the Arkansas bank swept a curtain of green across it, it was gone.

That night they played Vicksburg. In the course of another week they played Natchez and Baton Rouge, and within a third week they were in New Orleans. Duff made two trips on the excursion steamer, to and from Saint Louis and fifty river towns along the way. He was learning, playing and listening in all those different places flanking the river where this kind of music was born. What was more, Jefferson — who, Duff soon discovered, had a good deal more genuine friendliness than the garrulous façade had indicated — taught him to read musical notation and featured him on a share of the songs.

"Look here now," Pearly said, spreading a sheet of music. "It's easy as Baby Ray. All those squiggles and dots and dashes, theyre not there to mix you up, they are there to help

you. Look what I mean. Here's this fellow with a round white
face — he goes slow. Give him a leg, like this one here, and he
goes twice as fast. Then black his face and he goes twice as
fast again, like Jesse Owens outrunning all those white men.
Put him a tail on the end of his leg and he doubles speed, eight
times as swift as the round-face white one. Another tail, that
makes it a flipper; he goes doubling up again. All the time
doubling, however many. Comprehend?"

"Two tails and he goes sixteen times as fast?"

"Co-rect. You catching on."

"That does seem mighty swift."

"Well, you got to remember — that white-face fellow, he
goes awful slow. We'll get to sixty-fourths before we're done.
And look at this. Where he sits on the ladder, high or low,
shows how he sounds, how shrill or rumbly. F, A, C, E, between the rungs: spells face. The higher he goes, the higher
you go with him. Here. Play me this line by the notes, and take
it easy. All I'm trying to do is teach you something on
paper that you already know in your mind."

Duff had the flannel trousers now and the coat of many
colors, but he could not wear the two-tone shoes because they
were only lent for the duration of the job. Like the jacket and
trousers they belonged to the boat, and the owner would not
allow him to slit them for his corns. But that was all right; he
had other compensations. In Memphis, on the trip back downriver, he bought a new cornet, a golden horn with easy valves
and a glitter like new money. He wrapped the old one carefully in burlap and mailed it back to the warden. *Here and
thanks*, he wrote in a note he inclosed. *Give it to some other
boy to learn on. I am fine.*

Jefferson played piano. After the second trip he persuaded
Duff to join him on a job in a New Orleans riverfront dancehall near the Quarter. With four other musicians, drums,
trombone, clarinet, guitar, they formed a combination known
as Pearly Jefferson's Basin Six. As a group — though they
made no recordings by which to prove or disprove it at this

late date, or even to argue or rave over — the Basin Six were
probably not as good as the cultists nowadays declare. They
were late in the tradition, too late for the "carving" contests
held on street corners in the days when rival bands played to
attract the public to their dancehalls and cafés, too late also
for the days when a band advertised its music by driving
around town in a mule-drawn wagon, the musicians hunched
in the bed between the pianist, who faced forward against the
driver's seat, and the trombone man, who faced rear and moved
his slide out over the tailgate. There was none of that left by
the time Duff Conway reached New Orleans. But late or early,
he was in the tradition. He played the same songs for people
who had heard them in the early days and he got to know
musicians who had grown old in the trade, who had sat on
the same rostrum with Buddy Dubray and Cleaver Williams
and were willing to talk about it: as for instance, how Buddy
would lean out of a window, pointing the bell of his cornet
toward the city, and "call his children home," meaning that
he would signal the customers to come on out, the dance
was getting started; he hadnt needed to go downtown to ad-
vertise. Duff's four years in New Orleans were not the years
of his greatest music, but they did more than any other years
to develop his final tone and style. Backed by the example
of Blind Bailey — who had never presumed to "teach" him
anything — they were the years that made him what he was
when, later, musicians who were supposed to know called him
the best horn man of his time.

In March of 1935 he accepted a job with Rex Ingersoll in
New York. Tall, handsome, light-skinned, with sideburns and
a hairline mustache, Ingersoll was billed as "the crown prince
of swing" in billboard and newspaper advertisements for the
motion pictures and radio programs which featured him. In
New Orleans two weeks before, he had heard Duff play and
had talked with him for half an hour. He was interested in the
Basin Six treatment of Maple Leaf Rag and had paid Pearly a
hundred dollars for what he called the "arrangement." Pearly

spent ten dollars of it on a wreath for Cleaver Williams' grave
(Williams had played the Rag that way, twenty years ago),
gave another twenty to beggars on the street (that was the way
Williams had wound up, begging on the street after he lost
a hand in a shooting scrape) and blew the rest on a beer bust
for the band. From New York Ingersoll telegraphed Duff an
offer of eighty dollars a week. Duff packed a cardboard suitcase and caught the first train north.

Ingersoll was waiting for him at Pennsylvania Station. From
there he took Duff straight to a tailor who measured him for
half a dozen orchestra suits. "We'll get that out of the way
first," he said. Then he took him to rehearsal. Afterwards he
told him, "Duff, you really blow that thing. It's great, kid,
really great. But it's a little different up here. On those passages that belong to you, go right on and ride it out; it's great.
But other times you have to hold back on it, sort of melt in
with the others. See what I mean?"

"Play it soft?"

"Yes, kid, background it. Tacet."

"All right, Rex."

He tried to do as he was told, but two days later Ingersoll
spoke to him again about it. "We've got to take out some of
the blare," he said. "Not that it's not great. It's really great.
But you know, kid, we got to keep the icks happy, not go
breaking their eardrums."

Duff tried this time, too. He kept on trying, right up to the
day when he couldnt even try any longer; he had to give it up.
Later he explained it this way:

"He told me to hold back on it, and I tried. But I couldnt.
So Rex put a mute in the horn and hung a derby over the bell.
That was all right, then — Rex said it was fine." Duff wagged
his head. "Maybe it was, to listen to, but my wind backed up
on me. What was suppose to be coming out the other end
got choked back down my throat. I like to bust. Rex said it
was great, kid, great, but it got me so wrought-up I couldnt
sleep. I'd sit up mornings, trying to woodshed it out of me,

but that didnt help any whole lot. So finally one night I stayed home.

"Next afternoon when Rex come round I told him how it was. 'I cant,' I told him. But he said I was wrong. He said music wasnt only for the ones that played it; it was for the ones that listened to it, too. He said it was up to us to give it to them the way they wanted it, and let the longhairs take care of the other and go hungry." Duff nodded gravely. "That sounded reasonable, you know. I figured he was right, being top man in the big time and all that. I figured he wasnt clearing any hundred thousand a year without knowing what he was talking about. And Lord knows I wanted to stay. All that money and high living, fine clothes and good food and smooth women — I like it well as the next man, all of it. But I couldnt; I couldnt even go back and try any more. I would have if I could have but I couldnt."

The following day a drummer he had worked with in New Orleans came to see him. The drummer said, "I heard you took off from Rex. What you planning now?"

"I dont know. Go back home, I reckon."

"Aint no sense to that, man; you just got here. Look. This friend of mine is opening a place right here in Harlem — a gin mill affair, nothing special; youd be playing for cakes at first. But come on in with us and we'll make us some music the way it ought to be made."

"I dont know, Juny. Seems like my horn dont suit this town. Rex ought to know."

"Itll suit this place. Come on."

There were no tin derbies at the Black Cat, no mutes, no music stands spelling R E X in blinking neon; there were no music stands at all, in fact. Opening night, the following Saturday, everything that had been pent up inside him for the past ten days came out loud and clear. From that first night it got better. Six months later he hit his stride.

"I dont know how it happened," he told Harry Van afterward, looking back. "It seem like the horn kind of opened up and everything I ever learnt come sailing out."

Harry Van had never heard jazz before, to listen to. It was something he accepted much as a person might accept Joyce or Brancusi, admitting there might be something there and even admitting it was probably sincere, but never caring to study it or give it any real attention. Van was twenty-seven, only beginning to compose the things he had always worked toward, music that was intellectual in concept and highly organized, with a good deal more stress on form than content. There were plenty of interesting ways to put notes together, and this way was the safest — meaning that it was the one least likely to lead to disappointment; the less you ventured, emotionally, the less you stood to lose. He was aware of the shortcomings of this approach but he excused them on the grounds that what he had done so far was student work, preparation; he was learning his craft, one of the most difficult in the world, and when the time came for what he called the breakthrough (he was anti-romantic, but he was romantic enough to believe in this) he believed he would find his material proceeding naturally from his studies; that is, he would find 'himself,' as so many others had done before him. After all, he told himself, there were plenty of interesting ways to put notes together if 'themes' were what you were after. Nothing had interrupted or even disturbed this belief until the night his harmony instructor took him to a Harlem nightclub.

Over the doorway there was an arched cat with green electric eyes and a bristling tail. The instructor rapped and a panel opened inward upon a face so black that the eyeballs glistened unbelievably white. The Negro showed an even row of gold teeth when he recognized the harmony instructor. "Evening, professor," he said, and the door swung open, revealing a dingy anteroom and another door. From beyond it came a pulse of music, like something under pressure in a bell jar. When this second door was opened they were struck by a violent wave of sound, the ride-out finish of China Boy, followed by one thump of the drum and an abrupt cessation, a silence so empty that, in its turn, it too seemed to strike them across their faces like an open palm, a slap.

On a low dais in the opposite corner there was a five-man group — drums, piano, cornet, trombone, clarinet — seen dimly through smoke that hung like cotton batting, acrid and motionless except when it divided to let waiters through and closed again immediately behind them as they moved among the small round tables where people sat drinking from under-sized glasses. Van looked for other instruments, unable to believe that all that sound had come from five musicians. As he and the instructor were being seated the drum set a new beat, pulsing unvaried; the clarinet began to squeal, trilling arpeggios with the frantic hysteria of a just-castrated pig; the trombone growled; the cornet uttered tentative notes; the piano brought out *One Hour* for sixteen bars (Van knew it as *If I Could Be With You*, from college dances) and subsided into a general rhythm of sustained chords. Then it happened.

The cornet man, whose skin had the reddish tint of cocoa, took a chorus alone. Wearing a pale blue polo shirt, high-waisted light tan trousers, and shoes with the fronts hewn out to expose white cotton socks, he sat with his legs crossed, the snub horn bunched against his face. His eyes were closed and he held his head so determinedly down that through the early measures he appeared to be blowing the notes deliberately into the floor, driving them there like so many silver nails, a lick to each. His playing was restrained; it sounded almost effortless; but, seeing him, Van got an impression that the cornetist was generating a tremendous pressure only to release a small part of it. Apparently this was the case, for near the end of the chorus, as if the pressure had reached that point he was building toward, the player lifted his head, the cornet rising above his face, and the leashed energy seemed to turn loose all at once, riding powerfully over what had gone before. It approached the limit at which hearing would renege, that farthest boundary of the realm of sound, soaring proud and unvanquishable beyond the restraint of all the music Van had ever known. "No! No!" and "Hey!" people cried from adjoining tables. Van just sat there looking, knowing that his life had reached a turning.

The harmony instructor left soon after midnight but Van was there when dawn began to pale the hanging smoke. He left when the musicians did. He went home, ate breakfast, walked the early morning streets for an hour, and went to class. Afterwards, looking back, it seemed to him that this day had the unreal quality of a dream not quite remembered, partly no doubt because of the lack of sleep (he had always followed a healthy regimen) but mostly because of his state of mind, his reaction to what he had heard. He was confused. Something had happened beyond his will, and he could not call it back or comprehend. It was not until three hours after dark, after a restless four-hour sleep, when he passed through the tandem doors of the Black Cat for the second time, that the dream state ended and he returned to the actual living world.

Knowing nothing of the schedule, he was early. The tables were empty and last night's smoke had dispersed. Four of the musicians were there, two of them with their instrument cases, cornet and trombone, on the floor beside their chairs. The crowd began to arrive. Presently, when the room was about one-third filled, the pianist mounted the dais and took his seat. Again it was like no music Van had ever heard; again it was without melody or, seemingly, even tempo — a vague tinkling in which the black keys seemed to predominate, a strumming such as might have been done by a performing animal, ape or seal, except that there was a certain intelligence to the touch, a tonal sentience beyond Van's comprehension. Then the clarinetist arrived. White, about forty, with a neat pale tonsure exposed when he removed his Homburg, he resembled a successful dentist or a haberdasher's clerk. As he crossed the room, the air already beginning to thicken with smoke, he took the instrument from the flat, booksized case beneath his arm and began assembling its five sections. He stepped onto the rostrum without breaking his stride, halted at the far end of the piano — an upright with its front removed to show the busy hammers capped with felt — and began to play the shrill, sliding runs of the night before. The other three members came forward together, as if this were some sort of muster signal, and during the trombone break Van recognized the melody and realized that he had been hearing it all along. It was *I Never Knew*, which had been popular at dances in his Yale undergraduate days.

He was there for the closing this second night as well, sitting alone at one of the back tables, the steel-gray smoke matting thicker and thicker between him and the bandstand. The following day he cut classes, but he stayed away from the Black Cat that night. He was dazed, like a survivor of some disaster, a dancehall fire or a steamboat explosion. 'All I have done adds up to nothing,' he told himself as he lay in bed unable to sleep after the day's idleness; 'now I'll have to start all over again.' He kept remembering the tone of the cornet, recalling whole passages of improvisation by the cocoa-colored Negro. 'Maybe he cant even read music,' Van thought. 'Maybe he came here from a cornfield somewhere, dropped the hoe and took up the horn and played what his grandfathers played in the jungle a hundred years ago.'

The following night he found that some of this was wrong. The cornetist could read notes, for one thing, anyhow after a fashion. His name was Conway; he had come up from New Orleans two years before and had already made a name for himself. Van learned all this from an enthusiastic young man who sat at an adjoining table. He wore a crew haircut and a hound's tooth jacket and explained off-hand, though with an edge of pride, that he was a writer for *Platter*, a trade magazine published by a record manufacturer. "Thats the most horn in the world," he said. "I thought everybody interested in music knew Duff Conway." He spoke a racy jargon which Van could not always follow, and he had a habit of pacing the music by patting the table with his palms and humming du-duh du-duh through his teeth with a rhythm which Van, at any rate, thought did not always conform to that of the musicians on the bandstand. The gold-toothed manager seemed impressed, however; he kept dropping by to ask how things were going and sent the writer a fresh drink every fifteen minutes without charge.

During a break the young man brought the cornetist to Van's table. "You been asking so I thought I'd bring him round," he said by way of introduction. He spread his arms and put his head back like a prize-ring announcer. "Comb them all — 52nd Street, the Loop, 12th Street in K.C., anywhere — you wont find a horn like this one. Mind what I'm telling you."

"I'm pleased to meet you," Van said.

"How do," Duff said, shaking hands.

He was twenty-four that month. His manner with strangers was nearly always awkward, but soon after meeting Harry Van he lost this awkwardness, at least in Van's direction. They became friends and were seen together in such diverse places as Swing Row and Carnegie Hall, the Village and the Metropolitan — one the son of a New England choir master and a sea captain's daughter, advanced student at one of the nation's leading music institutions, already composing music which even the conservative officials of the school called "promising" with considerable more enthusiasm than usually hid behind the word; the other the son of an itinerant guitarist and a Mississippi servant girl, horn man in a Harlem gin-mill, whose name spoken casually was enough to evoke superlatives from his followers and whose recordings were beginning to be collectors' items. For two years this relationship grew, Van being drawn steadily away from the music he had known and into the orbit — or maybe vortex — of the music Duff represented, until finally he was composing things like those he formerly had believed were without melody or harmony or sometimes even rhythm. At first his friends at the institute talked against it; it didnt make sense, they said. But now he seldom saw them. He was at work on a four-part composition made up of jazz themes with variations based on Duff's improvisations. Later he was to abandon this. Indeed, the jazz influence is hardly apparent in his work today. But he had got what he wanted by then; he had made the breakthrough, and the influence remained, if not the signs. What he wanted was an approach, and jazz had shown him that. An inferior art by virtue of its limitations, it involved great drive and marvelous technique and little else; but jazz men — anyhow the good ones, and where the emotions were so naked, thrown out in such a spendthrift fashion, it was obvious from the outset which were good and which were not — never let technique be anything but a means to an end. This was what he mainly got; this was what had struck him that first night in Harlem (though he did not know it then, or at least could not identify it) and this was what stayed with him after he left jazz behind.

Van had completed about two-thirds of this four-part composition, almost as far as he was to go with it, when Duff began to admit a weariness in his arms and legs. He had felt it for some time, but now he began to admit it, at least to himself; he had lost weight, and some nights he was so tired he could barely hold the horn up to his face. So he began drinking to fight it, keeping a waiter on the move between the bandstand and the bar. This took away some of the weariness, or seemed to. But toward the middle of August, 1939, something happened.

It was near closing time and he was just entering the chorus of Body and Soul, one of his best numbers. As the horn mounted toward the final, unbelievable note he felt something rise at the back of his throat, an insistent tickling like a feather against his pharynx. He fell off the note. There was a moment of flat silence; waiters froze in midstride, and here and there about the smoky room people sat with glasses halfway raised. "Fluffed," someone said, dismayed and loud against the sudden quiet. Duff coughed and there was a taste of salt at the base of his tongue. He stood there on the platform, looking over the cornet at the crowd, and wiped his mouth with the back of one hand, still holding the horn. When he saw the darker red against the flesh he coughed again, harder, and a bright bubble of blood broke from his lips, running down his chin, onto the horn and onto the front of his shirt.

Van took him home and sat feeding him cracked ice until morning. At the clinic, when the examination was over and the x-ray had been taken, the doctor said: "Come back at five and we'll see what there is to this. Go back to bed till then."

He was a mild, gray-haired man with beautifully laundered cuffs and a collar like mother-of-pearl; he prided himself on never being hurried. When Duff and Van returned, late afternoon sunlight lay in soft yellow bars across the doctor's desk, filtered through a slatted blind. The doctor held the negative against the light. "Here you are," he said, indicating the x-ray like a portrait at a private showing, himself the painter.

At first Duff could not see what he meant. Then, as the doctor's finger moved among the smoky branches of the ribs, he discerned a gray smudge about the size and color of a tarnished silver dollar. He had been watching it for a good while before he became conscious that the doctor was still speaking.

". . . prescribe in a case like this. What you need is bed rest. I cannot tell how long it will take to cure you, if at all, but I can tell you anyhow it will take less than six months to kill you if you stay in that airtight smoke-filled room blowing your lungs out on a trumpet every night."

"It's a cornet," Duff told him.

"Cornet, then. Isnt that worse?" Duff did not answer. The doctor said, "Do you want me to arrange accommodations at a sanitorium for you?"

"No, thank you, doctor." Duff rose, holding his hat, and Van rose with him. "I'm going home."

Every morning, on her way out, Nora would set the pitcher of milk and the glass on the bedside table. Duff would lie there

watching them through the long quiet day. Just before sundown he would tilt an inch of milk into the glass, sloshing it
around to stain the glass to the brim. When he had drunk it —
painfully, sip by finicky sip — he would set the glass back on
the table, take the still-full pitcher to the kitchen, and being
careful not to spatter any drops his mother might discover
on the sink, pour the remainder down the drain. Then he
would compose himself in bed for her return.

He took the inactivity fairly well. Some days, however, a
speculative expression would come on his face as he lay there,
and after a while he would get up and cross the room to the
bureau. The cornet lay in the drawer beside Nora's pistol.
He would not touch it; sometimes he would not even open
the drawer, for he could see it clearly in his mind, thus juxta-
posed, the dull shadowed gleam of gold beside the brighter
glint of nickel. He had been in the room for three months
now, hearing newsboy voices cry Hitler and the ruin of
Poland while the tree outside the window, like something in a
hackneyed movie interlude, turned from dusty green to the
hectic flare of Indian summer and then stood leafless in the
steady rain of late November; winter came early that first
war year. Christmas Day he took up the horn for the first time
since he put it away, four months ago. He carried it back to
bed with him and played it for an hour as a sort of self-given
Christmas present, holding the quilt over the bell to deaden the
sound.

After that he began to play it for an hour every afternoon, and by the end of January he was playing it mornings
too, without the quilt. But it was March, the tree budding in
the abrupt Mississippi springtime, before he left the cabin with
the horn. Except that now he left by the front door — Nora
slept on the cot in the kitchen, having surrendered the front-
room bed to Duff — it was like the nights a dozen years ago,
when he would steal away to hear forbidden music on Bantam
Street.

That was where he went, this time, too. As he walked up the
steps of the Mansion House he heard the piano going strong on

Deed I Do. Looking across the dance room, through the smoke and around the heads and shoulders of the dancers, he saw Blind Bailey's broad blue back and his gray head bobbing in time to the music. A young man in overalls sat wooden-faced beside him, strumming a guitar. Duff crossed the room and stood behind the piano, watching the heavy hands move over the keyboard. Some of the keys were dead or badly out of tune, from stretched strings or missing hammers, but Blind Bailey knew how to avoid them; he only struck them for special effects. Duff raised the cornet, waiting, then came in on the beat, carrying it wide open for sixteen bars before fading for the piano break, and they took it together for a ride-out finish, the guitarist straggling along as best he could.

"Lord, Lord, Duff, it's good to hear you," Blind Bailey said, lifting his head. The spectacle lenses were blue disks, flat and opaque as target centers in the glare of the lightbulb. "How you been so long?"

"Fine as fine," Duff told him, smiling. "Just you play me some more of that mean piano."

At the cabin four hours later the lamp was burning and Nora was waiting. This was like the old days too. As was her custom, she had got up in the night to see if there was anything he needed. Finding the bed empty, she dressed and went straight to Bantam Street. From the sidewalk outside the Mansion House, along with a crowd of others who could not afford the twenty cents admission, she heard the cornet. Then she came home, lighted the lamp, and waited.

When Duff had closed the door and turned to face her with the horn in his hands, she said calmly: "I aint going to try and reason with you, because you grown now and besides I learnt better long ago. But aint you got no more sense than to be at that place, blowing that thing with them wore-out lungs that the doctor his own self's done told you wouldnt last a half a year that way?" She waited for him to answer, then said again, "Aint you?"

"Noam."

"All right. Go on to bed. Satan can call you his own where I'm concerned."

At first he went to the Mansion House twice a week, rationing his pleasure. By the middle of April he was there every other night, and before the end of May he was not missing a session. But by that time, with spring an actuality, not a promise, and the long hot days of summer drawing in, the trees and flowers in full leaf and bloom before the press of heat made them wilt, there was more to draw him than the music. There was a girl.

Her name was Julia, a light brown girl with a wide mouth, sloe eyes, and a boisterous manner. She had the loveliest laugh he'd ever heard. Nineteen, slim, high-bosomed, she had come to Bristol from Vicksburg when her parents opened a café on Bantam Street; their name was Kinship. She had her faults and Duff saw them from the beginning — a capacity for cruelty, for example, in any connection that clashed with her self-interest — but they were the faults of youth and were therefore not only correctible but were also as charming as her virtues, at least in his eyes. With his New York clothes and haircut and his aura of fame, Duff attracted her from the start, but the first time he noticed her was one night when he had just finished a fast chorus of *Wish I Could Shimmy*. She was wearing a knee-length red silk dress and suddenly, out of nowhere, she leaned forward and threw her arms around his neck.

"Oh people, people!" she cried. "Look here at my horn-blowing man!"

"Back up, gal," Duff told her, almost gruffly. "Back up and I'll blow one just for you."

This kind of thing had happened before—on the river, in New Orleans, and up in Harlem — but this time something in him answered. He played the Corn Crib Blues, and for the rest of the night, on into morning, whenever he looked out over the dance floor he saw Julia either watching him or performing for him, switching the red dress and preening like a bird. When the last number was over and the room emptied, she was waiting for him. After coffee at the All Nite Café he walked her home, and from the porch swing they watched the dawn come through. There appeared to be two sources of light, one descending from the sky, one rising from the earth; when they touched, joined, it was broad open daylight. He had never noticed this before.

In the three weeks that it lasted Duff experienced much else that he had never known before. Except for his music and his illness he had never been involved in anything he could not walk away from. His mother had not held him, for all her wiles, and even at the reform school he could look forward to a time when he would be released. But there was no such assurance here. Sick as he was, his system upset by coughing fits that were growing more frequent and more violent all the time, he was conscious of his inability to hold her. Within a week of the night she threw her arms around his neck and called him her horn-blowing man, Julia began letting him know his shortcomings. Wherever they were he was always aware that he did not satisfy her wants, whether at the All Nite Café, where she expected raucous talk to impress her friends — and even strangers — with his life in the big time, or in the high back room of the Mansion House, where she would rail at him with all the passion he was unable to assuage.

There were really only two considerations that kept her by him even for the short three weeks it lasted. One was her wanting to get full benefit of the reflected fame, which was there whether he would boast of it or not; the other was a lack of anyone to take his place. Two weeks were enough to exhaust the first, and the second was filled by the end of the third week. But Julia could not be satisfied with just leaving Duff for another man. She wanted to be won, preferably after a contest that would display her as the object of contention. The man she chose was likely to furnish whatever violence she desired.

He was Chance Jackson, a gambler well known in the

region for his instant willingness to bet on almost anything, as well as for his loud clothes, his pearl-gray derby, and the big yellow diamond studs he wore in place of buttons on his shirtfront. Born and raised in Oxford, where his mother worked in the home of the president of the University of Mississippi, he had been given his mother's employer's official title, Chancellor, as a first name. Faculty members and townspeople thought it a ludicrous name, until he began growing up and it was shortened to Chance. Then they realized how apt it was. While still in knee breeches he became known as a master at dice, coon-can, pitty pat, and all the other Negro gambling games. When he had cleaned out his section of the state he widened his field, and now he went from town to town, staying no longer than the winnings were good; 'pickings' he called them. He was nearing forty. There were men who had saved between visits for more than twenty years, awaiting an opportunity to skin him, not so much for the money — though it would have been considerable, by their standards — as for the prestige, the sake of being able to boast about it later. It had been known to happen, but the satisfaction was short-lived; they either had to face him when he returned, or decline the contest, or move outside the circle of his glory. All the same, they kept waiting, hoping, trying, and they kept losing.

Bristol was on his itinerary; he came here twice a year. A section at the rear of the Mansion House dance room was partitioned off by an old theater curtain nailed along its top edge to the ceiling, thus forming an alcove in which two blanketed card tables and a canvas-bottomed dice table stood under steel-blue cones of down-funneled light. Whenever there was a hush on the dance floor, which was rare, the rattle of dice and the cries of gamblers came through the curtain. Foot-high letters across its center spelled ASBESTOS and there were faded advertisements of harness shops and restaurants, gunsmithies and clothing stores, whose dead proprietors had never guessed the final room their names would grace.

Duff was resting on one of Blind Bailey's special numbers when he saw the gray derby above the red silk dress. He watched, brooding, for Chance had a reputation for handling women that almost equaled his reputation for handling cards and dice; it was a bad sign that he had forsaken the gambling alcove for the dance floor. But when the piano stopped, Julia came to the rostrum. "Make him leave me lone," she said. "I'm scared of that man."

"Whats he doing?"

"Nothing. But I'm scared. He *holds* me funny."

"Stay away from him then," Duff told her.

Half an hour later he saw them together again. He could see that they were talking while they danced, Julia with her head tilted back, looking up at Chance, who was looking toward Duff on the bandstand. Though he could not hear what they were saying, Julia was telling the gambler that Duff had said he would beat her if she danced with him again. "He'll do it, too," she added.

"Him?" Chance peered through the smoke at Duff. "He aint going to bother *no*body. Watch here." He danced toward the rostrum. "Hey, boy," he said. "Was you wanting to beat on somebody?"

It was between pieces; Blind Bailey had just finished the special, and Duff sat with the cornet in his lap. The gambler's diamonds flashed yellow as he leaned forward, one arm around Julia's waist. His face was close; his nose was large, fleshy and powerful-looking. "Was you?" he insisted. Duff did not answer. Chance leaned closer and spoke again. His voice was soft, almost caressing, his face less than six inches away. "I said *was* you?"

"Move on and let that girl alone," Duff told him.

What followed happened so quickly that he was not aware of any sequence of events until it had ended. Without taking his arm from around Julia's waist, Chance raised the other hand. Then — not making a fist, not even using the flat of his palm — he touched Duff under the chin with the tips of his fingers, lifted him gently clear of the chair, and toppled

him over backward. There was a loud thump as his head hit
the floor, and then, his ears still ringing, Duff heard a clang
as the cornet struck.

"Watch out there, whoever!" Blind Bailey cried. "Quit that
horseplay round the bandstand."

Looking up, Duff saw the pearl-gray derby haloing the
smiling chocolate face. "Just who was you going to give that
beating to?" Chance asked.

The cornet, on the planks beside Duff's head, had an ugly
dent in the column, just behind the bell. He saw this first;
then he saw Julia. The gambler's hand, still clasping her waist,
showed dark against the red silk of her dress. She was smiling
now, and Duff realized that he had heard her laugh as he
went over, a laugh that had been a cry, a squeal almost, not
only of nervous excitement but of delight.

Afterwards he was to tell himself that the smile had caused
what followed; the smile stayed in his mind even more than the
laugh, for the smile was in cold blood. He had expected to
look up and find her striking at the gambler with one of her
high-heeled shoes. Instead he found her smiling. There were
other factors, too. His nerves were upset from knowing the
girl would not stay with him, and his music had been getting
worse because he had been holding back to stave off coughing
fits. All this combined and contributed, so that when he went
over backward, sent sprawling not by a blow from a fist or
even a slap from an open palm, but by the almost gentle lift and
nudge of fingertips, when he saw the scarred cornet and then
looked up to find Julia smiling approval of what had been
done to him, he reached the end of misery and he knew already
what he was going to do. Curiously enough, however, he felt
no particular hatred toward Chance; hating the gambler would
have been like hating the car with which a careless or spiteful
driver had run him down. He went out, carrying the dented
horn, and behind him the crowd was laughing.

He walked fast, went up the cabin steps and into the room,
crossed straight to the bureau, and opened the drawer. For

a moment the cornet and the pistol lay side by side, nickel and gold, as they had done through the months he spent in bed. Then he turned with the gun in his hand and heard the canvas cot squeak in the kitchen. "Duff?" Closing the front door behind him he heard his mother's voice again, sharper this time: "Duff!" He left, walking fast, the pistol heavy in his pocket.

Blind Bailey was banging out Tin Roof Blues as he came up the steps and into the dance room. Chance and Julia were dancing in a far corner. Duff shouldered his way through the crowd until he was within ten feet of them. Then he took out the pistol and waited. The other couples faded toward the walls; the room was hushed except for the loud piano and the cries from the dice table beyond the curtain; "Come on, *eight!*" a voice shouted with all the fervency of prayer. Chance and Julia, cheek to cheek in a slow turn, did not notice any of this. The gambler's head continued to revolve until beneath his lowered lids he saw the glint of the pistol: whereupon, the gyral movement half completed, he stopped, still clasping his partner. He moved Julia slowly aside, never taking his eyes off the pistol. It was as stylized as ballet.

Chance had time to raise one hand, the palm showing pink in a gesture of protest; "Wait a minute, boy," he said, maneuvering for time to reach for the pistol everyone knew he carried under his waistband. Then the gun went off — louder, Duff thought, than anything he had ever heard; he had never been that close to a shot before. The piano stopped like a dropped watch as the gambler went back against the theater curtain and slid down it to the floor. The bullet had passed through his outstretched palm, ranging upward; it entered his forehead, just above one eyebrow, and came out high at the back of his head. The gray derby rose, and now it fell, spinning on its crown to show a new red lining matching the red of Julia's dress.

There were hurried patters and scrabbling sounds as dancers and gamblers went out through the two doorways and the windows. For a moment the curtain billowed like a sail in a strong wind; then it hung straight, becalmed. There was silence again, and Duff and Julia and Blind Bailey were alone in the room with the body of Chance Jackson, who appeared to muse profoundly upon his shoetips. Forgotten cigarettes raised their plumes among overturned chairs and half-empty beer bottles. Julia began to back away, eyes bulged, one hand against her mouth. "Dont," she said, looking into the muzzle of the pistol. "Dont . . ." Duff watched her until the end of the curtain lifted and she was gone.

Alone on the bandstand, under the steady glare of the naked bulb, Blind Bailey sat with his hands suspended above the keyboard, the flat blue disks of his spectacles reflecting no light. "Whoever you are, God bless you," he said. "And please dont shoot a blind old man."

Then there were footsteps on the porch and at the door. Dropping the pistol, Duff turned and saw the policeman at the end of the room. A sand-colored snapbrim hat cast a parabola down the top half of his face. Beneath this shadow the mouth moved steady and thin-lipped.

"Dont try nothing, boy," the white face said. "Just stand there."

He was in jail three months awaiting trial for having done violence against the peace and dignity of the State of Mississippi. It was held in early September, the hottest weather of the year. The judge sat behind his high bench, an old man who wore a black alpaca jacket and a string tie, despite the heat, and had a habit of clearing his throat with a rattle of phlegm to signal his displeasure as he watched the opposing lawyers around the stem of a bulldog pipe. The jury was out less than half an hour; the district attorney had made much of the fact that Duff had left the dancehall for the pistol and returned; here was premeditation indeed, he said, and here was the chance for right-thinking people to show the lawless element whether they intended to put up with all these barrel-house killings or not. Duff's lawyer, a young man just out of law school and appointed by the court, sat there helpless though he tried to earn his fifty dollars by objecting as often as possible. When the jurors had filed back into the box and the foreman had reported ("Guilty as charged," he said, without recommendation of mercy) the judge leaned forward and peered at the prisoner over the swoop of his pipe. This was the last case of the term; tomorrow he would make another halt on the circuit.

"Do you have anything to say before sentence of the court is passed upon you?"

No one heard Duff say anything but those on the forward side of the rail saw his lips form the words No Sir. Overhead the paddle-blade fans made a creaking. The judge paused, leaning forward, forearms flat along the bench. He watched the prisoner intently. Then, seeming to gather his strength for some particularly energetic pleasure, he spoke slowly like an actor measuring up to his big speech:

"I sentence you to be committed to a felon's cell, and there to be safely kept until the tenth day of October in the year of our Lord nineteen hundred and forty, at which time you shall suffer death by electrocution, and may God have mercy on your soul."

There was a sigh, a collective suspiration; then the spectators rose and filed for the door. They showed an unaccustomed politeness toward each other, having been in the presence of death, though once they were out in the hall they threw it off. A deputy led Duff down the stairway, across the rear lawn of the courthouse, and back to his upstairs cell in the county jail. The door closed behind him with an iron clang like the final stroke of a clock. But that was all right; he was used to it by now, after three months in the cell; today was not much different from yesterday. He sat looking up at the barred window, the high hot bright blue September sky.

Next morning when Nora came to see him she carried a bundle wrapped in freshly laundered flour-sacking, the creases still crisp from ironing. Even before he unwrapped it he could feel the familiar, compressed shape of the cornet. There was

no instrument repair man closer than Memphis, so Nora had
taken it to a local gunsmith to have the dent smoothed out; it
was her way of asking her son's pardon for having told him
Satan could call him his own. Duff played the horn whenever the turnkey would let him. The other prisoners didnt
mind. They liked it, the white ones in their individual cells and
the Negroes in the bull-pen. The notes were less blary now,
for his lungs were worse, but the tone was as clear as ever.
Every day there would be a sizable group in the yard below
the cell window, sitting under trees or leaning against the
weathered concrete wall of the jail itself, listening.

When Harry Van first heard the horn he was halfway to the
county jail. It caught him in midstride, as if he had crossed
an exact circumference into a circle of sound which had for
its center the golden bell of the cornet, and though it grew
louder as he drew near, the tone was no clearer beneath the
cell window than it had been a block away.

He had taken the midnight train out of Memphis — the one
natives called the Cannonball, in derision — south through the
fields that were white as if with incongruous snow in the
warm October moonlight. The trip was one hundred and
fifty miles and it lasted beyond eight hours; the coach bucked
and rattled, halting at every hamlet along the way and even
backing onto spur tracks to make those stops that were off
the main line. During the final two hours he could see the
countryside quite clearly, first in the pale, misty dawn which
came through slowly, like a scene on a photographic print
in the process of being developed, and then in sunlight, the
corrugated metal gins whining soprano with queues of mule-
drawn wagons lined up for the sucker pipe, the slow willow-
bordered creeks and drainage ditches with their rackety
bridges, the flat, ash-gray fields where pickers moved down the
rows dragging nine-foot sacks that bulged at their lower ends
with the fiber which had resembled snow in the moonlight.

Van had never before seen cotton growing, and in fact,

though he had made two European crossings, had never been
south of Philadelphia. In rumpled tweed, with his soft hat and
careful collar, Scotch-grained shoes and black knit tie, juxta-
posed among salesmen sleeping on their sample cases and ex-
cursionists returning from two-day flings in the city, he was
like a visitor from a future generation or even another planet;
the other passengers looked at him once and then let him
strictly alone. When at last the conductor passed down the
aisle announcing Bristol, Van took his pigskin bag from the
overhead rack and went out on the platform. He stepped down
onto a graveled quay, deserted except for an old Negro who
wore a dusty tailcoat and a frayed white panama.

"Pardon," Van said, and to him his voice sounded rusty
from not having used it for such a long time, "but could you
direct me to the county jail?" The old man watched him
curiously, puzzled by the Eastern syntax and vocabulary. "The
county jail," Van said again. "Where is it?"

The old man raised one arm, pointing. "Yonder ways," he
said at last. "Two blocks twill you sees the soldier: thats the
cyote-house. Hit's in back, behindside."

Now it was Van's turn to be puzzled. However, he took up
the bag again and began walking down the sidewalk in the
direction the old man had indicated. Behind him what was
obviously the main street, lined with store fronts, ran westward into a steep, grassy sort of earthwork which he did not
recognize as the levee. He had known the river was there,
having heard Duff speak of it and having seen it on the map,
but 'river' to him meant the rivers of New England, France,
and Italy; he had expected to find a village sprawled along its
bank, all green and peaceful, with white church spires and
cottages in ordered rows, each with its brass knocker. Instead
the town looked gimcrack, characterless with its false storefronts, unclean with its litter of trash and dust. He would have
been even more dismayed, and perhaps alarmed, if he had
known that instead of the town overlooking the river, the
river — from behind its earthwork, which he did not recognize; he saw no sign of the river at all — overlooked the town.

What was worse, he had left the bright, hazy riot of Indian summer, with a tinge of woodsmoke in the air, but now it was if he had traveled not only southward through space but also backward through time. It was summer indeed, and the clothes he wore were too heavy for the weather; he was sweating, wilting the careful collar which gripped him now like a damp hand at his throat.

All this was forgotten, however, even the press of heat, when he crossed the circumference of the music. He paused for an instant, then continued forward, moving now within the rich circle of sound, hearing again after all those months the proud, soaring tone of the cornet known to jazz musicians and their followers everywhere. But to Van it did not seem that he was hearing it again. It seemed, rather, that he had never stopped hearing it since a night almost three years ago, when his harmony instructor took him up to Harlem, under the arched back of that green-eyed cat.

When Duff left New York, the morning after the interview in the doctor's office, he said he would be back within a year. Perhaps he even believed it, at the time. But eleven months later a waiter at the Black Cat told Van that Duff had been tried for a roadhouse shooting and would be executed in October. That was in late September. Van wrote and waited ten days for an answer. Then he took the train for Memphis. And now, walking along the southern street, hearing again the cornet which had become for him the ultimate expression of all music, he thought in a kind of rage: 'There ought to be two sets of laws, one for us and another for the few like him. It's enough that they carry the burden and the anguish of their talent and their genius; it's not right to expect them to follow something set down and codified in books for men who dont even think the way they do, if they think at all.'

He crossed the intersection toward a wooded lawn where a marble column gleamed pale among oaks and sycamores, magnolias and elms, still wearing their dusty summer foliage. Surmounting the shaft, the Confederate faced south, his blanket-roll tied neatly across his left shoulder to leave his shooting arm unencumbered; he stood with one foot a bit advanced, both hands clasping the muzzle of his musket, and his eyes were bland, impervious, the pupils dimpled into the stone eyeballs, under the shadow of a hatbrim as stiff and unyielding as if it had just been lifted from the stamping machine; he seemed not to have gotten word of the surrender. This was the soldier the old Negro at the depot had told Van to watch for, and the ugly brownstone structure with its new cupola was the courthouse. Behind it there was a square two-story building of harsh concrete, bars slatting the windows and a heavily grilled door blocking the entrance.

It was the jail, and a man sat on the stoop. He wore khaki trousers and a faded denim shirt with half-moons of darker blue beneath the armpits. As Van approached, carrying the pigskin bag, the man looked up. His eyes were a pale green, as if they had been washed in too-strong soap and the color had not held, and there was a lax, mobile expression about his mouth. He held a knife and a whittling stick. Van halted in front of him, looking more out-of-place than ever in his city tweeds. "May I see Duff Conway?"

The man dropped his glance. Without looking up, he shaved a long curl of pine from the stick. "From up his way?" he asked. There was a big ring of keys at his belt.

"Yes."

"Figured you were." He looked up. Van, whose knowledge of such things was limited to what he had seen in the papers and magazines, wondered what would happen next; he had no taste for being involved in one of those 'southern' incidents. The man rose, brushing shavings from his lap. "Sho now. You can see him." He swung the iron door ajar and led the way. "Put your suitcase there," he said. "Wont nobody bother it." His voice was not strong but it had a staminal quality. "I understand he got sick up there or something, and come down here to get well. But it dont matter now. My cousin Luke Jeffcoat is going to give him the big treatment tonight."

"Treatment?"

"The chair — the 'lectric chair. He comes around and sets it up; calls it his old shocking chair. Sick or well wont make any nevermind then. Were you acquainted with him up the country?"

"Yes."

"Lawyer?"

"No: friend."

"Ah?" The turnkey looked back over his shoulder. They were climbing a steep circular staircase. "Then maybe you can bring it home to him. I'm a religious man, myself; I always have been. But I cant talk to him, seems like." He toiled ahead, speaking over his shoulder with the same unflagging volubility. "I can talk to most of them, bring them round before the end, but not this boy. He listens but it dont get through. So you tell him. Tell him to lay that horn aside and get right with his Maker."

'Oral personality,' Van thought, remembering the term out of a far-off psychology classroom as he followed the faded broad blue back, the shifting khaki hams just at eye level. 'Does he ever stop?'

"Most of them we have to kind of put the damper on, they get so wrought-up and sanctified with all their kinfolks there in the cell and two or three jackleg preachers yelling about salvation at the top of their voice. But this one cant seem to get it through his mind the time aint long. Wont see a preacher, wont even pay his mamma any mind: just sits there all day long with that durn horn, playing them honky-tonk songs like his soul depended on it. He'd be blowing it all night too, I reckon, if I'd let him."

They had reached the second story by now; the turnkey led Van down a corridor flanked with cells. Convicts in striped trousers and sleeveless undershirts watched through the bars, the eyes of the Negroes rolling white in the gloom of the bull-pen. "Full house," the turnkey said. "But thats all right. The long-chain man will be here a week from Monday to take them up to Parchman." Van felt the need for a guide book and

a two-way dictionary. There was a combined odor of creosote
and mildew, of perspiration and urine, of rust and sweating
iron and much else, anonymous and myriad. The sound of the
cornet filled the jail; it was Tailgate Ramble, near the finish.

"Well," the turnkey continued, unwearied, against the soar
of the horn, "he can blow it tonight if he wants. Most of them
ask for a quart of corn and a woman, but I reckon he'll want
the horn. The sheriff always gives them what they want. If
it's possible I mean, because we had one to ask us for a
hacksaw. He could joke at a time like that. Last January we
had a boy wanted watermelon; wouldnt nothing do but that,
he said. In January, mind you. And we got it for him out of the
cooler at the icehouse. Fellow that owned it had been saving
it for something special, a wedding or an election, some such
rumpus, but he didnt begrudge it. No sir. He never begrudged
it a-tall, since that was the one thing the poor boy wanted.
I think youll find the folks round here are like that, by and
large, with some exceptions."

While he told about the watermelon he stood at the cell door
with the keyring in his hand like a badge of office. Finally he
selected one of the big keys and fitted it into the lock. It
turned with a clanking of tumblers. Then he swung the door
ajar, performing a gesture of presentation with one hand.
"Company, son," he said.

Duff did not hear him. In fact he appeared too busy, too
concentrated on what he was doing, to hear anything but the
music. Riding out the coda of Tailgate Ramble, he was jack-
knifed into the lower section of the double bunk, hunched
against the wall with his knees drawn up and his heels against
the bed frame. The cornet was lifted toward the window,
catching the light as in a golden bowl. While the final note
died away he turned and saw Van standing in the doorway.
He did not seem surprised. He lowered the horn and smiled,
and his teeth were white and even against his cocoa-colored
face.

"Hello, Harry," he said then. "You a long ways from home."

At first, in the dim light from the high window, Van thought that Duff had changed very little. He did not wear convict stripes as Van had expected; he had on the peg-top trousers and polo shirt of his Harlem days. The skin fitted closer to his skull; that was all, Van thought at first. Then — either because his eyes had become accustomed to the light, or else because his mind was recovering from the shock — he saw the difference, and once he had seen it he saw little else. The skin did indeed fit close; the face was like one of those African masks, the lines of suffering and sickness grooved deep into the wood with all the exaggeration of the primitive, wherein the carver pits the force of his emotion against his lack of tools and training. Duff's voice had sounded even lower than usual, a hoarse whisper, and now Van saw that this was because the lungs were almost gone; he breathed with difficulty, high in his throat. His arms and legs were thin as famine. Only the eyes and teeth remained unchanged, yet even so they had a terrible kind of beauty, frightening by contrast.

Van had come twelve hundred miles but there was little he could find to say. He was too conscious of the haunted mask, the sticklike arms and legs, the shallow breathing. Smalltalk was an effort, like a constant lifting of weights, yet anything but smalltalk would have been outrageous; death was like a presence in the cell. Also, though he was patient and polite, Duff was obviously waiting for them to leave so that he could return to his music. Within nineteen hours of the chair, he belonged to another world already, and now Van understood why Duff had not answered his letter. He had known it would be like this.

The three men sat in the cell for about twenty minutes, the turnkey doing most of the talking. At last, when Van got up to leave, Duff looked at him quietly and said in a hoarse whisper: "Dont be feeling bad about all this. There wasnt anything anybody could do, Harry. It's just I ought not ever have left home. Going off like that I lost touch with everything I was born to be with. I been thinking about it, some. I ought to stayed at home where I belong."

Standing in the corridor while the turnkey locked and tested the door, Van said, "I'll tell them hello for you when I get back."

"Thanks," Duff said, and still it was as if he had to make an effort to be a part of the world. He looked down at his hands, holding the cornet; they were thinner, too. "But you better not make it hello. Make it goodbye."

He raised the horn toward the glittering eyes and teeth. Van turned, following again the broad, faded back of the turnkey. Halfway down the corkscrew staircase he heard the first note. This made him hurry. He took up the pigskin bag and stepped out into the sunlight.

"So long," the turnkey said.

"Goodbye," Van said in a choked voice, not looking back.

Crossing the lawn he could hear the cornet, well into *Didnt He Ramble*. The vivid, brilliant waves of sound swept over him, surging past the dusty trees and the ugly brownstone courthouse, past the pale Confederate, undefeated on his marble shaft, and into the street beyond, where people on the way to work were pausing to listen, their heads cocked toward the high cell window. The power behind the music was gone yet the clarity and sweetness were still present. There was more than an hour before time for the northbound train, but Van walked fast, wanting to be out of range of the horn.

The sheriff and Hoskins brought him into the cell, walking on either side of him, their hands supporting his elbows. His shaved head glistened like mahogany. He was thin, slight and frail between the florid sheriff and the husky deputy, and his slit trouser-legs flapped about his ankles. His eyes glittered, the pupils contracted in the sudden light. His teeth looked false, too white to be true and too large for his mouth, which was drawn in what appeared to be a grimace or even a smile though it was neither; it was fright. Roscoe followed them into the cell; Dr Benson and I and the district attorney watched from the rear wall. Luke Jeffcoat, who had stood beside the chair and watched them come in, stepped forward now and took over, beginning the running commentary, the oration he supplied with every job. He spoke with the full-mouthed accent of the old-time stump orators, sometimes addressing the condemned man, sometimes the witnesses.

"All right," he said. "Here you are for that last fast ride they promised you in court. Dont be troubled in your mind; youre in good, professional hands." He led him to the chair. "Have a seat," he said with grave formality; he even made a shallow bow, one hand out, palm up. Then he secured the straps at the wrists and ankles, going onto his knees for these last, and the larger strap across the chest. "Now dont you be trembling, son. Sit up straight and tall and take it cool, so when I tell all your friends how you stood it theyll be proud. Do you have anything to say?"

He stepped back, waiting, but there was nothing. Then he secured the plated cap and the hood. As he worked, the snakes tattooed on his arms seemed to writhe. "Ive had them all kinds," he said. "Some moaned and groaned. Some didnt. But they all went, every man jack of the lot, the way youre going. So dont you fight it; dont fight back . . . Hey there!"

The switch clicked and for a moment there was that deep, pulsing hum and that odor of burning.

"Yair!" the executioner cried. "One quick bump on the road to glory and he rode right out of this world never knowing what hit him. Yair. Steady, folks; we'll hit him again. Not because he needs it, no, but because the law says do it and the law's almighty. Yair!"

There were footsteps hurrying through the door of the cell, and as I came forward with the stethoscope we heard the young district attorney being sick in the hall. I leaned over the chair, then straightened up and pronounced the prisoner dead.

A MARRIAGE PORTION

This was in the middle Twenties, back before the flood. Snooky said he was coming by to pick me up a little after seven, but you know Snooky; he says one thing, then he does another. Only this time he came early. "Well, just tell him he can wait," I said, all soapy, and Buster went downstairs and told him. He told Buster, "Tell her if she's not down by seven, sharp, I'm long gone." So Buster came back up. Poor Buster: all those stairs. He was the houseboy, as you may have gathered, gray-haired, well past sixty, and though his bottom lip hung slack from feeble mindedness, he was very good at building fires, carrying messages, and such. He died two years later. I was just getting out of the tub; he had to talk through the door. "Tell him I'll do my level best," I said, and Buster went back down.

Snooky was sitting talking to Daddy; Daddy had just come in. Mother had been dead three years that month, October. He was still long-faced and of course he had those wisps of cotton all over his clothes, the way they always do that time of year. He's a cotton man. Buster stood there, dignified in his white jacket, till Daddy came to a pause in what he was saying. Then he delivered the message. "Looks like youve bout got her tamed," Daddy said, but Snooky didnt say anything; he just sat there looking determined, or anyhow his notion of determined. Buster waited to see was there any answer. When there

wasnt, he went back to the kitchen with Louiza. She was his
wife and she looked after him all those years until he died.
You know how Negroes talk; "I slept true to that man," she
used to say. All the same, she remarried within the month, a
strange coal-black lantern-jawed man almost seven feet tall if
he was an inch, and moved straight up to Memphis. After
cooking for us for eighteen years, seven days a week, she barely
took the time to say goodbye. Thats how they are, thats
typical; there's never been a one of them had ulcers.

When I got down at seven-twenty Snooky was downright
purple in the face. He didnt say anything or even help me
into my coat, just followed me out to the car. The porch light
glistened on his hair, the part like a streak of white light down
the middle. The car was a cut-down Essex with writing all
over it, even under the fenders: *Chickens here's your coop.
Fragile, handle with care. Shake well before using* — things
like that. He had on his yellow slicker and there was writing
on that as well: *Oh Min! This end up. Yes we have no bananas*,
and so forth. I wont go into details except to say we drove up
to Rosedale to a dance and didnt get home until almost four-
thirty. By that time we werent speaking. The last thing I said
to him when he kissed me goodnight on the steps (he tried to
put his tongue in my mouth, among other things) was, "I dont
care if I never *see* you again!" I meant it, too. He left, racing
the motor down the block the way he always did when he was
mad.

It had happened before, more or less exactly, but this time
he really scared me. He didnt call for nearly a week. Then
he did and we were married in April, during a cold-snap. Our
wedding night was in Jackson, at the Robert E. Lee Hotel.
He had a bottle of real champagne; it was his daddy's, left
over from before the war, but we couldnt get the bellboy to
bring ice (there was some kind of convention going on, Baptists or something, all with their names on little squares of
cardboard pinned to their lapels) so Snooky tried to cool it by
holding it under the cold-water faucet in the bathroom. It
fizzed all over the place when he popped the cork out. I

drank almost half of it, luke warm like that, the first alcohol I ever really tasted except the sugary bottoms of Daddy's toddies when I was little, and next thing I knew I was standing under the shower, dripping wet, and all in the world I had on was a horrible nigger-pink bedspread wrapped around me and the wave had come out of my hair and I was bleeding. It was awful. Whats more, Snooky didnt understand at all; he kept yelling for me to come back to bed. "Come on back to bed!" he kept yelling. He had been drinking whiskey too, and finally he stumbled into the bathroom (like a fool I was so flustered I forgot to lock the door) and tried to wrestle the spread away, the only stitch of covering I had. I was more than a match for him, though, even in my condition. He fell and bumped his head on a corner of the washstand, then sat on the cold tiles, rubbing his head and mumbling over and over, "Some wife. Some little wife. Some little wife *I* got." It was horrible, watching him squat there, naked like that, mumbling. His hair had always been smooth before, glossy as patent leather, but now it stuck out all around his head, like spikes. Then all of a sudden a solemn expression came over his face, as if he was about to pray or something, and he turned and threw up in the toilet with his chin hooked over the seat. Mind you, I had to stand there, watching, because I was afraid if I went back into the bedroom he'd recover and follow. He just kept on heaving, heaving, long after he was empty. It's no wonder I got disillusioned early.

I sometimes think I married him just to get him out of my system. Not that I didnt admire him; who wouldnt? He was so much older, twenty-four to eighteen, and such a sheik. He played the ukulele, wore wider-bottomed trousers than anyone, had a car and all those things. Also his folks had money, lots of it, and Daddy had lost our money on the market years ago. I knew if I didnt marry him I'd regret it all my life. Then too, everyone kept saying he could 'handle' me, get me 'tamed' as Daddy said. That was what I wanted, after what had happened between my parents; I wanted what my mother didnt have.

A while back I said she died but thats not true, or at least
it's only true in a manner of speaking. What she did was she
ran off with a man. It was an awful shock — I was terribly
impressionable in my teens. It gave me an absolute horror of
anything vulgar, and of course almost everything was vulgar
in those days. I didnt understand at all but now I think I do.
She wasnt bad. It was the times, the war being over, women
doing the shimmy on dining-room tables, bobbed hair, short
skirts, all that. And the truth was Daddy was lovable but dull,
and not only dull but soft; he couldnt handle her at all. So
I married Snooky and you know how that turned out, from
the very first night in the Robert E. Lee Hotel.

He wasnt like they said. He was hard on the outside, all
right, but soggy inside. I'd suspected it all along, but of course
I had to find out for myself. Well, I found out soon enough.
He turned to whiskey round the clock, what they call a night-
drinker. His daddy sent him up to Keeley several times
though it never really took. Then one afternoon I came home
from playing bridge and found him in the living room with a
hammer — killing flies, he said. You should have seen it, what he
did to all my lovely things; the silver service from Aunt Agnes
was mashed down to little wads of tin. So then I signed a
paper and they put him in an institution. He didnt stay long,
less than a year, but by that time I had the divorce. He soon
married again; I heard she gave him a hard time, some Yankee
who pronounced her final g's and all the r's. It served him
right. Soon he left her and married another — a California one
this time; I hear she's just as bad if not worse. Not that I
care. I dont care. He can do whatever he likes, provided that
check comes through on the first of every month. I gave
him my youth; if we didnt have any children it wasnt my
fault.

There now; I've talked about it and made myself all sad.
Life *is* sad and there's no good in men. Feel those tears. I
guess youd better get up now and go; I think thats daylight
peeping through the shade.

CHILD BY FEVER

Old Mrs Sturgis lived all her life in the house her grandfather built fifteen years before she was born. Unlike most of the houses in the region, which grew piecemeal, room by room being added in flush years on alternate sides of a shotgun hall until they reached the baronial proportions so much hoped for and sought after, this one was that way from the start, a big, soaring structure of cypress and brick, set on pilings to protect its hardwood floors from the high water every spring. It was past its hundredth year when they tore it down, in accordance with instructions in her will, and converted the grounds into a public park — called Wingate Park for her father, Hector Wingate — a grove of oaks and sycamores, cottonwoods and cedars, with graveled paths and occasional benches where Negro nursemaids take their charges to while away the sunny afternoons, the former in aprons and headrags, the latter in prim chambray or belted corduroy, strolling its formal pattern with the precise intentness of figures in a minuet. She had always been public spirited, and this was her final gesture, six months after she died.

Every year on her birthday for the past quarter-century, first when she was sixty and last when she was nearing ninety, the newspaper ran a feature describing how her plantation had become the residential district of the town, the three thousand acres subdivided and parceled out under her supervision. With the story there was always the same two-column cut of an old lady in a wheelchair, the photograph looking somewhat blurred or out-of-focus until you looked closer and saw that this was because the face was a network of wrinkles. The fixed, archaic expression about the mouth was more like a grimace than a smile, but the eyes behind the octagonal spectacle lenses were bright as agates, even in the newsprint reproduction. Year after year that face looked out from the page, just as it had looked on the hot June day, ten and twenty and thirty years ago, when the itinerant photographer huddled beneath his cloth, palming the bulb, and saw it upside-down on the ground-glass plate. The text itself might change a bit from time to time, successive cubs and editors adding or subtracting particular flourishes, but the caption over the picture was always the same: *Esther Wingate Sturgis*, it always called her, *Mother of Bristol.*

This is not primarily a history of the life of Mrs Sturgis, but since her life was the backdrop against which her son's was played, overlapping it broadly on both ends — especially the latter; for years before she finally died people were saying she would live forever, baked to durability in the oven of the fever — a proper examination of her life is the best means of looking into many of the questions of his own. Here as always it was a question of action and reaction, hers and his. If a posy were needed to decorate a page or point a theme, perhaps the most suitable would be that biblical verse which tells of the children's teeth being set on edge by grapes the parents ate.

He was called Hector too; she named him for her father, just as later she would direct that the park be named for him, with his name on a wrought-iron archway spanning the entrance. Hector Sturgis has been dead for better than forty years. Not many people nowadays ever heard of him. Even fewer ever saw him, and no one at all ever knew him.

Yet there were those who claimed to know his story: know it so well, they said, that between the time when Mrs Sturgis died and six months later, when the house was razed, they could take you into the attic and point out the rafter beneath which he had brought it to a close: or so they claimed. It had a certain charm for those who told it, or if not charm then anyhow a certain fascination, partly because so little was known and there was therefore plenty of room for conjecture, but mainly because there was a ghost in it. That was what drew them, the lurid element: that and of course the boast of having inside information, being privy to events in the secret lives of the highborn. Actually, however, no matter how they embroidered and invented, his life was as uneventful as most lives are when they can be looked back on, when events have lost their immediacy, when the texture has raveled and the pattern run to gray. There were only three main dates to hang it on — 1878, 1899, 1911: the years of his birth, his marriage, and his death — which is as much as most men have, and more than some.

So this is primarily a history of the life of Hector Sturgis, and it begins with the time of his birth, or at least with the time of his mother's marriage. The two dates were uncomfortably close to coincidence, and therefore there was scandal from the outset.

Townspeople viewed the wedding mainly as a come-down for the Wingates. They knew that Mrs Wingate, so recently widowed, who dressed her daughter New Orleans style, sent her away to school, and taught her that she was somewhat better than anyone else and considerably better than most, had planned for Esther — called Little Esther to distinguish her from her mother, whose name was Esther too — something higher than marriage with the son of an Irish barkeep. His prospects were good, it was true, but after all they were no more than business prospects, which in Mrs Wingate's eyes was worse than having none at all. The bride was eighteen, the groom twenty-four. The wedding was in early March, a time of bitter cold. The child, a son, was born in mid-September.

This was 1878, the year of the fever. People should have been sufficiently occupied with troubles of their own. Yet, looking back from the day of the birth, they scarcely needed to count the months on their fingers. It was an event of the kind they had desired so long, giving occasion for them to strike at Mrs Wingate through her pride, through what they called her 'airs,' her high-and-mighty ways, that they told themselves they had known it all along.

"Why, certainly," they said. "Certainly. I knew it at the time. Who ever heard of a wedding in early March, with real spring weather just around the corner?"

Esther was an only child, born in 1860, and her father — he was one of four brothers; the other three were single — had stayed home from the war, under the twenty-Negro clause of the Conscription Act, to tend the plantation and look after his wife and daughter and the slaves. Of the three brothers, one was killed at Holly Springs, commanding a horse company under Van Dorn, and the other two survived four years' fighting in Barksdale's old brigade in the Army of Northern Virginia. All through the war, while news came of victories and defeats, both in a swirl of glory, and afterwards, when those who had returned formed veterans' organizations and staged parades and barbecues, Hector Wingate resented the wife and child who, along with the property and slaves, had kept him first from the glory and then from the gatherings.

His father, the first Hector, a younger son of an Ohio merchant, had come to the delta in 1835, after the Treaty of Dancing Rabbit cleared the Choctaws from the land. He bought a wooded tract almost five miles square at less than two dollars an acre, cleared and bounded it, grew rich on cordwood and cotton within ten years, and built the fine big house which apparently had been his dream from the start. However, he

had little time to enjoy it. Within a year after its completion
he died fighting in Mexico, a line officer in the First Mississippi Rifles, near the point of the V his colonel, Jefferson Davis,
formed to win the Battle of Buena Vista. His son, the second
Hector, Esther's father, having missed the war for Southern
independence, felt that he had failed his heritage. He turned
bitter.

Mrs Wingate, Esther's mother, was the daughter of a levee
contractor who came south from Missouri in 1850, the year of
the Compromise. His name was Pollard. The Wingate-Pollard
wedding, two years before the war, drew guests from all over
the delta, so that afterwards it was remembered as the prime
social event of antebellum Bristol. That in itself was not much
of an accomplishment, the town being mainly a roughneck
place in those days, but there were at least two factors that
made it memorable. The bride wore a gown by Worth, delivered by fast packet and overland stage, all the way from
Paris, and a visiting Missouri senator, a big, florid man with a
snuff-colored beard that grew high on his cheekbones and
hands that trembled violently unless he held them clasped and
massaged the palms, died of apoplexy the following morning,
having amazed the other guests with his capacity for chilled
oysters and champagne punch and extemporary stumping.
Bride and groom left by steamboat for New Orleans. From
there they sailed on a year-long Mediterranean cruise, including a barge trip up the Nile. Then they came home to Mississippi, to the delta, to the fine free life which already had begun
to bluster its way into the war that ended it.

After the war, when her husband had turned bitter, Mrs
Wingate, repulsed and estranged, went through a period during which all her love and energy were pent up like a hard
knot in her chest. She could feel it there. But then she succeeded in canalizing it by attempting to give her daughter
everything she had planned for herself in the days before her
marriage soured. Previously she had left the child to a nurse;
now she and the girl were seldom apart. She would spend

hours dressing her, and later devoted much of her time to
planning balls she would give for her daughter's coming-out,
brilliant affairs at which champagne would flow and fiddles
play for the young men and women whose hearts would pump
the best blood in the delta. When the year arrived for the
coming-out, however, Hector Wingate's violent death and
then the yellow fever, which followed soon, delayed it until
the girl had indeed come out, though in a manner her mother
had never considered, much less intended.

Esther herself, all through girlhood, had felt as strongly as
her mother the resentment her father took no pains to hide.
It was directed as much toward the daughter as toward the
wife; he somehow held her responsible for her own birth.
Like her mother, then, she might have turned to the next
closest person for consolation — in this case Mrs Wingate —
except that Mrs Wingate turned first; so that, instead of having
to seek compensatory affection, Esther was forced into the
defensive position of having to avoid being smothered with
it. What was more, she knew quite well, with all the wisdom
of children in such matters, that the affection was not really
for herself, but rather, like an investment made with an eye
to the return, was for the benefit of the person who bestowed
it. She would tremble with something akin to nausea whenever
her mother stroked her with those soft white hands and called
her darling every other word. During the interminable fittings,
the lessons in elocution and posture and china-painting, she
would stand demurely, head bent, plotting for the time when
she would be on her own. Her voice was soft, her movements
prim; she had learned her lessons in deportment well. But her
bright blue eyes, which were no less sharp for being solemn,
made her seem wise beyond her years.

After her fifteenth birthday, when she was sent to a New
Orleans seminary, she thought perhaps she had found a chance
to break away. But this was not it, or even anything like it.
She was as sheltered from the world as ever, the only diver-
sion being secret nighttime talks with other pupils, most of

them as limited as herself. She returned to Bristol with a glut of useless knowledge (she spoke French now, after a fashion, and could read music and even parse a simple sentence with very little assistance) and then set out to win her liberty. She had no idea of how to go about it, but she found a way soon after joining the choir.

When she came home from two years at the seminary Mr Clinkscales, the new rector, paid a special call on Mrs Wingate. He was young and pink cheeked and persuasive, where the rector before him had been old and rather incompetent and gruff; it was years before the ladies of the congregation recovered from the heady surprise engendered just by contrast. Then too, his predecessor had been struck by lightning while conducting a pauper's funeral, and this gave young Mr Clinkscales an added attractiveness, as if he were braving danger, like the soldier who snatches up the flag when the color-bearer pitches forward with a bullet through his heart. He had heard that Esther had received voice training in New Orleans, and through her mother he invited her to become a member of the choir. Mrs Wingate was pleased. "My daughter will be glad to serve," she told him, and she brought Esther to choir practice on Tuesday and Friday evenings after supper. She would sit in the Wingate pew for a while, listening to the singing, the voices reverberant in the empty church, more like demons than angels, and then leave, the rector having promised to see Esther home in safety and propriety.

John Sturgis, who had a sweet Irish tenor, was a member. He wore tall celluloid collars and needle-tip shoes and drove a buggy to and from choir practice, picking up the other members at their homes and returning them when it was over. The buggy was not really his — it belonged to the feed and grain company for which he worked as a salesman — but it might as well have been, and indeed it seemed likely that it soon would be, together with much more; people were predicting that he would own a share in the business before long. He was forever making jokes and he had a sizable repertory of comic songs in which the characters were immigrant Irishmen whose brogue he could imitate to perfection. With his pale green eyes, his upturned nose a bit knobbed at the tip, his high-colored face and carroty hair, his jaunty manner and whinnying laugh, he was like no one Esther Wingate had ever known. Sometimes when they stood together, singing, sharing a hymnal, his elbow would touch hers. It was like electricity. Sometimes when he took a long note, letting it rise and rise, his face reddening with the rush of blood and his eyes bulging from the effort, she would look up at him, her lips parted in admiration. Then he would break off and smile down at her, his face still red but his eyes no longer bulging, and that was like electricity too.

It was December, the air frosty; the choir members' breaths floated in front of their mouths as they came out of the darkened church where the stained-glass windows admitted no moonlight though the world outside was flooded with it. On the homeward ride they sang popular songs — *Whoa Emma, The Lost Chord, Silver Threads Among the Gold, I Hope I Dont Intrude* — the voices getting fewer and fewer until at last, the Wingate house being the farthest out, there were only three of them in the buggy, Esther and the rector and John Sturgis. The singing would end, and from beyond Mr Clinkscales, who chatted pleasantly in the middle, Esther would watch the young feed salesman, her eyes narrowed with speculation. Sturgis felt her watching him that way, with narrowed eyes; but though he recognized the symptoms — he had had considerable success in that direction, along with his success at salesmanship — he could not quite believe his luck. Besides, Mr Clinkscales was always there.

He was, that is, until a night two weeks before Christmas, when he tripped and broke his ankle. He was making a genuflection, and when he straightened up, feeling behind him for the step, he missed his footing and toppled backward down the short, carpeted flight of stairs, snatching frantically at emptiness as if for the rungs of an invisible ladder. There were cries of alarm, a flurry of excitement; Mr Clinkscales lay flat on his back with a look of profound surprise on his face and one foot crooked sideways at an unaccustomed angle. He did not know that he was hurt until he tried to stand. Then he saw the twisted foot; "Look at that!" he cried, astonished, pointing downward. The men carried him back to the parish house, where the women helped his wife prepare a basin of hot salt water to draw the pain. The rector kept shaking his head as if he could not quite believe all this had happened. He muttered to himself, his black serge trouser-leg hitched up and his foot in the hot water: "Five thousand times I must have done that in the past five years, at school and all, but nothing like this ever happened. Nothing like this ever happened," he kept saying, wagging his head with astonishment and unbelief while the women cooed to soothe him and the men stood in the background with long faces.

So when Sturgis had dropped the others and turned the mare out toward the Wingate house, there were only the two of them in the buggy. The hoofs went clop clop, clop clop, somewhat muffled by the dust of the road. There was a full moon low in the eastern sky. A string of geese went across it, contracting and expanding like elastic — there, then gone, leaving it empty, a disk of burnished gold. Afterwards, at the time of her father's death and through the weeks of waiting, Esther was to tell herself that it was Providence, their being given the chance to be alone: else why should a man of the church have broken his ankle in the moment of placing himself in the hands of God?

That was a Tuesday. She did not tell her mother about the rector's accident. Friday evening after supper the coachman drove her to choir practice; Mrs Wingate was indisposed (this was Providence, too, Esther told herself) and when Sturgis brought her home, having dropped the other singers along the way, her victory was complete. The only thing it lacked was that, as she looked beyond the grain salesman's shoulder, seeing the big yellow moon now barely on the wane, and felt against

her back and hips the little hard round buttons that studded
the buggy seat like a handful of pebbles tossed in, Mrs Wingate
was not there to watch.

These were their only two times alone. By Tuesday the
rector was onto crutches, and ten days later, on Christmas
Eve, Hector Wingate, hard-faced now in his middle fifties —
he had gotten so he rarely spoke to anyone, and whoever spoke
to him risked offense, either given or received — was killed by
a Negro tenant following a disagreement over settlement for
the '77 crop. Thus at last he achieved his heritage of violence;
it had been a bloody death, if not a hero's. The tenant was
caught late that night, treed by dogs in a stretch of timber
east of town, and lynched early Christmas morning. That was
the one they burned in front of the courthouse.

In late February Sturgis came to Mrs Wingate and asked for
her daughter's hand. Mrs Wingate was in widows' weeds;
Esther stood beside and slightly toward the rear of her mother's
chair. When the young man had spoken, Mrs Wingate's first
reaction was to turn and look at her daughter. Then she
turned and looked at the young man. "When?" she asked,
almost in a whisper, who had never before been known to
lower her voice for anyone.

"Soon, Mrs Wingate."

"How soon?"

"Soon as possible."

She turned again and looked at Esther. "Couldnt . . ." She
stopped and cleared her throat. "Couldnt you wait until your
father is decently cold in his grave?"

They did not reply, but something in their faces — hesitancy
and embarrassment, but urgency and certainty too — caused
her to pause. Once more she was about to speak and again
thought better of it. She made no further objection; she sat
looking at the young man, at the carroty hair and the celluloid
collar. She did not know that she had ever seen him before,
and she fervently wished that she had never seen him at all,
certainly not under the present circumstances.

The fact was she had seen him, although not to recognize. His father, Barney Sturgis, had come to Bristol twenty years before, a widower with three children, directly from Rathfryland, County Down, and had gone to work as a bartender at the Palace Saloon. He worked there still; the Palace was owned by a man named Lowry, who was his cousin and had sent for him. Barney spoke with an Ulster brogue, emphasizing the aitches and the ars. Short and broad-shouldered, he had a florid face, the long, meaty upper lip of the Irish, and bulging eyes. He wore his hair brushed in a damp, neat parabola across his forehead to hide a tendency toward baldness, and about his biceps he wore fancy elastic sleeve garters to keep his cuffs out of the suds. Armed with a bung-starter he was known to be formidable when it was necessary, but it was seldom necessary after the first few times, and his manner was otherwise mild. He would lean forward, both hands flat on the bar, to take an order. This was because he was slightly deaf, but it gave him a confidential air and caused him to have to listen, or at any rate to have to seem to listen, to a great many endless confessions about the secret, troubled lives of his customers. He had never betrayed a confidence; actually, however, that could have been because he heard very little of what was told him. "Is that so?" he'd say, interjecting the words appropriately; "Ye dont tell me." He was an Orangeman, a Protestant, and had contempt for those of his countrymen born nearer Dublin. It was known that his wife was dead. His life gave him no occasion to speak to women, and he appeared to prefer it so. At least he never remarried.

John was just out of skirts when his father brought him and his two older sisters to Bristol. He grew up there, leader in school of all the boys within a year of his age and a dozen pounds of his weight. Though he was far from the scholastic top of his class, he had a quick enough mind and a forthright manner and an instant readiness with his fists; he had never been known to back away from a challenge. In times of excitement he spoke with traces of his father's brogue, which also

earned him a certain respect. Finishing high school he went
to work for one of his father's customers. It was the one favor
Barney ever asked in return for having listened or seemed to
listen to all those dithyrambic confidences delivered across the
bar, and the feed and grain merchant never had cause to regret
it. The boy did well, first in the warehouse and then on the
road. He was liked and even admired, and now in his middle
twenties after six years in the business world he was being
pointed to as a man on the way to success, an example of
what could be done in that world by a young man who would
apply himself, keep cheerful, and not grouse about salary or
overtime. There were mothers who preened their daughters
for him, considering him quite a catch, and there were daughters who, although their mothers would never have considered
him under any account and their fathers would absolutely have
reached for pistols at the thought, watched with approval as he
rode past in the feed and grain buggy and tipped his hat and
cocked his eye.

No matter what success seemed to lie in his path, however, no one was prepared for his marrying into the Wingate
family. "Well!" they said when they heard it, especially the
hard-eyed mothers and the fathers who kept their pistols
handy. But that was all. It was a time of fever, the first
cases; within another two months the dead wagon was making the rounds every morning and they were burying their
friends and relatives by the twos and threes; there was little
time for comment. Even so, no one was more surprised than
Sturgis himself. Marriage had been a long way from his mind.

There was no proposal, certainly not in any accepted sense,
though the request for her hand had been formal enough even
by Wingate standards. In the weeks following the Tuesday
and Friday evenings when they had had the buggy to themselves he thought of Esther frequently; he would find her
coming into his mind at the most unlikely times — in the
middle of a sale, for instance, or when he was out with another girl in the buggy. He was rather proud of himself,

seeing the affair as a successful sortie into a social group above his own. The pleasure had been small, however, except in this sense, and consequently, though he did not forget her, he thought about her less and less in the course of the two months since they had been together. Then he received a letter, a note. On good stationery, folded precisely and sealed with a monogram in wax, a *W* looped and scrolled to illegibility, it told him she was going to have a baby, and requested that he call the following morning.

His reaction was surprise, then alarm, then dismay, then downright fright, all four in rapid succession, each giving way in turn until the fourth, which remained and which he never lost though at first he misunderstood its source, its basis, believing it was fear of Mrs Wingate. He had never presumed even to bow to her from the boardwalk as she rode past in her carriage. Yet now he must go to her with this request, this knowledge; he must climb those steps, cross that high gallery, walk into that house he had never believed he would enter, and face her in that parlor. This seemed as thoroughly presumptuous to him as he knew it would seem to her. Though he had the advantage of strength proceeding from an established fact — Esther was pregnant, and had summoned him — he also had the guilt, and guilt was a burden no man knew the weight of till it was loaded on his back.

Then in a moment of revelation, the chain reaction continuing, the fright became pure terror, which passed to panic. He realized that it was not the mother he feared; that was just something to hide behind, to conceal himself from himself, from his own thoughts. The one he really feared was the daughter. That Friday night in the buggy, driving back toward the heart of town, his prayers having been answered after the flesh, he had indulged in a daydream, a fantasy in which Esther came to him at his boarding house, and there in front of his fellow boarders told him, 'I cannot live without you. Marry me'; 'All right. Gladly,' he said, and they were married with the approval of her parents and the town; they lived happily ever after, in the Wingate house and on the Wingate money. Yet now that something very like this had occurred — though in fact she had not come herself but had sent a summons, and though the words were not the same — Sturgis did not feel elated; he did not say 'Gladly,' or feel it either. He felt fright. For now he saw that behind the demureness and the inexperience Esther was formidable, maybe even inexorable. He remembered the eyes narrowed beyond the chattering rector; "It's early yet," she had said, watching the string of geese go across the moon, and when the opportunity came she had not so much surrendered her virtue as flung it from her, and flung it with a shudder not of passion and abandon but rather of revulsion and determination, accomplishing conception in a single connection — as if that too had been an act of will, he realized suddenly. Now that he was confronted with the necessity for marriage there began to be considerable doubt in his mind as to who had been the aggressor in the seduction, if seduction was the word.

Then too, like any other man, he had had his plans, and they were no less real for being vague. He had intended to hang onto bachelorhood as long as he was able; then would come a wife and a home, small and neat and snugly run, with children and friends who laughed at the jokes you laughed at, and old age and earned money as the goal. Sturgis had not known how much all this meant to him, how desperately he wanted what he had not even formulated, until now that he was confronted with the loss. He might have gone away, absconded (and in fact that was precisely the advice given him by a voice inside his head, like shouts of warning: "Run! Pack! Get aboard the midnight train! Get out!") but he did not. He went and faced Mrs Wingate and her daughter. Man enough to meet his responsibilities, he was not man enough to run. It was the saddest day of his life, not only because it marked his entrance into an existence for which he was unsuited, but also because it was the day when he first faced the fact that he had limitations as a man.

The wedding was at the Wingate house, in that same parlor,

because the first cases of yellow fever had appeared by then and gatherings were forbidden even at church. Besides the minister and the principals there were only the mother and the two bachelor brothers-in-law, the veterans. One gave the bride away; ten days later he was dead of the fever, and the other was dead of the same cause before the end of summer; he had been best-man. Sturgis had not suggested that his father attend, and neither Mrs Sturgis nor Esther brought it up; apparently they had never heard of Barney Sturgis. At the wedding Mrs Wingate was as stiff and proud as ever, like a general at a surrender following a battle lost to guile and superior numbers, but she unbent as far as she was able so that not even her husband's brothers might suspect that she had been maneuvered into something.

There was no honeymoon. Trains and steamboats had suspended operations south of Cairo, and even if the bride and groom had managed to reach one of the outlying cities, Nashville or Atlanta, say, they would have been locked in a pest house as soon as it became known that they were from the fever-ridden Mississippi Valley. Sturgis moved directly into the house, into the upstairs front left bedroom which Mrs Wingate assigned them. He brought everything he owned in an imitation-leather suitcase and a cardboard packing case tied around and around with rope. Mrs Wingate spent the wedding night with friends, as was the custom, but she was back next morning for late breakfast.

So they took up their lives, the three of them in the high-ceilinged mansion built in the days when Bristol was no more than a nameless river landing where steamboats took on cotton and firewood without staying long enough to affect the pressure in their boilers. In time, however, though it was scorned by the floating palaces, the landing became a stopping-off place for flatboatmen. They had slept and worked off the after-effects of their Memphis excesses by then, Memphis being a hundred and fifty miles upriver, and by the time they reached Bristol they were primed for another bender —"carrying a load of steam," they said, that would not wait for Vicksburg, another hundred miles downriver. The settlement grew from a cluster of grogshops, fiercely competitive over the chance to wet the brawlers' thirsts. Originally the Wingate house was more than a mile beyond the remotest shack of the hamlet (it was built in 1845 nearly two miles east of the landing, not quite out of earshot of the roistering flatboatmen) but gradually during the antebellum years and rapidly during the post-Reconstruction building boom, which was in full swing in 1878 when the fever epidemic brought it to a temporary halt, the town extended eastward in the direction of the Wingate plantation, foreshadowing a time when the house itself would be surrounded by bright, one-story, boxlike bungalows, as if it had spawned or littered overnight, and townspeople would point it out to visitors as a landmark, a relic. "This used to be country, out here," they would say. "Look how Bristol has grown."

But that was still in the future, beyond the present. No part of the plantation had yet become part of the town, and for John Sturgis now it was as if he had entered another world indeed, a place where all values were reversed, where the qualities he introduced, those upon which his business success and his general popularity had depended, were alien and contemptible. His whinnying laugh was no longer infectious. It caused, rather, a stiffening of backbones, a pursing of lips, a raising of bland eyebrows. His voice was too loud for the echoing rooms; he had trouble understanding that a larger space called for a smaller voice. Yet as soon as he understood this, as soon as he began to speak with something less than a shout, his camaraderie paled. It had been mainly a matter of confidence anyhow, and now that the confidence was gone he felt trapped. He showed it, too.

The three of them would sit at meals, Mrs Wingate at the head of the table, the two young people halfway down the polished walnut that reflected them foreshortened on its surface like two ghosts, facing each other yet seldom looking at

each other, any more than they looked at the older woman
at the head. Esther was more swollen every day with the
unmistakable burden which her mother continued to ignore,
and Sturgis was like a hostage held in an enemy camp or a
recently captured animal crouched in a cage and darting sidelong glances, uncertain whether it is about to be fed or be
eaten. He stayed in the house no longer than was necessary;
he would leave immediately after meals, folding his napkin
and stuffing it awkwardly into its ring while he mumbled
something about a carload of feed to be consigned or a batch
of invoices waiting to be tallied, and would return as late as
possible every evening. His original misgivings, the fear called
up when he received the note with the unreadable *W* stamped
into the wax, turned out to have been well founded. Now,
though, he was more or less inured. Sometimes it seemed
to him that he had never had another life, much less an
enjoyable one. No longer pointed out as a young man on the
road to success, he had abandoned the Pat-Mike jokes and the
dialect songs; he no longer tipped his hat and cocked his eye
at the girls who, with or without their mothers' encouragement, admired him from the boardwalk; all that was behind
him, far away. Life was no joking matter now. There was
little to smile at, and the corners of his mouth turned sharply
down.

The child was born in mid-September, neap tide of the long
hot summer of fever, in an upstairs bedroom while Sturgis
and Mrs Wingate waited in the downstairs parlor. They did
not speak, for even now, while it literally was taking place
directly above her head, Mrs Wingate continued to ignore
the birth just as she had ignored the pregnancy, and there
seemed nothing else to talk about. The room was quiet behind
the minute, rhythmic clack of her knitting needles. From time
to time, at intervals more and more closely spaced, they heard
groans and smothered cries from the room above, as if someone were being tortured up there, a suggestion of thumbscrews
and the rack, the boot and the iron maiden. But Mrs Wingate

paid it no mind; she went on with her knitting, and Sturgis continued to cross and uncross his legs, careful not to wrinkle the crease in his trousers. He had been awake since before daylight, when Esther woke him with news that the water had broken. After going for the doctor, sockless and with his nightshirt hurriedly tucked inside the waistband of an old pair of pants, he came back and put on his best suit and a clean white shirt, freshly polished shoes and a black silk tie, as if for an extra solemn funeral. It had seemed to him the proper, highborn thing to do; yet now, sitting in the parlor with his mother-in-law, he saw that she had contempt for him for dressing so; 'Irish!' she seemed to say. When the doctor came downstairs at last and told them the child was born, that Sturgis had a son and she a grandson, Mrs Wingate folded her knitting and went out to see after her roses.

Sturgis went upstairs. Esther (she was still called Little Esther and it was fitting, for she was never more than an inch over five feet tall and after the birth of the child she dragged one leg with a limp which, though barely noticeable, subtracted a bit more from her height. Later, in her old age, that was what put her finally into the wheelchair) — Esther, then, lay in the big four-poster, the baby swaddled in flannel beside her. Her face was swollen, the lines of strain clearly marked, but now that the fright and exertion were past, the pain alleviated, there was a peculiar glint in her eyes. This was final victory; this was better, even, than the night when she saw the barely waning moon beyond the grain salesman's shoulder and felt the buggy seat buttons against her back.

When he came into the room she turned toward him and raised her head clear of the pillow. "What did she say?"

"Her?" Sturgis paused. "Nothing. She went out to look at her roses."

Esther was quiet, considering this for a moment before she smiled, apparently satisfied. Then she turned back a flap of the flannel and Sturgis saw his son, the face like an angry fist, livid and toothless, eyes tight shut, and a hand alongside the face like an old man's hand in miniature, with tiny perfect fingernails, trying to clench but unable. "I named him for father," she said, watching her husband. "Hector Wingate Sturgis is his name."

△

Within two years of the Christmas Eve death of the hard-faced man who had failed his heritage and turned bitter, who was not yet a grandfather and never suspected how soon he might have been if he had not got into the wrangle with the tenant who gave his life the violent end he apparently had been seeking, the Wingate dining room was the scene of one of those reduction-and-growth periods which recur at more or less regular intervals in family histories and which sound, to the disinterested listener at any rate, like a too-simple problem in elementary arithmetic. The room itself did not change; the Wingate silver and crystal continued to gleam on the sideboard and the dark-faced servants continued to circle the candlelit table as lesser planets revolve about the sun. What changed was the people themselves, by addition and subtraction. There were three: then the father was dead and there were two: then the daughter married and there were three again: then the highchair was brought down from the attic and there were four.

Hector grew up under the guidance of the distaff side of the family. His father, whom his mother called John and his grandmother called You, was seldom there during the waking hours; he was like a visitor, or at best a boarder. Hector had only an impression of a high-colored face and hurrying legs that ended in button shoes. This was his father, he knew, and the younger woman was his mother. But the one he respected, the one he felt closest to, was the gray-haired one at the head of the table. She commanded the servants and owned the house; 'My house' she called it, where the others just said 'home' without a pronoun. They were afraid of her; he could tell, and he admired her with a child's admiration for strength, just as, conversely, he disliked the others with a child's dislike for weakness. She had a way of making the others not only look small but feel small. He could tell that too.

There was a tension in the house, a three-way pull, for the younger two were by no means united against their common enemy. Even before he learned to speak he felt it. By the time the highchair was returned to the attic and he was allowed to sit on a regular dining-room Chippendale chair, with the unabridged dictionary for a chock, he had begun to store in his memory those otherwise unrelated scenes and scraps of conversation which, contiguous to nothing, would remain with him always, though with an air of unreality, like thoughts of a previous incarnation or happenings in dreams. Once, for instance, when the word *Irish* came up (who had said it was no part of the memory, though in later years he was to wonder) his mother staged one of those fits of rebellion which even Hector knew would lead only to defeat but which she could no more resist than he could resist scratching when he itched, if only to irritate the itching. She turned sideways in her chair, addressing Hector though it was clear that the words were for her mother's benefit.

"You must never be ashamed of your Irish blood," she told him. As she said this she looked across the table at her husband. He did not return her glance; he kept his eyes down, both hands busy with something on his plate. So she turned back to Hector. He too was looking at his plate. "The Irish had as much to do with building this country as anyone."

"Indeed," his grandmother said promptly, and as usual the calm clarity of her voice made it seem louder than her daughter's, though in fact it was lower. She addressed Hector too, holding a sliver of chicken poised on her fork. "Indeed they did. Never underestimate the Irish. I can remember my father saying it: 'Never underestimate the Irish. They never underestimate themselves.' He knew them well, you see. In the olden

days our levees were built by Irish wheelbarrow laborers hired
at fifteen cents a day because the planters along the river would
not risk their valuable Negroes at such work. It was entirely
too dangerous."

The fork continued along its short arc to her mouth and
returned to the plate with a slight click, loud against the silence.
She smiled as she chewed, but narrowly, and her eyes had no
share in the smile. When Hector looked toward the other two
he saw that his mother was glaring at the opposite wall and his
father still kept his eyelids lowered as if he were studying the
food on his plate. Mrs Wingate had more to say on the subject,
however. She took a sip of water and continued.

"Yes, indeed; nor was that all. For I also remember hearing
my father say that in those oldtime levee camps whenever anything happened to one of the laborers, anything drastic I
mean, such as having a load of logs fall on him or getting bitten
by a cottonmouth or kicked in the head by a mule, since there
was no one to claim the body, not a soul who cared — for of
course none of them had any people, in spite of the fact that
many of them had crossed the ocean together to get away
from the potato famine back in '47; they never had any sense
of family, such as the Jews had or even the Chinese — the
poor fellow was buried where he fell, and thus became part
of the levee. It meant one less barrowload of dirt for the others
to haul. Yes. So you see, Hector, your mother is right and
you must never forget it. Give the Irish their due. For even
now, long after they are dead and gone, their dust and bones
are part of the sod that made the levee and are helping to keep
the river off our land."

There were other scenes more frightening still, in which the
participants figured singly or in pairs. Hector was in the parlor with the two women, the younger one's voice growing
more and more shrill and bitter, launched on the flood of another of those arguments she knew she would not win, and
suddenly, though he never knew what prompted it — the violence of what followed abolished any memory of what had
gone before — she caught him fiercely to her chest, squeezing

him breathless, and screamed beyond his shoulder, full in the older woman's face: "*I'm* your mother! She's not your mother; *I'm* your mother!" Terror overcame him, partly at not being able to breathe, but mostly because of the violence in her voice. He kicked and bit and lashed out with his fists: "Let go! Let go!" "For shame. For shame," his grandmother said. But that was all.

Worse by far, however, were the scenes between his parents late at night in the room adjoining his own. This wife had contempt for her husband: Hector saw that by daylight and heard it at night. She had married expecting deliverance; she had thought he would take her away or join her in revolt. Yet he had knuckled under more abjectly than she herself had ever done — he had joined the opposing conspiracy, the cabal. Hector would hear her in the night, in the adjoining bedroom, her voice rising and falling, hissing with fury: "I know why. I know *why* all right!" She repeated her sentences this way, to italicize a word or rearrange a phrase for emphasis. "You want her money; thats what *you* want! Do you know what you are? Youre a scoundrel. An underbred scoundrel: thats what *you* are!"

Hector would lie there, clutching one corner of the pillow, frightened by the fury in her voice, the way it shook and trembled until sometimes he could not distinguish the words; all that was communicated was the naked fury, the frustration. His nurse slept on a pallet beside his bed. She heard it too, that choked, furious voice, and she was frightened, too, he thought; he thought he heard her sobbing and he saw her shoulders shake. But one night, worse than usual, when he slid down onto the pallet to hug her back, to comfort and be comforted in an extremity of fear, he discovered that she was not sobbing as he had thought. She was not even frightened. She was chuckling; she was laughing, and her shoulders shook with the effort to suppress it, keep it quiet. She was enjoying the frantic bedroom monolog, the white folks' nighttime trouble, the recriminations and the bitterness. This frightened him, too,

though in a different way. He got back into bed, alone, and
lay there hearing his mother's voice with the nurse's chuckling
for an undertone, until at last his father's snores came through
the hissing and his mother snorted and stopped and went to
sleep.

He was troubled with nightmares. Somewhere in one of his
grandfather's books he saw a drawing of a grizzly. It stood
beside a log on an empty plain, looking out at him, man-tall,
taller, with eyes too small for its face. In the background there
was a mountain, dead-looking, with snow down one slope and
on its peak. He had never before seen snow, much less a bear.
When he first saw it he was so frightened he dropped the
book and ran. It had a fascination for him, though, and from
time to time he peeked at it again, always clapping the book
quickly shut to keep the bear locked in. Finally he told his
nurse about it, calling the bear a pig.

"Less see," she said. But when he showed her the drawing
she laughed and shook her head. "That aint no pig, child.
Thats a bar," she told him. Her name was Emma. He held
tightly to her apron string, peering around her shoulder. "They
eats little boys," she said gravely, frowning at him. He hid his
face. "But dont you fret, child," she added, patting the back
of his head, stroking the cowlick where the hair stood stiffly
up; "Emma aint ghy let no old bar git *her* boy. No sir she
aint."

Now he began to see the bear in his dreams. In the background was the mountain with snow on its peak, and the bear
walked upright like a man in baggy underclothes, taking awkward steps and balancing its big ungainly head on narrow
shoulders. Its fur was shot with gray; its tongue lolled wet and
red; its eyes were small, with pink whites, bloodshot, and
glowed when the way led through shadows. There were
others who came to join the first, alike except in different sizes
and all ferocious in a lumbering, flat-footed, shaggy, stiff-
kneed manner. Always in the dream they were chasing him,
tottering after him with their elbows held in close to their

sides, limp-wristed, the big paws dangling. They did not run
very fast but they never tired, and that was where the terror
lay, in just their persistence. They wanted to hug him and
there was no place to hide, and they knew it and they kept
coming, shaggy and ponderous. He would wake up sobbing
just as the bear in the lead, the original bear from the drawing, was about to hug him to its chest. But his nurse was always there, bending over the bed to calm his fears.

"It was the bar, Emma, the bar — "

"Shh: hush now. Dont you fret. Emma aint ghy let him eat
you. Hush."

A gangling, limber-jointed woman with amber eyes, she was
past fifty and had Indian blood; so she claimed, and apparently
she did. She was the coachman's wife. Though she was a bit
'touched' she was esteemed an excellent nurse and had a way
with children. She told Hector stories, each one taking up
where the one before left off; "Where was we?" was the way
they all began. The hero was Dobby Hicks, the guardian angel
of Negro character. He was less than five feet tall, she said,
dressed in a polkadot tie and a claw-hammer coat with the
tail down over his heels, and every time you were about to do
wrong he would stand on your toes, looking up at you, and
shake his finger in your face, plain to you but invisible to anyone else, and if you didnt mind him you had trouble. She had
a collection of charms, 'mojoes' she called them, to keep off
evil spirits and hants. She kept them in a cigar box, each in its
individual tobacco sack tied with different colored string.
There were charms for love and charms for hate, powders
and unguents bought from hoodoo men, fast-working or slow,
depending on how you wanted it, and all infallible. She would
take out the mojoes and tell him their names, mostly in what
must have been an African dialect, though she did not know
this any more than Hector did.

Every night she put him to sleep with a rhyme that had been
used on her as a child, back in slavery days:

> *Be quite — go to sleep:*
> *Eyes shut: dont you peep.*
> *Hush now or he just moans:*
> *Raw head and bloody bones!*

and Hector would lie with his fists clenched under his chin, too frightened to relax for fear his eyes would accidentally open and he would see the monster thing with the fleshless head and nothing but shreds of meat on its bones.

Emma indeed had a way with children. But it was his grandmother who dominated the majority of these remembered scenes. He was with her most, and she was the one who bought and taught him to wear the tight serge knee-breeches, the hightop button shoes and ribbed black stockings, the hard round hat like a truncated cannonball fitted into a rim, the wide black satin bow tie that rode up under his chin and made his throat hot. Other boys of good family were dressed more or less this way on Sundays and on special occasions, but this was Hector's everyday wear. Mrs Wingate smelled of orris root and sachet, and he never dared to ask her why he was not allowed to dress like other boys.

She took him with her in the carriage when she rode out for her weekly inspection tour of the plantation. Emma sat on the jump-seat facing rear, holding a parasol over their heads in fine weather when the hood was folded back, and Samuel the coachman, Emma's husband up on the box, wore a plug hat and drove with his elbows high and wide, as Mrs Wingate required. Hector watched and admired her; he could hardly take his eyes away from her long, fine-bred face with its layer of rice powder, the way she smiled and spoke with her mouth awry to hide the gap where a front side tooth was missing, the blue-pink cameo at her throat (it was said to resemble her mother) which her father had presented to her for Confirmation in Missouri forty years ago. Her hair was almost white now, but that was by a certain magic he could not understand — she put bluing in the water when she washed

it. Collectively these things made her seem like a queen to
Hector, and the plantation was her kingdom. It had POSTED:
NO HUNTING signs nailed to trees and fence posts along its
boundaries, and the tenants standing beside their plows at the
turnrows removed their hats with a sweeping gesture, like
subjects of her kingdom, when the carriage came abreast. The
manager, big and hale, with a shovel beard and an enormous
rat-colored hat, rode alongside on a sorrel gelding that broke
wind steadily, a rapid series of backfires in rhythm with its
stride. Mrs Wingate seemed not to notice this, but it embarrassed Hector.

On every such trip, if the fair weather held, they got out
of the carriage to inspect one of the tenant cabins. Each had
a vegetable patch out back, as Mrs Wingate required, and
there was always a woman standing in the doorway, barefoot,
usually with a punched dime worn on a string around her
ankle, more naked-looking in a one-piece cotton dress than
she would have looked without it. She rode a child on one
hip and cried, "Hush up, sir! Hush up, sir!" at the invariable
flop-eared hound that came belling from under the gallery as
soon as the carriage stopped, and for some reason the dogs all
had yellow eyebrows like a pair of inverted commas, one on
each side of its forehead. Inside the cabin there was a special
odor compounded of many things, most of which remained
anonymous, though among them Hector learned to identify
coal-oil, corn starch, and stale bread, vanilla, lye soap, and old
newspapers. Wooly-headed children, their eyeballs and teeth
standing out incredibly white, looked at him in a solemn, not
unfriendly way, but when he or his grandmother spoke to
them they hung their heads or hid behind their mother. The
woman would follow them through both rooms, her bare feet
making a hissing sound against the floor planks. She called
Mrs Wingate 'Old Miss,' saying "Yessum, Old Miss" or "Noam,
Old Miss" depending on which was applicable. Hector never
heard one of them say anything else; apparently it was all
the vocabulary they had. Riding home in the carriage, he felt

as if he were returning from a visit to another world. "Someday all this will be yours," the grandmother said from time to
time. It made him feel uneasy.

Mrs Wingate also took him to town with her on shopping
expeditions. Sometimes she would let him get out of the carriage and go into one of the stores with her. She was a meticulous shopper; her life was a long war with Bristol tradesmen,
every purchase being preceded by a skirmish. She could not
abide having a clerk suggest an item. "Never mind, sir," she
would say. "I know what I want. Just show me what I ask
to see, and that will be sufficient."

At the market she would not allow her grandson to accept
a wiener from the butcher, as he saw other boys do when
they were with their parents. "No, Hector," she would say.
The butcher stood by, hands folded respectfully into his
apron. "How do we know what they use to stuff those things?
Wait till we get home where we grind our own." It was the
same with lady fingers at the bakery. "Dont you know they
make those things with the leavings?" And the baker, too,
would be standing beside her, listening. Though the tradesmen never allowed it to show as long as she faced them, whenever Mrs Wingate turned her back, even for an instant, Hector
saw that they looked at her with cold hostility in their eyes.
It lasted only as long as her back was turned. As soon as she
faced them again the look was gone, replaced by one of defer-
ence and even solicitude. They were afraid of her; they hated
her but they were afraid of her. Hector saw that and it made
him proud that she was his grandmother. It was almost worth
the loss of the wieners and lady fingers which went to other
boys and which, after a first time, neither the butcher nor
the baker ever offered him again.

There was a period every afternoon when he had time to
think of all these things, an hour after dinner — the midday
meal — when everyone went to take a nap, each to his own
room. Hector would lie in bed in his underwear, thinking
about 'life' and the world outside. If a thing occurred in the

morning he would watch without deduction, saving all analysis
for naptime; 'I'll think about that this afternoon,' he would
tell himself, watching and storing impressions. Sometimes he
invented stories, modeling them on the ones his nurse had told
him, except that where she had made herself the princess in
distress, he saw the events from the position of the hero with
the sword. In time he even learned to look with the eyes of
the dragon, who after all had his side too, and that was better yet.

Sunshine, beating against the outer wall, was strained through
the shades, lending the bedroom a false, thin-gold twilight.
The only sounds were the buzzing of flies and the muffled
breathing where Emma lay on her pallet with the quilt drawn
over her face in even the hottest weather. Her feet stuck out
at the bottom, black on top but with soles as pale as his own;
the long toes stood apart like fingers on a hand, ready to grab,
and the nails were crusted yellow-gray, like little oyster shells.
When he lay there that way, awake when everyone else was
asleep, it was like living a secret life that no one shared.

He had never been really alone, out of arm's reach of someone assigned to watch. But now — cautiously, lest Emma stir
and wake and catch him — he began to slip out of the room,
to move about the upstairs hall while everyone else lay profoundly relaxed in sleep. They slept with their doors ajar for
coolness: he could see them. His mother, her hair spread fanwise on the pillow, lay flat on her back with her arms flung
akimbo, as if she had fallen out of the sky. Sometimes she
talked in her sleep, a fitful murmur that could not be de-
ciphered though Hector thought it was probably addressed to
her husband and her mother, the quarrel continuing through
sleep. His grandmother, sleeping with her face toward the
door, on guard like a good soldier even in slumber, clasped
both hands to her chest in an attitude of prayer that made
her resemble a tombstone angel tipped sideways off its pedes-
tal. She wore a nightcap frilled with lace, the drawstring
tied at the nape of her neck, and in sleep she still held her
mouth twisted bitterly to hide the gap left by the missing

tooth. Hector stood in the hall, opposite first one doorway and then another, looking at the sleepers. This way he was not only living a secret life, he might indeed have been the only person left alive on earth — a small figure, barefoot, wearing knit one-piece drawers-and-shirt with a slash in the seat and a row of bow-knots down the front because Mrs Wingate believed that buttons were uncomfortable and should never be used on underwear. His light brown hair, which caught the glimmer from the windows at the end of the hall, was cut Dutch fashion with bangs across the front, the sides clipped squarely along the line of his jaw. His nose was snub; he had it from his father. His eyes were blue-green, or rather, chameleonlike, depending on the color of his clothes, they seemed to change from blue to green and back to blue again. They bulged and glistened. This, taken in conjunction with the damp, slightly gaping mouth, gave his face a somewhat imbecile look when he was thinking, though at other times it had a small-boy sweetness. His voice was high and reedy, like Mrs Wingate's.

At the rear of the hall, to the right of the staircase, there was a door he had never seen anyone use. He wondered about it; it was like a door in a fairy tale, enchanted and forbidden. Then one day he tried the knob and it turned with a dry click. The door came open. Unlike any other he had ever seen, however, this door did not open into a room; it gave directly upon a flight of stairs, the first step flush with the sill and the others leading steeply toward a high dim dusty rectangle of light. He stood there, looking. Then, since naptime was nearly over, he went back to bed and lay thinking about it until Emma roused and got him dressed for their afternoon walk. He did not mention his discovery. This was one thing he would keep to himself.

Next day, as soon as Emma was breathing in muffled groans beneath the quilt, Hector went directly to the door and opened it. He stood holding the door ajar and looking up the dusty flight of stairs, gathering courage. Sunbeams filled with dustmotes slated the rectangle. It was like looking up out of a well.

The stairs were steep; he took them a step at a time, pausing with both feet on each step as if waiting for the echo of his footfall. When his head came through the opening, on a level with the floor of the attic, what he saw was like nothing he had ever seen before. The place was cluttered with discarded furniture, broken or outmoded, stacked aimlessly among trunks of wornout clothes. He saw cracked mirrors, a row of damaged chamberpots, and other things he could not identify, including a canvas fencing jacket with a heart sewed on the left breast and a screen-wire mask like an empty face. This was the overflow of half a century; no Wingate ever threw anything away; the conglomerate litter included articles the first Hector had brought from Ohio fifty years ago, ten years before the house itself was built. Dust was everywhere, velvet underfoot, coating everything with its soft insistence, mouse-gray in the shadows but gleaming like old silver where sunlight struck it. On the opposite wall, suspended from nails by their collars, his dead great-uncles' army uniforms dangled side by side like hanged men. Their buttons (CSA) were tarnished, and so were the gold-braid bars and loops at the collars and cuffs and the two swords leaning against the wall beside two pairs of boots with their tops flopped over.

When he had lain in bed, thinking, it had been like living a secret life, and that was good. Then when he had roamed the upper hall, looking at the sleepers on their beds, it had been like being the last person left alive on earth, and that was better. But now in the attic, barefoot in the velvet dust, it was as if no one had ever lived at all, or if they had lived they had not merely died, they had been abolished, abrogated; and that was best. He had a world all his own, like a polar explorer on a wide cold waste no man had ever seen before or a balloonist alone in the high far ether with nothing but clouds below. If he had had any notion of what he intended to do up here, it was forgotten. He only stood and looked at the clutter, at the overhead beams and rafters crisscrossed with sunbeams lanced from the front and rear mansard windows and the louvers set into the gables at each end. When the time was up he went back down and lay in bed waiting for Emma to waken.

"Look here, boy," she said when she came to rouse him. "How you git the bottoms of yo feet so potty black?"

But he would not tell her. "Maybe it was Dobby Hicks," he said, his face innocent. The attic was his hideaway, his secret kingdom, and he refused to share it with anyone. Returning from their walk an hour later, he would look up at the high windows, rose-colored in the sunset, and think how what was behind them was his and no one else's, a secret place that no one knew about.

There was more to life than this, however. There was Bristol as he saw it when he sat beside his grandmother in the carriage and Emma balanced the parasol over their heads. Bristol had come a long way since the days when flatboatmen swaggered down the stageplanks with blood in their eyes, heading for the grogshops and calling for the bully of the town. Two main streets ran eastward from the levee almost half a mile to the depot, intersecting the railroad at a point where, coming from the north, it bent west in a long curve, its parallel silver threads describing an arc subtending the town, bounding it on the east and south as abruptly as if the ramp had been another levee or a fortified wall in the Middle Ages. Outside the ramped, twin-thread arc lay cottonfields and random cuts of timber; within it, shops and hostelries, saloons and one-story false-front offices were clustered near the river; the rest was residential. The streets were lined with trees, live oaks older than the town, whose overarching branches touched from opposite curbs to form a tunnel, cottonwoods that filled the air with fluff, black-trunked magnolias with blooms like exploding stars and boat-shaped leaves with waxy tops and fuzzy undersides, chinaberries with delicate lavender flowers and later with fruit that fermented in the sunlight and made the robins so drunk they tumbled to the ground and were gathered in sacks and baskets, themselves like fruit, to be cooked into pies. Hector saw these and others whose names his grandmother taught him, sycamores

with shaggy bark that peeled of its own accord to show an
underskin as smooth and white and shapely as the naked arms
of women, pecan and walnut and hickory, the wisest three,
which never put out their tender shoots till spring had come
to stay, silver-leaf maples and weeping willows and poplars
that shivered in the slightest breeze, redbuds whose limbs were
sheathed with purple flame like the bush Moses saw burning
in the Bible. This had all been forest before the white men
came, and even today whoever grew up in Bristol grew up
in their shade, breathing the springtime perfume of their blos-
soms. The days were sleepy and quiet for those who moved
along the leafy tunnels, but even Hector, detached as he was,
could sense the teem of life below the surface.

For one thing, there had been a war and a way of life that
was lost when the war was lost. The men who had fought in
it were veterans now. They sat on benches at the depot, sun-
ning themselves and whittling while they watched the trains
come in, but on holidays they donned uniforms and staged
parades, the younger ones sucking their stomachs in and skip-
ping to keep step, the older ones already hobbling on canes.
It was hard to connect their rheumy eyes and empty faces
with the shot-torn flags and the tumult, yet sometimes when
the carriage was held up at the crossing he would hear them,
and the names of the battles came through the drone of talk
— Manassas, Shiloh, Gaines Mill, Malvern Hill, Sharpsburg,
Second Manassas, Fredericksburg, Murphreesboro, Chancellorsville, Gettysburg, Vicksburg, Chickamauga, The Wilderness, Spottsylvania, Cold Harbor, Brice's Crossroads, Ken-
nesaw Mountain, Big Shanty, Atlanta, Petersburg, Spring Hill,
Franklin, Nashville, Five Forks, Appomattox: he heard them
all — the Biblical, Indian, English names of cities and hamlets
and creeks and crossroads throughout the South, for the most
part unimportant in themselves until the day when the armies
came together, more or less by accident, to give the scattered
names a permanence and to settle what manner of life Hector
Sturgis, for one, was to grow up under.

Three-fifths of the population of Jordan County, of which Bristol was the county seat, were Negro. Twenty years ago they were slaves. Ten years ago they had held the most important public offices, sheriffs, judges, senators; "Bottom rail on top!" they cried. But there had been some sort of revolution-in-reverse (something about night riders and smut ballots; nobody spoke of it now, however, not even in whispers; evidently there had been some necessary acts of shamefulness better left unmentioned) and now the bottom rail was back on bottom. They lived apart, in separate sections of the town, one called Lick Skillet, the other Ram Cat, and on weekdays that was where you saw them, the women in shifts or flour-sacking dresses and headrags, the men in ragged overalls, sitting on their porches in split-bottom chairs. But Saturdays they came downtown and that was a sight to see, the women in gored skirts and bright red shirtwaists, carrying india-rubber sponges to sop their faces, and the men in swallowtail coats and button shoes, sporting horseshoe tie pins and big-link watch chains. No matter where you saw them, though, blinking in the sunlight on their porches or standing on the boardwalk in their finery, their faces were dark masks. "We know a secret or two," they seemed to say. "We know things that we wont tell." Even when they laughed, which they frequently did, tilting their heads to show their golden teeth, their faces were inscrutable: "We know a secret — "

This was a brooding force, a fuliginous backdrop against which the town, mindful of Haiti and John Brown and Reconstruction, played out its life. But there was another, as dark, as brooding, and even more inscrutable. Bristol was a river town. Tawny, mile-wide, humped by boils and dimpled by eddies, the river came out of the north, gliding between Mississippi and Arkansas with a faint, insistent whisper against the bank. All afternoon the shadow of the levee, ragged along its rim because of the grass, edged eastward down the two main streets, moving from door to door: Bristol merchants told time by its progress until the sun was gone, then barred and locked their doors and hurried home through the gathering twilight. In mid-spring, when the river was on the boom, people in the streets looked up and saw the cupolas of steamboats sliding against the sky above the levee with the smooth, unreal progress of floats at carnival, each with a pilot who stood with his hands on the big wheel like the master of a lottery.

The pilot in turn looked down and saw the town spread out beneath him, first the business district, directly below in the shadow of the levee, where the upturned faces were as pale and small as the petals of flowers, then the residential district, a crescent of overarching trees pierced at random by church steeples raising their spires and crosses to his level, and finally, half a mile to the east, the silver curve of the railroad drawing its arc about the limit of the town. Here at times the pilot saw — and sneered at, having nothing but contempt for this land-going, malodorous, railbound mechanism which was one day to replace him — a chuffing locomotive dragging a blanket of smoke from its funnel stack. Beyond the area thus circumscribed, thus ringed with steel and water, beyond this hive of humanity devoted to money and dedicated to Progress, the pilot saw the very heart of the delta, level as a table top as far as the eye could follow and resembling a tapestry laid flat, its pattern mainly one of cottonfields, ash-gray and corrugated, marbled with dark green fingers of woodland hugging the creekbanks and starred with scattered two-story whitewashed-brick plantation houses and the glinting metal roofs of barns and gins.

These four — the trees, the war, the Negroes, the river — rose out of the past and cast their shadows on the present. They were the dominants of the scene where Hector grew to manhood, as if life were indeed an action on a stage and these were the properties. No matter where he was, whether padding about the sleeping house or alone in the attic he called his kingdom or riding in the carriage with Mrs Wingate, these four were with him whether he knew it or not, and from time to time, singly or in pairs or all together, they came forward and made their presence felt.

Manhood was still a long way off, however; he was yet in childhood, with boyhood and youth still to be passed through, and there was another remembered scene, one that was to stand out in his memory as if against the aureate glare of lightning. It was strange. This time his grandmother had left him in the carriage with Emma, saying she would only be gone a minute. Samuel walked the horses up to a watering trough, and Hector sat under the parasol, amusing himself by looking at the storefronts and spelling out the names printed across them in block letters. He would enter school that fall and Mrs Wingate had begun to prepare for this by giving him reading lessons; they sat on the veranda every morning, holding the primer between them, and at night after supper she took him on her lap and read fairy tales out of an illustrated book, pointing out the words with the tip of her finger so that he could follow the text as she read. He had made good headway, and that was why he was able to read the names on the storefront windows and over the doors.

The doorway opposite the watering trough was different from the others along the street. It had swinging half-doors, slatted like jalousies, and beneath them he saw a floor strewn with sawdust. Above these doors, in block letters whose gilt had tarnished and peeled, he spelled out:

PAL CE SALOON

He could discern the weathered outline of the missing A but he could not identify either word: not the first — though he had seen it often in the fairy tales — because it was mutilated, nor the second because he had never seen it before nor even heard it spoken.

Men entered and came out. When they paused in the doorway to adjust their ties or set their derbies straight, Hector would catch a glimpse of the dark interior. Then two men came out together. They stood there, talking, holding the doors ajar, and he saw what seemed to be a long box, narrower

than tall, extending the length of the opposite wall. It was covered with sheet marble and a polished rail ran along its base
like a line of yellow light from a bull's-eye lantern held just
clear of the floor. Above this dark, oblong box an oil painting
in an ornate frame was fastened to the wall. It showed a
woman reclined on a couch. Her hair was as bright as the
brass of the rail, and she wore no clothes. Beneath the painting, posed with both hands palm-down on the marble slab
like an Olympian deity against a backdrop of glasses and bottles racked in rows, Hector saw a broad-shouldered old man
in shirtsleeves, as motionless as the woman in the painting.
He wore a high collar without a tie, and the point of the
collar button was a tiny gleam of gold. He was looking at
Hector, eyes narrowed, and Hector was looking at him. Then
the two men separated ("So long" — "So long"); the doors
flicked shut, then open, then shut, and Hector never saw him
again.

Emma had seen him too, for when Hector turned his head
he saw that she was watching him with something like a smile
on her dark face. She leaned forward, still balancing the parasol, and whispered hoarsely: "Thats yo grandaddy!" Then he
saw her face assume a blankness, the eyes as expressionless as
a pair of musket balls, and he too heard his grandmother's quick
firm step on the boardwalk beside the carriage.

"I was longer than I thought," she said.

Somehow he knew better than to ask Mrs Wingate what
his nurse had meant, or even Emma herself as long as his
grandmother was there. As it turned out, he never asked anyone. But he did not forget it; he simply let it move to the back
of his mind.

In the fall following his sixth birthday Hector began to
attend the Bristol public school. He still wore the serge knee-

breeches, the ribbed stockings, and even the satin tie; the
coachman drove him there every morning and called for him
every afternoon. It was a new world, peopled with Lilliputians. There was a bell for everything, one to begin and one
to end and one each for the many things that came between.
First they had a morning prayer, asking God to make them
good and thankful, then a song as they stood in the aisles:
"Good morning, dear teacher, good morning to you." Then
they sat, hands clasped on the desk tops, all eyes on the teacher
who said solemnly, "Now we'll put on our thin-king caps,"
making a two-handed motion as if she were pulling a sack
over her head, and all the children did the same; "Now we'll
put on our thin-king caps!" they chanted, more or less in unison, performing that same curious head-in-sack motion, groping at the air beside their ears.

As a result of the reading lessons Mrs Wingate had given
him every morning out of the primer he would use in school,
Hector was far ahead of the other pupils. He could read
straight through whole pages, moving glibly down lines of
type that caused the others to falter and sweat and tangle
their tongues in their teeth. Whenever a particularly difficult
passage came up, one that prompted a general squirming and
a hiding of eyes out of fear of being called on, the teacher
assigned it to Hector, who not only read the words correctly
but read them with expression as well, pausing for commas
and inflecting the exclamation points and question marks like
an actor arrived at his most effective speech. The other pupils
turned in their desks and watched him with a certain awe,
for sometimes like an orator he made gestures as he read. The
teacher always smiled when he had finished and gave a little
series of nods of approval. "Very good," she would say. "Very
good, indeed. Why cant the rest of you do as well?"

At noon recess he sat apart and ate his lunch from a japanned
box which the cook had packed according to his grandmother's
instructions; Mrs Wingate had definite opinions about diet.
He had a particular place where he sat to eat, on the side
steps leading up to the principal's office, and a group of chil-

dren always collected to watch. For them it was like Christmas morning, watching what came out of the fancy box, one good thing after another and always a surprise for dessert, a cookie with colored icing, a strawberry tart, or a gingerbread man with raisins for eyes and three more raisins in a row for the buttons on his coat. They stood at the foot of the steps, their eyes growing larger, their mouths gaping wider with each good thing that emerged. For Hector there was something embarrassing about having them stand that way, gawking. He thought they were probably hungry; they looked it. But once when he offered a boiled egg to one of the watchers (there was always a boiled egg, with two twists of waxed paper, one for salt and one for pepper; "They build bone," his grandmother said mysteriously) the boy put his hands quickly behind him, his eyes wide as he looked at the egg on Hector's palm, and backed away. "Go on, take it," Hector said. "I dont want it anyhow." The boy turned and ran.

Presently his brother, a big fourth-grade boy with a shock of yellow hair high on his head and a saddle of freckles across his nose, approached the steps. He came striding, then stopped with his face thrust close to Hector's and said in a gruff voice, "Keep your old done-up grub to yourself, Mister Fancy Pants."

"Well, I will," Hector told him.

"Well — all right," the boy said. He paused. Then, considering that this was a note perhaps not forceful enough to end the exchange on, he thrust his face closer and added still more gruffly, "You want to make something *of* it?" The freckles stood out large and brown, and his younger brother peeped around his shoulder.

"Well, no," Hector said. "I dont."

"Well — all right," the fourth-grader said. And deciding that this was probably forceful enough after all, he said no more. He just stood there, glowering and clenching his fists. All the watchers laughed and whooped until Miss Hobbs, the principal, came to the door at the top of the steps and scattered them.

"Hush this hubbub!" she cried, and they ran, exploding outward as if a bomb had gone off in their midst. She held a sheaf of papers in one hand and brandished a ruler in the other, a tall gray-haired woman wearing an alpaca skirt, streaked and splotched with chalkdust, and a horn-rim pince-nez from which two strands of ribbon drooped to a gold pin at the breast of her shirtwaist. The ribbons fluttered in the breeze.

Hector returned to his lunchbox. He sat there eating as if nothing had happened. Miss Hobbs turned to go, then paused with one hand on the door knob, looking down at Hector. "Why didnt you stand up to them?" she asked. Her nippers glinted in the sunlight, vibrating with the flutter of the ribbons. "Even if that tow-headed one had hit you, it would have been lots easier than what they will do to you now." Hector stopped chewing. He looked at her, his jaw bulged with food. She watched him, not unkindly, waiting, but he only looked at her with that same vacant stare, eyes bland, expressionless. "Well, maybe you know best," Miss Hobbs said. She entered her office, closing the door behind her, and Hector resumed his chewing.

This ended that early, brief period during which the other children stood in awe of and even perhaps respected him. Now whenever the teacher assigned him a difficult passage they turned and watched as always, except that now their faces expressed not awe but derision. They smirked and sniggered at the way he dramatized the words, and sometimes when he made one of those oration gestures with a free hand to emphasize an action or a happy turn of phrase, the teacher had to rap smartly on the edge of her desk with her ruler to stop the catcalls of the boys and the giggles of the girls. It was as Miss Hobbs had foreseen.

Outside the classroom it was even worse. Beginning with the day of the boiled egg incident, it became part of the school life for a group to assemble at the carriage block for his arrival and departure. They would stand solemnly watching him climb into the carriage with the lunchbox under one arm and an oilcloth book satchel under the other. Then, as if by prearranged signal, at the moment when Samuel lifted the reins to flick the horses into motion, they would hoot and jeer, shouting "Fancy Pants! Mister Fancy Pants! Fancy Pants!" running alongside until the carriage picked up speed and left them behind. Hector kept his eyes to the front. High on the box Samuel muttered angrily, "Trash. Nothing but trash; thats all. White trash."

But that was not all, for soon it began to pale; it was not enough, and two weeks later a gang of boys waylaid him. He had seen them whispering behind their hands all morning, watching him out of the sides of their eyes. Obviously were plotting something, but he did not discover what until that afternoon. The group at the carriage block, assembled to give him the jeering send-off, was much smaller than usual. He thought nothing of this, however, until the coachman slowed to turn a corner two blocks from the school and a band armed with barrel staves and lengths of lath came charging out of a clump of mulberry trees and began to beat on the sides of the carriage, cheering each other on and screaming their battle cries.

For a moment Hector was terrified by the din of sticks against the fenders and running-boards, the mass of wild, excited faces with open mouths and tossing hair. Then, drawing on some atavistic reserve — received perhaps from the man who fell near the apex of the V at Buena Vista — he stood on the seat, facing backward over the tonneau, and swung the oilcloth book satchel at their heads. He held it by the long carrying-strap and swung it with all his might. It was a gift from his grandmother, the latest model, with special compartments for books and tablets and a row of pencils stuck through little loops of elastic, each with his name stamped in gold on its shank near the rubber eraser. As he swung it he could hear the tablets and books slapping against each other and the dry, brittle sound of pencils breaking. Samuel looked back over his shoulder. "Give it to um, Little Mars!" he cried. "Give it to um!"

That was just what Hector was doing. The satchel made really an excellent counter-offensive weapon. But the first time it landed squarely against one of the upturned screaming faces, he felt the shock of resistance travel up the strap, the momentary give of flesh and then the solidity of bone beneath: whereupon, all of a sudden, there was a flutter at the pit of his stomach and a sour taste at the root of his tongue. He dropped the satchel onto the seat and, turning, sat for an instant with a stricken, dazed expression of revulsion on his face. Then he leaned deliberately forward, placing his head between his knees, and threw up on the floorboard of the carriage.

"What you want to quit for?" Samuel said, forlorn on the box. "You was just gitting going good."

The waylayers had been startled by the counterattack, as unexpected as it was violent, and when the satchel struck one of them they fell back. However, they recovered quickly — except the boy who had received the blow; he was nursing his face — and began to gather rocks and clods of dirt from the roadside and fling them after the carriage. One knocked Samuel's plug hat clean off; he barely managed to grab it before it rolled into the road. Another caught Hector above the left eye just as he was straightening up. These were the only two hits, though other clods and rocks continued to clatter against the rear of the carriage until it was out of range.

When they turned in at the house Mrs Wingate was standing in a rosebed beside the drive. She wore a heavy leather gauntlet as if for hawking, with a pair of snips in one hand and some dead stems in the other. First she saw the dent in the coachman's hat and then the cut above her grandson's eye. She took Hector up to her room, and when she had cleaned the wound with camphor she made him tell her what had happened, from the beginning. He had been all right up

till then — in his mind at least, for the vomiting had resulted
from an impulse in his stomach; it had nothing to do with his
mind, he told himself — but now, as he stood in front of his
grandmother, breathing the clean, medicinal smell of camphor,
feeling it tingle the gash above his eye, and tried to tell about
what had happened since the day of the boiled egg, he began
to cry. And that was the greatest shame of all; it made him
cry all the harder. When at length he had finished both the
weeping and the telling, Mrs Wingate gave him his first lesson
in the mysteries of human relationships.

"Now listen," she said. Placing both hands on his shoulders,
she looked directly into his eyes and held him so that he had
to look directly into hers. Whenever his eyes tried to wander
or lose focus she gave him a shake that brought them back
where they belonged. "There are really only two classes of
people in this world, those who have and those who wish they
had. When those of the second class . . . Mind what I'm telling you," she said sharply. She gripped him tighter, and when
his eyes came back into focus she resumed. "When those of
the second class begin to realize that they will never catch up
with those of the first, they jeer. All right: listen. Those of
the first class (which includes you," she said, releasing one
shoulder to give him a prod, then grasping it again) "must
realize that the jeering goes with the having. Besides, when
you are older and able to strike back at them, by foreclosing
their mortgages or causing them to be dismissed from their
places of employment, they will not jeer where you can hear
them. They wont dare to; no. And what is said behind your
back cannot matter, first because you cannot hear it and second because it is a sort of underhanded compliment in the
first place. It's a certain sign that they acknowledge your position, a proof of membership. You understand?"

"Yessum," he said, responding to another shake. But he did
not.

That was his last day in a public school; he did not go back
even to clean out his desk. Mrs Wingate engaged the mathe-

matics and science teacher from Bristol High School to come
to the house every afternoon and tutor him. This was Professor Rosenbach, a German with a dark brown beard and
inward-slanting teeth: Professor Frozen Back he was called,
for he walked with a stiff Prussian carriage as if he were pacing off the distance between barriers for a duel. However,
there were those who said that he had left the fatherland as a
youth to avoid military service in the war with France, and
now he walked this way either to make up for it or to mis-
lead suspicion. This may or may not have been true; in any
event it was certainly malicious, being repeated mainly by
pupils or former pupils who resented his stern classroom
discipline and who could give first-hand testimony as to
his zeal with the birch. But there was no doubt that he gave
an impression of militarism. The seals on his watchfob made
a little chinking sound wherever he went, reproducing in
miniature the clink of a saber chain, and there was a cica-
trice high on one cheek that might have been a dueling scar,
direct from Heidelberg, except that it was rather small and
neat and had been acquired in the high school chemistry
laboratory when he was rinsing a beaker in which a careless
or ingenious pupil had left a pellet of sodium.

The professor believed in memory work. It developed the
mind, he said; he frequently referred to the mind in this manner, as if it were a muscle or a savings account or a combination of both. He sat in an armchair in the upstairs parlor
during the lessons, holding the book on his knee and marking
the place with a finger between the leaves, while Hector stood
opposite him, arms straight at his sides, fists clenched, like a
choir boy trying for a high note, and recited the multiplica-
tion tables or the rules of spelling and grammar. "Good. Very
good," Professor Rosenbach would say, stroking the underside of his beard with the backs of fingers whose nails were
filed straight across like those on the statues of Greek athletes.
"We are making progress. Now give me the nine-times table."
Then he would resume that curious rotary motion with his

hand under the short dark beard, nodding his head in time
to the chant of arithmetic, and when it was finished he would
nod once more, with a sudden, ponderous motion, and shine
his eyes. "Good. Good," he would say. "Very good, Master
Hector."

At first it was queer, being at home all morning while the
others were at school and only beginning his lessons after
the others had finished. Some mornings he would think about
them, the way they stood in the aisles beside their desks, heads
bent, reciting the prayer, then lifting their heads and shuffling
their feet and singing, "We're all in our places, With sun-
shiny faces; Good morning, dear teacher, Good morning to
you," while the teacher beat time with her ruler and sang
louder than anyone, wishing herself good-morning. But after
a while he seldom thought of them. The six weeks at the public school were a period far in the past; he might have dreamed
it. Education was Professor Rosenbach, opposite him there in
the armchair with the book held on one knee. If other children
were herded together in an atmosphere of chalkdust and con-
fusion, with a bell for this and a bell for that and bells for the
hundred things that came between, obliged to chant in unison
and wear invisible thinking caps, that was their misfortune.
His grandmother had explained it, and though he did not understand the explanation, it was comforting at any rate to be
told there was one.

When he was twelve and had completed a course of study
roughly corresponding to the one covered by the local grammar school, he went away to boarding school in Virginia. By
the time he was into his second year in the East, Bristol was
secondary; he had come to think of it mainly as a place where
he spent three more or less pleasant months doing nothing
every summer. In dormitory conversations he dropped ref-
erences to "our Mississippi plantation," saying the words with
an off-hand, studied carelessness to imply that it was one of
many, just as other boys up here said "our Newport place"
or "our Pennsylvania holdings." It was that kind of school;

Mrs Wingate had chosen it after a good deal of correspondence around the country. Bristol people (which included his mother and father, but not his grandmother) became a faraway conglomerate of faceless automatons who did not wear the clothes he wore or speak with the accent he spoke with or think the things he thought. It was rather as if they were all in a cage, provincial, and he was on the outside looking in.

The center spread in his American History book was a relief map of North America. On it he traced the Mississippi River from its source to a point where it made two sharp curves, like an S laid on its back, and that was Bristol (or at any rate it might have been, for the river had many such double bends); "Thats my home," he said, placing the tip of one finger on the lower curve. The map showed none of the man-made boundaries, only the natural formations, rivers and their tributaries, like lengths of string, and mountains like brown wrinkles on the page. It was strange, being able to point to this one spot out of all that veined and crinkled mass of brown and white, and tell someone "Thats my home" as if he owned it, river and all. He did not say it with any real conviction.

Christmas of 1892, when Hector was fourteen, he came home for the holidays for the first time in two years. He brought two classmates with him. They were out of Maryland, city boys from Baltimore, and when they had not understood what was said to them, they did not say Sir? or Maam? after the usage taught in Mississippi; they said Pardon? which would have made people think them abrupt and rude if they had not had such good manners otherwise and such expensive clothes and luggage. The highlight of their visit was the Christmas trip around the plantation. They went with Hector and Mrs Wingate in the carriage, and more than anything they were impressed with the way the tenants approached their mistress with their hats off, bobbing their heads and showing their teeth and saying, "Crissmus giff, Ole Miss: Crissmus giff! En you too, Little Mars: Crismuss giff!" and the way Mrs Wingate took silver dollars from a canvas sack

on the seat beside her, handing them out one at a time with
a stern expression and calling each of the Negroes by name
as he stood bobbing and grinning above the hat he held in
both hands like a basin.

"You wouldnt have believed it," the Maryland boys said
afterwards. "It was like something out of the Middle Ages.
It really was."

That was the way they told about their visit when they
got back to school in Virginia. They had gone down there
half expecting to find it one big swamp; they admitted now
that they had had misgivings. But they had been wrong and
they wanted to make amends. Life in Mississippi — "the Delta,
they call it, though it's not all the way down at the mouth of
the river" — was fascinating (that was the word they used,
back in Virginia) and Mrs Wingate was "a lady of the old
school, one of the few that are left." Others listened while
the travelers told about life on the plantation, especially the
silver dollars distributed from a sack — "like something out
of the Middle Ages. It really was" — and Hector's stock went
up. They had never called him anything but Sturgis, yet now
they began to use his first name and even abbreviate it. They
called him Heck, a devil-may-care sort of nickname. It was
almost as if he had made the varsity. Classmates who formerly
had cut him dead now nodded to him on the quad. There
was nothing really effusive about it, but all this was quite different from anything he had ever known before.

Also, now that it had brought him this, he began to see in
his homeland values he had never sensed before. He saw it
with new eyes, the eyes of strangers, and in a different light.
It was indeed romantic, he saw now, where formerly he had
thought of it as just the opposite. The Negroes, the overarching trees, the river, all the things he had taken for granted
while he lived among them — even the giving of silver dollars out of a canvas sack, since that apparently had impressed
the visitors most — now had an enchantment lent by distance
and praise, and Hector told himself that when he got back

home he would appreciate them. He would study them in
this new light. Even his grandmother, whom he already admired to what he had thought were the limits of possibility,
acquired an added value now that the Maryland boys had de-
fined her singularity — "a lady of the old school, one of the
few that are left." In her case, too, he told himself he would
make a reassessment; he would appreciate her even more when
they were together again.

It did not work out that way, however. They were never
together again. The fever intervened.

Mrs Wingate wrote to him once a week, and that was how
he learned of its return. First there were just a few scattered
cases, nothing really unusual for the time of year. Then there
were more, and more, until at last it had become an epidemic.
He no longer had to wait for information from the letters.
News of fever deaths was featured in all the papers. Yellow
fever was general all down the Valley, and though it was not
as serious as it had been fifteen years ago, in the season of
Hector's birth, it was serious enough.

Then there was a week when no letter came. He told himself it was nothing. The authorities had quarantined the mails,
or railroad workers had refused to handle anything out of
the delta, even letters, or she was too busy to write. He told
himself all these things and more, doing everything he could
to keep one certain thought out of his mind. Then, when it
passed from a notion to a conviction, he told himself not to
think about it at all. It would work itself out; any day now
he would get a letter in his grandmother's angular script ex-
plaining the lapse. What he finally got was a telegram signed
by the family doctor, which put an end to wondering:

> GRANDMOTHER FATHER DEAD BUT MOTHER WILL LIVE
> I THINK. DO NOT COME HOME TIL EPIDEMIC PAST.

He had not believed Mrs Wingate would ever die. Sitting
in the dormitory cubicle, the sheet of yellow flimsy in his
hand, he could hear her speaking to him the way she had done

through his childhood, telling him of Irish wheelbarrow laborers in the oldtime levee camps and of the two classes of
people, the havers and the wishers, teaching him how to tell
time with his dead grandfather's watch and how to blow his
nose and tuck his shirttail, the long, involved, tortuous sentences grinding on, the convulsive syntax causing the language
to turn back on itself like a snake devouring its tail. But she
was dead now: dead, and so was his father: both were dead
and probably buried, and he would never see them again. He
kept saying it over and over in his mind, in order to accustom
himself to thinking of them in the past tense.

It was difficult in his grandmother's case, for he could see
her as clearly as if she were with him now in the cubicle, the
mouth held a bit awry to hide the tooth-gap and the hair that
was white because of the strange alchemy of bluing. But when
he tried to think of his father he found that he could not
shape the face. He could recall it in outline; his father had
begun to get fat and his face was redder, too. But when he
tried to fix the features, they faded and there was only the
blank oval. He tried to remember words that his father had
spoken to him, something, anything at all, but there was
nothing. Then, as he had done before, he told himself not to
think about it. It would work itself out in time, he told himself.

In mid-June there was an exchange of wires: SCHOOL IS OVER
CAN I COME HOME NOW? and then the answer: FEVER STILL
EPIDEMIC. DRAW ON BANK FOR FUNDS. It was signed MOTHER.
So he went to Baltimore, returning the visit of the Maryland
boys. He wrote home, telling where he was, and waited for
an answer. For two weeks there was nothing. Then in the
third week he got a letter, and when he saw the envelope his
heart gave a leap. It was addressed in his grandmother's hand.
But when he tore it open and looked at the foot of the single
sheet (Mrs Wingate had always written at least three pages)
the signature said *Mother*. It inclosed a check for a hundred
dollars and instructed him to return the following week. That
was all it said.

Previously the trainride had been one of the best things about coming home for the holidays. This time it was different, partly because there were no other young people on the train, but mainly because he was riding toward his first realization of death; he could not believe in his grandmother's death until he saw for himself that she was gone. He wired from Memphis and the carriage was waiting at the Bristol station, just as always except that Samuel was alone. During the ride to the house he observed that the town was expanding eastward toward the Wingate property. At last they were there, and when he saw that the house had not changed, that it even had a new coat of paint like the old one, he realized that he had expected to find it dilapidated, as if the epidemic would leave a path of destruction like Sherman or a cyclone. But the driveway gravel had been raked as neatly as ever and there were not even weeds in the rosebeds. Then, going up the steps, he saw Mrs Wingate's shawl folded over the arm of her rocker on the gallery.

The shawl was what did it, brought it into the open. When he saw the shawl he began to suspect, quite consciously, that this was all a hoax, an ugly joke prepared and staged to test him, to show him how much his grandmother meant to him. And now that he had begun to suspect quite consciously, it seemed to him that he had never believed in the absence of letters or even in the telegram that followed. She was not dead: they had only told him that. The feeling, the conviction grew as he entered the house. Upstairs, when he stopped with one hand on the newel post and peered through the twilight of the upper hall, into Mrs Wingate's room where the only light was what filtered between slats of the drawn blinds, he saw that his suspicions were true. She was propped up in bed, asleep, wearing one of her quilted jackets and a nightcap with frill as stiff as icing on a cake. Her hands rested outside the covers, the fingers half curled into fists. She lay so profoundly motionless that for a moment he thought they had saved her body, had postponed burial all these weeks until he got there to see her before she went down into the grave. Then, as he stood watching, her hands twitched in sleep, the rings glinting.

She was not dead: they had only told him that. But as he started forward, intending to waken her, he saw that she had indeed been sick. She was thinner, and even in that dim light he could make out new lines in her face. He looked at her carefully, closer now. Somehow the sickness had reduced her stature; her feet were a long way from the footboard. Then, without any preliminary flicker, the eyelids lifted. She was awake, looking at him, and her eyes had changed too. But it was only when she spoke to him, saying his name with the different inflection, that he saw his mistake. It was his mother.

The fever had wasted her, the ash-blonde hair gone to gray and the body under the counterpane was like a loosely tied bundle of sticks. She was convalescing now, allowed only the morning hours out of bed, but already she had assumed charge of the house. She had wanted the whip hand for so many years that as soon as it was hers she would not delay using it, not even for the fever. When she had passed the crisis and they told her Mrs Wingate was dead (she already knew about Sturgis, though they had moved him into the room where Hector dreamed of bears; she watched through the doorway while he died, and unlike the news of her mother's death — though it was true she was sicker at the time — it seemed not to affect her one way or the other) her reaction took the form of a violent impatience that would not be quieted until she was moved into the dead woman's room across the hall. The ravages of fever had caused her to re-semble Mrs Wingate, or at least had heavily underlined a re-semblance formerly made vague by the span of years between them, and she took pride in this, doing all she could to em-phasize it. As soon as she was able to sit up in bed she began to wear the dead woman's clothes; she even held her mouth awry, irked and bitter-looking, though there was no gap to hide.

People were considerably taken aback at this manifestation of what they thought was grief and respect for the dead woman. They had rather supposed there was bad blood between them; they had not realized she loved her mother so. "It just goes to show," they said. "You never miss the water till the well runs dry. You cant tell about people, no way in the world." This was because they did not understand. What they called manifestations of grief and respect, and even love, was in fact the celebration of another victory, one by which all her others paled in comparison. She had not only outlived her enemy; she had assimilated her personality, her looks and character and actions, to the extent that the world would never know she was gone, much less miss her.

During the summer of her convalescence and afterwards, when Hector returned to the preparatory school, she extended her activities to include not only the running of the house but also the supervision of the plantation. Mrs Wingate had always watched the crops and checked the books and had weekly conferences with the manager, but Mrs Sturgis did more. She subscribed to and read periodicals on the new diversified agriculture, and in good weather or bad she rode the turnrows in her mother's carriage, taking the bows of the tenants, a small, bustling woman with a quick eye for a dollar and a sharp tongue for whoever crossed her. She had learned her lesson well and made her plans, and now she used them.

When Hector came home from his second year at the University of Virginia, a rather plump young man by then, wearing Eastern clothes and even a straw boater with a gaudy band and a shiny black, wet-looking length of string that drooped like fishline from its brim to the buttonhole at his lapel to keep it from blowing away, he discovered on his ride from the station that Bristol had indeed expanded eastward. The railroad no longer drew its noose about the limits of the town; a new, more fashionable residential district had sprung up beyond it. Mrs Sturgis had subdivided the West Hundred, a cut of buckshot bottomland where the crops had

never been good, and people already were building houses
there. Two years later, when he came home from graduation,
a bachelor of arts, the new houses extended to within shouting
distance of the Wingate house itself.

That was 1898. All down the seaboard, then westward
through Atlanta and Birmingham, he had seen brass bands
parading and lamp posts strung with bunting and cheesecloth
lettered boldly lest people forget to remember the *Maine*.
They were parading in Bristol, too, and when Captain Barcroft, who commanded the local volunteer company now being
organized, approached him with the offer of a position as
adjutant, Hector accepted. It carried the rank of lieutenant, and
he was to be sworn in the following morning. They were expecting marching orders any day, first to Jackson for field
training with the regiment — the old Second Mississippi, in
which his great-grandfather had fought and died, down in
Mexico under Jefferson Davis — then to Cuba.

He did not tell his mother about it until that night when
they were alone in the parlor after supper. He tried to make
it casual in the telling.

"I'll be sworn in tomorrow," he said in conclusion.

Mrs Sturgis looked up sharply from her knitting. "I reckon
not," she said. "This is no time for you to be gallivanting off,
playing soldier." Her spectacles glittered in the gaslight. "Is
that how you intend to use a fifteen thousand dollar education?"

"Noam. But I told Captain Barcroft —"

"So?" she said. "Well, you can just untell him."

When the volunteers entrained the following week at the
Bristol depot, amid the hoarse shouts of old men and the
fluttering handkerchiefs of the ladies, Hector Wingate Sturgis
was not among them.

2

Those who stood on street corners in Bristol that summer after his graduation and saw him drive past — always in a hurry but going no place, an outlander, rakish and modern, sitting ramrod straight with his elbows up, wearing hard bright yellow dogskin gloves to match the hard bright yellow spokes of the surrey — watched him with amusement and even admiration, but with hardly any envy. Their imaginations simply would not stretch to the extent of seeing themselves in his place. For even if, inconceivably, it had been offered them, they would no more have accepted the Eastern education than they would have worn the dogskin gloves or held their elbows so. They watched him. They sniggered as he drove past. They nudged each other. They said, "It's that Sturgis boy, home from college, a dude. I bet you he's hell with the ladies."

The gloves were his own idea; he had brought them home from Charlottesville. But it was his mother who, approving of the gloves, had bought him the surrey and the blooded mare they seemed to require to set them off. He was her chief possession and she intended to be proud of him. She gave him everything he wanted, provided it made him shine in the eyes of the world, and since she intended for him to be actively as well as ornamentally successful, she turned over to him the back issues of the agricultural digests, with critical passages underscored and additional notes in the margins. She was a confirmed reader of these publications herself, using them to supplement her already considerable practical experience in the field, and now she passed them on to her son.

"Here. Look these over," she told him. "You might get some notions for improvements on the place."

Hector took them, not letting the casualness of her tone disguise the importance he knew she attached to them, and dutifully read them from beginning to end. Yet they might almost have been written in Sanscrit for all the good he got. There was one article that interested him, however. It suggested the use of burr clover in rotation with cotton; there were statistical tables and complicated graphs to demonstrate what was called "the nitrogen curve." Even more important, the margins of these pages were filled with cryptic notes by his mother. But when he told her about it, speaking with an edge of pride at being able to show at least that he had read the periodicals, she said: "Yes, we tried it and it worked fine, every way except financially. Look again."

He tried once more, this time with a plan for raising beef cattle. But this was even worse. "You must not have read it very carefully," she told him. "Thats for people with land unfit for anything but grazing." So he did not try again. The husbandry journals lay in three tall stacks on the floor beside the desk in his room, untouched except by the maid who dusted them every morning.

Mrs Sturgis, watching his progress — or rather, his lack of it — with misgivings and forebodings, told herself that they had gone at farming hind-part before. What Hector really needed, she decided, was practical experience in the field. But that worked no better. The agricultural digests had given him a superficial, technical knowledge of farming, an academic approach, always with an eye for innovations and a tongue that wanted to know not 'how' but *why*: so that the manager, who was charged with the instruction, would begin to mutter in his beard whenever Hector approached. Crowding sixty, he had been in charge of the plantation for more than twenty years, since back in the Wingate days; he was the one who had ridden alongside the carriage on the flatulent horse, a gruff, unsociable individual with an instant, violent dislike of anything new. After two weeks of seeing the young man daily and taking him with him wherever he went — Eastern clothes, proper accent, and all — the manager told Mrs Sturgis that she must make a choice; it would have to be himself or Hector. He knew he was safe. The twenty-odd successful years had given him a reputation, and good managers were beginning to be scarce. Any plantation owner in the delta would hire him at any reasonable figure he might name.

"I can farm the place," he said. "Or maybe I can learn that boy to farm it. I cant do both."

Mrs Sturgis made the foregone choice. That night she told Hector, "We were wrong, thinking you could move right in like that. What you need is a rest from all those years at school. Take yourself some time off. Take the balance of the year getting settled and meeting people all over again. We'll see how it works out."

Thus he began a social interlude, during which people on street corners watched him go past in the bright-spoked surrey and called him a dude and bet he was hell with the ladies. This last was based on the yellow gloves and the surrey — for without them there was little that was prepossessing about him. His features were vague, the eyes somewhat bulging and pale gray, the nose broad at the base and sharp at the tip, the mouth with down-tending corners and a heavy upper lip, the chin short and recessive. His hair was dark brown; he wore it parted far on the left, brushed straight across, with a cowlick at the back as if that patch had been sprinkled with a special tonic that made it always dry and fine and tufted, paler than the rest. He was thin in the arms and legs, especially the biceps and thighs, but at twenty he already had the beginning of a paunch. Probably no one seeing him in a crowd on the street or at a ball would have recognized him ten minutes later in a parlor.

At the preparatory school he had learned to see his homeland with new eyes, assigning new values after hearing how the Maryland boys spoke of it after their visit. But that was just at school. When he came home it was no different, in its physical aspect, from what it had been when he went away. The distance-lent enchantment having faded, he was faced with things as they were, essentially drab, even grimy, and he spent his vacations waiting for the time to return to school. Now, however, there would be no return. School was behind him, and he was busy learning at first hand, by necessity, what his homeland had to offer a young man settling down.

It had a great deal to offer, as he soon began to learn. There were dances at the Elysian Club, gala occasions that drew young people from all over the delta, four big ones a year, a dance each season, with numerous lesser ones interspersed to keep the months between from growing dull. There were hayrides and boating parties on Lake Jordan, down at the south end of the county, a sheen of moonlight on the water, girls in gauzy dresses and young men in white flannels and blazers, plucking mandolins. Hector made one among them. He was willing enough, even eager at times, but the girls' mothers were apt to regard him more agreeably than their daughters did. The daughters thought him stiff — 'stuffy'; they could not *talk* to him, they said; they said he was no 'fun.' The Eastern clothes, the scrupulous accent, attributes of eligibility in that other world where he had got his schooling, were like a weight upon him, holding him down and back. Sometimes when he went toward a couple on the dance floor, intending to cut in, he would see the girl watching him over her partner's shoulder and suddenly, in the middle of a dip or glide, they would stop and cross the ballroom to the punch bowl, hand in hand; Hector would be left alone among whirling couples, looking sheepish. It could happen to anyone, he told himself; but it happened to him too often.

The year moved into winter, and the young men who had gone with Captain Barcroft came home from soldiering, those who had survived the embalmed beef. They were tanned and fit, Bristol's first new veterans in more than thirty years, and though they had seen no battle they spoke of camp life in Florida as if it had been more eventful than San Juan Hill or Manila Bay, as if sand fleas had a sting that beat the bullets. There was a general reclaiming of girls, a reallotment, and those men who had not gone felt envious and resentful, seeing they could have had the glory with so little attendant risk. Hector was restless, fidgety, unable even to read through those evenings he stayed at home. That was odd, for books had been his chief pleasure. One summer, waiting to return to the university, he read straight through Walter Scott, thirty volumes without a pause between them. But not now. He was too fretful even for Scott.

"I know what you need," his mother told him, watching from behind her spectacles. "You need to find yourself some nice, congenial girl."

She made the remark off-hand, looking arch. Later she was to tell herself that this had been the cause of what followed.

What followed came two nights after Christmas. She was sitting alone in the downstairs parlor, knitting. Hector had gone to the holiday ball at the Elysian Club. Near midnight she had begun to nod (she had been troubled with insomnia since the fever, and had taken to sitting up until she felt she could sleep) when she heard the driveway gravel crunching under the thin tires of the surrey: 'He's home!' she thought, rousing out of a half-sleep. Footsteps crossed the veranda; the door came open, letting in the wind, and Hector entered with a girl on his arm. At first she thought she was dreaming.

"Hello, mother," he said. "I'm home early. Guess why."

Startled thus out of slumber, seeing their flushed faces and her son's excited manner, Mrs Sturgis thought that he had been drinking; he had the false, selfconscious exuberance of the adolescent tippler. He did not stop talking. Apparently he could not. It was as if he feared that if he stopped she would say something to injure him.

"It's Ella," he said. "We got married."

Then he did stop; he stopped short and stood there grinning foolishly as his mother came past him and closed the door against the cold wind coming around it. "Whats that?" she asked, turning with both hands behind her, holding the door-knob. "Whats that you said?"

"This is Ella, mother: Ella Lowry. Ella, this is mother."

Hector made a one-handed, flipper-like gesture of introduction, indicating each in turn. The girl at first seemed undecided whether to curtsy or hold out her hand. Then, since Mrs Sturgis only stood and looked, with both hands still behind her and leaning now against the door as if in need of support, Ella did neither. She performed instead a supple, gooselike motion with her neck and bobbed her head.

"Pleased to meet you," she said.

Mrs Sturgis looked at her, still not moving. Then: "I believe I know your mother," she said hesitantly, hoping against hope. "Mrs Lowry?"

"Yessum," Ella said. Her voice was rather shrill, partly because she was frightened, being here in the Wingate house where she had never been before, and partly because it was always so, as if raised against the blare of music at dances.

She had grown up in Bristol. Mrs Sturgis had seen her from time to time in the course of her carriage excursions and shopping trips downtown, but she had heard of her more often than she had seen her. Anyone but Mrs Sturgis, secure in her insularity, would have recognized the girl on sight. Perhaps even Mrs Sturgis did, behind the shock, the outrage, but she wanted to delay admitting even to herself this new daughter-in-law's identity. Ella had been strikingly pretty as a child, which won admiration first from older people, then from girls at school, classmates, and finally from boys. Many Bristol girls won their popularity on a basis of birth and station; Ella won hers in spite of it. Her father had been a railroad man, a brakeman in the C&B: 'had been' because he abandoned his wife soon after their child was born. They never saw him again, but Ella knew what he looked like from a picture in a tortoise-shell frame on Mrs Lowry's night table, a daguerreotype of a small man neatly buttoned into what was obviously his Sunday suit. His hair, heavily pomaded, was brushed in pigeon wings above ears that were strangely pointed like a fawn's. He wore a low collar without a tie; it was too tight, which gave his throat a naked, swollen look — but that was all right; apparently the tightness made him feel more dressed-

up. All this, together with the humorous wrinkles at the outward corners of his eyes, was in contrast to the stern black
mustache that lay like a bar across the middle of his face. He
seemed to be hiding behind it; he seemed to wear it with guile.
Ella thought for years that the mustache was false (it looked
false, as if he had dressed hurriedly on the way to a mas-
querade or a highway robbery) but one day, apropos of
nothing, her mother told her how proud he had been of it,
how he would sit in front of a mirror to groom and admire it,
and how he wore a bandage over it whenever he was working,
a little hammock of gauze that hooked behind his ears like
spectacles.

"He thought the world and all of that mustache," Mrs
Lowry would say, and a dreamy look would come into her
eyes.

He had left with another woman — "gone to Texas," Ella
heard, the refuge of absconding bankers, seducers, and errant
husbands; that was all she knew. But there were postcards, as
many as four or five a year and always one for her birthday,
lithographs of the Southwest, desert scenes with cattle skulls
bleaching in the foreground or village squares with court-
houses and churches built of mud and men in wide hats and
striped blankets asleep in the shade, and on the reverse, scrawled
in pencil or a sputtering post office pen: *How is my little girl?*
Am fine hope your the same. Daddy. Ella kept them in a
dresser drawer. There were over fifty of them, alike as carbon
copies, when her mother received the letter that said he was
dead, fallen between two cars, and the postcards stopped. The
second wife, or maybe it was the third, got the insurance.

Mrs Lowry was from Alabama, the eastern terminus of the
railroad for which her husband was a brakeman at the time
they met. He saw her at a church supper during a lay-over
between runs, and after the marriage ceremony he brought
her home to Bristol in the caboose. "Ive done enough running
round," he said. "It's high time I was settling down. I'm saying
goodbye to all that." He seemed to mean it, though obviously
he was fighting something in his blood, some heritage, some

pattern of behavior. They were together a little more than a year. Then he left with one of the dancers from a tent show that came to town in the fall after Ella's birth — 'Little Egypt' she was called, a belly dancer in baggy pink silk trousers, a girdle of pearls worn low on her hips, a halter, and shoes with upturned points; her hair had a glint like brass, and she emphasized her brows and lengthened the corners of her eyes with the soot from burnt matches. All his resolution went like smoke at that first sight of her. Those men who did not condemn him envied him openly, and some among those who condemned him loudest, those who had seen her dance at any rate, also envied him most.

At first, in her despair, Mrs Lowry considered following him wherever he had gone, collaring him and bringing him back to face his altar-sworn responsibilities. It was clearly what he deserved; everyone was agreed as to that, especially the ones who envied him for having what they had not dared to try for and probably couldnt have gotten if they had dared. But before she could make up her mind how to go about it, just which point of the compass to strike out on, a strange thing happened. Her legs began to swell.

Within a week they were twice their former size. The doctor, who could discover no organic cause for the swelling, put it down as dropsy (after all, he had to put down something) but predicted that this manifestation of bereavement (such he considered it, privately) would cure itself within a week. He was much interested in abnormal maladies; they were a sideline with him, along with false asthma, sinus, mysterious headaches, and the bloat. But he was wrong in his prognosis. By the end of the week she could not get across the room without someone on each side for her to lean on. "Hm," the doctor said, shaking his head. It was strange. Eventually the swelling stopped, but it never went down. So now there was no question of following the wayward husband, nor of finding another to take his place. Mrs Lowry was left with no one to turn to, without support for herself and her child.

That was when she put the sign out. She lettered it herself,

with red enamel on a cypress shingle: ELIZABETH LOWRY. SEAM-
STRESS, nailed to a pillar beside the steps, directly opposite
another shingle nailed to the other pillar: ROOM & BOARD. APPLY
WITHIN, nailed there fifteen years ago by the landlady when
her husband died.

The landlady was the one who gave Mrs Lowry the notion.
"Look here," she said, a gaunt, mannish woman who wore
her hair in a bun at the top of her head. "You have my heart-
felt sympathy and all that. I know how you feel; I do indeed.
I know what it means to lose your only man. Why, when
Mr Simmons passed I like to died. I did; I did indeed. But a
woman's got this world to live in, man or no."

"You had this house, Mrs Simmons, and all that went with
it. What can *I* do, me with these bad legs?"

"Do? Goodness. Just look at here." They were sitting face
to face, Mrs Lowry holding Ella on her lap, and Mrs Simmons
leaned forward and fingered the hem of the baby's dress. She
pursed her lips as she did so, nodding positively. "Let me tell
you, thats as nice a piece of stitching as ever I saw. Thats
one thing you can do."

So the two signs, one weathered and the other shiny new,
decorated the pillars on opposite sides of the boarding-house
steps. After the shingles had been exposed to two years of
rain and sun, alternate heat and cold, anyone without particular information would have thought they had been nailed
to the flanking pillars at the same time. By then Mrs Lowry
was established. She had a straight-back chair equipped with
casters so that she could move about the room without having
to stand on her swollen legs. Her skill with the needle was
praised for miles around. Mothers from surrounding towns
and plantations throughout the central delta brought their
daughters to her sewing room for fittings whenever the dress
was to be a special one. They could recognize her work from
across a ballroom and they pronounced the name Lowry with
the same tone of respect and awe that women in other parts
of the world adopted when they said Worth or Fortuny.

Ella grew up with the rapid stutter of the sewing machine

constantly in her ears. Her mother's customers cooed with
admiration; "*Such* a lovely child!" they cried, partly to curry
favor with Mrs Lowry but mostly because it was true. At
school the other girls liked to be with her because she drew
the boys. By then she was not as pretty as she had been, for
this was a transition stage; the prettiness was changing into
beauty, and also into something else which the boys could
recognize by instinct though they could not identify it as
readily as the men who saw her on the street, still in ribbed
stockings and button shoes, carrying school books. Her popularity held, being based now on talk of her promiscuity. For
the past five years, up to the month preceding her sudden
marriage to Hector Sturgis when she was nineteen, her only
concern had been young men (but she never called them
that; she called them 'boys') and thus she had acquired a reputation. When she was fourteen the watchers downtown would
see her pass the barber shop or pool hall window, legs wobbly
on high heels and wearing the flimsy, violent-flowered dresses
she persuaded her mother to make for her — a juvenile Lillian
Russell, emphasizing the bosom she already had — and returning, out of the tail of her eye, the stares of all the watchers.
She not only seemed not to care what they thought, she
seemed to go out of her way to make sure they understood
that she did not care: so that, in the end, she showed how much
she did care after all (but in reverse) and they responded
with the frank, lickerish stares and the gossip she not only
provoked but invited; it was reciprocal.

In those days she would be with girls older than herself
and usually from families who disapproved of their being in
her company, the disapproval of course adding to her attractiveness in their eyes. The watchers observed her moving with
a sort of vicious jerkiness — slouched posture, high-colored
cheeks, and languid eyes — to the murmurous accompaniment
of their gossip. Presently, however, she left the girls behind.
They saw her in the Kandy Kitchen drinking sodas with high
school boys, ululant, head backflung, lips parted and damp.

Then she left the high school boys behind. On their way home to their farms, they saw her emerge from lonely back-roads, high on the seats of buggies with the blotch-faced youths of the town. And the watchers, farmers in Bristol for haircuts or pool or just for conversation, would return the following Saturday and tell about it, until finally it was mentioned only in passing — "I saw that Lowry girl again, out Dundrum way with a gig full of boys." "Yair?" "Yair" — like fair weather or international politics. They had worn it out with too much talk, just as a popular song can be worn out with too much playing.

Then something changed all this. Suddenly, without any preliminary gesture so far as anyone observed, Ella sloughed her promiscuity. It was puzzling to the watchers, especially to those who had compounded it with her. Certainly something must have caused the reformation, or anyhow led up to it; or maybe not, maybe it just happened. Anyhow, for whatever reason or lack of a reason, she no longer welcomed the advances of the rounders nor addressed them with the encouraging smile and sidelong glance of Lilith on the lookout; she wore instead the mournful, slightly soured expression of Magdalene redeemed.

Some among the watchers, unable to account for it otherwise, claimed that her mother had straightened her out; but even those who said this did not believe it. For, two years earlier, when a delegation of Baptist ladies, members of the Bible Union carrying out a decision reached in caucus, called on Mrs Lowry to acquaint her with the talk about her daughter, the seamstress received them with smiles and an offer of tea, until the member previously appointed began to tell her why they had come: whereupon she cursed them from the room in a fit of indignation and passion, herding them out of the door like frightened sheep, the casters of her chair making a clatter like roller skates on the floorboards of the sewing room, and would never accept a dress order from one of them again.

Whatever else Ella gave up, she did not give up dancing. The Christmas holidays began, the series of dances that would continue through New Year's, and Hector saw her as if for the first time. She had always gone with older boys; he had entertained no hopes, considering her beyond him. But now he did — and she saw him, too; he could tell. Abnegation lent sorrow to her face, a new, profounder beauty supplementing that which always had caused half the stags to cluster about her portion of the dance floor. With a suddenness and force that knocked all other thoughts from his head, Hector believed he had found the answer to every problem that had ever come his way. *Love* was his release from the burden coming-of-age had thrust upon him; Love was his consolation for all failures, all short-comings; he perceived now that nothing could ever be really unbearable if a man had Love to turn to. Also, she needed him. This alone, in Hector's mind, was enough to recommend marriage. In point of fact, however, he was gone before he ever suspected a bait or looked for a reason. He was wooed, snared — thrown — by the old eternal feminine, the nun-like attitude of fallen women who have changed their ways if for no other cause but a whim.

He proposed on the fire-escape landing at the Elysian Club; they had stepped out for a breath of air between numbers, and Ella did what she had every cause to do; she accepted. They left at once, not going back through the ballroom because she had a date in there; woke up the old j.p. who filled out the license and married them, his wife and spinster daughter standing by in wrappers and curl-papers, two gray loveless ghosts; and then drove home in the surrey, all before midnight. They were in evening clothes, Ella's satin dance slippers peeping from under the hem of her gown. Hector kept talking, talking; his eyes glittered with excitement and his starched white shirtfront flashed cold in the moonlight, like a shield. Ella had never seen him like this before, nor had anyone else. However, as they rode out toward the Sturgis house along the quiet, moon-silvered road, the mare's hoofs clopping with a hollow sound like drumtaps along the way to a scaffold, he became less and less hilarious and more and more preoccupied. The euphoria was playing out.

'He's scared of that old woman,' Ella thought. 'Of what she'll do.'

She was right; he was frightened — and so for that matter was she. For Mrs Sturgis was formidable, especially when challenged on her own ground, which was where they were headed now in the surrey. Hector was her chief possession, the one to which all others — house, plantation, bank account, even the highborn insularity — were adjunct. Ella imagined the scene she believed would greet them. Yet presently, as the three of them stood in the parlor, mother and son and daughter-in-law, it was not at all as she had feared. Mrs Sturgis did not rave and wring her hands or tear her hair. Rather, she was remembering a similar scene a generation back, in the time of fever, when the red-faced feed and grain salesman with the celluloid collar and the carroty hair had come into this same room and spoken for her hand with such well-founded assurance. She remembered the sound of their voices: "When?" "Soon" — "How soon?" "Soon as possible," and the way her mother had looked at the young man with a curiously combined expression of pride and defeat. (Six months later Hector was born and they swathed his hands in oil-soaked cotton and told callers he had no fingernails.) But this time it was a woman being brought into the house, and somehow that seemed a greater desecration. She herself was in her mother's position, faced with what the diplomats called a *fait accompli*, having to accept what she could not alter. There was nothing she could do about it, any more than there had been anything Mrs Wingate could do about it twenty years ago. Remembering that time, Mrs Sturgis crossed the parlor and sat in the chair her mother had sat in when the roles were reversed.

She assigned Hector and Ella the upstairs front left bedroom where she and Sturgis had lived. Her room, formerly her mother's, was directly across the hall. Sometimes in the night she would lie awake, hearing the muffled voices and the profound silence and then the voices again, and she would hate them in her heart for having what she had lost, for having what she perhaps had never known. She would lie awake in the cold wide bed and hate them out of envy and regret, with a taste in her mouth like brass and a tight, constricting hoop about her chest. There was satisfaction, though, in suspecting that her mother had felt the same things in her time, fifteen and twenty years ago, when she was the one who lay awake in this same bed, tasting brass and breathing pain, while her daughter in the room across the hall took her pleasure, emitted those little choking sobs, never knowing how soon it would end, how soon the wheel would come full circle and passion be replaced by emptiness.

But Hector entered this new world without considering anything from the old one. He was young in it, quite unaware that anyone ever before had had what he was having. Sometimes at the breakfast table, after all that had happened in the night, he would look at Ella, the pale loveliness, the big green eyes, the mass of dark hair crowning the triangle of brow and chin, and his hands would become so awkward that he could not hold the fork; he would sit with his head lowered, feeling turmoil in his chest, the pounding that came whenever he looked at her and told himself that she was his, that they belonged to each other. It was like nothing he had ever suspected. When the three of them were together this way and Mrs Sturgis happened to have her attention drawn aside, giving instructions to one of the servants, Ella would look at him covertly, smiling that slow, secret smile, and he would feel the hair stir at the nape of his neck and his mouth would go dry.

It continued like this, with nothing to distract him. He did not even wonder where she had learned all she was teaching him. The academic Why he had brought to farming was forgotten; now his only concern was How. Then one night in early February they lay in bed talking, and Ella said suddenly, almost casually, as if it has just occurred to her: "Did you know we're kin to each other, sort of?"

"What do you mean, kin? How kin?"

"I dont know exactly, for sure. But we're kin, all right."

Ella was quiet for a moment. Then she told him. "My great-grandfather, my father's grandfather, brought your grand-father over here from Ireland after his trouble. Your father's father, that was. My great-grandfather had a saloon here in Bristol called the Palace, and he came over to work for him. They were cousins. Second cousins, once removed I think. What does that make us?"

Hector did not answer. He was recalling something. It floated up from the dark well of the past, and when it broke the surface he saw again the hunch-shouldered man posed against the backdrop of racked bottles, looking at him with narrowed eyes out of the cavernous gloom while he sat in the carriage outside in brilliant sunlight; he heard Emma as she leaned forward, balancing the parasol like a tightrope walker, and whispered: "Thats yo granddaddy!" He had never seen him again, for when he came back from his freshman year at Virginia the saloon had been remodeled and there was a different bartender, a young man in a drill jacket. Hector went into the saloon for the first time in his life. "Old Barney?" the new man said. "He died last winter," and that was all.

"What kind of trouble?" Hector asked.

"Hm?"

"You said your grandfather brought him—"

"*Great*-grandfather."

"— brought him over from Ireland after his trouble. What kind of trouble was it?"

"Oh," Ella said. She paused. "I thought you knew. They always kind of kept it in the family. Mamma told me about it years ago; she heard it from Daddy. I thought surely your father would have told you. He was there and saw it, and any-how he must have heard about it afterwards, even if he was too young to remember."

Hector lay staring up toward the invisible ceiling, his breath coming quicker and sharper while Ella told about Barney Sturgis, a farmer in one of the worst farming countries in the world. He had lived on rented land in County Down with his young wife, children coming regularly — there were three, two girls and a boy; the boy was the youngest — and one morning he came back unexpectedly from the field and found his wife in the house with a man. They were in bed, the two heads on one pillow, looking at him in the doorway. At first the wife was frightened, but at length, as Barney continued to stand there looking foolish and too hurt to speak, she began to smile. Maybe it was from nerves or embarrassment or even fright; he told himself later that he could have forgiven it. But then the man smiled too, the two smiling faces on the one pillow. That was what did it, the smiles. Barney went to the woodpile and returned with the ax, running. He killed his wife right there in the bedroom, one blow with the blunt end, and killed the man, still running, when he caught up with him half a mile from the house. The way Ella heard it, the man ("He was what they call a tinker, and traveled round in a pony cart mending pots and pans and grinding scissors") ran the last fifty yards with the bit of the ax in his skull and the helve down his back like a queue. The children looked over the low stone wall flanking the road the two men ran their race along; they saw the whole thing, round-eyed.

So Hector came to believe that what he had seen in those eyes, fifteen years ago — they inside in the darkness, he outside in the sunlight — was a reflection of the thing that had brought Barney Sturgis thirty-five hundred miles across the ocean, then southward down a strange continent to tend bar in Mississippi. It explained why he had never had anything to do with women, not even for the sake of having one to raise his children, the two daughters married and gone by the time they were into their middle teens. Hector believed also that it perhaps explained much of what he had never understood about his father, who had been so gloomy, so melancholy, the dark-souled Anglo-Saxon hidden behind the flashy clothes and the salesman's smile and smalltalk. He thought of his father as a child in faroff Ireland, not even old enough to go to school, leaning over the wall to watch the tinker run down the road with the bit of the ax wedged into his skull and the helve down his back like a wooden pigtail, then going into the house, maybe even into the bedroom spattered with his mother's blood shed by his father. John Sturgis had grown up with that; it stayed with him always, no matter how young he had been at the time. Probably from year to year, whether in Sunday school as a boy or later in fireside conversation with a garrulous preacher improving the shining hour, there had been talk about the mark of Cain —

And then it came into Hector's mind that the same impulse must flow in his veins, the stain of blood carried down from father to son and from father to son. He tried to remember, but could not, the Bible verse about the sins of the fathers being visited. It said something about the third generation: "Yea, even unto the third and fourth generation . . ." He would remember to look it up, or ask Mr Clinkscales.

"I thought you knew," Ella said. She had raised herself on one elbow and was looking down at him. He could barely see her in the gloom, the face above the faintly luminous shoulders.

"I didnt know."

She let herself down. Again they lay side by side, as removed as two corpses in a winter tomb, both looking up toward the ceiling. Then she turned her head on the pillow and spoke with her lips close to his ear. "Well, goodness," she said, "dont take it so serious. He had every right. Besides, it was a long time ago, way off in Ireland."

This shadow moved over the first year of their marriage, was cleared momentarily by the birth of a son — called Hector too: Hector the fourth, in January of 1901 — but then moved back, even darker than before.

△

Two: then three: then four in the house, around the dining room table — mother and son and daughter-in-law and grandson, entering the new century: thus it progressed through a time without subtraction. Bristol continued its growth east-

ward from the river, first to and then beyond the house
(called the Sturgis house now, except by a few older Bristolians who still called it the Wingate place, out of habit and
a determination never to give way); Mrs Sturgis had subdivided another Hundred, and this was Hector's vocation, or
anyhow his occupation; he drew the plans.

Mechanical drawing had been his favorite subject at school,
and now he spent all his time at it; farming had gone by the
board. He even kept regular hours — 'office hours' he called
them, and so they were. His downstairs study was equipped
as a draftsman's office, including a desk with an adjustable
lid, lamps to throw the light just right, India inks in all the
colors of the rainbow, and T-squares hung like gripless broad-
swords on the wall. Here was where he drew and redrew
plans for the subdivision, tree-bordered avenues named for
historically prominent Mississippians from the state at large
and cross-streets named for early Bristol settlers. It was more
for amusement than in earnest, however; he enjoyed it too
much to be able to think of it as work, and Mrs Sturgis used
the plans or not, as she saw fit.

That was at first. A time was coming when she would prize
them, would use them as a blueprint for East Bristol, over-
riding her advisory engineers whenever they suggested a
change — even in such small matters as the location of a fire
hydrant ("I want it precisely the way it is on the map." "But,
Mrs Sturgis, the pipe line . . ." "I want it this way." "Yes
maam") — and would offer them as the Wingate bid for a
place in the world of art. But that was later; that was ten
years after he put ten years of work on them.

It began at the suggestion of his mother, while Ella was
far along in pregnancy. They had Mr Clinkscales out for
supper one night; he had recently lost his wife and the pa-
rishioners were taking turns at trying to console him. They
were in the parlor, having coffee, when Mrs Sturgis began
to speak of her plans for extending the subdivision.

"You took that kind of work at school," she said to Hector.

"Maybe you could block it out for me. It doesnt have to be anything special, just sketches I could use to show the men who do such things approximately what I want. They gave me the address of a man they said could do it, but I dont know. Do you think you could?"

"I think I could."

"You could?"

"I think I could."

"A truly noble conception!" Mr Clinkscales suddenly cried. He sat forward on the edge of his chair as he said it, and for the rest of the evening he spoke with enthusiasm of the notion of a mother and son working together to build a new Bristol. It appealed to him morally and esthetically, so to speak. "Who knows?" he said. "Who can tell? Together, with God's blessing — which surely He will not withhold — you may perhaps be laying the groundwork, the foundation for a future Athens, an Athens of the South. Yes. And this young woman's child, so soon to be born," he added, indicating Ella with a deferential nod, "will be one of its leading citizens, the one perhaps under whom it will come to flower, a beacon for the South, a torch held out."

His voice had regained its old resonance. Mrs Sturgis beamed with pleasure, for up until this outburst of enthusiasm no one had been able to bring him out of the despondency into which he had sunk when he buried his wife three weeks before. Then, the notion having served its purpose, she would have forgotten it. But next morning Hector went downtown immediately after breakfast and returned with a roll of drafting paper, a packet of thumbtacks, and a box of hard-lead pencils. He rummaged in his trunk until he found his drawing instruments, then took them out of their plush-lined case and polished them. While the cook looked on resentfully, he commandeered the big biscuit board from the kitchen, tacked a sheet of the drafting paper to it, and set to work.

That was the very beginning. The old fascination the work had had for him in school returned, the precise, mathematical beauty, the neat geometrical simplicity in which a single line, drawn clear and sharp, was as mind-filling as the most complicated theory any philosopher ever contemplated and evolved. Hector wondered why he had forgotten how much pleasure it gave him, both to do the work and to look at it after it was done. He began with a small-scale drawing, but new ideas came crowding fast. By the time he was half way through it he had conceived the project which, in one sense, was to be his life's work. Gridding the sheets into sections, he reproduced these sections a sheet at a time, on a scale of one to one hundred — "A shade more than an eighth of an inch to a foot," he explained, showing them to his mother.

He was enthusiastic from the start, and though Mrs Sturgis was a bit perturbed at seeing him race off with her suggestion in this manner (his hands trembled with excitement, holding the sheets for her to examine) she was glad to see him interested in something besides Ella and she encouraged him to continue with the work. It solved another question, too — the question of what he was going to *do* — for after all, this was not Europe; even the highborn Wingate tradition could not support an idler. Ever since he had failed at farming, Mrs Sturgis had had the problem of finding an occupation for her son. It could not be a menial job, such as weigher in the gin, yet apparently he could not fill a responsible position. Now there was this, and she welcomed it because it automatically made him something more than an idler and a husband. She paid for whatever special equipment he ordered. "Go right ahead. Whatever you need," she told him. Soon his study was crowded with the paraphernalia of draftsmen.

The total absorption came later, in the troubled years. It was in those years that he began to add colors, green for trees and lawns, blue for the water in drainage ditches and artificial ponds, red for underground installations, mains and sewers. By then black was reserved for details such as carriage blocks and arc lights, streetcars and delivery wagons, and finally the people themselves, as seen from above, going about their work and their pleasures. In the end it became compulsive, obsessive. He would see a thing while out for a stroll, for instance a group of boys running after the ice wagon, and would hurry home to get out his instruments and put it on the map, crowding them in one after another, colors and details overlapping, until at last the sheets resembled a futuristic painting, a bird's-eye view of Utopia, one to one hundred.

But that was later; that was during the troubled years immediately ahead, when he turned to the work for more consolation than he needed now. Now he was just beginning. It was twenty years later, ten years after all his troubles were over, that Mrs Sturgis — 'Mother of Bristol' by then — collected the drawings, had them bound in tooled morocco with watered silk end-sheets and his name stamped in gold on the cover, and presented them to the city council in a ceremony which included a speech of acceptance by the mayor. She instructed that they be placed on display in the foyer of the city hall for all the people to see, and it was done. They stayed there through another twenty years, on display under glass, and the people came and looked at them — the crowded, multicolored sheets that had begun as maps and wound up resembling work done by a latter-day amateur Bruegel or Bosch looking down from a seat in the clouds — and found in them confirmation of their suspicions ("Look! Look at there," they said; they sniggered and nudged each other; "I *told* you he was crazy as a betsy bug. Look how he spent all those years!") until finally Mrs Sturgis was dead in her turn and the map-drawings were removed to the belfry, filed among the dusty clutter of old records, deeds and resolutions, council minutes and building permits, all jumbled together for the pigeons to coo and strut over and stain with their droppings.

Now, however, he was only beginning the work; it was still in simple black and white and on a small scale, used mainly to fill the hours while he waited for his child to be born. Ella went past her time, unbelievably swollen, and at last the pains came on her. They were protracted. When the doctor said,

"Bear down; bear down, now," she bore down and chewed at her under lip to keep from crying. No one had told her it was going to be like this. The doctor stood beside the bed, sleeves rolled, watching over the tops of his spectacles, calling her 'mother' to encourage her. "Bear down, Mother. Be brave," he said, and she tried. She had decided at the outset that this was her chance to show Mrs Sturgis that there could be bravery under adversity even where there was no trace of the Wingate strain.

That was what she intended, but by the end of the first day she was too taken with pain and exhaustion to be concerned about anything except the sensations of the minute. She stopped chewing at her lip, and now whenever the pain returned and shook her, she filled the house with her screams. Between times, she called on God to forgive her her sins. By morning of the third day she was begging to be allowed to die.

Hector was not with her then; he had not been with her since the start. On the evening of the first day, believing that she needed him, wanted him by her or anyhow close at hand, he went upstairs and stood outside her door. Until an hour ago she had kept control of herself, chewing at her under lip, but since then she had been making a steady whimper, punctuated from time to time with groans. He meant to knock, then put his head around the door and wish her well, anything to let her know that he was standing by, sharing her travail so far as he was able. However, as he raised his arm to rap on the panel, Ella suddenly broke into a new series of cries, high yelps like those he once had heard a hurt dog make, and he lost his nerve; he dropped his arm and broke. He was halfway down the stairs before he realized he had run.

Next afternoon he tried again. He went upstairs and stood outside the door, and this time he saw her. It was during a lull. As he stood there, trying to make up his mind to knock, the door came open; a Negro woman faced him with a basin in her hands, and he saw beyond her shoulder into the room. Ella sat in the center of the bed, leaned slightly forward, gripping the knotted ends of two sheets tied to the footposts. Posed thus in an attitude of terrific exertion, like an oarsman collapsed on his sweep at the end of a course, she glistened with sweat. Her gown had been slit up the front, from hem to neckline, the pale enormity of her belly filling the fork of her thighs, and her breasts, formerly so beautiful but large as melons now, sagged obscenely. Her face was toward him, the lips bloodless, the jaw dropped slack, and though her eyes were open, staring out of bruised sockets, she did not see him. She obviously did not see anything.

"Shut that door!" the doctor shouted.

"Scuse me," the woman said.

Hector scurried aside, and as she came past him, holding the basin shoulder-high like a tray held by a butler on the stage, he saw the monogrammed *W* at one corner of the crumpled towel that had been laid across it. That meant it was one of the fine pieces of linen brought from France by his grandmother after her wedding tour. 'Oh-oh,' he thought. 'I hope Mother doesnt see theyre using that.'

A son was born the following night, soon after supper, and weighed eighteen pounds at birth. That was a record. When the news spread around the town there were a dozen variants of the same old joke, "Who does he suspect?" for people remembered the time when Hector was born, when a report was circulated that he weighed less than four pounds and had no hair or fingernails. Ella of course was unaware of this; she was not aware of anything except relief at having emerged from three days of labor. When Hector finally came into the room to congratulate and thank her, leaning down to kiss her cheek, all she said was "Dont. Dont shake the bed."

Next morning, though, lying with the child beside her, she seemed to say to the world at large and to Mrs Sturgis in particular, 'I may not have done it exactly the Wingate way. It's true I yelled; I certainly did, and loud. But look. Eighteen pounds!' She exulted, and Hector exulted with her, sucked into the rearward vacuum of her pride.

"He looks like one of those Japanese wrestlers," he said, careful not to nudge the bed as he stood there looking down at his son.

Even Mrs Sturgis had to admit there had never been such a baby born in Bristol. She had indeed been outdone. But she also asked herself if it didnt verge on the common for a new-born infant to be so big and strapping.

No one could deny, however, that he was well-behaved. He seldom cried, not even when he had such a bad cold three weeks later and had to be put under a sheet with the croup kettle and wear a camphor poultice on his chest. The doctor was more concerned than he let them know. Finally the cold was cured; there seemed to be no ill effects. Two days later, though, when the nurse was changing the baby's diaper, she called Ella and showed her something. "How come that?" she said.

Too embarrassed to ask Mrs Sturgis for advice, Ella spoke to Hector about it that night in bed. She hesitated, undecided how to phrase it in this connection, though she would have had no difficulty otherwise. Then she told him. "His thing," she said. "It's turned sort of blue on the tip."

"His what?"

"*You* know . . ."

By morning the blueness had spread; the baby's lips were a darker red and his face was flushed. The doctor came and made another examination with the stethoscope hooked in his ears and a worried expression on his face. "Keep him wrapped up warm," he said. "Try not to let him exert himself. We'll see in a couple of days."

"But, Dr Clinton — "

"We'll see. Dont worry; we'll see."

The condition grew worse, the dark red of the baby's lips shading toward purple. His eyes were dull, unresponsive, his breathing labored. There was no fear that he would exert himself, for he had become torpid, lying quite still and taking a deep breath every once in a while, as if he were breathing

a rarified atmosphere. He never cried; yet somehow, to Ella
and Hector at any rate, that only made it worse. A sick child
was supposed to cry; that was the way they told you they
were sick. But this one lay in silent misery, not even fretful.

Dr Clinton spoke to the three of them, Mrs Sturgis and
Hector and Ella, after a second examination two days later.
He employed the detached, somewhat distant manner of medi-
cal men when the case is no longer in what they call the hands
of science, and as he spoke he looked over the rims of his
glasses, first at one and then another of the trio, undecided
whether to address Ella and Hector as the parents or Mrs
Sturgis as the head of the household, the one who paid the
bills. He ended by dividing his glances about equally.

"To go back to the beginning," he said. He paused, studying the toe caps of his brightly polished shoes. He was a
bachelor. "That wasnt just a cold we brought him through.
It was pneumonia, and I dont mind telling you I was considerably worried, concerned. Then I felt better; he seemed
to come out of it fine. Now it turns out I was right to worry."
He removed his glasses and began to rub the lenses with a
clean linen handkerchief which he took from the breast pocket
of his salt-and-pepper jacket. His eyes looked weak and naked,
out of focus. There was a red pinch-mark on each side of the
bridge of his nose. "The pneumonia has affected the heart.
Rheumatism — rheumatic. It's like a rheumatic arm or leg:
wont function properly. The blueness, now. That means the
blood isnt being distributed properly. It's a matter of faulty
circulation because of the damaged heart. You follow me?"
He put his glasses on and his eyes seemed to spin back into
focus.

"Yes," Mrs Sturgis said. Ella and Hector nodded doubt-
fully.

"Wellp — " Dr Clinton rose, holding his satchel; "I never
believed in withholding the facts." Hector helped him into
his overcoat. "Thanks." He paused with his hand on the
doorknob and stood there for a moment, head lowered. "Well,

we'll see how it comes out," he said as he opened the door;
"We'll see," and left. Hector and Ella noticed that this time,
in contrast to the last time he had said 'We'll see,' he did not
add 'Dont worry.'

The child was six months dying, which left it not a year
old at its death. During this period Ella was possessed by a
terrible sense of helplessness, a knowledge that there was
nothing she or anyone could do. All her life she had heard of
rheumatism as a fever of the joints, to be treated with liniment and massage, yet in this case there was not even a medicine that could be prescribed. She began to have a nightmare,
recurrent throughout the six months of the baby's dying.

She dreamed she was in the center of an amphitheater, and
people in white costumes were seated in the gallery. They
leaned forward, watching. An arc light, overhead, glinted on
the enameled table in front of her; she recognized it as a table
from the kitchen. Her baby was on the table. Arranged in a
convenient row beside it were a paring knife, a threaded
shoemaker's needle, and a bottle of brown liquid which at
first she thought was whiskey. The voices of the spectators
made a rising murmur beyond the down-funneled light, tiers
of faces in the outward darkness, but every now and then an
authoritative voice would shout for silence and the murmur
would stop, then resume on a lower key, rising again.

— Quiet! the voice commanded.

The murmur ceased.

— All right, miss. Begin.

It was as if she had been rehearsed. She took up the paring
knife, made a neat incision high on the left side of the baby's
chest (there was hardly any blood) and took out the heart. It
was shaped like the hearts on valentines; it seemed to be made of
pink satin, with a sheen in the brilliant light from overhead.
Around the amphitheater the murmur rose, individual voices
coming through:

— Look.

— She cut out her baby's heart.

—Look!

But she would not be distracted. She raised the bottle, poured a few drops of the brown liquid over the heart (it was liniment; she could smell it now) and began to massage gently, being careful not to put any strain on the little rubber tube that ran from the tip of the heart into the body, through the incision. At this the voices rose excitedly:

—Ella! Ella!

That meant they knew her. She did not know whether she knew them, though occasionally, despite her determination not to be distracted, she heard a voice she thought she recognized. But were they cheering or were they angry? The murmur grew to a roar as she replaced the heart, took up the curved needle, and began to stitch the lips of the incision with the waxy shoemaker's thread.

—Quiet! Quiet! the authoritative voice commanded.

But they would not be quieted. They would still be roaring in her ears when she came awake with a start, to find Hector shaking her shoulder and calling her name in a tone that was at once a plea and a reproach:

"Be quiet, Ella, be quiet." The smell of liniment, brought out of the dream, seemed to be strong in the room. Then it was gone. "You were having that nightmare again," Hector would say. "Are you all right now?"

There was always the hope that the heart would cure itself; the doctor had said it might, and indeed that was the only chance. But the torpidness, the labored breathing, the discoloration grew worse. When the milder weather of early summer set in and there still was no improvement, Dr Clinton told her to take the baby out into the sunlight. "Fresh air and sunshine," he said pontifically, holding up one finger. He was glad to be making some sort of prescription, and he made it more for Ella's sake than for the child's, which he had given up already. So she dressed it in the knitted suits it had outgrown even before it was born, put it in the perambulator, and walked up and down in front of the house, pushing.

People approaching along the road, no matter how they tried to be polite, could not keep their eyes off the baby. It was so big, bulging Buddha-like out of its clothes, and so obviously a representation of death: it had a monstrous fascination for them. With those dark lips shading toward purple, that liver-colored skin, it was like something displayed at a sideshow, in a vat. Though they did not want to seem to be snubbing or pitying her, they would struggle to turn their heads as they drew near, or at least hold their gaze above the level of the perambulator. Yet they could not keep their eyes away, no matter how they tried; they could not keep the look of horror off their faces. They twisted their mouths into sickly smiles, raised their hats, and wished her a good day. Then they hurried on, not looking back for fear that she might look back, too, and catch them at it.

Still, no matter how much they might seem so, six months were not forever. Summer burnt itself out, gave way to fall; fall was prolonged, and then on a morning in mid-November, a time of woodsmoke and reddening leaves, Ella woke, turning to the crib beside the bed, and a miracle had happened in the night. The discoloration was gone; the blood-colored mouth had returned to pink and the skin was pale as ivory. Her heart gave a leap, then held and throbbed as she saw her mistake. The baby was dead.

They buried this fourth Hector the following afternoon in the Wingate plot, a cedar grove where the first Hector, dead in Mexico, had a marker, where the second, dead by violence too, was buried, and where the third would someday join the fourth. They would lie sleeping with their wives, all the Hectors except the first and the last.

Mr Clinkscales' voice reached Ella through a mist of tears: "Suffer the little children to come unto me, and forbid them not: for of such is the kingdom of God."

"It's better off, poor thing," people said. "Better for it, and better, too, for everyone concerned."

In time even Ella came to think so. Recovered from both the

birth and death of her child, she turned to Hector with the old urgency — the low moan so deep in her throat that it was almost a growl, the busy hands that knew just where to touch him, the clasping thighs with a heat to their inner surfaces like fever — and found no resurrection of the flesh. Ever since her second day in labor he had been haunted by what he had seen in the bedroom past the shoulder of the woman in the doorway. When he looked at Ella now he saw her as she had been that day, the animal agony, the eyes in the bruised sockets, the swollen body glistening with sweat. No matter how he tried to put it aside (as for instance he had done at the time, by worrying because the doctor was using one of his mother's fine linen towels for a sopping rag) it stayed with him, along with the reproach of having been the cause of all her suffering.

Then the child was born and there was a lull to this. After all, eighteen pounds: perhaps it was worth it. Women had gone through this, to some degree, since time began. He told himself that and he felt considerably better. Then this other thing happened; the child fell sick. What began with a blueness of the glans, a slight discoloration — an ailment with a somewhat comic tinge — had spread until he no longer had a son, he had a monster. The doctor spoke of rheumatism; a rheumatic heart, he said. But that was no answer, that was merely a fiction to fill a gap; after all, he had to speak of something, if for no other reason than to earn his fee. What was it, really? Hector asked, and then a terrible question came. Was it the curse, the sin carried down? He lay in bed or leaned across the drawing board and asked himself these things, and from then on, whenever he looked at Ella he saw her in the agony of labor, like an oarsman collapsed on a sweep, and whenever she touched him, even by accident, he felt his flesh grow cold beneath her hand.

She gave him six months. For she knew his life, how he had failed as a planter, as a man-about-town, as a father, and now that he had failed in this way too, she considered six months a liberal wait. When the time was up, she struck out on her own.

The husband and the mother-in-law both knew it from the start, of course, yet there was nothing they could do but wait for her to reach a stage of revulsion like the one she reached a month before her marriage. It could happen again, they told themselves; nothing ever happened for once and for all. In point of fact, however, despite the outrage to her sensibilities — nothing like this had ever happened in the family before, except perhaps her brief affair with the man she later married — Mrs Sturgis waited because she was afraid that any action on her part might alienate Hector, and Hector waited because he was too filled with a sense of his inadequacy to risk the chance of being shamed with it.

He had not realized *how* inadequate, though, until a night soon afterwards when Ella came in late and found him sitting fully dressed in the bedroom, waiting for her. Her clothes were rumpled and she walked unsteadily; he smelled whiskey. "Where have you been?" he asked her, spacing the words. He stood there pale and trembling, yet with considerable dignity, and when she came past without a sign that she had even heard the question he struck her with his open hand. It made a sound as abrupt and sharp as a pistol shot in a theater. Ella sat on the floor with a sudden, collapsed motion, her hair falling over her face. Then, to his horror, he saw her separate the strands with her fingers crooked and look up at him, smiling. His palm tingled.

"Come on," she said, speaking softly. "Hit me. Hit me again."

It was more than he had bargained for, more than he could bear. It was much the same as it had been, twenty years ago, when he stood on the carriage seat, swinging the book satchel at the upturned faces, and felt the shock of resistance travel up the strap. But this time it was worse; this time it was flesh to flesh, no strap to act as conductor, no Samuel to shout encouragement, no carriage to draw him away, and she was sitting there with the mark of his hand on her cheek, watching him through the parted curtain of hair, her eyes gone tender, her voice soft, loverlike, asking him to hit her again.

This time, however, he did not throw up. He went instead to the bed, lay down across it with his face in the pillow, and wept. Presently Ella got up from the floor and came to him, still walking unsteadily. She began to comfort him, patting his shoulder and saying, "There, there. There, there." And as he went on weeping, the taste of tears like salt at the back of his mouth, it was as if he were standing outside himself, looking down at the two of them — Hector Sturgis and Ella his wayward wife; he could see them, the man with his face in the pillow, sobbing, and the woman crouched beside him on the bed, stroking his shoulder, fondling the back of his head, comforting him for his inadequacy. "There, there," she said. "There, there." Experienced from within, there was something terribly degrading about it; yet seen this way, impersonally, it gave him a strange, vicarious pleasure.

Thus he set the pattern for those future scenes between them, staged in the upstairs bedroom when Ella returned from her hours with other men. Hector would sit there, fully dressed, waiting sometimes until the windows were gray with dawn. Then she would arrive, and the scene that followed always conformed to the pattern already established, leading to a climax like that first one, the night he slapped her. He would fall in a heap, moaning with his face against the carpet, and she would sit beside him on the floor; she would take his head in her lap, stroking his hair and purring to comfort him, until her thighs were damp with his tears. And when, his voice trembling with emotion, he asked why she committed the acts that provoked these scenes, she would cradle his head in her arms, rocking it against her chest, and say: "Now, now, sweetheart, dont you fret. If you want to have your fun this way, you mustnt fuss about how I have mine."

Sometimes it seemed to him that all this had happened overnight. It had come about so quickly, he was embroiled before he even had time to realize trouble was coming. One day he

was riding the streets of Bristol in a yellow-spoked surrey, a
bachelor home from college. Then he had seen the immemorial
face of repentance. It had snared him, and now he was engaged in a nightmare with no exit, unable to relieve the tension
except through hysteria.

"Is this me?" he asked himself; "Is this really me?" — knowing well enough what he had come to, and even perhaps where
it was leading him.

He knew the result, but he wanted to know the cause. His
mind beat at its barriers and achieved a curious belief. He
believed that Ella was trying to provoke him into doing
what his father's father had done. She wanted him to kill her,
out of revulsion and despair, and thus fulfill his destiny. It
was all a plan that got underway the night she told him the
story of what had happened in Ireland between old Barney
and the tinker; she had told it by design. His only two ex-
periences with violence, first the day he swung the satchel,
second the night he slapped her, had shown him how poorly
he was equipped for it. Nevertheless, soon after it occurred to
him that their relationship was in truth a contest in this
manner, he went down to the hardware store and bought himself an ax. He bought the finest they had, a double-bitted
woodsman's model, razor sharp along both cutting edges,
smuggled it into the house in a roll of drawing paper, and
hid it behind his dress suit in the chifforobe.

He did not put it there to use — for that was the contest
as he saw it: she trying to provoke him into using it, he
resisting the provocation. He put it there, rather, as a challenge
to himself, a reminder never to relax. In this he believed he
was like a master at chess, who draws an opponent along in
confidence up to the final moment; "Check!" the challenger
cries, so intent on victory that he has forgotten the possibility
of defeat; "Checkmate," the master says. Thus some night
he would produce the ax, showing it to her, perhaps even
brandishing it. Then, craftily, at the instant when she thought
she had succeeded, he would put it aside, smiling, and say,

"See? You thought youd won; you thought you could make me use it. But I wont. And never will." He was really that far gone.

All the traveling men knew her by now. They discussed her on trains and in Memphis hotel lobbies. A drummer on the way out would give an incoming man the tip. "There's a little married woman down in Bristol, name of Sturgis. Tchk!" He made that sudden clucking sound of approval, bringing his tongue down sharply off the roof of his mouth. "She's a looker, man. And loves it, too. Her husband dont treat her right, if you see what I mean."

This continued. Hector was well along with his project of plans for the subdivision by now; he had begun to put in the colors. Across the hall, Mrs Sturgis was biding her time, waiting for the day when she could reclaim her son. And night after night he sat alone in the bedroom, waiting and knowing the ax was in the chifforobe. He did not need to touch it or even look at it; he knew it was there, and for the present that was enough. Later, however, there was an urge to look at it. He would open the chifforobe door and hold the clothes aside and there it would be, as bright as new. Then he would close the door and see the ax in his mind, the two cutting edges like bright identical arcs clipped from a circle of ice. This too continued; he was satisfied, until finally there was a compulsion to touch it, to lift it out of the gloom. Now he began to sit alone in the bedroom with the ax in his lap, waiting. But as soon as he heard Ella's step on the veranda he would return the ax to its hiding place.

The months merged into years; it was 1910, and one night he sat waiting for the sound of her footfall, when suddenly — as if by the glare of lightning — the windows were bright with daylight. He looked at the bed and Ella was lying in it, asleep. Then he looked down at his lap, and there was the ax. He had fallen asleep in the chair and slept straight through. She had come in and found him asleep with the ax in his lap; she had stood and looked at him, in full knowledge of how he had waited all those nights; and then had gone to bed. He rose, holding the ax with both hands, crossed the room, and stood beside the bed, watching her sleeping. Something troubled her just then; she stirred, making a little moan, and one of her breasts tumbled sideways into the V of her gown with a slow, pouring movement like flowing batter. It looked up at him, the sagged sack of woman-meat, like a blind little face, and he hated her with a fierceness beyond any hate he had ever known.

He could have done it then, he believed: could have wakened her, shown her the ax, said "See: you thought I wasnt man enough," and killed her. He stood beside the bed, balancing the ax and looking down, leaned slightly forward like a man looking down into an abyss, and for a moment time stood still. Awake or asleep, inhale or exhale, people were frozen in motion all over the world; Time was that unbearable ultimate instant before dynamite goes. Then it flowed on; the paralyzed clock-tick passed, and Hector put the ax back into the chiffo-robe.

There was no feeling of defeat. It was quite the opposite, in fact. He had made up his mind to kill her, but he would not do it now, in anger at himself because he had fallen asleep and let her catch him with the ax in his lap. He wanted to kill her for her sins, make her the victim of an avenging angel, and he wanted this to be as clear to her as it was to him. In the moment when she saw the ax come down, its twin arcs glinting in the gaslight, he wanted her to understand, to see it as a stroke from Judgment, not from a brain that was sick with shame and self-pity.

Two weeks passed before he got his chance. But that was all right; this was no unusual span between outings. Besides, waiting was easy now that he had made up his mind and could see an end to waiting. It was a night in early August, a time of heat. Ella left soon after supper, and Hector went into his study to work on his maps. There had been a fire that after-noon, the engine going past with its plunging horses, its clanging bell, children on the sidewalks cheering and half the stray dogs in Bristol running after it. He sketched this scene in full detail and was pleased with the result, particularly the horses and dogs, for they were horizontal creatures and looked best from overhead. Occasionally he glanced up from the drawing board, listening to the quietness of the house. At midnight, when Ella still had not returned, he removed his sleeve protectors, put away the instruments, and went upstairs.

As he climbed he heard the bedsprings creak in his mother's room, and then her voice: "Son?"

"Yessum?"

"I just wanted to know if it was you."

"It's me," he said. They repeated this scene, word for word, each night when he came upstairs.

"All right. Good night."

"Good night."

He went directly to the chifforobe, took out the ax, and sat with it in his lap. The house was quiet. He was utterly sure of himself.

A little less than half an hour later there was a sound of wheels and hoofs on the driveway, a moment of silence, then the squeak of buggy springs and footsteps crossing the veranda. Always before, she had made them let her out at the road; but if she was getting bolder, all the better. He was completely calm. He knew there was no doubt that he would kill her, and he waited for her footstep on the stairs.

Instead there was a rapping at the door.

Hector did not move, but he gripped the ax handle tighter and began to pant a little, thinking: 'It's a trick. She guessed what I would do.'

The rapping came again, louder now, insistent. 'Something's happened,' he thought. He went into the hall, then to the head of the stairs. "Son?" he heard his mother say. He did not answer. As he picked his way gingerly down the stairwell, a descent into darkness, the thought returned: 'It's a trick. She's hired someone to kill me.'

But when he opened the door it was the constable, a big man with a walrus mustache. He wore a khaki shirt and a

wide-brimmed hat and the revolver at his hip twinkled in
the moonlight. "How do," he said. "I come to see you about
Miz Sturgis."

"She's upstairs, asleep."

"Ah? No sir — I mean your wife."

The constable stopped short and Hector saw that this was
because he was looking at the ax, which also glittered in the
moonlight, matching the twinkle of the revolver; Hector had
forgotten he had it. He leaned it against the jamb and said
cautiously, "What about her?"

"Something's happened, Mr Sturgis. I want you to come
with me."

"Happened?" It occurred to Hector that Ella might be having him arrested. "Whats happened?"

With his bloodhound eyes and drooped mustache, the constable looked quite sad. He hesitated, then spoke, and the last
word came like a drumbeat. "Mr Sturgis, I — I think she's
dead."

△

There was a full moon, late risen and so bright now that
the shadows of trees, cast on the streets which the constable's
buggy followed on its way toward the heart of town, stood
out in sharp contrast of black and gold, like filigree, each leaf
along the ragged edges as distinct as a saw-tooth. Northwest
beyond the river the comet flared, its tail upraised like the
tail of a horse on fire, and the stars were spattered thick
and hot against the pale gray velvet of the night. Hector had
not spoken since the constable told him he thought Ella was
dead. They had come down off the veranda, climbed into
the buggy from opposite sides, and the constable offered no
further information or explanation. Now Hector sat with his
hands limp in his lap, gazing straight ahead and listening to

the rhythmic clip-clop clip-clop of hoofs on the moon-dappled pavement. The sound had that smooth, effortless quality of something in a dream.

Indeed, there was something dreamlike about this whole affair. The constable had said he *thought* she was dead. What did that mean? Was she dead or was she not dead? Or had he said that in an attempt to soften the news, to give him some doubt to cling to until he saw for himself? Or was it all a lie, told to make him docile on the way to jail? These questions came fast, one behind another, but Hector made no attempt to answer them. He waited for the illogical to work itself out, the way it always seemed to do in dreams. Meanwhile the shadows flowed over and past them, alternate black and gold. The constable's nickel-plated revolver twinkled in the moonlight, gleamed in the shadows, and suddenly it occurred to Hector that, though the delta was a widely recognized hunting country, he had never touched a firearm, even a pistol.

This took on an importance in his mind. Like not having learned the names of the stars, it seemed a serious lack. He forgot the questions, forgot even Ella, and concentrated on suppressing a desire to touch the revolver. He told himself that he should not do this, that the constable (his name was Mullins, Pete Mullins, and somewhere Hector had heard that he had killed five men, two of them white) might be alarmed, might even be offended, and any man who had killed five men, two of them white, was no man to offend. The desire, however, was stronger than the fear. He was just reaching out to touch it when the constable reined in the horse. "Here we are, Mr Sturgis," he said. They were in front of the Bristol Hotel.

A red gig belonging to the fire department was drawn up at the curb. Hector observed that the horse, head down, knees locked in sleep, wore an almost new straw kady, its ears standing stiff and hairy through the holes cut into the brim. Otherwise the street was deserted, stretching long and empty under the drench of moonlight. While the constable waited

at the hotel entrance Hector stood in front of the sleeping
horse. ("He looked like he was studying it," the constable
said when he told about it later. "Like he was thinking about
buying it, maybe, that old swayback nag that ought to been
out to pasture years ago. Thats the trouble with having money;
you think about buying almost anything you see. Imagine —
at a time like that. And mind you I'd already told him his wife
was most likely still dead in there.") After waiting a full
minute, which seemed considerably longer, the constable
cleared his throat, first tentatively, then louder. When that did
no good he said cautiously, "Mr Sturgis —"

Hector looked up, startled. He had been sketching the horse
in his mind, planning to put it on the map, asleep with its ears
thrust upward through the holes in the brim of the kady.
"What?"

"This way," the constable said.

The lobby was empty when they first came in, as deserted
as the street, but the tinkle of the bell on a curved spring
above the door brought the night clerk out of a rear passage.
Short, narrow shouldered, his flaxen hair so heavily plastered
with brilliantine that he seemed to have just emerged from
swimming or a heavy shower of rain, he had the bright, darting
eyes of the habitually curious and the limber upper lip of
the talkative man. Entering, he wore the solicitous mask of the
professional greeter, showing the edges of his teeth. When he
recognized Hector Sturgis, however, he stopped and sipped
his breath; he performed a shallow bow, shaping the words
Good Evening with his mouth but making no sound, as if he
had considered and decided that it would be indelicate to speak
aloud at such a time. Hector returned the bow with a nod,
looking doubtful. There was something too decorous about
all this, something too like Frenchmen in cartoons.

He followed the constable, the night clerk bringing up the
rear, and as they entered the passageway the latter had emerged
from, he began to hear a steady, ghostly sighing. It came from
the end of the corridor, a series of low moans, suspirant

and profound — human yet not-human too, somehow too big for human, as if an elephant lay dying of pneumonia in one of the far rooms. The last door on the left was all the way open, but the others along the passageway were only slightly ajar: held so, Hector saw as he came abreast, by hotel guests wearing nightshirts and standing with the doorknobs in their fists. They all faced the same direction, like alerted sentinels, and their eyes caught the flicker of the gasjets.

"It's the husband," they said as he came past. He could hear them murmuring from door to door and from opposite sides of the hallway, their voices touched off in a chain reaction, the whispers reaching him louder than shouts; "It's the husband."

Just short of the open door, the last on the left, the constable stopped and turned around, intending to prepare Hector for what he was going to see. All the way out to the Sturgis house in the buggy, then all the way back to the hotel, he had thought about what he would say. Up to now, however, he had not been able to bring himself to say anything, and this was his last chance, just short of the door. He raised one hand, palm forward, facing Hector with the great sad bloodhound eyes and the mustache like a big straw-colored U suspended upside-down beneath his nose. His mouth was set for speech, the words of condolence he had rehearsed to himself in the buggy, but Hector brushed past him; he even jerked his arm away when the constable touched his sleeve. It was as well, for when he reached the doorway and halted at last, looking into the room, he knew that beyond what he had already gathered from hearing the hotel guests whisper down the corridor — "It's the husband!" — nothing the constable might have said, either in the buggy or in the hall, could have prepared him for what he saw.

Two firemen were in the room, both still wearing gum boots though they had removed their slickers and souwesters and thrown them in a corner. One stood over some kind of machine, turning the crank of what resembled a coffee grinder mounted on a metal cylinder; the other, kneeling on a wide double bed that had been pulled into the center of the room, held the ends of two hoses that ran from the machine. Soft rubber masks were attached to the hoses and the fireman was holding them, one in each hand, over the faces of two people lying crossways on the bed.

One was covered past the shoulders with a sheet. The other, a man sprawled on his back, was uncovered. He wore only a pair of knee-length drawers, candy-striped and wrong-side-out. They had been improperly buttoned, apparently by other hands and obviously in a hurry. Air from the machine — Hector recognized it as a pulmotor now, though he had never seen one before — was being forced into, then drawn out of the man's lungs. It went in with a thin, reedy sigh and came out with a quavery moan choked off at the end by a sob of final exertion, as if he were lifting weights beyond his strength. Each breath made the man's chest expand almost to bursting, and with each expansion and contraction the blond hairs at the top of his chest glinted like scraps of copper wire under the glare of the chandelier directly above the bed. Presently the fireman moved aside for a moment and Hector saw what he had known he would see.

The face beneath the other mask was Ella's. They had spread her hair fanwise over her head; it was dark and there was even more of it than he remembered. Her breaths were drawn almost an octave higher than the man's, so that the two of them, lying side by side on the rumpled bed, their four legs dangling in that profound and ultimate relaxation of death, were chanting the not-human duet which Hector had heard from the lobby.

This continued for two more hours, the firemen alternating at the crank. But it did no good. Whenever the masks were removed the breathing stopped; their hearts never beat.

Hector and the constable waited, sometimes in the hall and sometimes in the room itself, though there it was difficult to keep out of the way of the firemen who clumped about in their gum boots and shirt-sleeves and suspenders. The guests had deserted their vigil by now. From time to time, however, one of them would return to his door, peep out, and then go back to bed. During this period of waiting the constable told Hector what had happened. Speaking with the tuneless Liebestod for background music, he told it in a halting, embarrassed manner. It was true that he had killed five men, four of them more or less in the line of duty, but nothing in his life had prepared him for imparting this kind of news; he kept imagining himself in the listener's place, with his wife where the listener's wife was, and that made it difficult. Besides, the version he gave Hector was considerably reduced from the one the night clerk had given, earlier in the evening.

According to the night clerk — in the unabridged version, that is — the dead man (he came through Bristol twice a year, representing a Massachusetts shoe firm) had called for ice water and towels at ten oclock. The Negro bellboy who took them to him was the last person to see him alive, and he saw only a naked arm extended around the partly opened door, a muscular arm with a fell of reddish blond hair glinting coppery in the dim light of the corridor. No one had known the lady was with him until the bellboy saw the way he took the ice water and towels, and even then the bellboy did not mention it to the night clerk.

"She must have snuck in the back way," the night clerk said. "She sure didnt come past the desk; I'd have seen her. This may not be exactly the cushiest house in the country, no Waldorf-Astoria by a long shot, but at least it's respectable. Or anyhow it tries to be till something like this hooraw comes along."

"I hear you," the constable said. They were in the lobby. He had just gotten there; he had taken one look into the room and now he was waiting to learn the particulars before driving out to the Sturgis house for Hector. "Get on with it," he said.

A little after midnight the bellboy reported a smell of gas.

When the night clerk went down the hall to investigate, there was a reek of it coming around the door. He knocked but no one answered. Then he used his pass key, and there they were. He had one quick look at them before the gas blinded him with tears.

"That room was full of gas as a balloon. The two of them were on the bed, mother nekkid, huddled up together like a pair of drownded people that got run over by a steamboat. It was something to see, all right."

"Never mind the trimmings," the constable said. "Just get on with it. What then?"

The night clerk stumbled around the room, his eyes streaming tears. Blinded, he had to feel his way, and this was particularly harrowing because he had a dread of touching the people on the bed. "Dont anybody strike a match!" he kept shouting, though there was no one to hear him; maybe he was shouting to himself. The window was stuck. He had a hard time raising it, getting angrier and more frightened every second. Finally, though, he got it up. It yielded all of a sudden, as if some force outside himself had jerked it, and he fell forward against the rotted screen, breathing night air through the dust and the rust. When the window and the door had been open long enough to clear the air in the room he found the trouble.

"That fellow must have accidentally kicked the lever on the heater alongside the bed. Youd think they would have heard the hissing, though; when I come in it sounded like a whole pit full of snakes. It's a good thing nobody struck a match. Lord God. Theyd have heard the boom in Bannard; we'd have all been blown to glory." He grinned. "What do you reckon that fellow was doing, to kick that heater on like that and never know he'd done it?" This was rhetorical; he broadened his grin, then continued. "They didnt hear it or smell it either, except maybe after it was too late, and maybe not even then. They sure must have been keeping occupied; you have to hand him that. Yair. I heard once of a fellow

took a girl off into a canebrake. It was over in Arkansas, the
way I heard it. He took her out for a buggy ride, and while
they were back in the canebrake on the laprobe, along came
a moccasin and bit her in the act. They — "

"In the what?"

"The act," the night clerk said. "It's a manner of speaking.
And they come back out and got in the buggy and started
back for town. They were about halfway home before she
begun to feeling peaky. That was the first she knew of being
bit. Fact is, she didnt even know it then. She like to died,
and they still didnt know what it was until the doctor got to
looking round (all in the line of duty, you understand) and
found the tooth marks, the punctures where the cottonmouth
had struck her. Yair; I always had a respect for that fellow . . .
But this one tonight has got him beat a mile." He sighed.
"You saw her, Pete. Tchk! All he had to do was measure up
to what luck brought his way; thats all. Even dead she looked
plenty good to me."

He paused. His face was suddenly serious. He was quiet
for a time, brooding upon mortality, and a little V appeared
between his eyebrows.

"I heard she was running round, though I never got in on
it myself; she favored out-of-towners, traveling men. It was a
kind of quirk with her. Everybody was talking about her,
saying she was hell-born, things like that. Well, *I* never blamed
her, considering what she married. Ive known him all his
life — him and his highflown ways. Bristol schools werent
good enough. He never even dressed like us, the others with
him in school I mean. You could tell just by the look on his
face how much better he thought he was than anyone else.
Let me tell you, Pete, if thats blue-blood I'm glad I didnt
have any to pass on to my kids. Come to think of it, maybe
thats why that baby swole up and turned purple and finally
died. Too much blue-blood. If it was his to begin with, I mean."

He leaned forward and tapped the constable on the forearm,
nodding earnestly as he spoke.

"I remember he went to public school for a while at the beginning. You should have seen him, the way he dressed, like every day was Sunday and school was an ice cream party. He thought all us others ought to kowtow to him. Once he tried to give something out of his lunch box to my kid brother, the way youd feed a monkey at the zoo. He came to me about it, crying; my brother I mean; his feelings were hurt. So I went up to the little overdressed dude — he was sitting on the side steps with that fancy lunch box on his knees. So I went up to him, as I said, there on the steps, and told him to keep his elegant grub to himself or I'd bounce one off his nose. 'Get up from there and I'll bounce one off your nose.' Thats what I told him, the identical words, and he just sat there and took it; he didnt budge. (He remembers it still — I can tell. He cant look me in the eyes to this good day, not even in passing.) And from then on, all the boys were onto him. We guyed and ragged him till his mama came and yanked him out of school."

He took out a pocket comb and ran it through his hair. It made a whispering sound, like a spoon stirring butter. The constable watched him without really listening; he was trying to decide how to go about breaking the news when he reached the Sturgis house. Down the corridor the firemen had gone to work with the pulmotor. The night clerk returned the comb to his breast pocket, and now he rubbed his palms together to wear off the brilliantine.

"I'll tell you, Pete," he said. "When a man's wife gets to running round, it stands to reason she's out after something she's not getting at home. Right?" The constable just looked at him, so the night clerk answered himself: "Right. And what would you expect? He grew up in satins and laces, cultivating the graces, the way the song says, and come back from college with a Yankeefied accent, wearing Yankeefied clothes. Then he up and married *her* and everybody says 'Oh-oh, now we'll see some fun'; they had known her of old, back before she married him. And sure enough he got more and more peculiar, keeping more and more to himself, till it wasnt long before she was back to her old practices. I'm telling you. Many's the time I stood behind this desk right here in the lobby and heard the drummers pass the word, telling each other about her, talking like she was a train youd ride, calling her the best jump between Memphis and New Orleans and counting up how many times and all her little tricks. Yair. But like I say, I never blamed her. What the hell. If a man wants his wife to stay home, cleaving her only unto him the way she swore at the wedding, he by God ought to nail her down. Give her what she's wanting, is what I say, and she wont want to roam."

"All right," the constable said at last, not in answer to anything the night clerk had said, merely as a sign that he was leaving. He had not decided how to break the news to Hector that his wife was dead in bed with another man, but he could not put off leaving any longer. He drove slow. Then he was there, and when Hector came downstairs with the ax, all the constable said was that he thought Ella was dead, meaning that he did not know how successful the firemen might have been with the pulmotor by then. Hector did not question him, and though the constable thought this strange he certainly did not regret it and he did not attempt any further explanation until he turned, just short of the death-room doorway, extending one hand palm-forward. Even then he did not really know what he intended to say, and this time too he was glad when Hector brushed past him, refusing to listen, determined to see for himself what he must have suspected he would see ever since he had begun to hear the chain-reaction of murmurs down the corridor: "It's the husband. It's the husband. It's the husband."

Presently, while the firemen continued to labor over the couple on the bed, Hector and the constable — who were merely in the way, particularly the former, for the firemen were distracted, sneaking sidelong glances at the husband of the woman on the bed — returned to the lobby and sat in over-stuffed leather chairs with a potted plant between them in the background. "Cigar?" the constable asked. His hand moved toward his breast pocket; he wanted to offer what condolence he could. Hector shook his head. It was the only sign he gave that he had heard. "Well," the constable said. He fell silent, too, looking uneasily about the empty lobby. Then he saw something he had not seen before. The gray-haired Negro bellboy was asleep in a straight-backed chair beside the registration desk, his chin down near his chest. "Hey — boy!" the constable cried, loud with sudden inspiration. The bellboy, startled, jerked awake, then crossed the lobby to where the constable sat with one arm already extended. "Take this and get us some coffee," he said, and he handed the bellboy a dime.

The coffee was a failure, too, as much so as the unproduced cigar. The bellboy returned in about ten minutes with two heavy white earthenware mugs, each wearing a plume of steam. The coffee was pale yellow, the color of river water, already sugared and creamed, and very hot, as if the cook had tried to make up in heat for what it lacked in strength. The constable drank his, taking finicky sips from under the straw-colored walrus mustache, but Hector sat holding the mug with both hands between his knees, gazing down into it as if it had been as deep as a well, with the answer to all his problems at the bottom. He sat thus for a long while, not drinking. The plume of steam disappeared; the coffee cooled; finally it was all the way cold, truly like river water now, and the constable leaned forward and relieved him of it. "Here," he said; "I'll take that." He set it, still full, untasted even, beside his own empty mug at the foot of the potted plant. "Well, Mr Sturgis, it's a trial," he said at last.

Shifting his great, sad eyes with their oversized bright red tear ducts, he avoided looking at Hector as he spoke. This was all he managed to produce out of all the words of condolence he had rehearsed in the buggy, riding to and from the Sturgis house. Hector still said nothing. He was more or less in a state of shock, and he looked it. From time to time the night clerk emerged on tiptoe, peered at them, then tiptoed back down the corridor to look once more at Ella and the drummer sprawled on the bed as if they had fallen from the ceiling. The firemen continued their work and the dead couple continued their thin, reedy imitation of breathing.

At last, however, the ghostly sighing stopped. It stopped quite suddenly, and somehow the silence that followed immediately upon it seemed louder than the sighing, like the vacuum at dead center of a typhoon. This was either a reprieve or a death knell, and Hector and the constable rose together. They went down the corridor toward where the night clerk stood in the doorway, leaning forward with a hand on each side of the frame. He had not heard them coming; he stood there until the constable touched his shoulder, at which he leaped as if from a bee sting or a boo. Then, looking back over his shoulder, he saw Hector. "Ex-ex*cuse* me," he stammered. He stood aside and Hector saw that the firemen were disassembling the pulmotor to carry it out to the gig. They had given up. The dead couple now were laid lengthwise on the bed, like any two sleepers anywhere, side by side and covered with one sheet. Except for the stillness, they might indeed have been sleeping, but this was a stillness beyond the stillness of slumber. The drummer lay on the far side, rather bulky. Ella's body, on the near side of the bed, looked very flat beneath the four-point lift of her breasts and toes, with a smooth, empty curve of sheet between the pairs of points.

"Mr Sturgis," the constable said —

Hector turned, as if the voice were a leash that had been tugged, and followed the constable into the corridor. There they encountered Harry Barnes, the undertaker. He evidently had just gotten the news, for he wore list slippers and had his nightshirt tucked into his trousers. "Leave everything to me," he said by way of greeting. He was always on hand for misfortune, among the first to arrive when tragedy struck, and for this reason was known as Light Hearse Harry. Sideburns framed his face, like the clamp of a vise, and his chin and upper lip were blue with stubble. His attitude was in-variably sympathetic, but there was a glint of curiosity in his eyes, so long intent on watching the various reactions to death.

"Go on home and get some sleep," he said. His voice was low and confidential; he always spoke this way. "I guarantee you, when I bring her out to the house this afternoon youll never have seen her looking prettier. Mind you, I dont make idle promises. When I say pretty I mean it, and I promise you I'll do a careful job. Let me handle all this, Hector; I'll take care of everything."

Dawn was coming through when Hector and the constable left the hotel. Bristol was still asleep, profoundly relaxed be-hind drawn blinds, awaiting another tomorrow, another tick of the giant clock of time, but the streets looked harsh in contrast to the way they had looked three hours ago, bathed in moonlight. The year was into the dog days, the heat a steady glow. As a fire burns to embers, hotter than flames, so summer had burned to its climax. The sky was a cloudless, smooth gray dome like cast-iron perfectly joined and tinted with rose at its eastern rim predicting the sun. A file of men in work clothes, whites and Negroes, walked home from the oil mill, their lunch buckets under their arms. They were the night shift, coming off. Sloping their shoulders, they scuffed their shoes on a pavement still warm from yesterday's sun, while behind them the oil mill ground its teeth, crushing the cotton seed with a hungry-making odor like broiling ham. Hector, who had never been to town at this hour before, saw them thus for the first time. They lifted their heads as he came past, the buggy intersecting their line of march, and he looked down at them. With their stubble-darkened jaws and work-splayed hands, their eyeballs etched with tiny red threads of fatigue, they might have been visitors from another planet. He looked at them and they looked at him, down and up, and he was vaguely afraid, without knowing why. He believed he saw hate in their faces.

The moon was still up in the daylight sky. As the buggy turned into the Sturgis drive the sun came up too; it broke clear of the landline with a sudden jump and quickly turned from red to fiery, blinding whoever looked eastward, throwing a yellow-pink glow over the front of the house and softening the gray planks and pillars. The first thing Hector noticed was the ax, a steely glint among the shadows of the doorway. The buggy stopped; Hector got down and went up the steps, not saying Thank You or Goodbye, not even looking back. But then, as he took up the ax and started through the doorway, he glanced over his shoulder and saw the constable watching him. He stopped. For a moment they looked at each other. The horse was already asleep in the shafts, its muzzle down near its knees, and the constable sat with the reins held loose in his hands. When Hector suddenly looked back, returning his gaze, the constable, startled thus out of contemplation, twitched the reins and made a clucking sound with his tongue (it resembled the sound the out-going drummers had used, describing Ella): "Tchk!" and the horse lurched into motion, still asleep.

Going into the house was like re-entering the coolness of night. As Hector passed through the lower hall he looked to the right, into the parlor, and saw his mother sitting in her armchair, a shawl about her shoulders and her hair a pale gleam in the dawn-shadowed room. 'She knows all about it,' he thought. 'She sat right there, speaking to no one and no one speaking to her, yet she knows all about it.'

Then, taking the first step on the stairs, he heard her say his name. He did not stop or even hesitate, any more than he had done three hours ago when she spoke from her room as he came downstairs to investigate the constable's rapping at the door. He could not afford to stop; he was hoarding that diminishing span of time before he would burst into tears. Climbing the stairs was like ascending a slope at a high altitude, each step demanding an exertion out of all proportion to the gain involved, where a degree or two of fever would

approach the boiling-point of blood. What was more, something seemed to be dragging his arm out of its socket. Then
he remembered the ax. He dropped it on the landing. That
was better, though not much better. Crossing the upper hall he
staggered like a man who has swum from a shipwreck a long
way through surf before reaching the beach. He went directly
to his room, sat on the bed, and began to unlace his shoes.
But he was too tired even for this. He had one shoe off and
the other half-unlaced when the weariness came down; he
sank back, staring wide-eyed at the ceiling. 'Now I'll cry,' he
thought, surrendering at last to what he had fought against for
the past three hours. But the tears did not come. He could
feel the tear ducts trying to function, pump, but no tears came.

He lay there, flat on his back and trembling, and suddenly
for no reason he remembered Sunday mornings at church
when he was a boy. He always went with his grandmother.
She wore a dress that rustled and Samuel wore a broadcloth
coat with fire-gilt buttons. All the way to church they heard
the bell toll; they got there just as it stopped, and the others
were all in their places, turning to watch as Hector and Mrs
Wingate came down the aisle. Mr Clinkscales apparently took
this as a signal, for then the service would begin, though maybe
it was coincidental; they were never really late enough for
Hector to know for sure. The pew had a smell of varnish
which he thought of as the special odor of sanctity. The dime
he held was sweaty by the time the plate came round. To
his left a stained-glass window showed an angel standing barefoot in a field of bright green grass that grew brighter and
greener as the sun shone fuller and fuller on that wall of the
church. The angel had one hand on the head of a fuzzy, blue-
eyed lamb. The scarlet of the angel's lips had been misplaced
in processing and lay outside the border of the mouth like
a lipsticked kiss of shame. Hector recalled, too, that the lamb
had carried a cross, one of its cloven forehoofs hooked around
the upright.

Remembering, almost dreaming, he lay on the bed. Then,

without having heard any sound precede it, he felt something cool and soft upon his forehead. His lids lifted and the shape hovering above him might have been a ghost, Ella come back; he caught his breath. But when he focussed his eyes he saw that the shape was his mother. "There, there," she said, stroking his brow as she said it. "There, there." This soothed him. He relaxed and the tears came at last; the tears welled up. "There, there. There, there," his mother said as he wept.

She had waited for this through all these years, and now she had it.

3

That was a Thursday. The funeral was Friday. Normally this would have been considered indecent haste, but people not only 'understood,' they even stayed away — out of delicacy, they said; that was the word they used. Many, however, did not forego the chance to ride past during the graveside service, some in buggies, some in automobiles, to see if their fellow townsmen (they said) had shown a like consideration. Just as that morning they had collected at the depot, craning over each other's shoulders to watch the drummer's coffin and sample cases being put aboard the northbound train, so now they formed a parade going past the cemetery, riding slow in order that only a thin screen of dust would obscure their view of the little knot of mourners about the grave, and lacking only hampers and blazers and mandolins to make it resemble the holiday outing it really was.

For thirty-six hours Bristol had hummed with the news. People heard it with incredulity and passed it along with an air of having foretold it. Women discussed it in grocery stores and over backyard fences, tipping their heads together and hiding their mouths with their hands as they spoke, as if in fear of lip-readers, their eyes at once shocked and eager, their cheeks flushed as if they were into the final stage of what was called galloping consumption. "Have you heard about Ella Sturgis? Did you *ever*?" Men gathered on street corners and reviewed her life over bars and café counters, philosophizing on mortality and the sanctity of marriage, much as the night clerk had done in conversation with the constable, in defense and condemnation, alternately saturnine and sardonic. This death seemed such a waste. "They say you cant take it with you. Ha. By golly, she took it with her."

It had been a crazy year, a keyed-up summer. There was a fat man in the presidency who was everything a fat man ought to be, jovial and expansive, yet the government was split on issues that were hard to understand. Society women up East were said to be smoking cigarettes, and at a private dinner in Washington when the Russian ambassador's wife asked for a light, the president himself had held the match. A man flew in an aeroplane from New York to Philadelphia and back, making a mile a minute some of the time. The comet hung in the sky like a warning sign from God, but in early summer when the earth was scheduled to pass through its flaming wake there had been neither a bombardment of meteors nor clouds of poisonous gases to choke them in their beds; there wasnt even any stardust in the streets, and after the first elation at having been spared the fire from heaven, there was also a feeling that God had forgotten them, a feeling that God had no care for either their enormities or their prayers. Then in the month just past, on the Fourth — which, except by scattered groups of unregenerate and pastless Irishmen whooping and blowing anvils, went uncelebrated still in Mississippi because that was the day when Vicksburg fell nearly fifty years ago — a white man and a Negro stevedore stood toe to toe on a roped-off square of canvas in Reno, Nevada, slamming away at each other for the championship of the world, fifteen rounds under a broiling sun, and the Negro won. Bonfires that night in Lick Skillet and Ram Cat lighted the northeast sky; there was dancing in the streets in front of the cabins, and a hum of voices: "Jack Jawson whupped that white man to his *knees!*" But next morning when they came to work in the kitchens and gardens there was nothing in their faces to show their feelings, nothing at all, except that the whites of their eyes were threaded with red in proof of the whiskey drunk.

Bristol now was a far cry from Bristol as it had been, back

in that other century when Hector was a boy and a young
man. Progress had caught up with it; the automobile had run it
down, and the saxophone moaned over the remains. Those four
dominants rising out of the past — the trees, the war, the
Negroes, the river — no longer cast their shadows across the
present and were not included in any calculations for the
future. Many of the trees had been felled to make way for
widening the boulevards, and others were dying of thirst,
choked by the concrete poured close about their trunks for the
new sidewalks; the leafy tunnels were badly gapped, as if
by shellfire, and dead leaves fell unseasonally. The veterans
who turned out for parades and barbecues were only a
handful now; blear-eyed, they went on canes, and none of
them sucked in their stomachs now or skipped to keep step
with the music; the battle names had been forgotten along
with the cause for which they were fought, the fields themselves planted in cotton or run to weeds. The Negroes had
worn out the gay-colored shirtwaists and swallowtail coats
and did not replace them, for they were too poor; their faces
no longer resembled masks, for they knew no secret; Haiti and
John Brown had no connection with such as these. The river
was not grand and glittery any more; the showboats were tin-
sel affairs, and the old luxury packets, the *Natchez*, the
Robert E. Lee, the *Big Jim White*, were bleaching their ribs
on mudflats all the way from Cairo to New Orleans, the pulsing throb and rumble of their whistles drowned by the pierc-
ing, one-note shriek of locomotives.

New dominants replaced them. The Opera House, which
had boasted occasional traveling companies playing *Ben Hur*
and the like, was the Bijou now, the first cinema palace in the
delta; beneath the lancing beam of the projector the audience
crouched in the gloom, serried like countrymen in the old
dank multiholed privies, their upturned faces drinking the
frictionless shadows of a nation's desire, changing the shape
of Woman to Mary Pickford and looking forward to Clara
Bow and Garbo. An automobile, snarling and malodorous, was

no longer a curiosity on the sparrow-infested streets. The telephone, already common in houses not yet wired for electricity, had given every man an extra voice, squeaky and inflectionless like Punch infuriated, punctuated by wire-hum instead of smiles and nods, as he spoke into an oblong box screwed to the wall, filled with wire and buzzers and fronted by a tulip-like funnel on a stalk that cupped and threw his breath back in his face.

Such a list could grow and grow, but these were the dominants. These were the things which the preachers, high in their pulpits, railed and cajoled against, quoting the eschatology of Jeremiah and Isaiah and Jesus — to no effect: for the people sat in their Sunday clothes, soberly nodding agreement with all the preachers said about impending doom on earth and searing flame hereafter, and came out Monday morning as before; they gave the Lord His day, and kept the other six for their own uses. Yet they were new to these involvements. These devices that saved labor agitated their brains, and there was an increasing dichotomy between the Business life and the Christian life; they began to have nervous stomachs. There were nights when they tossed sleepless in their beds, counting the small hours by the courthouse clock, and suddenly, out of nowhere, dread was like a presence in the room; hell yawned and the trumpet was about to sound; cold sweat broke out on the palms of their hands and feet, and they knew fear.

The summer of 1910 was filled with such nights, the comet flaring like a rocket and a Negro beating a white man for a purse containing more money than most of them would ever see. All this and more went into making them ready and even anxious for some sort of personal, or at least local, outrage or affront; they were primed. So when they heard of Ella's death, how she had been found asphyxiated in the hotel bed with the drummer in candy-striped drawers, their minds leaped at, fastened onto, and examined it inside-out. Women philosophized less than their husbands, being mainly concerned with the facts in the case, but men who had experienced her

early or late promiscuity found in her death an occasion for
parading what they knew for the entertainment and envy of
their friends, using her light moments as a basis for conjecture
into profounder mysteries. Some who had never known her at
all, or had known her only to nod to, adopted an air of
reticence, implying that there was much they could tell if
they had not scrupled to betray a confidence or show disrespect for the dead. Others downright lied, unable to resist
this easy irrefutable chance to strut and posture. Those who
had known the drummer, had bought his goods or shared a
bottle with him, told what a ready eye he'd had for the girls.
"A rounder," they said, laughing, and added: "I hope when
my time comes I go like that."

Generally speaking, however, he was merely adjunctive,
supplementary. It was Ella — and, by inference, the Sturgis
family with her — who held the limelight. Hector was responsible, with Mrs Sturgis behind him. "If thats blue-blood,"
the night clerk had said, "I'm glad I didnt have any to pass
on to my kids. If a man wants his wife to stay home, he by
God ought to nail her down. You see what I mean?" They
saw; they followed all the clues and suggestions. For thirty-
six hours the talk had been of little else — where she had been,
whom she had been seen with, her partiality for traveling
men — and when the thirty-six hours were up, they formed a
parade out past the cemetery, just short of the lip of the grave.

What they saw, through the trailing screen of dust like
smoke, was hardly worth the trip. Only five persons attended:
Mrs Sturgis and Hector, Mr Clinkscales and Harry Barnes,
and Mrs Lowry. The first four of these were ranged along one
side of the grave, the minister at the head with the prayer book
held so close to his face that his nose was almost between the
pages; his eyes were failing though he was not yet ready to
admit it. Mother and son were in the center, standing close.
The undertaker was at the foot, not quite on line with the
others since, as he said, he never presumed to push forward
socially on a basis of professional advantage. Mrs Lowry

remained in the carriage because of her swollen legs. Her shoulders hunched, she wept into her handkerchief, producing a smothered, rhythmic moaning like a woman being tickled or drowned or maybe sawed in two. Anyone hearing her without knowing the occasion which brought forth these sounds would have thought she was being shaken by uncontrollable laughter: Ah, ah, ah, *ha!* The ha! that ended each series of ah's was a sob of final exertion, like the ultimate gasp of a lifter of weights.

Mr Clinkscales read from the book: "Jesus saith to his disciples, Ye now therefore have sorrow: but I will see you again, and your heart shall rejoice, and your joy no man taketh from you."

Standing beside the grave Hector heard it all, the text along with the sobs from the nearby carriage — ah, ah, ah, *ha!* — but the former had no more meaning for him than the latter. The only safe and sensible thing in the world was his mother's hand, which held firmly onto his wrist and gave it a squeeze or a comforting pat from time to time.

"In sure and certain hope," Mr Clinkscales read, droning fervently.

The coffin sank on its patented rollers, going down into the earth while Mr Clinkscales prayed with his head tipped back, looking up into the sky. He was reciting poetry now, the rhymes coming through at regular intervals out of the surrounding words; death had no sting, the poem said, quoting Paul. After a silence broken only by the moans and sobs like Olympian laughter, Hector felt a tug at his sleeve. He had been feeling it for some time now, he realized, and when he looked up, Mrs Sturgis spoke to him again: "Come along, son."

He got into the carriage, opposite the rector and beside his mother, who sat facing the weeping seamstress.

"The Lord giveth," Mrs Lowry said between sobs. "The Lord taketh away."

As the carriage passed beneath the gateway arch (HOME OF

PEACE it spelled in wrought-iron letters) Hector turned, looking back, and saw two Negroes in overalls come from behind
the hearse where they had been hidden during the service.
Under the direction of Mr Barnes they removed the bright
green mats of artificial grass from the raw mound and began
to throw pale yellow dirt into the grave. Their shovels, polished silvery by digging, flashed in the sunlight, but distance
and the sound of the tires on gravel drowned the hollow clatter
of clods on the lid of the coffin; Hector heard them only in
his mind.

"The Lord giveth," Mrs Lowry said.

She wept more quietly now, as if the final fact of death, not
as one stunning blow but as a presence that would be with
her all the balance of her life, had reached her at last with its
strange comfort. Presently she dried her eyes, using one
corner of a silk dance handkerchief a little less than half the
size of a bedspread, and sat watching the houses flow past. For
a time she said nothing. She sat watching. Then suddenly:
"My, *my*," she said, her voice sounding quite loud after the
silence, "so many *new* ones. Bristol certainly has grown!"

It was the first time she had left her room since the flood
of 1903. Her legs bulged beneath her skirts and petticoats. Her
eyes, pale green under lids inflamed from weeping, blinked
weakly in the unaccustomed sunlight, and her flesh had the
bluish tinge of soured milk. "Who lives there?" she asked from
time to time, pointing with the hand that held the handkerchief so that it fluttered like a banner on a rampart. She had
begun to sweat and the secret, unwashed parts of her body
gave off a rancid odor, faintly ammoniac. The bruise-colored
circles under her eyes came almost to her cheekbones.

They had fallen into the passing column, the parade of
Bristolians who had foregone the actual funeral, the graveside
service, but who could not forego having at least what they
called a look-see. It wound from somewhere south of the
cemetery, northward into the heart of town, inescapable and
avid. The people in the surrey just ahead turned their upper

bodies with sudden birdlike movements, darting glances, and from time to time one of the vehicles toward the rear would pull out of line to catch a glimpse of the Sturgis carriage. An automobile, whose driver was more adventurous than the rest, clattered past with a sound like pieces of scrap iron being shaken in a wooden tub, and though its occupants sat with their bodies held severely to the front, like cannoneers on dress parade, they twisted their heads slightly to the right as they came past, examining the quartet of mourners out of the corners of their eyes.

Mrs Lowry wore a black taffeta tea gown, stylishly cut, which a client had never called for. She told them about that, Mr Clinkscales and Mrs Sturgis and Hector, as well as the coachman high on the box. The latter did not look back; he sat as stiff as a department store dummy, and the others were frozen in various attitudes, surprised by her sudden volubility. They avoided her eyes, which flicked from one to another while she spoke.

"It was for Mrs Crenshaw, a dear lady; I think I might even say friend. She was looking forward to wearing it for her daughter's coming out. God rest her soul, she passed away the night I got it finished. You remember: it was awful sudden. She'd been in the best of health right up to the day. At least we thought so. Apoplexy took her and we never even knew she had it; she never looked the least bit apoplectic, to my mind. Well, I sent word to Mr Crenshaw it was ready, in case he wanted it for her for the occasion. She'd have liked that, being buried in it I mean, after all the pains she took getting the pattern and having it fitted and all. But he never answered, then or later. You know how it is at times like that: I suppose he had enough on his mind, poor man. Dont you?"

'My God,' Hector thought. 'My God, my God, my God.'

Then, without waiting for an answer and without even any change of tone (the transition was clear in her own mind, if not in anyone else's; she had mentioned Mrs Crenshaw's daughter and Mrs Crenshaw's death) Mrs Lowry said abruptly, "People said things about her I wont repeat, but they didn't know. What did they know? They made them up because of their idle minds. Elly was a good girl, good as gold. Who could know better than me? Why, I could tell you things she done for me. . . ."

She paused and dabbed at her eyes with one corner of the big plum-colored handkerchief, beginning to weep again. It was a bright clear day, very hot and still, the leaves hanging motionless, the sky intensely blue, almost to cobalt, not at all in keeping with the scene now being staged in the carriage. For a moment Hector had hopes that she would not be able to continue, but she recovered her voice soon afterwards.

"When Mr Lowry went away, ran off that is, and I begun taking in sewing, little odd jobs, piecework in the beginning, never any too sure where my next fifty cents was coming from, she used to say: 'I know what youre doing for me, mamma. *I* wont forget.' Mind you, she was just a little girl. (Wait." Mrs Lowry counted on her fingers, and then for some reason pointed one of them at Mrs Sturgis like a pistol. "She was barely six.) And then some nights when my poor legs were aching me too bad for me to use, she'd get down on her hands and knees under the machine and pump the pedal, going even and smooth with hardly a breathing-space until I'd make her stop and rest a spell. Nobody knows what a comfort she was to me in my misery. Lord love us, nobody *knows!*"

She threw back her head and roared this last, and the moans and strangulating sobs resumed: Ah, ah, ah, *ha!* Ah, ah, ah, *ha!* while the remaining three people in the carriage avoided not only Mrs Lowry's eyes but, now, each other's as well, seeking to occupy themselves, in the presence of a common embarrassment, with various trivialities apart from the action at hand. Mrs Sturgis smoothed her skirt, watching the cloth ripple under her fingers and the glitter of her rings against the black. Mr Clinkscales took out his watch, a big one, turnip-sized in a hunting case, which he always laid face-up on the lectern at

the beginning of every sermon; he joggled it now on the flat
of his palm, raising and lowering it as if trying to estimate its
weight for the first time in all the years he'd worn it, as intent
as if he were absorbed in solving the riddle of Time. Hector
was the only one who apparently did not feel obliged to occupy himself in some such manner. He kept his head down,
hoping that now at last Mrs Lowry would be unable to continue.

But it was not so. She soon recovered. In addition to wiping
her eyes, this time she blew her nose loudly twice, like
trumpetings, and then resumed. Now she spoke with bitterness.
Her voice was cold and, in comparison, calm.

"Yes. And mind you that wasnt the worst I had to bear,
oh no, because when she was coming up, barely out of pina-
fores, they couldnt keep her name off their filthy tongues. I
was dressing her fine as any lady in this town and they
couldnt bear it. They couldnt bear it. And why?" She paused,
eyes narrowed. "I'll tell you why."

This time it was not Mrs Sturgis she chose to address in
particular. She leaned across the minister's knees and shook a
finger in Hector's face for emphasis. Mrs Sturgis continued to
smooth her skirt and watch the glitter of her rings, still trying
to pretend for the benefit of the public-at-large that nothing
out of the ordinary was happening in the carriage, but Mr
Clinkscales drew back in alarm at the sudden aggression, the
seamstress leaning across his knees, and almost dropped his
watch. Hector raised his head, watching Mrs Lowry with
unbelief as she continued to rail.

"Because she made their skimpy little knock-knee girls look
silly. Thats why! Yes. And then to have a whole delegation
of Baptists (and me a Methodist and always have been) come
marching into my sewing room with their mouths screwed
tight as buttonholes, prunes and prisms, prunes and prisms,
telling me I'd have to keep her off the streets of Bristol because she was proud of the legs and the gorgeous bosom God
had give her, and was already more of a woman at sixteen
than any of them would ever be."

"Dear lady — " Mr Clinkscales said, putting the watch back into his waistcoat pocket for safe-keeping. But she ignored him, or more probably had not heard him at all.

"Yes! And them the same identical ones as used to bring their pipsqueak little scrawny-chested girls in for fittings and ask me please to tack some padding into the bosom but, shh, dont tell a soul, whatever you do — as if they wasnt all out after the selfsame thing: a man: else why would they want to be pretending to be having what they aint?"

"Really, madam," Mr Clinkscales said —

"You think I dont know them? I know them, all right. And when she up and married Hector Sturgis I thought theyd die. Die!" she cried, leaning again across the rector's knees, her face quite close to Hector's face. He could see the individual pores in her putty-colored skin, the mad grief in her eyes. She was speaking directly at him and she sputtered as she spoke. "Because you know as well as me the way they set their caps for you. I dont mean the girls; I mean the mammas. You may not be much man (and in fact I warned her at the time; I said, "Baby doll, I'm afraid thats not much man") but that was all right, where they were concerned, so long as the —"

"Dear lady, I must ask you," Mr Clinkscales managed to say. But for a third time she ignored him, not even pausing.

"— Wingate money was there and they could get their hands on it. But that didnt stop them, oh *my* no, even after she was sitting up there in that fine big house with servants to fetch and carry for her and hand her things on a plate. Marrying you wasnt their notion of the reward she ought to have gotten for the kind of life theyd been saying she was leading, not by a long shot. No sir, that didnt stop their limber tongues from wagging. You might think I dont hear things, cooped up there in that sewing room with a pair of legs that went bad on me when my man took off for parts unknown with a cootch girl. But I hear them; I hear them, all right, when theyre sitting there waiting for fittings, talking out of the sides of their mouths. I hear them all right: 'I heard she did this'; 'I heard she did that'; 'Did you hear about the other?' "

Here Mrs Lowry performed an imitation of the gossips, hunching her shoulders to the level of her ears, screwing up her eyes, and hiding her mouth with her hand as she spoke. It was a credible performance, though rather broad. By now the others in the carriage had abandoned all pretense of being variously occupied; they watched her with wide eyes, frankly horrified, as she dropped back into character and continued, speaking faster all the time. It was as if she feared that some outside force was going to stop her before she finished saying all she had stored up through all those years.

"They doted on it; it was their bread and butter. Well, it's easy enough to explain. Theyve got such empty lives anyhow; you could almost forgive them, except the harm they do. When their men come home at night from bending over desks all day and counting other people's money, theyre too tired, too wore-out to treat them right. Yes: thats their trouble, for a fact. That might explain it, right enough, but it dont forgive them what they done. It dont forgive them provoking Elly into what happened to her. It dont forgive them murdering my child. Bitches!" she cried suddenly, her voice mounting toward some unattainable shrillness, perhaps beyond the furthest range of hearing. "Bitches! Bitches!" she cried, over and over, wringing her hands and shaking the tears from her eyes.

During this last the carriage drew up at the curb in front of the big gray boarding house where Mrs Lowry had two rooms on the upper floor. However, she took no note of this; she remained launched on the flood of bitterness, her voice mounting higher and higher, until two of the men boarders (they were night shift workers from the mill and had come onto the porch to watch the fun) responded to the rector's gestures by coming out to the parked carriage, where they clasped each other's wrists to form a four-hand basket carry, then lifted her clear of the seat and across the yard.

Her legs bulged enormous in black cotton stockings and the
workers panted under the load, their faces drawn from exertion, the tendons of their necks standing out like cords, the
corners of their mouths pulled sharply down. Mr Clinkscales
ran alongside, uttering quick, chirpy cries of caution and
fluttering his hands, which were pale and large and, now,
apparently boneless. Overhead, the cloudless, cobalt vault, with
its limitless intensity, still lent the scene an atmosphere of too-
vivid unreality, as if it were being played on a stage or
even by the glare of lightning and must therefore end in darkness, suddenly, like the end of the world. Mrs Lowry, thus
transported, was still weeping, still screaming and calling the
Baptist ladies bitches, when the men took her up the steps,
between the two shingles on the flanking pillars, and into the
house.

All down the block, on both sides of the street, her neighbors
(they were mostly women at this time of the day; their husbands would be home between five thirty and six oclock)
leaned out of windows or came out onto the sidewalk, already
beginning to tell each other what they had seen and heard,
rehearsing what they would tell their men when they got home
from work.

"Did you see her? Did you hear the way she bellered?"

"Did I? Oo!"

"She really told them, didnt she?"

"*Did* she? Oo!"

"She did. She did, indeed!"

Two hours ago they had watched the departure, the Sturgis
carriage drawing up and Mrs Lowry being carried out and
deposited in it, greeting the others with considerable decorum
and settling back against the button-studded cushions as the
carriage pulled away, like any duchess out for an airing in her
black taffeta tea gown. It had all been very polite, very
sedate, and therefore something of a disappointment. The return was more to their liking; they leaned out of windows and
across hedges, commenting on it with delight.

"She really told them, didnt she?"

"Did you see the way she yelled it in their faces?"

"Did I! My oh *my*."

They said these things with a considerable element of pride, lifting their voices higher than was necessary to span the gaps between. It was as if Mrs Lowry had championed a common cause, and now they took courage and followed the example she had set.

Hector and Mrs Sturgis did not look at them or even at each other. Their faces empty of expression, they waited for the rector to return. Presently he did, a nervous, gray-haired man who by ordinary retained the elaborately cordial manner he had brought to Bristol forty years ago as a young minister with a boyish, pink-cheeked face that caused the older ladies of his congregation to coo and flutter over him, who also had played unsuspecting chaperon at Esther Wingate's courtship, and who still walked with a slightly rolling limp like a sea-faring man because of the badly knit ankle that brought Hector Sturgis into the world or at any rate contributed toward his conception. But he was worried now for fear that he would be blamed for the scene just past. It had been his suggestion that Mrs Lowry go in the carriage with them, though he knew that the two women had never met; Mrs Lowry's legs prevented her making calls, and certainly it had never occurred to Mrs Sturgis that she should make the overture, even at the time of the marriage that connected them, any more than her mother had made any overture to her son-in-law's barkeep father, back in her own time.

Mr Clinkscales climbed in at last, flushed from exertion and the difficulty of his position. "My dear Mrs Sturgis, I cannot tell you how much I regret — "

But she cut him short, speaking for the first time since they left the cemetery and losing control of her voice for the first time since the old days when she quarreled with her red-faced feed-salesman husband, dead of the fever almost twenty years. "Drive on!" she cried in a cracked voice, prodding the coachman with the ferrule of her parasol.

The coachman, a young saddle-colored Negro — old Samuel

had been retired four years ago — had sat motionless and
wooden-faced through Mrs Lowry's tirade, as well as through
the period of waiting which had followed. Startled by the
shrill command and the sudden jab between his shoulder blades,
he slapped down smartly with the reins. The fat, asthmatic
carriage mares leaped forward, translated instantly from a
standstill to a headlong, plunging gallop. Watching them was
like watching a motion picture scene from which fifty interior
feet of film had been carelessly snipped. One second they were
drowsing at the curb, heads down, somnolent in the August
heat, and the next they were involved in a wild-maned swirl of
motion, lifting their knees like circus ponies and traveling at
the tip of a funnel of dust. People on the sidewalks and
lawns and porches gave them a cheer. Mr Clinkscales clung
desperately to the edge of the seat, crying "Madam! Madam!
Madam!" until the coachman brought them under control and
they proceeded, wheezing, at a walk.

△

But for Hector things were never the same again. Mrs
Lowry's tirade, on the way back from the cemetery and in
front of the boarding house, had given him a glimpse into a life
he had never suspected during all the ten years he had shared
it. After circling the town to let Mr Clinkscales out, the
carriage finally pulled up at the house and Hector went straight
upstairs to his room and lay on the bed. It was deathly still,
the curtains hanging rigid as carved marble.

'I stood here with the ax,' he thought.

'And I'd have used it, too,' he told himself.

He could not admit that he would not have used it; in his
mind that would have amounted to admitting he had not loved
her. While the sunset burned and faded beyond the river he
shaped her name with his lips: *Ella, Ella,* over and over again,

and when his mother came in the twilight to tell him supper was ready, he gave no sign that he knew she was standing in the doorway.

She spoke his name softly: "Hector . . ." and then again, a little louder: "Hector? Supper's ready."

"You go on," he said at last. "I dont want any."

He spoke with his face turned sideways on the pillow. Mrs Sturgis left and he lay there, and presently the evening breeze came up, stirring and rustling the lace curtains. Alive, they moved languidly, in and out; they sighed her name. He could see in a shadowed corner the chair in which he had sat for so many nights, nursing the ax, his brain full of murder, while she was out with other men. Feeling the ten-year indentation her body had made on the opposite side of the mattress, he imagined a faint glow of warmth beneath his hand. Suddenly he remembered that night two weeks ago when he stood beside the bed, looking down at her lying as in a shallow trough, one breast spilling into the V of her gown with a smooth, pouring motion; he remembered the hate he felt, the way he gripped the ax while time stood still throughout the world. 'And I could have done it, too,' he thought. He still told himself that, for the room was pregnant with her, or with her ghost.

Mrs Sturgis watched and waited, and that was the way it was from this day on. He kept to his room except at mealtimes, as oblivious to what went on around him as a man engaged in counting his heartbeats; he would enter and close the door, and there would be nothing but silence. Mrs Sturgis, who had waited all these years to have her son to herself again, was willing to wait still longer. She had got into the habit. Besides, she told herself, this was merely a period of bereavement and readjustment, something to be outlived as the other had been, and she reassured herself with the thought that now she had no rival. Some nights she would get out of bed and steal across the hall, moving quietly in the darkness until she stood outside his door in her batiste nightgown,

catching the moonlight like a figure on a tomb. There was
only silence. She believed that this would reach an end, as
the other had done in its time, one way or another, and she
waited.

But whether she knew it or not, she still had a rival, a new
one more formidable than any she had faced before. That
evening when Hector came home from the funeral and lay
on the bed, repeating the dead woman's name to soothe his
grief while he fumbled at her imprint on the mattress and
mistook the warmth of his hand for the warmth of her body,
he began to realize for the first time that what he had thought
was hate was love; he was in love. It came to him as he lay
staring upward. He was in love as few men ever had been,
sincerely and with all his heart, calmly and with infinite ten-
derness — not infatuated, as he had been on the night of the
elopement: nor entranced, as he had been during his initia-
tion into the rites of marriage: nor bewitched, as he had been
through the years of inadequacy and torment. He knew all
this, and he trembled with the strength of his desire. Knowing
that the object of his love was dead was no deterrent; no man
was ever inadequate with the dead. Besides, he intended to
bring her alive again in his mind. He saw his task clearly.

The first step had been shown him by Mrs Lowry that
afternoon in the carriage when she revealed things about her
daughter which Hector had never suspected. He determined
now to reconstruct her life, their life together. He would join
fact to fact with all the patience and skill of a paleontologist
reconstructing a skeleton from what few bones had been dug
up, with all the devotion and industry of a biographer piling
scene upon scene with the use of jotted notes until the figure
grew rounded and warm and breathed beneath his touch.
When she had been alive he had thought he wanted to kill
her, but now that she was dead he wanted to bring her back
to life.

That was his task as he saw it. And best of all, he told himself, when he was done she would be exclusively his. She would

never demand more than he could give. She would never be unfaithful, at least not without the permission he might sometimes grant for the sake of the comfort that followed forgiveness. He set himself this task; he began it that first evening after the funeral, and he began it in the classical manner, invoking her spirit by calling her name, repeating it in his mind until even the curtains sighed it.

Once past the invocation, however, he struck an impasse. All his sources of information were blocked. He could not go to the various men she had known, especially not to those who could tell him most, for even if he could learn their names and locate them — which was highly improbable, scattered all over the country as they were, drumming up trade for their products — they would mock him with their eyes and tell him nothing. "It's the husband," they would say, like the nightshirted people lining the hotel corridor that night. Nor could the women help him; all they knew was gossip, and he had ruled out hearsay evidence. Then, to his dismay, the one source on which he counted most was cut off from him. Three days after the funeral Mrs Lowry died of a cerebral hemorrhage.

She had continued her tirade after being carried into the house by the two workers. She sat in her castered chair, flailing her arms and shouting at the boarders and neighbors who gathered in her room. Her excitement mounted. Then suddenly she halted in midsentence, mouth open, one arm raised; a surprised expression came onto her face; she fainted, then passed into a coma. She lay unconscious Saturday and Sunday, filling the house with the uproar of her breathing. The doctor called it brain fever — the same doctor who had diagnosed her swollen legs as dropsy. Monday she died and Wednesday they buried her. Mrs Simmons took the shingle off the pillar and rented the two rooms to a foreman from the oil mill, a man with seven children.

So now there was only himself, and in time he learned to believe that it was better this way. He kept a ten-cent copybook locked in a drawer of the night table beside his bed. On the first page he printed in block capitals: ELLA LOWRY STURGIS, and centered beneath it in smaller letters: WIFE OF HECTOR WINGATE STURGIS. At the foot of the title page he wrote: *B May 80: M Dec 98: D Aug 10 — These are Facts.* The second page was blank. The third page was about half filled:

> *Her Mother said (Mrs Elizabeth Lowry, seamstress):*
> *(1) Worked pedal as girl to save paralyzed legs. And was comfort to her in misery.*
> *(2) Dressed better than other girls.*
> *(3) Had developed legs & breasts at 16, which classify under Biological, future page.*
> *(4) No Four, only gossip which omit.*
> *NOTE — These are Opinions save perhaps pedal. Source (Mother) died same month. Biassed but cannot check.*

And that was all. The remaining half of the page was blank, as was the rest of the book. He had intended to make it a solid fund of fact. In time, for all he knew, the drawer might overflow with copybooks, each bursting at the seam with information on which to draw for the projected *Life of Ella Sturgis.* Then, perhaps, he would turn to his own life, recording it in this same fashion, with scrupulous exactitude and honesty, and later maybe the two could be combined, in literature as in life, to constitute a whole called *Hectorella.*

He had written rapidly through the first three notes, had set down the Four in parentheses, and then had paused, chewing on the penstaff. There was no Four; there never would be, now that Mrs Lowry was dead. Looking at the scant half-page of notes, he realized the hopelessness of his task. Half a page in a dime copybook held all he would ever know about her from any source outside himself, and even that had to be qualified: "Biassed but cannot check."

All that was left was what was in his head, a hopeless clutter of half-remembered scenes, conversations about nothing

definite, dresses she had worn on forgotten occasions, her way
of pronouncing certain words; 'Yes,' for instance, had always
had two syllables. It was little enough to work on. He wished
now that he had thought to keep a diary, noting what she had
said and done on particular days, the songs she hummed, the
color of her eyes and hair ——

He stopped, astounded. Her eyes were green, her hair
brown; yes. But what shade of green, what shade of brown?
He did not know. Already she was escaping him, just as she
had done in life, and there was no way to call her back.

Suddenly he remembered the sound of her laughter, the
peculiar ringing quality it had, pitched on a rising note. He
was filled with wonder at why this memory of her laughter
should come to him now that he saw how much else he had
forgotten. Then he realized, with considerable shock, that
memory had nothing to do with it. He was not remembering
her laughter: he was hearing it. It was here in the bedroom
with him, not loud but quite clear — so clear, indeed, that he
could place it exactly. She was in the far corner, laughing at
him; she had escaped him, gone the other side of death, and
now she had returned to mock him. Invisible in that far corner, she was laughing at him, or her ghost was.

It was shortly after this that the servants began to avoid
his room. The upstairs maid, a cocoa-colored, high-strung
girl, keeping an eye on the door for fear it might blow shut
(or something) while she was in there, never stayed any
longer than was required to make up the bed and flick at the
furniture with the dust cloth on her way out. In mid-October,
when at last Hector denied admission even to her, the other
servants began to say the thing that had frightened the maid
from the beginning. He was carrying on with a ghost, they
said. Their eyes rolled balefully, displaying a good deal of the
whites. They said they heard his voice starting and stopping
irregularly beyond the locked door, the intervals filled with
something profounder than silence, and they went past on
tiptoe, in a hurry.

"He's got him a spook in there," they said.

By then the house had been prepared for winter. The curtains in his room were now of velvet, full length, with heavy silken tie-ropes. During the daylight hours he kept them closed. At night, however, when he drew them apart, people passing along the street or the sidewalk would look up at the tall windows and into the room where the bedside candle twinkled and guttered like a lamp in a shrine. It gave them at once a feeling of awe and pity and excitement.

They had begun to talk about him all over Bristol, at lotto and poker gatherings, retelling things they had heard from their servants, who in turn had heard them from the Sturgis servants at lodge meetings and religious celebrations. But the white people did not say that he was haunted; they left that kind of talk to the Negroes. The white people said he had lost his mind.

Women in the Kandy Kitchen for sodas, or in each other's parlors for tea, discussed it in the particular way they had. One would advance a piece of information, received perhaps from her cook that very morning; then the others would hunch forward, eyes sharpening over the glasses or cups, and pass it back and forth, with variations and embellishments.

"They say he just sits there in the bedroom, mumbling, and wont let anyone in. Nobody at all."

"Talking to him*self*?"

"Yes."

"Thats bad. Oh, thats a bad sign."

"Yes. And wont let anyone in for anything. He just sits there, round the clock they say, mumbling. Hour after solid *hour*, Louella says."

"Did you ever. Mrs Sturgis must be worried sick."

"Well — you know *her*."

"Thats true; yes. But how would you feel if your only son took it into his head to — " And so forth.

Men at the Elks Club or at their places of business used it to fill an interval while waiting for the cards to run or customers to happen in. They sought the humor in the situation.

And though they were more cautious with their information, being inclined to qualify it with disclaimers, their ultimate flights of fancy soared as high.

"You mean he just sits there?"

"Thats right: talking to himself. So they say."

"Then he must not have all his marbles. Hey?"

"Something like that I reckon; yair. But I dont know. Maybe it's his way of grieving for his wife."

"Check. If I'd had that to call my own, then up and lost it overnight, I reckon I'd do some grieving, too. Tchk! I'd let them hear me the other side of the county."

The year declined, the first sharp cold of late October bruising the late-blooming flowers, then the flare and haze of Indian summer, the air scented with woodsmoke and red leaves piled shoetop-deep in the yards. After a shirtsleeve Christmas — "Wont it ever get cold?" people were asking — winter came, and came with a vengeance, the bitter, icy winter of 1911. The earth was frozen iron-gray, hard enough to strike matches on, and the fields were gridded with long silver pencilings of ice in the furrows. In the leafless trees the sparrows huddled in ruffled groups along the boughs, like clusters of feathery fruit, looking out through slits of eyes. Pipes burst and sleepers woke to find the water in their bedroom basins frozen firm as marble.

"Well," people were saying now, shivering, shaking their heads, "we asked for it. Now we've got it."

Mrs Sturgis, who had waited before, did not change her tactics now that her adversary was what people were calling a ghost. She continued to wait, believing that Hector's mind would clear in time and the ghost would be gone. Then she would step in and claim her own, but not before. The thing she feared most was that, by word or gesture, she might provoke him into taking a stand against her. Once he and the dead woman were joined against a common enemy — in his mind, that is — the ghost might never fade. The main thing, she decided, was to give it nothing to feed on. Her attitude in this resembled the treatment old-time physicians prescribed for tuberculosis, placing the sick man on a diet of moss and goat's milk in the belief that the ailment, being more fragile than the body it occupied, would starve before the patient, who then would be left weak but uninfected.

She decided, however, to speak to him about plans for a vacation the following spring, a six-week stay at Cooper's Wells for the benefit of the waters. "Youre looking a little peak-ed," she ventured to say. Yet she had no more than mentioned the trip when he turned on her with a peculiar expression, one she had never seen before, half blankness and half hatred; so she took it no further. He was sick in his mind and Mrs Sturgis knew it. The cure would have to come from within, not from any outside influence; she preferred no cure at all, in fact, to a cure at such a price. So she told herself, and she waited, maintaining the insularity that had given her life its meaning.

A cold rain fell the final week in January. The wind came out of Arkansas, then veered clockwise and blew steadily from the north, out of Tennessee, driving the rain in scuds. At length the wind died, but the rain drummed on, turning at last to sleet, a constant, icy sifting mixed with flutters of snow like tiny feathers that floated about and never touched the earth. This continued through the night, and next morning the town lay blanketed with white, a wonderland. Telegraph wires were sheathed in ice. Trees wore brittle armor, the air filled with the sound of limbs breaking beneath the weight of frozen rain; they fell like cutglass chandeliers, scattering diamond-bright, prismatic fragments up and down the street. The schools declared a holiday, and boys invented sleds from scraps of lumber and rode them, whooping, down the eastern slope of the levee and the steep banks of the Indian mounds scattered about the county. Everyone else stayed indoors as much as possible, close by their stoves and firesides. Bristol lay cramped corpse-fashion under its shroud, a bit of New England translated south to Mississippi.

Hector came to the door of his room every morning to pick up the two scuttles of coal the houseboy left in the hall for him, and usually he came downstairs for meals, sitting bemused, uncommunicative over food he often left untasted. Otherwise he kept to his room, the door bolted against intrusion. This continued until the week of the big freeze, when he began to take long walks in the woods beyond town. He would come out and lock the door behind him, putting the big old-fashioned key into an inside pocket beneath layers of coats and scarfs. Some days he would be gone for hours, without explanation. He took slices of bread and leftover biscuits with him to feed the birds. When he returned, half frozen, he would go immediately to his room and lock himself in. If anyone spoke to him, either in the house or while he was out walking, he would not answer. He would not give a sign that he had heard them or suspected in any way that they were near, not even a nod of the head or a flick of the eye; he would stride on or just stand there. Apparently his whole life was in the room, behind the bolted door. He wanted no other contact, human or otherwise.

She had come to him readily enough that first time, unbidden, when she mocked him with her laughter, but it was weeks before she spoke to him. They had all their old troubles, holding off from one another. And when she finally did speak to him, one night late as he was falling asleep, her voice was so weak he could hardly believe it was Ella who had spoken.

"You dont sound like yourself," he said.

— It's mee, all right.

Her voice was reedy, worn, like a voice over a long-distance telephone line with a faulty connection. Some of the words were lost entirely; others had a false, drawn-out emphasis, usually misplaced so that the effect confused her meaning. This angered him, for he thought at first that she was speaking thus on purpose, to mystify him with the mumbo-jumbo spiritualists were supposed to practice on their clients in the belief that it lent verisimilitude; which perhaps it did when the seance was false, but which in this case merely made him angry. She explained it to him, however. It was caused by the deterioration of her vocal organ. She seemed embarrassed at having to speak of this, like a person obliged to mention a distasteful subject.

"Will that keep on?" he asked, frightened at the thought of someday losing her voice completely. "Will it keep on getting worse?"

— Yess.

The word died away with a hissing sound, as if her tongue would not fit properly against her teeth.

First he felt revulsion; then he was angry. The two emotions held; then anger won. She might have known this would happen, he told himself. He had so much to ask, a thousand things, not only about her life but also about his own, and yet she had waited. What was worse, however, was that even now, with no telling how little time left, she would not answer his questions, except those to which he already knew the answers. Otherwise she ignored them.

She was intent on something else, a subject Hector did not want to talk about: the ax.

— Youd never have used it.

"I would."

— You thought you would but you wouldnt.

"I would. I would."

— N-no, Hector. Never in all this world.

"I would!"

He sat bolt-upright, angry and ready to defy her, no matter at what cost.

— No, you wouldnt. Not when it came right down to doing it. You know how you are; I dont believe you even thought you would. Not really.

"I would! I would!"

He was shouting now, but he knew it was no use. She was no longer there to hear him.

That was the beginning. She came to him from time to time

in this manner, always at will and seldom at his bidding. He learned never to cross her, for as soon as he began to disagree with her, her voice would diminish; it would grow weaker and weaker, and finally he would be left addressing the empty air. That was her advantage, and she had always been one to press advantages, as he well knew. But he had certain advantages, too. Realizing that he had been almost childish that first time, shouting and clenching his fists as he had done, he learned now to be sly in their relationship. Sometimes he could even outwit her. Originally he had feared that she possessed extraordinary powers — the ability to read his mind, for instance — but this was not true, even though at times it seemed to be.

He discovered also that she was governed by some sort of regulations, a list of do's and donts, for when he tried to steer the conversation into certain channels she would cut him off. It's not *allowed*, she would murmur. He had to learn to curb his curiosity, for if he persisted she would leave him. If he became violently insistent, as he had done the first time, she would not return sometimes for days on end.

For one thing, though it was the very purpose for which he thought of himself as having called her up, she would tell him nothing about her past life. It's not *allowed*, she would say with a note of warning in her voice, and that would end it. For another, she would not appear to him: not because it was against the regulations (at any rate she never said it was) but rather on her own account. She had always been vain, and now she seemed ashamed of her appearance. He did not yet know why, though he suspected.

In the course of time he became reconciled to not collecting facts for the notebook. Besides, now that she was with him again, he no longer felt the need to reconstruct her life. Even the talking, which was quite trivial in the main and might have passed between any two people seated by any fireside, served for little more than to assure him that she was there. Except for needing this assurance — Ella being invisible — he would have been content to sit quietly, saying nothing. But from week to week her voice faded more and more. He could see that a time was coming when she would no longer be with him. When that time came, as it surely would, he would want to return to the biographical project.

So he would slip in an occasional question, trying to catch her off guard, to trick her into giving him forbidden information. They would be talking about some commonplace thing and he would ask her, without any change of tone, without any note of urgency in his voice: "That drummer at the hotel: where did you meet him, Ella?"

— Well, I was downtown that morning, shopping, and. . . .

But he never really fooled her. She always caught herself before she told him anything vital.

— I've told you time and again, it's not allowed.

Another time, under pressure of a jealousy he had never felt before, he asked her if she still saw the dead drummer, off in that other world.

— Mm: I see him sometimes.

— Ah. And do you . . . ?

— No, no. There's nothing like that. He's just like you, now, Hector. There's no blood, you see.

But then she stopped again and would go no further. He never really fooled her. So finally he explained it to her, told her his predicament. "Youll go and I'll be left alone. I'll turn back to that notebook no better off than I was before. I'll have it all to go through again, from back where I started months ago. Why, *why* wont you help me, Ella? It's for your sake, after all."

— No it's not; you know it's not. It's for your own sake. Youve been self-centered all your life, Hector Sturgis. And besides, youre worried about something there's no need for.

"But arent you going to fade?"

— I'll fade. I'm fading now.

"Then what will I do? What will I do when youre gone?"

— Dont fret, Hector. We'll be together.

"Not if you keep fading, we wont. Even if you were here I wouldnt know it; I couldnt be sure. How would I know you were with me? How would I know?"

— Shh.

Then he thought he understood what she meant. "Do you mean I'm going to die? I'm going with you?"

— Shh. We wont talk about it now.

"But I *want* to talk about it; I want to know!"

He called after her, cried her name. "Ella! Ella!" he shouted. But it was no use. She was gone. He was alone.

This time he was afraid that he had taken things too far; he was afraid that she was gone for good. For five days he sat in the room, alone and miserable, bereft. When she returned at the end of that time, she warned him not to try to find out things that were not allowed, and she made him understand that this was a final warning. She made it clear, for once and for all. There was something in her voice, cracked and broken as it was, that told him she was dreadfully in earnest. It was no longer a game. Whatever future risks he took, he would take against heavy odds, the possibility of losing all his life seemed meant for now.

Outside, the world was sheathed in ice and people stirred as seldom as possible. They wrapped their heads in shawls and turned their collars high about their ears, lumbering along the streets like bears. They did not pause to speak to one another, satisfying themselves with quick, furtive waves of recognition. Rabbits and squirrels and birds, the woodland creatures, were locked in rigid misery; the earth itself was stiff and cramped with cold. But here inside the room, behind the bolted door, Hector had a different world — a universe within a universe, like Chinese boxes, and the fireplace was its glowing heart. If the temperature did not suit him, all he had to do was tilt the scuttle at the grate. No misery, human or otherwise, could reach him except at his bidding. It was as if he had seceded from the race. If doubts came (was she real? or was it all a delusion born of grief and regret and an inability to admit that she was gone for good, with so much left unspoken and undone?) she herself came to reassure him. For the most part, her kindness and consideration were far beyond any he had ever thought her capable of showing. No doubt was ever valid once she had allayed it; she was real as real. As for the decomposition — the one problem for which she offered no solution, no consolation — he told himself he would worry about that when the time came. There was plenty of time, here at the glowing heart of his particular universe, his nestled box.

He would have been content to stay here, never stirring, but finally she told him it was wrong to keep himself cooped up the way he did. It was not only wrong, it was unnatural. People all over town were talking about him.

"Talking?"

— Yes.

"What do they say?"

— They say. . . .

"Yes?"

— They say youre crazy, Hector.

So he yielded to her in this as well. Heavy snow had come behind the sleet storm, and he began to go for long walks in the woods, carrying bread in his pockets to be strewn for the birds; the snow had blanketed their food. Thus it was that farmers, riding along the slushy roads on their way from town, saw him standing alone in a wilderness of snow and fallen branches, making a sluing motion with one arm, broadcasting crumbs for a semicircle of hungry robins and blue jays and sparrows. When the farmers got home they told their wives about it. "He feeds the birds," they said, as if this were the final, irrefutable proof of his insanity.

They told it in town as well, the next time they came in.

"He leaves the house now," they said, sitting in the perfumed warmth of the barber shop, the air redolent of lather and bay rum, the razors making an intermittent, luxurious rasp against napes and jowls. "Guess why."

"Why?"

"To feed the birds."

After a silence someone said from down the line, "Maybe he thinks he's Saint Francis. Somebody told me he was growing a funny-looking beard."

"Or Napoleon," another added, the voice muffled under a hot towel. "Was he wearing a three-corner hat? Did he have one hand in the front of his coat and a spit curl on his forehead?"

They would laugh at this for a while — rather moderately by now, however, for it was beginning to wear a bit thin already — and pass on to another, newer topic.

The women were the ones who kept it going. They continued, ohing and ahing over scraps of information, much as a dog will worry a chip or a rag.

"Feeds the *birds?*"

"Yes. Henry saw him the other day."

"Actually *saw* him?"

"Yes. Off in the woods, feeding them."

"Oh. Oh, thats bad."

"But thats not all. *Henry* says — " And so forth.

Hector knew nothing of all this, beyond the recent information that they were saying he was crazy. He was happy and oblivious, having Ella with him. Always now, when he came back from walks in the woods, he found her waiting for him. She never failed him now; he had never known such a period of happiness. But her voice became weaker and weaker. He had to strain to hear her now. It was only by the closest attention that he was able to distinguish what she was saying, and even then he lost most of the words. He did not ask her to repeat them, however: partly because the topics of conversation were so trivial that the loss did not matter, and partly because he knew that it embarrassed her to have him call attention to these evidences of her deterioration.

All the same there was no doubt that she was slipping from him. Soon he would be left alone, with all the anguish loneliness would bring, and he would not have seen her even once during all these visits. He tried again to persuade her to make

herself visible to him; she had never denied that she could do
so at will. But she refused. At first she was almost coy about
it, assuming a tone of modesty and shame quite out of keeping with her character in life. Later, though, she threatened
to leave for good and all if he kept harping on the subject.
This frightened him into being satisfied with what he had,
out of fear of otherwise having nothing.

Through all these months, while winter lost its grip and
spring came on, he never saw her but once, and even that once
was only in a dream.

In this dream he wakes suddenly out of a sound sleep. Lying
flat on his back he looks down the length of his body, beyond
the foot of the bed and across half the width of the room, to
where Ella is sitting in the chair he used to sit in while he
waited with the ax. It is between dawn and sunrise; a faint
glow of daylight, pearly and sourceless, comes through the
windows at his left.

'It's Ella,' he thinks. 'She has come back. She has finally
come. After all these months of waiting and hoping, hoping
and waiting, she is here.'

He sees her vaguely, in outline as it were, and it stirs a
memory of something he once saw in a Washington theater
when he was at school: the figure of a woman seated behind
a diaphanous curtain on a dimly lighted stage. She is slouched
in the chair, her legs crossed at the shins, one hand relaxed
in her lap, the other supporting her head from the rear, the
elbow resting against the low back of the chair. She seems
infinitely patient, infinitely calm. This too is memory: he
identifies it as the classic pose which he has seen in the attitudes of the women on Grecian urns. She is looking at him,
her head tilted slightly back, eyes limpid in dark sockets, a
limpidity amounting almost to liquefaction, as if they held
their shape merely by surface tension; a shake of her head
might break the tension and cause them to trickle down her
cheeks, like tears.

But no matter how he strains he cannot make out the features of her face. He can see them in outline; they are there,

all right—mouth, nose, chin, brow—but they are ill-defined, as in a photograph blurred by motion or poor focus. At first he thinks this is because of some fault of vision, because his eyes are still heavy with sleep and will not function properly; but when he looks more closely, raising himself in bed, supporting his weight with both hands behind him on the mattress, and straining his eyes in the poor light, he sees that this is because the face, each individual feature of the face, has decomposed, has crumbled into ruin.

— You shouldnt have waited so long, he says.

— What?

Apparently it has affected her hearing too, even those small bones of the inner ear which murder-story writers tell us are the last to go, even in the searing heat of a furnace, and therefore serve to establish a corpus delicti.

— You should have come sooner, Ella.

— I havent come at all, she says. Youre only dreaming, Hector. Look behind you.

He looks over his shoulder and sees himself lying full-length on the bed, asleep, corpse-quiet, arms rigid at his sides, the incipient beard dark against the waxen face, the nose like a beak arching upward. Then he looks back at Ella, halfway across the room. The light is weak but lucent, without shadows, and now that he has learned the cause of what he thought was faulty vision on his part, he can see her face quite clearly. The chin moves with a curious up-and-down motion, like that of a ventriloquist's dummy, between slits extending vertically from the corners of her mouth, downward past both sides of the point of her chin, and as she speaks she makes a scratching movement with the hand at the back of her head.

She goes on speaking, telling him it is only a dream, a dream within a dream. But he is not listening; he is getting out of bed, moving cautiously for fear that she will see him. There must be something wrong with her sight as well, for she does not see that he is approaching; she goes on speaking, her face toward the figure asleep on the bed. The ruin is more apparent at close range. One cheek has crumbled nearly away, and

the flesh of her throat is mottled with yellow and purple, a
marbled effect. He is alongside the chair by now, passing to
its rear, when he sees something that stops him.

The hand he thought was scratching the back of her head
is actually working a lever which extends from a hole in her
skull; she moves it up and down with her fingers as she speaks.
Evidently a system of wires and pulleys connects the lever
with her chin, for he can hear them creaking as they move.
He is horrified past caution.

—Ella! he cries.

She sees now for the first time that he has left the bed, has
discovered the extent of her disintegration, the secret lever.
She is embarrassed, flustered, and she turns her head to hide
the mechanism. However, she soon recovers her composure.

—You neednt be so ill-mannered, she says primly. We're
all this way, this side of death. Youll see.

And she begins to fade. He calls after her, Ella! Ella! but
she has faded; "Ella! Ella!" he called. But he was alone in the
room, sitting bolt-upright in the bed with both arms stretched
toward the empty chair, and dawn had not even broken.

February went out raw and windy, with blackbirds in
startled flight like dashes of pepper blown across a page, but
March brought a week of warm rain that melted the snow in
the secret shady places, sluiced the dirty ice from fields and
gutters, and pattered monotonously against the window panes.
This in turn gave way to a spell of sunny weather. Birds
hopped and sang in the tasseling oaks; cottonwoods popped
their buttons, and the sky was high and dazzling. The cold
returned for a three-day Easter snap; then the pecan trees
put out their pale green leaflets and spring came in to stay.
Barefoot children all over Bristol leaped and shouted in the

puddles, and people once more took the time and trouble to speak to one another on the street.

But no matter how much wind might veer and bluster, or rain come down, or April sunlight pave the streets with gold, there was little change inside the Sturgis house. Hector's mother continued to avoid provoking him. He seemed almost happy nowadays, for all his absent manner, and she accepted this as a sign that he was making progress toward the day when he would be cured — 'himself again' she called it. She watched and waited and let him strictly alone. As the year wore on, however, moving now toward summer, the long hot days with the sun like hammered brass, she began to note an increasing discontent. He was as preoccupied as ever, communicating with no one; but he was restless, fretful.

He had developed a facial tic that twitched one corner of his mouth, agitating the beard which had been growing since the time of the big snow. The hairs grew thick and soft about his lips and on his chin, the color of burnt-over grass or sunbleached hay, but they thinned out along the lower planes of his cheeks and did not grow at all on his upper jaws, where an adolescent fuzz tapered down from the sideburns. Negroes called it a Chinaman's beard, and it did in fact give him rather a Mongolian aspect. Much else had changed as well. In the old days he had been meticulous about his clothes, making a complaint if the washwoman ironed wrinkles in his collars or his shirtfronts, insisting that his suits be sponged and pressed each time he took them off, and wearing the latest styles ahead of their general adoption. For all this the town had called him a dude and made conjectures about his prowess as a lover. But now when he went for his afternoon walk he wore rumpled trousers without a belt and a shirt without a tie. There were days when he neglected to comb his hair, and sometimes in setting out he even forgot to change from carpet slippers.

Mrs Sturgis of course observed all this and she worried more as time went by, though it did not show in her face.

She had not aged perceptibly in the seventeen years since
her ordeal with the fever that had killed her husband and her
mother. (Nor did her appearance change appreciably in all
the years that followed. It was as if she had been baked by
some ceramic process in the fever oven; all that Time could
do to her had been done in that one month, with her fellow
townsmen dying all around her and the bell of the dead
wagon sounding through the streets. Perhaps the secret of
her longevity was that no germ could live where all those
stronger ones had raged and been defeated. For when, eventually, the machine wore out by pure and simple friction and
they put her into the ground at last, she looked almost exactly
as she had looked on the afternoon when Hector arrived
from the depot, found her asleep in bed and mistook her for
her mother.) But now, no matter how little it showed, she
was worried about her son. She thought perhaps she should
call in a doctor or try again to persuade Hector to go somewhere with her for a consultation, inventing any pretext. Then
she remembered the look on his face when she suggested
Cooper's Wells, half blankness and half hatred, and more than
anything else she feared, she feared that he would hate her.

Daily on his walks, skirting the woods two miles beyond
the house, Hector went past a cabin where Samuel and Emma,
the coachman and his wife, had lived since Mrs Sturgis pen-
sioned them off, five years ago. She gave them the cabin to
live in and an adjoining half-acre garden plot where Samuel
raised vegetables which he sold in Bristol, either to the markets or from door to door whenever the markets would not
take them, for enough small change to keep a bait of sidemeat
and molasses in the larder, coffee in the coffee pot, and coal-
oil in the lamp. They were both incredibly old, older Hector
thought than any two people he had ever known, and they
lived apart from the world. Other Negroes, on the way from
town in their Sunday clothes, would take off their good shoes
and go half a mile across muddy fields to keep from having
to pass the cabin after dark. Emma was supposed to have
powers of evil at her command.

She had always been peculiar, from back in her nursemaid days, but a little over five years ago she went out of her mind completely. It happened at a religious gathering, a sanctifying held on the banks of Moccasin Creek. Though Emma had never been especially religious, at least so far as anyone had known, the Spirit moved her this day, and she came through with such fervor that she never recovered from it — another instance, perhaps, of the medieval legend depicted in woodcuts, showing the devil in church whispering into the ear of a maiden who knelt in prayer, though of course it might have been much simpler; maybe she just went 'off.' At any rate, Mrs Sturgis had had to let her go soon afterwards, and Samuel as well. Nowadays Emma sat by the fire (there was always a fire on the cabin hearth, big and roaring in the winter, smaller in the summer, a glow of embers) watching it through a pair of old-fashioned, octagonal spectacle frames that had belonged to Mrs Wingate. Hector remembered the day his grandmother dropped them out of the carriage; Samuel got down and picked them up, and Mrs Wingate let him keep them for 'pride specs.' Emma claimed them soon afterwards; she had kept them ever since. One of the eyepieces was empty. The other held a jagged star; it glittered in the flicker and dance of flames on the hearth.

Samuel was suspect too, since he lived with Emma and suffered no resultant hurt. When he went into town with the sack of vegetables across his shoulder, small children ran from the sight of him in fear that he would carry them off in his sack, as their nurses had told them he would do if they misbehaved, and older ones ran after him to prove their heroism, chanting "Sam, Sam, the conjure man! I aint scared of the conjure man!" but keeping safely out of reach of the stick he brandished. The bravest of them threw clods at him. Age had bent him; he had the wrinkled, grimacing face of a gnome.

Day after day Hector went past the cabin, a sway-backed, paintless two-room structure of home-ripped plank, built in his grandfather's time, before the war. The yard was grassless and the gallery sagged upon the rotting steps. When the weather was fine he would see a little man standing in the vegetable plot, leaning on a spade to watch him pass. He did not recognize Samuel until one day the former coachman left his spade stuck upright in the earth and came running out to the road to meet him, crying "Marster! Little mars!" Hector stopped and he approached, bobbing and grinning. "Lord a mercy," he said, wheezing from the run, "I like not to knowed you with all that hair on your face. Aint you got a kindly word for old Samuel helped to raise you out of knee pants? Seem to me lak you ought to have, all them times we spent together."

From now on Samuel greeted him in this way every afternoon. He seemed glad to have found someone to speak to. "I mind the time you whopped them town boys with the book sack. He-he! You really whopped um." Another day he said, "You look something lak your grandpappy with the musstache cross your face." (Samuel had skipped a generation; he meant the original Hector, the one who lost his life in Mexico. The second Hector had been beardless.) "Yassah, and he was a proud, tall man in his day — a proud tall man I'm here to tell you. They dont grow um lak that no more. I members the morning he rode off to war, the one before the big one, and never come back, till all they was was a marker in the graveyard. I was stable boy then. But I dont know. It appear to me lak everything is shrunk, and me along with um. Even the watermillions is little bitty."

Hector scarcely replied, except with nods and headshakes; but he stood and listened willingly enough, which was certainly far more than he had done with anyone else for a long time. There was a certain kinship established. Both of them had rejected the world, or had been rejected by it, and this was their one connection.

In June, after a month of such encounters, Samuel asked him: "Little mars, dont you want to come in the house and see old Emma used to nurse you when you was a child?" He spoke hesitantly but with a quality of urgency in his voice. "She aint just right in her mind nowdays, and it mought do her good. People talking about she's crazy. Emma aint crazy; Emma's lonesome, that what *she* is." He led the way toward the cabin, across one corner of the vegetable patch, and Hector followed.

Half an hour later, at home again after a two-mile run through the midsummer heat, when he looked back on what had happened in the cabin, all he could remember was the sudden scream that rose in terror and the swirl of motion on the hearth where the woman crouched and hid her eyes and called on God to save her from the devil.

They had crossed the sagging gallery, Samuel muttering at Hector's elbow, and when he first entered the cabin, out of the blaze of sunlight, it was as if he had stepped downward into a pit. Soon, however, his pupils dilated; objects began to appear. They came out one by one at first, then a whole cluster in a rush. All he saw at first was a dancing gleam of orange where firelight flickered in the grate on the opposite side of the room. Then the gloom paled rapidly, and he saw — so suddenly that she seemed to appear by magic, materialized out of empty air — a Negro woman turned sideways in her chair, looking at him with a querulous expression. It was Emma.

"Who that there?" she said.

She had aged; she had aged indeed, so completely gaunted to skin and bones that if he were to grasp and shake her by the shoulders, Hector thought, her body beneath the voluminous skirts and petticoats would give off a dry, fusty clatter like pine kindling shaken in a sack. The cabin had that nigger smell of clean quilts and cornstarch, the walls covered with newspapers; beyond Emma's shoulder a headline shouted the loss of the *Maine* with an exclamation-point six inches tall. She looked at him, the face like a mummy's face behind octagonal spectacle frames, the skin stretched nearly transparent over Indian cheekbones, the headrag drawn so tightly over her scalp that it shone like naked bone. Mrs Wingate would look like this if she had lived, he thought, for they were of an age.

"It's me, Emma," he said. "Ive come to see you."

Perhaps it was his voice that caused it, he told himself after-

wards, alone in his room, still panting from the two-mile run
down the dusty road; he had not spoken in such a long time,
it probably sounded as creaky as an unused hinge. Or perhaps,
like him — for he stood in the doorway with the light at his
back — she had to wait for her pupils to dilate after having
looked for so long into the soft orange gleam and flicker of the
fire. First there had been blackness, a sense of a presence there,
a shape, and then she had blinked and seen a strange, bearded
white man standing in her cabin door where no one dared to
come. At any rate, whatever caused it, as soon as he had spoken
Emma threw up both hands, the palms showing pink in the
gloom, like dancing flames with the reflection of the fire, and
began to scream.

"I knows you!" she cried. "I knows you, old Satan: I knows
you walks the earth lak a natural man!" She tumbled from
the chair, fell to her knees on the hearth, and covered her
eyes with her palms, both hands beneath the spectacle frames.
"Save me, Lord Jesus! Save me!" The two eyepieces were over
the backs of her hands, one empty, innocent of glass, the other
holding its shattered star which flickered rose and yellow in
the firelight. As Hector turned, already running, he heard her
beginning to pray in earnest: "The Lord is my shepherd: I
shall not want. I'll lay down in the pasture and store my soul."

The hot dust of the road was ankle deep in places. It filled
his carpet slippers as he ran, each grain like a live spark. But
he did not mind. He ran head-down, fists clenched, numb with
terror at what he had seen, at having been identified with the
devil, the powers of darkness. Ahead, at the side of the road, a
Negro boy shuffled the dust, moving his feet in time with the
words he sang:

> I knows, hey I knows a woman got gret big legs
> Takes little bitty steps lak she walking on eggs
> — I'm telling you.

When Hector came past, his carpet slippers pounding the road
in a series of small explosions, each with its accompanying puff

of dust at the heels like smoke, the voice cut off abruptly. The
boy stood stock still, looking after him, halted in midstride,
eyes bulged; "What was that?" he said aloud. Hector ran on.
A brown thrasher sat on a rail fence beside the road, the steady
yellow bead of its eye watching him approach, the long bill
turning in profile until he came abreast: whereupon the bird
sprang away from the rail with a single quick motion, its
wings and narrow tail the color of dusty cinnamon, and was
gone. Thus, in Hector's mind when he looked back on it later,
he had been rejected in his time of need, both by mankind and
by the woodland creatures he had befriended during the time
of snow and ice, leaving his cozy nestled box to do so. He
ran on.

He had run from things all his life, in one way or another,
but never as far and as hard as this. When he was back at the
house, safe in his room, the door bolted behind him, the
curtains drawn, he lay on the bed, breathing hoarsely from
the exertion and from fright, which was still upon him. It
gripped him like a hand gripping his heart, and it was more
than physical; it was spiritual fright as well, so to speak. Samuel
and Emma had been a possible wedge of re-entry into the
world. Needing each other the way all three of them did,
almost anything might have come of the relationship. But the
moment he made his first attempt at comfort, concerning himself even for an instant with another person's troubles, he
heard himself identified with Satan.

'No wonder I ran,' he told himself. 'And besides, it may be
true for all I know.'

So now his renunciation was complete; he abandoned the
walks and never left the house again. He had a world of his
own, right here in the room, a world with a population of
two — or one and a half, more strictly speaking; or even one
and a quarter, to stretch it finer — withdrawn from the public
eye and the heat of the sun. Since he seldom came downstairs
any more, not even for meals, Mrs Sturgis sent up a tray three

times a day, with instructions that it be placed on a chair in
the hall outside his door. He left it untouched more often than
not; usually he did not bother to lift the napkin and see what
was there. These nights when she tiptoed across the hall there
was nothing for Mrs Sturgis to hear, only the sound of his
breathing. The one-sided conversations, on which she had
eavesdropped for so many months, making of them what little
she possibly could, had been discontinued.

Day and night he lay on the bed or sat in the chair beside
the curtained window. He believed he never slept (he did sleep
very little, it was true) and he moved as seldom as possible,
for motion made his head ache. Though his education had not
included a course in anatomy or even zoology, he had heard
or read somewhere that the brain had lobes. He reasoned that
there were eight of these, distributed among the semi-quarters
of his cranium; he could feel them individually throb and ache,
and when he moved they rubbed against the incasing bone and
became inflamed, particularly the one above his right eye. His
brain was like a badly mangled octopus, nursing its eight
throbbing stumps.

Now that he had gone back into his box, Bristol's interest
flared again. They had second-hand reports from their servants,
who had them first-hand from the Sturgis servants. "What do
you suppose he really *does* in there?" they wanted to know.
They had rejected all the talk about a ghost, not only because
it was improbable, but also — even mainly — because they
were tired of it. They were agreed on one thing, however:
"He's crazy as a betsy bug, and always was."

Professor Rosenbach, now superintendent of the Bristol
public schools, was a prime source of information. He still
wore the chinking watch-fob and the beaker scar, and he
looked more severely military than ever, with his roach of
grizzled hair and his neatly clipped beard which he stroked
beneath the chin with the backs of his fingers. He dressed in-
variably in gray and wore facings on his vest.

"Ah yes," he said. "I tutored him in his childhood, as a favor to his grandmother Mrs Wingate. *There* was a lady of the old school . . . Yes, I tutored him. And let me tell you, in all confidence, there was something wrong with that one from the start. *I* at least was never sanguine in my expectations where he was concerned. Youve noticed his eyes? Shifty. He could never look at me squarely. You know what I mean?" (At this point the listener would attempt to look at the professor 'squarely,' but it never came off very well.) "I always tell by the eyes, and his were shifty. I predicted trouble from the outset. And I was right, sir; I was right."

That was more or less the way they talked before the final flare and sputter. Hector of course knew nothing of it. Even if he had known, it would have seemed an anticlimax after having been prayed against as the devil himself come up to walk the earth like a natural man. As it was, his mind was occupied with other things.

He had foreseen the time when Ella would be gone from him, his world reduced to a population of one, and now that time was at hand. It was August again, the month of her death, the dry, heat-labored climax of the long delta summer. Her voice was reduced to the tiniest, sibilant vibration, like a breath against harp strings or the sympathetic humming of a piano when an instrument across the room is struck. There were no words now, only a vague intensity, stepped up or diminished to indicate approval or dislike. All that week she was with him, and she made herself visible at last; for now there were no longer any grounds for modesty. She was only a shimmer of light, a phosphorescent glow of putrefaction.

She was so calm, so comforting all through that final week, like a woman dismissing a lover who has been tender. But on the final night, the anniversary of her death, she seemed to be trying to tell him something. She buzzed and hummed with urgency:

— *Zezz, zezz.*

"What is it, Ella? What is it you want?"

— *Zezz, zezz.*

The shimmer kept moving insistently to the window and
back. Finally Hector got up; he went to the window, parted
the curtains slightly, and looked out. But there was nothing.
The street was empty and all the houses were dark. *Zezz, zezz!*
The moon had risen late; it hung in the trees across the way,
swollen into the third quarter, gibbous and tinged with green,
flooding the yard with a thick rich golden light.

"I dont understand," he said.

But she hummed and buzzed, urging him on, and he put his
hand out, holding the curtain aside. The vibration grew more
intense like a bumblebee:

— *Zezz! Zezz!*

His hand moved along the velvet, fumbling, and when it
touched the curtain rope the humming suddenly pitched itself
an octave higher, insistent, exultant, a high thin tremulous
whine; Yezz! Yezz! The line of light danced up and down and
vibrated rapidly, shimmering and humming affirmation: Yezz!
Yezz! Then he understood.

She had never left the room with him, and in fact he had
thought perhaps the regulations allowed her no existence outside it. But now she did. She led the way, first into the hall,
then down it to the door beside the stairwell. He followed,
carrying the length of silken rope which he had torn loose
from the curtain and the wall; it hung slick and heavy, thick-
bodied, like a dead moccasin. As he climbed the attic stairs
the musty odor of desolation brought him a memory of
childhood, of afternoons when he was a boy and stole away
from Emma during naptime; he had crept up here to be alone;
he had called it his kingdom.

There was a scurrying of mice. A dressmaker's dummy, like
a headless statue, thrust its bosom to the moonlight streaming
through the mansard window. Big, gilt-framed paintings, long
since tarnished, leaned against the wall, indistinguishable
under their layers of dust. Four generations of discarded furniture loomed in jagged silhouette, including a table laid on its

back, its four legs in the air. Behind the wainscot the mice made frantic scrabbling sounds. He could imagine them crouched in fear or reared back on their haunches, twitching their whiskers, their eyes like bright little blisters of jet, their ears pricked as they listened to the footsteps of the invader who had returned after all these years, a grown man.

Hector had no will now; he only followed the glimmer, moving like a man in a dream while it led him to the proper rafter, one with a chair at hand. He climbed up, balancing carefully because the chair was frail, put the rope over the rafter, knotted the dangling ends together, then knotted them again, less than a foot above, and with the abrupt deliberation of a housewife threading a needle, put his head through the double strand between the knots. It was a close fit, and he had trouble getting the bottom knot past his chin. Looking down and sideways, with his neck in the silken yoke, he saw that the glimmer was almost gone. Her year was almost up, to the hour; she was only a pale line of light, but the vibration was sharp and steady with approval.

He did not hesitate, for he was quite sure of himself. But the moment he let down, feeling the chair tip backward from his kick, something happened that caused him to change his mind. The vibration switched to a new key; it was more like laughter now — the same mocking laughter he had heard almost a year ago, pitched on a rising note. 'This is wrong,' he tried to say, but the words would not come past the broken voice-box. Then he stopped hearing the laughter. He was alone for an instant of cold and terrible breakage, the grinding thorax and the pounding blood.

But it was only an instant. After its dreadful dance, like a limber-jointed doll jerked on a string, the body turned slowly, first one way, then another, more dreamy than fretful, and then hung motionless, the head thrown sideways and joined to the long wrung neck at a crazy angle, the lower knot pulled tightly under one ear, the rope like an iron bar hooked over

the rafter. The attic was deathly still for a term, but after another interval of tentative scurrying, the mice came out to
play.

Two days later Mrs Sturgis was still trying to decide
whether to notify the sheriff that Hector was missing. She
thought that he had wandered off on one of his walks and then
had just kept going. She believed that he would be back soon,
and she still did not want to antagonize him, especially in the
way a searching-party would do. Perhaps, indeed, this was the
final crisis that would restore him, just as certain illnesses develop the fever which is their only cure. By sundown of the
second day, however, she had changed her mind; she was on
her way to the telephone when there was a sudden commotion,
a steady, hysterical bellering from the top of the house. It
was the upstairs maid, who had been sent into the attic by the
cook.

"Go up there and see," the cook had said. "It smells to me
like something must have died."

Harry Barnes came with the sheriff to cut him down, and
they buried him the following afternoon. Mr Barnes took considerable pains with what he always called the 'arrangements.'
In after years he spoke of it as his masterpiece. "I really fixed
him nice," he said. "And if you dont think I had a job on my
hands, try hanging a side of beef in a shut-up attic for two
hot days in middle August and see what kind of shape it's in
when you go to take it down. There's more to this profession
than folks know."

For the rest of that year, and for the first six months of
the year that followed, people in Bristol and surrounding towns
heard and retold the story in at least a dozen versions, each
a shade more improbable than the one that went before. Then
it paled; they had overdone it, exhausted its possibilities with
too much enthusiasm, in much the same way as they had done
in Ella's case. When his mother presented the pictorial maps

to the city and they were placed on display it was revived, though no one who had known the original facts would have recognized the ones that were sworn to then. Years afterward, while the maps collected dust in the foyer of the city hall, and still later, when they were put into the cupola where pigeons swooped and fluttered and cooed in organ tones, it was mentioned occasionally that Mrs Sturgis had had a wayward son who had been involved in some sort of scandal: "He took some money or something. Maybe it was a woman caused it: I dont know." It was all quite obscure. Finally they classified it under sorrow: "She had some kind of sorrow in her life. A son went crazy or something: I dont know." It was rarely mentioned. Longevity conquers scandal every time.

Then she died too, and the house was razed, the grounds converted into a public park. Two years ago a man came down from Memphis, an art critic, or so he called himself, a columnist from one of the papers; he had heard about the maps. They got them out of the cupola for him and dusted them off, the multi-colored one-to-one-hundred representations of people going about their joys and griefs, seen on the streets of Bristol from above. He called his column "The Last Romantic" and spoke of Hector Sturgis as an undiscovered genius. There was a revival of interest in the maps; they stayed on display in the foyer again for a while. But then it faded, even faster than before, and they were put away. Maybe the man was just wanting to fill a column. Certainly they are romantic in a different way from our current 'tough-minded' brand of that endemic sickness. Perhaps when their true time comes, if it does come, they will be brought down to stay.

At any rate, nowadays when people ride past Wingate Park, where children and nursemaids stroll in the dappled shade, the name on the wrought-iron arch means almost nothing to them. They just remember that the park was donated by an old woman who died with no one to leave her money to. From time to time, however, they are reminded who she was by the story in the newspaper, revived by the editor at the request of

the Chamber of Commerce, anxious to show how much the
town has grown. The engraving is always there, the old lady
in the wheelchair, her eyes like agates set into the sockets of
a skull, and the caption always calls her the mother of Bristol.

THE FREEDOM KICK

You ask about that old time. It aint nothing I cant tell you. Kluxers, smut ballots, whipping-bees, all that: I'm in a position to know and I remember, mainly on account of my mamma. That woman loved freedom like nothing ever was. She was the daughter of a free man, a barber, and when she married my daddy it like to killed him — the barber I mean. A barber had a position in those days; the shop was kind of a gathering place where the white men would sit around and talk, so he knew all the business deals and the scandal, who-all was messing with who-all's wives, and so forth. When he got the news his only child had up and married, he butted his head against the wall, kicked at the baseboard so hard he lamed himself in the foot for a week, and threw two of his best porcelain shaving mugs clean across the shop. My daddy you see was a slave from the beginning, and he had looked a good deal higher for her than that. I'm still talking about the barber, but the fact was I didnt know him. He died of a sudden seizure around the time I was born, five months after the wedding. He just thought she'd been putting on weight, when all the time it was me.

He should have known better how to handle her. Ever since

she was a little girl, if you wanted her to have something, even medicine, no matter how bitter-tasting it might be, all you had to do was act like you were going to keep it from her. I know, for Ive got children of my own, including one marriageable daughter, and I wouldnt cross her for the world. Then, too, he had a lot of blood-pride — claimed we had African chiefs somewhere in the background. But I dont know; I never put much stock in all that talk. You used to hear lots of such claims among the colored. If it wasnt chiefs it was French blood. Maybe we caught it from the white folks. Anyhow, he certainly didnt want the son-in-law he got.

You see, my daddy was a kind of artist, high-strung and determined. He belonged at one time to a rich lady, a widow; she gave him his freedom in her will when she died. Maybe she sort of spoiled him. Anyhow he always wore a black silk tie under a soft collar and kept his hands smooth. He was a photographer, had his tent right down by the levee at the foot of Marshall Avenue, and country people theyd get their picture taken every time they came to town with twenty cents. Whatever else Mamma's daddy wanted, he certainly didnt want any twenty-cent artist.

But that was what he got, all right, and he butted his head and took it. What else could he do? That was during the war; I was born the day after Vicksburg fell on the Fourth. I dont remember the war, howsomever, though sometimes I think I do. The first I remember, really, was afterwards — what I'm telling now. The surrender was some time back and I was maybe six or seven. My daddy didnt come home one night. Then next morning here he came, with a lump beside one eye. "Where you been?" Mamma asked him, hands on hips, eyes blazing. She was worried and angry too. But he just stood there in the doorway, kind of weavy on his feet. So she got the camphor bottle off the shelf and some cotton and began to swab at the lump. The camphor fumes helped to clear his mind, and while she swabbed he told her.

"I'll tell you the plain truth, Esmy," he said. Mamma's full name was Esmeralda; Daddy called her Esmy. "I was standing on the corner Third and Bird, minding my business. It wasnt even late. This man comes up, big, so tall, with a derby and a cigar, a mouth full of gold. Say, 'What you doing, boy?' I aint no boy. I look back at him, eye to eye. Then I look away, across to where the Pastime Pool Hall was. Say, 'Answer up!' —like he had every right. Did I say he was wearing a brass watch chain? Well, he was, and every breath he took it made a little line of fire run across his vest. I said, 'Whats it to you what I'm doing?' Thats what I told him. He was already solemn but now he got more-so. He clouded up: say, 'Dont jaw back at me I ask you something. Come along.' Then it happen; I see what he was wearing. He let his coat kind of slide ajar and there it was. A badge. I turn to run and Blip! all I saw was stars and colored lights; the Pastime Pool Hall run round in a circle. He done hit me slap up side the head with one of them billy things, birdshot wrapped in leather. Next thing I knew it was the jail and a white man looking at me through the bars. I said, 'Captain, what was that?' 'Was what?'—the white man talking; he run his hand through the front of his hair where he had his hat tipped back. 'That man, Captain,' I ask him, 'was that a colored *policeman*?'"

Mamma went on swabbing at the lump. I was sitting there watching, smelling the camphor. She was so mad her face just swole up with it. I could see what was coming next, and here it came.

"Sue," she says.

"Sue who?" my daddy says. As if he didnt know, the same as me that was going on seven or eight.

"The town of Bristol," Mamma says. "The Law. Who else? They cant knock you round for sport and then just turn you loose like nothing happened."

"Cant?" my daddy says. He sat there for a minute, saying nothing. He was a high-strung man; God knows he was. But not that high-strung. So he told her: "You sue," he says, "but not in my name. I already got one knot up side my head."

It was the times; thats what it was — the carpetbaggers coming to town with cotton receipts already signed and the number of bales left blank to be filled in later, the fine-dressed man selling bundles of four painted sticks for you to use to stake off your forty acres come Emancipation Day again, and the night-riders pounding the roads in their bedsheets with the pointy hoods and the hoofs like somebody beating a drum along the turnpike. They burnt crosses every night all round us, and a man who'll burn what he prays to, he'll burn anything. It was the times, the whole air swirling full of freedom and danger; it was catching, you see, and Mamma already had it bad in the first place.

What happened next I didnt see, for she didnt take me with her. She left, walked out the door with that swole-up look still bulging her face, and was gone a good long time, till afternoon. Then here she came, back again, looking a good deal worse than Daddy did. He just had him a lump on the head but she had that and more. I broke out crying.

She went there looking for damages: "For what you done to my husband," she told them, right there in the town jail with the prisoners watching through the bars. At first the constable and this other man thought it was some kind of joke; they couldnt believe it. But then she got angry and started to yell in a loud voice about freedom and justice, right in their faces, and of course they couldnt stand for that, there in their own jail-house with the prisoners looking on. So they hit her, knocked her down. They almost had to, to get her to stop. But she wouldnt. She was still hollering in a high voice about freedom and justice and the vote, lying there on the floor where they had knocked her; she wouldnt quit. And then one of the men did something I cant justify, even considering all the disruption she was making. He kicked her full in the mouth, twice, cut both her lips and knocked several of her teeth right down her throat. That stopped her, for the time being at least, and then he kicked her once more to make certain. They didnt arrest her — which they could have done. When she came to, she picked herself up, holding her mouth, and came on home. I took one look at her and bust out crying; I was high-strung like my daddy in those days. But she wouldnt tell us anything. She went to bed without even the camphor bottle, and pulled the quilt up over her face and lay there.

Next day she had a nervous diarrhea, passed three of the teeth, and she picked them out of the slopjar, rinsed them off, and put them on the mantel to remember freedom by. That might sound like an ugly thing to you: I can see how it might. But to me it always seemed real fine, since it showed how much her love of freedom meant to her even after all it got her was three hard kicks in the mouth. It was the times, all that new liberty and equality coming so sudden before we had a chance to get used to them. But it worked both ways. You think we didnt laugh at all those white men cutting head-holes in their wives' best sheets and eye-holes in the pillow cases? We did indeed. It was a two-sided thing.

For a while then — most of her teeth being missing on one side, I mean — she didnt much look like herself. She'd always been such a fine-looking woman; her barber daddy had kept her dressed in style. But we got used to it in time, and Mamma was downright proud. It was like she'd sued and won. She held her head high, showing the missing teeth and the sunk-in cheek. You couldnt down her.

She didnt live long, though. She had some kind of stomach ailment; it went into a tumor and she died. I was nine or ten. The night she died she put her arms around me and her tears fell onto the back of my head. "Youll be free, Emanuel," she told me, her last words. "Youll have freedom and the vote and youll be free."

But I dont know. It was true; I got them, but it seems like they dont mean so much as they did back then with the Kluxers riding the roads to take them from you. Thats how it is, even with freedom.

My daddy he outlived her many years. He had two more

wives in fact, including the one that outlived him. I inherited all his clothes — and wore them, too, till I started putting on all this weight. Now all I can wear is these ties, a whole drawerful of silky bow ones. I got the business, too, this tent and all; I'm an artist like my daddy, with a wife and four grown children, one on Beale, one in Detroit, one in New Orleans, and one to help my wife keep house. You want me take your picture?

PILLAR OF FIRE

Ankle deep in the dusty places, the road led twelve miles
from the landing, around the head of a horseshoe lake and
down its eastern shore where the houses were. We left the
gunboat at eight oclock in brilliant sunlight, two mounted
officers wearing sabers and sashes and thirty Negro infantry-
men in neat blue uniforms; at noon the colonel halted the
column before a two-story frame structure with a brick
portico and squat, whitewashed pillars. He sat a hammer-
headed roan, an early-middle-aged man with a patch across
one eye.

"Looks old," he said, rolling his cigar along his lower lip. He
faced front, addressing the house itself. "Ought to burn pretty,"
he added after a pause, perhaps to explain why he had not
chosen one of the larger ones in both directions. I saw that he
was smiling, and that was as usual at such a time, the head
lifted to expose the mouth beneath the wide pepper-and-salt
mustache. Behind us the troops were quiet: so quiet that when
the colonel turned in the saddle, leather squeaked. "Walk up
there, Mr Lundy, and give them the news."

The troops stood at ease in a column of fours, the rifle
barrels slanting and glinting. Above their tunics, which were

powdered with dust except where they were splotched a darker blue at backs and armpits from four hours of hard marching, their faces appeared cracked as if by erosion where sweat had run.

"Orderly," I said. A soldier stepped out of ranks and held the reins near the snaffle while I dismounted on the off side, favoring my stiff right leg. I went up toward the house. When the colonel called after me, something I could not distinguish above the sound of my boots crunching gravel on the drive-way, I halted and faced about. "Sir?"

"Tell them twenty minutes!" With one arm he made the sweeping gesture I had come to know so well. "To clear out!" I heard him call.

I went on — this was nothing new; it was always twenty minutes — remembering, as I had done now for the past two years whenever I approached a strange house, that I had lost a friend this way. It was in Virginia, after Second Bull Run, the hot first day of September, '62. The two of us, separated from our command in the retreat, walked up to a roadside cabin to ask the way, and someone fired at us from behind a shuttered window. I ran out of range before the man (or woman; I never knew) could reload, and by the time I got up courage enough to come back, half an hour later, no one was there except my friend, lying in the yard in his gaudy zouave uniform with his knees drawn up and both hands clapped tight against his belt buckle. He looked pinch-faced and very dead, and it seemed indeed a useless way to die.

That was while I was still just Private Lundy, within a month of the day I enlisted back home in Cashtown; that was my baptism of fire, as they like to call it. After that came Antietam and Fredericksburg, where I won my stripes. The war moved fast in those days, and while I was in Washington recovering from my Chancellorsville wound I received my commission and orders to report directly to the War Depart-ment after a twenty-day convalescent leave. I enjoyed the visit home, limping on a cane and having people admire my new shoulder straps and fire-gilt buttons. "Adam, youre looking fit," they said, pretending not to notice the ruined knee. 'Fit' was their notion of a soldier word, though in fact the only way any soldier ever used it was as the past tense of fight.

When I reported back to the capital I was assigned to the West, arriving during the siege of Vicksburg and serving as liaison officer on one of the gunboats. Thus I missed the fighting at Gettysburg, up near home. It was not unpleasant duty. I had a bed to sleep in, with sheets, and three real meals every twenty-four hours, plus coffee in the galley whenever I wanted it. We shot at them, they shot at us: I could tell myself I was helping to win the war. Independence Day the city fell, and in early August I was ordered to report for duty with Colonel Nathan Frisbie aboard the gunboat *Starlight*. Up till then it had all been more or less average, including the wound; there were thousands like me. But now it changed, and I knew it from the first time I saw him.

He looked at me hard with his one gray eye before returning the salute. "Glad to have you aboard," he said at last. A Negro corporal was braced in a position of exaggerated attention beside a stand of colors at the rear of the cabin. "Orderly," the colonel said. The corporal rolled his eyes. "Show the lieutenant his quarters."

Next morning at six oclock the corporal rapped at the door of my cabin, then entered and gave me the colonel's compliments, along with instructions to report to the orderly room for a tour of inspection before breakfast. I'd been asleep; I dressed in a hurry, flustered at being late on my first day of duty. Colonel Frisbie was checking the morning report when I came in. He glanced up and said quietly, "Get your saber, Mr Lundy." I returned to my cabin, took the saber out of its wrappings, and buckled it on. I hadnt worn it since the convalescent leave, and in fact hadnt thought I'd ever wear it again.

The troops were on the after deck, each man standing beside his pallet; the colonel and I followed the first sergeant down the aisle. From time to time Colonel Frisbie would pause and lift an article from the display of equipment on one of the pads, then look sharply at the owner before passing on. "Take his name, Sergeant." Their dark faces were empty of everything, but I saw that each man trembled slightly while the colonel stood before him.

After breakfast Colonel Frisbie called me into the orderly room for a conference. This was the first of many. He sat at his desk, forearms flat along its top, the patch over his eye dead black like a target center, his lips hidden beneath the blousy, slightly grizzled mustache. There was hardly any motion in his face as he spoke.

When Vicksburg fell, the colonel said, Mr Lincoln announced that the Mississippi "flowed unvexed to the sea." But, like so many political announcements, this was not strictly true; there was still considerable vexation in the form of sniping from the levee, raids by bodies of regular and irregular cavalry — bushwackers, the colonel called them — and random incidents involving dynamite and disrespect to the flag. So while Sherman sidestepped his way to Atlanta, commanders of districts flanking the river were instructed to end all such troubles. On the theory that partisan troops could not function without the support of the people who lived year-round in the theater, the commanders adopted a policy of holding the civilian population responsible.

"They started this thing, Mr Lundy," the colonel said. "They began it, sir, and while they had the upper hand they thought it was mighty fine. Remember the plumes and roses in those days? Well, *we*'re top dog now, East and West, and we'll give them what they blustered for. Indeed. We'll give them war enough to last the time of man."

He brooded, his face in shadow, his hands resting within the circle of yellow lamplight on his desk. I wondered if this silence, which seemed very long to me, was a sign that the conference was over. But just as I was about to excuse myself, the colonel spoke again. He cleared his throat. "Lieutenant, does that knee bother you?"

"Not often, sir. Just when — "

"Never you mind," Colonel Frisbie said, and moving one hand suddenly to the lamp he turned the wick up full and tilted the shade so that the light was thrown directly on his face. His expression was strained, the patch neat and exact. "Theyll pay for that knee, lieutenant. And they will pay for this!" He lifted the patch onto his forehead. The empty socket pulsed as red and raw as when the wound was new.

During the year that followed, the colonel spoke to me often of these and other things. Every morning there was a meeting in the orderly room after breakfast — 'conferences' he called them, but he did the talking. I understood how he felt about the eye, the desire to make someone pay for its loss; I had felt it myself about the ruined knee and the death of my friend in Virginia, until I reminded myself, in the case of the knee, that the bullets flew both ways, and in the case of my friend that it was primarily a question of whose home was being invaded. I had more or less put it behind me, this thought of repayment; but with Colonel Frisbie it was different, and for many reasons. He was a New Englander, a lawyer in civilian life, an original abolitionist. He had been active in the underground railroad during the '50s, and when war came he entered the army as a captain under Frémont in Saint Louis. These were things he told me from time to time, but there were things he did not tell, things I found out later.

He had been with Sherman at Shiloh, a major by then, adjutant in an Indiana regiment which broke badly under the Sunday dawn attack. He was near the bluff above Pittsburg Landing, using the flat of his saber on stragglers, when a stray minié came his way with a spent whine and took out his left eye: whereupon he went under the bluff, tore off his shoulder straps, and lay down among the skulkers. There were ten thousand others down there, including officers, and only a few of them wounded; he had better provocation than most. Yet he could not accept it in the way those others apparently could. When the battle was over he bandaged his eye with a strip from his shirt, rejoined his regiment, and later was commended in reports. There were men in his outfit, however, including some of his own clerks, who had also been under the bluff, and he saw them looking at him as if to say, "If you wont tell on me, I wont on you." Soon afterwards he was assigned to courts martial duty with the Adjutant General's Department. When the army adopted its reprisal policy in the lower Mississippi Valley, he was given another promotion and a gunboat with special troops aboard to enforce it.

Patrolling the river from Vicksburg north to Memphis, two hundred and fifty airline miles and almost twice that far by water, One-Eye Frisbie and the *Starlight* became well known throughout the delta country. Where partisan resistance had once been strongest, soon there was little activity of any kind. It became a bleak region, populated only by women and children and old men and house servants too feeble to join the others gone as 'contraband' with the Union armies. The fields lay fallow, last year's cotton drooping on dead brown stalks. Even the birds went hungry, what few remained. The land was desolated as if by plague.

The only protest now was an occasional shot from the levee, which was followed by instant reprisal in accordance with the Army policy. Colonel Frisbie would tie up at the nearest river town, sending word for evacuation within twenty minutes, and then would give the *Starlight* gunners half an hour's brisk drill, throwing explosive shells over the levee and into the empty buildings and streets where chickens and dogs fluttered and slunk and squawked and howled. Or he would tie up at the point where the sniping occurred, lead the troops ashore, and march them overland sometimes as far as a dozen miles to burn an isolated plantation house.

I was with him from the beginning and I remember him mainly as straddled in silhouette before the lick and soar of flames. Dispossessed, the family huddled somewhere in the background. At first they had been arrogant, threatening reprisal by Forrest or Jameson or Van Dorn. "You had better burn the trees as well," one woman told us. "When we first came there was nothing but woods and we built our homes.

We'll build them again." But when Atlanta was besieged their defiance faltered, and when Sherman had taken the city and was preparing for the march that would "make Georgia howl," they knew they were beaten and their armies would never return. There had been a time when they sent their plantation bells and even their brass doorknobs to be melted for cannon, but not any more. Now the war had left them; they were faced with the aftermath before the finish.

Colonel Frisbie looked upon all this as indemnity collectible for the loss of his eye and his courage at Shiloh. Saber and sash and gray eye glinting firelight, he would watch a house burn with a smile that was more like a grimace, lip lifted to expose the white teeth clamping the cigar. That was the way I remembered him now as I continued to walk up the driveway toward the house. Around one of its corners I saw that the outbuildings had already burned, and I wondered if it had been done by accident — a not uncommon plantation mishap — or by one of our armies passing through at the time of the Vicksburg campaign. Then, nearing the portico, I saw that the door was ajar. Beyond it I could see into a high dim hall where a staircase rose in a slow curve. I stood in the doorway, listening, then rapped.

The rapping was abrupt and loud against the silence. Then there was only vacancy, somehow even more empty than before.

"Hello!" I cried, my voice as reverberant as if I had spoken from the bottom of a well. "Hello in there!"

I had a moment of sharp fear, a sudden vision of someone crouched at the top of the staircase, sighting down a rifle barrel at me with a hot, unwinking eye. But when I bent forward and peered, there was no one, nothing. I went in.

Through a doorway on the right I saw a tall black man standing beside an armchair. He wore a rusty clawhammer coat with buttons of tarnished brass, and on his head there was what appeared to be a pair of enormous white horns. Looking closer I saw that the Negro had bound a dinner napkin about his jaws, one of which was badly swollen, and had tied it at the crown of his head so that the corners stood up stiffly from the knot like the ears on a rabbit. The armchair was wide and deep; it faced the cold fireplace, its high, fan-shaped back turned toward the door.

I said, "Didnt you hear me calling?" The Negro just stood there, saying nothing. It occurred to me then that he might be deaf; he had that peculiar, vacant look on his face. I came forward. "I said didnt . . ."

But as I approached him, obliquing to avoid the chair, I saw something else.

There was a hand on the chair arm. Pale against the leather and mottled with dark brown liver spots, it resembled the hand of a mummy, the nails long and narrow, almond-shaped. Crossing to the hearth I looked down at the man in the chair, and the man looked up at me. He was old — though old was hardly word enough to express it; he was ancient — with sunken cheeks and a mass of white hair like a mane, obviously a tall man and probably a big one, once, but thin now to the point of emaciation, as if he had been reduced to skin and skeleton and only the most essential organs, heart and lungs and maybe bowels, though not very much of either — 'Except heart; there's plenty of that,' I thought, looking into the cold green eyes. His chin, resting upon a high stock, trembled as he spoke.

"Have you brum to run my howl?" he said.

I stared at him. "How's that?" I asked. But the old man did not answer.

"He hyar you, captain," the Negro said. His enormous horns bobbed with the motion of his jaw. "He hyar you well enough, but something happen to him here lately he caint talk right."

This was Isaac Jameson, who was born in a wilderness shack beside the Trace while his father, a South Carolina merchant, was removing his family and his business to the Natchez District as part of a caravan which he and other Loyalists had organized to escape the Revolution on the seaboard. Thus in later years, like so many of the leaders of his time, Isaac was able to say in truth that he was a log cabin boy. But it was misleading, for his father, who had prospered under the Crown back east, became even wealthier in the west, and Isaac grew up in a fine big house on the bluff overlooking the river. From the gallery he could watch Spanish sentries patrolling the wharf where steamboats, up from New Orleans, put in with goods for the Jameson warehouse. He was grown, twenty years old and four inches over six feet tall, when John Adams sent troops to take over for the United States and created the Mississippi Territory. The Republic, which his father had come seven hundred miles to escape, had dogged his heels.

Isaac was sixth among eight sons, and he was unlike the others. It was not only that he stood half a head taller; there was some intrinsic difference. They were reliable men, even the two younger ones who followed the removal. Reserved and proper, useful in the mercantile business, they knew their responsibilities; they stayed within their class and they knew the uses of dignity. But Isaac would not stand at a desk totting figures or checking bills of lading. He was off to cockfights or horseraces, and he spent more evenings in the Under-the-Hill section than he did in Natchez proper. He liked a brawl and he knew he could always find one among the river people. They came off their boats with their heads backflung, calling for the bully of the town, gesticulating with a curiously combined bravado and deadly seriousness: "Hear me, all you town galoots! I'm a combination rubber ball, wildcat, and screaming maniac! I'm a ringtail roarer!" Then Isaac would come forward, in decent broadcloth and imported linen, and it would be claw and gouge, no holds barred, best man on his feet when the thing was over.

His father, remembering the shack by the Trace, the panthers screaming in the outward darkness while his wife was in labor, believed that his son — wilderness born, conceived in a time of revolution — had received in his blood, along with whatever it was that had given him the extra height and the unaccountable width of his shoulders, some goading spark of rebellion, some fierce, hot distillate of the jungle itself. But while this might explain his excesses, or anyhow account for them, it did not make them any easier to correct or to abide, and neither the elder Jameson nor the seven brothers felt much regret when Isaac disappeared in the fall of 1804. He did not say where he was going, or even that he was leaving. He just went.

They did not see him for ten years. When his name failed to appear in the testimony at the Burr trial three years later, they believed he was dead. "He must be," the father said. "Otherwise he'd be involved in it somewhere. It's too wild for him to have missed." He could have been at the bottom of some creek or river, with a belly full of gravel; that was the way the Trace bandits, Murrel and the Harps, disposed of bodies. But not long afterwards they heard from a planter just returned from New Orleans that he had seen Isaac sipping claret in a Royal Street cantine with Jean Lafitte and Dominique You. "So thats it," the father said; "he's a pirate. We should have thought of that at the outset."

There followed a five-year period during which they heard nothing. Then one of the brothers met on the street in Natchez a ragged man who had fought alongside the missing son against the Creeks at Burnt Corn. A year later they saw Isaac himself.

He had come home to die, and he looked it. Four men brought him off the steamboat and up from the wharf on a stretcher. He was unconscious. Laid out, he appeared even taller than before, but he was considerably gaunted. His eyes were far back in their sockets and he had grown a wide blond beard that crawled with lice. One leg was wrapped full length in a rag bandage which was stained with suppuration and stank of gangrene. He had been wounded at the Battle of New Orleans — whether fighting under Jackson or Lafitte they did not know, though they thought it was probably Jackson since Lafitte took better care of his wounded than this. After two weeks in a riverfront hospital he had used a derringer to stand off the surgeon who wanted to amputate.

"Youre being a fool," the surgeon told him. "That thing has mortified, and now it will spread and kill you."

Isaac did not lower the derringer.

"Then let it mortify in peace," he said. "If I die I'll die with both my legs."

When the surgeon came back that night, intending to find him asleep, Isaac was gone. He had got someone to help him board the steamboat and was on his way upriver, though by the time the boat reached Natchez he was in delirium and barely managed to direct the stretcher bearers to his father's house at the top of the bluff.

He woke and instead of pain there was warmth and comfort, smooth sheets, and a pleasant feeling of falling slowly through space. Then he recognized the furniture in his room; the ten years might have been a dream. Remembering his leg, he sat up in bed to look for it, and it was there; the only thing that was missing was the beard. He was a year mending. Then he spent another year trying to make up for lost time. But it did not go right. There were still the cockfights and the grog shops and the women under the hill, but the old life had paled on him. He was thirty-nine, a bachelor, well into middle age, and apparently it had all come to nothing.

Then he found what he had been seeking from the start, though he did not know he was looking for it until some time after he found it. Just before his fortieth birthday — in the spring of 1818; Mississippi had entered the Union in December — he rode into the northern wilderness with two trappers who had come to town on their annual spree. This time he was gone a little over two years. Shortly after the treaty of Doaks

Stand opened five and a half million acres of Choctaw land
across the middle of the state, he reappeared at his father's
house. He was in buckskins, his hair shoulder length, and he
had the beard again.

Next day he was gone for good, with ten of his father's
Negroes and five thousand dollars in gold in his saddlebags.
He had come back to claim his legacy, to take this now instead
of his share in the Jameson estate when the old man died. The
brothers were willing, since it would mean a larger share for
them when the time came. The father considered it a downright bargain; he would have given twice that amount for
Isaac's guarantee to stay away from Natchez with his escapades
and his damage to the name. He said, "If you want to play
prodigal it's all right with me. But mind you: when youre
swilling with swine and chomping the husks, dont cut your
eyes around in my direction. There wont be any lamp in the
window, or fatted calf either. This is all."

It was all Isaac wanted, apparently. Between sunup and
nightfall of the following day — a Sunday, early in June —
they rolled forty miles along the road connecting hamlets
north of Natchez. Sundown of the third day they made camp
on the near bank of the Yazoo, facing the Walnut Hills, and
Wednesday they entered the delta, a flat land baked gray by
the sun wherever it exposed itself, which was rare, from under
the intertwined branches of sycamores and water oaks and
cottonwoods and elms. Grass grew so thick that even the broad
tires of the Conestoga left no mark of passage. Slow, circuitous
creeks, covered with dusty scum and steaming in the heat,
drained east and south, away from the river, each doubling
back on itself in convulsive loops and coils like a snake fighting lice. For four days then, while the Negroes clutched
desperately at seats and stanchions in a din of creaking wood
and clattering metal (they had been warehouse hands, townspeople, and ones the brothers could easiest spare at that) the
wagon lurched through thickets of scrub oak and stunted
willow and over fallen trunks and rotted stumps. It had a pitch-

ing roll, like that of a ship riding a heavy swell, which actually did cause most of the Negroes to become seasick four hundred miles from salt water.

They followed no trail, for there was no trail to follow. There was only Isaac, who rode a claybank mare as far out front as visibility allowed, sometimes half a mile, sometimes ten feet, and even in the latter case they sometimes followed not the sight of him but the sound of snapping limbs and Isaac's cursing. Often they had to dismount with axes and chop through. Just before noon of the eighth day, Sunday again, they struck the southern end of a lake, veered right, then left, and continued northward along its eastern shore. Two hours later Isaac reined in the mare, and when the wagon drew abreast he signaled for a halt. A wind had risen, ruffling the lake; through the screen of cypresses the waves were bright like little hatchets in the sunlight. "All right," he said. "You can get the gear unloaded. We are home."

Thus he began the fulfillment of a dream which had come to him the previous month. It was May then, the oaks tasseling; he and the trappers had reached the lake at the close of day. While the sun went down, big and red across the water, they made camp on the grassy strip between the lake and the trees. Isaac lay rolled in his blanket, and all that night, surrounded by lake-country beauty — overhead the far, spangled reaches of sky, eastward the forest murmurs, the whisper of leaves and groan of limbs in the wind, the hoarse night-noises of animals, and westward, close at hand, the lapping of water — he dreamed. He dreamed an army of blacks marching upon the jungle, not halting to chop but walking steadily forward, swinging axes against the retreating green wall. Behind them the level fields lay stumpless and serene in watery sunlight, motionless until in the distance clanking trace chains and clacking singletrees announced the coming of the plowmen. Enormous lop-eared mules drew bulltongue plows across the green, and the long brown furrows of earth unrolled like threads off spools. What had been jungle became cultivated fields, and now the fields began to be striped with the pale green lines of plants soon burdened with squares, then purple-and-white dotted, then deep red with blooms, then shimmering white in the summer heat. In a long irregular line (they resembled skirmishers except for the singing; their sacks trailed from their shoulders like limp flags) the pickers passed over the fields, leaving them brown and desolate in the rain, and the stalks dissolved, going down into bottomless mud. Then in the dream there was quiet, autumnal death until the spring returned and the plowmen, and the dream began again. This was repeated three times, with a mystical clarity.

"Wake up. Wake up, Ike."

"Dont," he said, drawing the edge of the blanket over his eyes.

"Wake up, Ike! It's time to roll."

In the faint dawn light the lake and forest had that same quality of unreality as in the dream. He was not certain he was awake until one of the trappers nudged him in the ribs with the toe of his moccasin and spoke again. "Ike! You want to sleep your life away?"

For a while he did not answer; he remained half-in half-out of the dream, which was still with him and which he knew already would always be with him. The trappers stood waiting, but he just lay there, looking out over the lake and at the forest. Then he sat up.

"You two go on," he told them. "This is where I stop."

He stayed there for three days, alone. A mile back from the lakeshore he found a deserted Choctaw village. The Indians had burned their shacks and gone; there was nothing left except an occasional shard of pottery in the ashes, and grass was already reclaiming the paths their feet had worn. During the past month he had seen them, or others like them, traveling single file, a people dispossessed, the braves in dirty blankets carrying nothing, the squaws with babies and utensils strapped to their backs, going north to land not yet ceded by the Chiefs.

On the fourth day Isaac rode south to Natchez and claimed

his share of the Jameson estate in cash and Negroes. Within two weeks of the night he and the trappers made camp by the lake he was back again, with the ten slaves and six mules, clearing ground and bounding the claim he had registered at the land office and paid for in gold. That was the beginning. During the next ten years he was joined by others drawn from the south and east to new land available at ninety cents an acre with few questions asked. Near the south end of the lake, four miles below Isaac's property, a North Carolinian named Ledbetter established a general store and trading post. Soon this was flanked by a blacksmith shop and a roadside tavern and hostelry called the Ithaca Inn by its owner, who claimed to have been Professor of Greek at an eastern university but who never enlarged on the circumstances that had prompted his change of careers. He did not stay long and soon no one remembered so much as the shape of his face. But that was no matter; by then the crossroads had taken the name of the tavern. When Jordan County was formed — this was 1827; men were leaving the land, abandoning their claims because of the collapse of cotton economy two years before — Ithaca was the leading settlement in the southern district, but Bristol, thirty miles upriver, had outgrown the earlier hamlet and was made the county seat, the legal as well as the industrial center.

The eighteen hundred acres of Isaac's original claim were increased to thirty-two hundred in 1826 when his neighbors north and south went broke in the crash. Two years later, though he had named his ten-square-mile plantation Solitaire in confirmation of his bachelor intentions, he got married. It happened almost accidentally. She was the youngest of four daughters; the other three were already married, and she herself was more or less engaged at the time to the blacksmith's assistant, two doors down the street. Her father, who came from Kentucky, had bought the Ithaca Inn from the wayward professor, and from time to time she took her turn at the tap. Isaac found her tending bar one warm spring evening when he rode down for a drink. He had seen her before, of course, though he had not really noticed. Now he did. He particularly admired her arms, which were bared to the elbows, and her thick yellow hair, worn shoulder length. That night he had trouble getting to sleep. At last he dropped off, however. He did not dream, but when he woke he thought immediately of her. Whats this? he asked himself. He returned to the Inn that evening, and the next. By then he had decided. He spoke to the father first. "I'm willing if Katy is," the innkeeper said. The daughter made only one condition. She would not marry a man with a beard, no matter what size the plantation he owned might be. So Isaac was clean shaven at the wedding. It was held at the Inn and the blacksmith's young assistant was there, bulging his biceps, drunk for the first time in his life. He got into three fights that day, though not with Isaac.

Isaac was just past fifty; the bride was five years less than half his age. Along with the plump arms and tawny hair, she brought to Solitaire the bustling, cheerful, apparently thought-less efficiency he had admired in the Ithaca taproom. The house, which they moved into on the wedding night, was little different from what it had been seven years ago when Isaac and the slaves first put it up. A cedar shingle roof covered three rooms grouped to form a truncated L and indistinguish-able one from another except for the casual presence of a stove to identify the kitchen and a four-poster the bedroom, the whole resembling a combination gunroom, kennel, office, and hunting lodge. It was musty of bachelorhood and cluttered with the incidentals of plantation living, old cotton samples and turkey-wing fans, split-bottom chairs and a Duncan Phyfe highboy, gnawed bones and in one corner half a dozen rusty plowpoints strung on a length of baling wire.

First Mrs Jameson drove the dogs out. There were eight of them, mostly hounds with long sad faces, scrabbling and yelping beneath her upraised broom. Then, commandeering three of the fieldhands, she had the rooms emptied of their conglomerate litter and scrubbed with lye water, floors and walls and ceiling, until the cypress timbers paled and wore a nap as soft as velvet to the touch. For nearly a week the house was damp and clean, empty of furnishings except for the bed and a box of clothes. She and Isaac left at last for Memphis on their wedding trip. After a single outing, when a clerk in a Main Street store referred to Katy as his daughter, he would not go shopping with her; he was afraid it might happen again. He stayed at the Gayoso bar while she made the rounds of the shops. "Just get whatever you think we'll need," he said. "Tell them to send the bill down home."

They returned to Solitaire five days later, living again in the almost empty house while Katy waited for her purchases to arrive. When the steamboat blew for a landing she was there with four wagons to supervise the unloading. Four wagons, Isaac thought; why four? Then he found out. He watched with amazement her transformation from girl-bride into mule skinner and section boss (all that was missing was the cursing) while the crates off the steamboat were being transported from the landing, along the twelve miles of road that led around the head of the lake to the house on its eastern shore. They were unloaded in the yard, uncrated there and carried in, carpets and draperies, a dining room table, lyre-back chairs and a grandfather clock, kitchen utensils of every imaginable size and shape and even a bathtub, the first Isaac had seen outside a hotel since he left Natchez. He watched with no less amazement, when the work was done and the house was to her liking, his wife's retransformation back to the girl-bride she had been before the steamboat blew for the landing. He had been in much the same position as a man watching what he thought was a spring breeze develop into a tornado, then back into a breeze again as soon as the holocaust was done. Standing among the new chairs and sofas and hangings and table lamps, she asked demurely: "How do you like it, Mr Jameson?"

"I, well, I like it fine. Just fine, Katy." Isaac looked and shook his head. "But I'm thinking youve spent next year's crop already."

"There will be plenty of years," she said.

△

That ended the first phase of his life, the fifty years spent running hard after trouble in any form, first among men — river bullies at Natchez-under-the-Hill, painted Creeks at Burnt Corn, British regulars at New Orleans; he had tried them all — and then against the cat- and snake-infested jungles of the South. Isaac, however, was not aware that it had ended until two years later, after Dancing Rabbit opened the remaining northern section of the state to settlers, when his neighbors, small farmers and planters alike, were selling their claims for whatever they could get, packing their carts and Conestogas, and heading north into the rich new land that lay between the lake and the Tennessee line. It was then, after they had gone and he had stayed, that Isaac knew his wilderness thirst had been slaked. He still would not admit it, though, either to others or to himself. He claimed it was because he had no one to leave in charge of Solitaire. "I'll go when I have a son," he told himself.

By then he had enlarged the house, first extending the arm of the L so that it formed a U, then closing the rear so that it became a rectangle with a dining room in the center and a kitchen behind it, across the back. What had been the kitchen, dim and hot and airless, became the store room, and in fact there was a general reshuffling of accommodations, much to Isaac's discomfort though by now he had resigned himself to the fact that it was his wife who ran the house. Its lines were long, by far the most imposing house on the lake, though it still had the low, cedar-shingle roof. This held him to the land but this was not all, for in the summer of 1832 he got what he had claimed would set him free. They had thought there would be many children, since both came from rather large families. For a time, then, he said to himself, "Maybe I waited too long." But presently his wife was pregnant, and in the summer their first child was born. It was a son and the doctor pronounced it a fine one. He and Isaac leaned over the foot of the bed, looking down at the baby swaddled in flannel beside its mother.

"A fine one," the doctor said.

"You think so?" Isaac asked, wanting to hear him say it again.

"I do," the doctor said. "I do indeed."

"Dont shake the bed so," Mrs Jameson told them.

A week later the baby died (it was stomach trouble; some kind of obstruction, the doctor guessed; he was not much doctor) and they buried it the following afternoon, three hundred yards south of the house, in a cedar grove which had been set aside for this when the house was built but which so far had remained untenanted. The Episcopal minister had come down from Bristol for the baptising two days before; he had stayed on to make it a three-day visit, as was the custom, and thus he was also there to officiate at the funeral. Again Isaac said to himself, "Maybe I waited too long," for he blamed the dead baby's unfitness on his age; young men were the ones for having babies. Yet he discovered that he had been wrong at least about one thing. He had been wrong about the effect of having a son. As he stood beside the small grave, hearing the rector pronounce the service ("Suffer the little children to come unto me") and then the somewhat muffled slither of loose summer earth being dropped on the box, he knew that now, with flesh of his flesh interred in it, he would never leave this land. He was linked to it for life.

Mrs Jameson was in bed two weeks, recovering from both the birth and the death of her child. Later, when she moved about the house once more, her eyes were nearly always wet with tears and often she would not reply when spoken to. It gave Isaac a strange, helpless feeling to see her thus; he was not accustomed to facing problems he could not take hold of;

yet he knew better than to interfere or offer help until it was called for. At any hour of the night he would wake to find her lying tense with grief, eyes shining as she stared upward at the ceiling. He did not know what to say or do, and he did nothing. Then this period passed, gave way to another in which the grief was lighter because it at least permitted action, but also was sharper because it let up on the dulling of her perception. From the southeast window of their bedroom she could see the cedar grove with its one small mound of raw earth, and now the full extent of her loss became apparent to her. This might have forced her back into her first prostrate condition, but it did not, for she busied herself with running the house. It was really that simple. She became a driver of servants because she could neither be idle herself nor bear to see them idle. All the furniture was rearranged, the carpets beaten, the woodwork scrubbed and waxed. In fact it was almost as thorough as the renovation she had staged when she first moved in. Again at night, too, she turned to Isaac with the old urgency abetted by a certain franticness, a passion that went beyond passion for its uses, and again Isaac observed all this with the amazement of a man watching what he had thought was a spring breeze develop into a tornado.

Then this passed too, as the other had done. Five months after the death of the infant, this second and furious period ceased. It did not play out: it just stopped, gave way to her original placative manner. The frenzy was finished, gone. She became calm again, almost bovine. Isaac recognized the symptoms, the quiet, careful movements, the attitude of inward listening. Ah, he thought. The child was born in August of 1833, the year the stars fell. (Wartime newspaper editors and, later, historians — Southern historians at any rate — were to make much of this. They saw in it an augury, and it lent a starry glitter to their pages.) Mrs Jameson named him Clive, not for any particular reason; she just liked the name. The dead one had been named for Isaac.

In the ten following years she bore six more children. They were all girls and were all either born dead or died within a week. They lay in the cedar grove, a row of crosses stretching eastward from the first. Mrs Jameson did not react to these deaths as she had done to the one in '32. She had become a pleasant-faced, bustling woman, rather full-bodied by now, expending her energy on a determination to keep the Jameson house the finest on the lake.

This took some doing: for, though nowhere near the extent it would reach ten years later in the expansive early '50's, there was already plenty of competition. Cotton was coming into its own, and the lake country was a district of big plantations, thousand- and two- and three-thousand-acre places which the owners ruled like barons. When the small farmers, settlers who had followed Isaac into the region after the Doaks Stand treaty opened the land, moved away to the north after Dancing Rabbit — usually with no more than they had had when they arrived, a wagon and a team of mules or oxen, a rifle and a couple of sticks of furniture, a hound or two and a crate of chickens or shoats, a wife and a stair-stepped parcel of children in linsey-woolsey, and perhaps a widowed mother or mother-in-law — their claims were gobbled up by those who stayed, as well as by others who moved in on their heels. These last, the second wave of comers, were essentially businessmen. They had no gift (or, for that matter, desire) for ringing trees and rooting stumps; their gift was rather for organization. They could juggle figures and balance books and put the profits where they earned more profits. Eli Whitney made them rich and now they began to build fine houses to show it, calling them Westoak Hall and Waverly and Briartree, proud-sounding names in imitation of those in the Tidewater counties of Virginia, though in fact the Virginians were few among them. They were mostly Kentuckians and North Carolinians, arrived by way of East Mississippi or the river, and for the most part they were not younger sons of established families, sent forth with the parental blessing and gold in their saddle-bags. Many of them did not know their grandparents' names, and some of them had never known their fathers. They were self-made men who had risen by ability.

For this they received due credit, but they also paid a certain price. Outside the field of their endeavor they had scarcely any existence. Few of them were more widely read than Isaac, for instance, who had been through no books at all since his boyhood years in Natchez, and none then except the handful he could not avoid. Their pleasures were few and simple and usually violent, limited mainly to hunting and poker. A favorite Sunday afternoon pastime was for them to assemble around the Jameson barnlot where a stake was driven with a chain attached to its top. A bull was led out and tied to the stake by the horns. Then a forty-year-old fieldhand named Memzy would enter the lot, bareheaded, and butt heads with the bull till the animal bellered with pain. The men cheered and laughed, leaning along the fence to watch, and give him dimes and quarters. "Hardest-headed nigger in all creation!" they cried. They slapped their thighs and shook their heads.

Isaac's original L-shaped structure, which he and the ten slaves had put up in 1820 soon after their arrival, had grown now to a two-story mansion with a brick portico and concrete pillars; the roof had been raised so that now all the bedrooms were upstairs. It was still called Solitaire though the name no longer fit. Isaac himself had grown handsomer with age. He was still a big man, six feet four, but he looked slimmer and, somehow, even fitter and more hale. Gray hair became him. Dressed habitually in broadcloth and starched linen, he had a stiffness, a formality that resembled an outward show of self-satisfaction and pride. In 1848, when he was seventy, people seeing him on the street in Ithaca, with his straight-backed manner of walking and his careful way of planting his feet, would point him out to visitors. "Thats Ike Jameson," they would say. "He was the first man into these parts. Fine-looking, aint he. How old would you take him to be?" The visitor would guess at fifty or fifty-five and his host would laugh. "Seventy. Seventy, by God. Youd never think it, would you? to look at him."

In September of that year he sent his son, who had reached

fifteen the month before, to the Virginia Military Institute. This was at the boy's insistence, and Isaac was willing: not because he wanted him to become a soldier (he wanted no such thing; he had known too many soldiers in his time) but because in preparation for the life of a planter it did not much matter what form the schooling took. In fact a military school was probably best, since the boy would be less likely to become seriously involved with books. A young man's true education began when he was through with school and had come back home to learn the running of the plantation, the particular temper and whims of cotton as well as the temper and whims of the people who worked it, meaning Negroes. Besides, the Mexican War was recently over. Young men throughout the South were admiring General Winfield Scott and old Rough-and-Ready Taylor, Captain Bragg the artilleryman who "gave them a little more grape," and Colonel Davis from down near Natchez who formed his regiment, the Mississippi Rifles, in a V at Buena Vista and won the battle with a single charge.

Early in June, nine months later, when Isaac went to Bristol to meet him at the station, Clive was in uniform, the buttons bright against black facings on the slate-gray cloth. All down the platform, people were looking at him. Isaac was impressed.

"I declare, boy, you look almost grown to me."

"Hello, papa," he said, and extended his hand. Always before that they had kissed.

Three Junes later, when he came home from graduation, tall, slim, handsome, blond, nineteen, he was the catch of the lake. It was not only his looks; he could be amusing, too, as for instance when he gave an imitation of his mathematics instructor, T. J. Jackson, who wound up every lecture covered with chalkdust and perspiration and who sometimes became so interested in solving algebra and trigonometry problems that he forgot the students were present and just stood there reasoning with himself and Euclid. Clive had much success with this; "Give us Professor Jackson," they would beg him in houses along the lake. Soon, however, his social horizon widened. He

was one of the real catches of the delta. Isaac and Mrs Jameson
were impressed, and so were the various girls; but the ones
who were most impressed were the girls' mothers. They
preened their daughters, set their caps, and laid their snares.
At dances and outings he moved among them, attentive, grave,
pleasant, quite conscious of the advantages of his position;
they found it really infuriating, the way he took what was
offered as his due.

Then he was twenty, within a year of his majority. *Now,*
the mothers thought; now he'll decide. But he did not. For
three more years he played the field. By then it was more than
a little infuriating; their nerves were beginning to wear. But he
still held off, as if he knew to the ounce his worth as a prize
— as if he knew already that he was offering, in addition to
present happiness, a place alongside him on the pages of future
history books. Yet in the end, of course, the mothers were
right. He decided.

He came home from a weekend in Bristol, late one night in
the spring of '55, and next morning he told his mother and
father. "I'm engaged," he said. They were at late breakfast,
seated on three sides of the long gleam of mahogany. "To be
married," he added, removing the crown from his egg. It
sounded casual, offhand, or at least it was intended to; but they
could see that it had been rehearsed, perhaps in front of the
mirror in his bedroom. He was considerably younger than he
would have had anyone think.

"Which one of them is it?" Mrs Jameson asked.

'It' was the third of six unmarried daughters of a Bristol
lawyer, a widower who had risen by his bootstraps, so far and
no further; he was only relatively successful — in the light of
his opportunities, that is — and though he was not downright
poor, he was considerably poorer than a man with six unmarried daughters had any right to be. There was a good
deal of surprise and even more of outrage when the engagement was announced. The various disappointed mothers, remembering the way Clive had moved among them, attentive

and pleasant, yet always with such grave assurance and always a bit removed — like a bachelor prince or, worse, a wealthy shopper in a bargain basement — considered themselves tricked. They took such solace as they could in reminding each other that his mother had been "practically a barmaid, after all."

But this died down and at length it even disappeared, the more quickly since the girl, who was dark-haired, with an earnest, heart-shaped face, saw her family after the wedding only to nod to from her carriage as they waved from porch or boardwalk. After her return from the European honeymoon tour, having moved into the big new house on Solitaire, she never saw them at all. This way, there was something grand and impersonal about her triumph. They did not resent it, neither the rivals-at-large nor the sisters, as they certainly would have done if she had continued to move among them, in which case her every phrase and gesture would have been interpreted as signaling her contempt. Even the mothers of rejected girls soon lost their resentment, recovered their equilibrium, so to speak, and were off on other pursuits. She made her success seem so conclusive, so inevitable in the light of all that followed; they could not imagine her in a different position.

The big new house was a wedding present from Isaac and Mrs Jameson, particularly the latter; it was her idea. The day Clive told them he was going to be married she told Isaac to send to New Orleans for an architect. By now she had had to relax her efforts to keep her house the finest on the lake. Bigger, grander ones, whose pillars were not of concrete but of fir or even marble, were being built all down the eastern shore, houses which the old house could not hope to equal by any amount of remodeling or addition. The architect came at once, a big man with frilled shirtfronts, a goatee, and hands that were always in motion while he spoke. He drew the plans and landscaped the grounds, settling down for a year in residence, and immediately after the marriage ceremony, four months later, presented the bride and groom with a list of appointments and furnishings for them to purchase during the tour of Europe.

When they returned at New Year's, after a six-month absence, the shell of the house was up. It had three stories and forty rooms, sixteen-foot ceilings and walls a little less than two feet thick. The bricks, kiln-dried to a warm, rosy color that delighted the architect, had been made on the place, from a clay deposit near the site of the Choctaw village Isaac had found deserted and burnt when he stayed here alone for three days in the spring of 1820; it had been a pottery center in Indian times, and plowmen still turned up shards of it in the fields every spring. Then the furnishings and appointments began to arrive in crates from Europe, half a dozen wagonloads a week, addressed in outlandish calligraphies to *Mr* — or *M* or *Hr* or *Sr*; they had done the full circuit — *Clive Jameson* (sometimes with an *Esq*) "*Solitaire*," *near Ithaca Mississippi*, *U.S.A.* As fast as they arrived they were unloaded and uncrated and installed.

In June the architect returned to New Orleans. "I leave you the best I'll ever do," he said, looking back at the house as the carriage pulled off for the landing. He had been there a year, and though other commissions were offered him up and down the lake, as well as in other parts of Jordan County, he wanted to get back to city life; he wanted other amusements besides poker, at which he lost consistently until he quit, and hunting, in which he took no part, and Negroes who butted heads with bulls until the bulls cried out in pain. He went home.

The house was complete, inside and out, two soaring wings flanking a low entrance with squat columns. It was set well back, with a lawn giving down to the road; from the veranda you saw the sun set bloody across the lake. Clive and his wife moved in. This was Solitaire now, not the smaller house where Isaac and Mrs Jameson still lived, and nothing in the region could rival, let alone equal it.

Now things moved fast. The young couple's first son, con-

ceived in Europe, was born in July. Then two more came in
rapid succession, in June and May of the following two years.
They were growing boys, the oldest already out of skirts,
when the war came. The younger Mrs Jameson saw her husband only between campaigns; at other times she heard of him
as everyone was doing, as the South and the North were hearing of him, the Starborn Brigadier, as the French peasants
heard of Bayard or the Hebrews the Angel of Death. When
he did come home — and he returned infrequently at first,
apparently to gather corn; he would drop back a hundred miles
with his cavalry brigade to harvest crops — it was like eating
and breathing and couching with an avatar or a thunderbolt.
At table he wore an aura of battle fury and shell glare, like
brimstone, as bakers at home disseminate an atmosphere of
flour and baking bread.

That was their marriage, up to the midpoint of the war,
when the fighting was still decked with plumes and roses. At
the time the house was building, Isaac — past seventy, nearing
eighty — could look back on a life divided neatly into two
unequal compartments, the first containing fifty years of wildness and the second containing twenty-odd — nearly thirty —
years of domesticity, with marriage like an airtight door between them. Now, though he did not know it and could have
done nothing about it anyhow, he was moving toward another
door which led to a third compartment, less roomy than either
of the other two, with a closer atmosphere, even stifling in
the end, and more different from both of the previous two
than those two had been different from each other. In a sense
beyond longevity he led three lives in one.

Since 1850, the year of the Compromise, planters in the lake
region had been talking disunion. As a topic for discussion it
had crowded out the weather and even the cotton market.
Seated on their verandas or in their parlors, clutching juleps
in their fists, they blustered. They had built their fine big
neo-Tidewater houses, displaying them to their neighbors and
whoever passed along the lakeside road, each as a sort of patent

of nobility, a claim to traditions and ancestry which they for the most part lacked. Insecurity had bred a semblance of security, until now no one questioned their right to anything at all. When Lincoln was nominated in 1860 they took it as a pointed insult. Not that they believed he would be elected; no; "Never in all this world," they said. "Those abolitionist scoundrels just want to flaunt this ape in our faces for the purpose of watching our reaction. Yes. Well, we'll show them something in the way of action they havent bargained for, if they dont watch out. Let them be warned," they added solemnly.

They admired the spirit and emulated the manner of the Texas senator, an ex-South Carolinian with a reputation as a duelist, who said to his Northern fellow-senators, smiling as he said it though not in friendliness at all: "The difficulty between you and us, gentlemen, is that you will not send the right sort of people here. Why will you not send either Christians or gentlemen?"

"Wigfall knows how to treat them," the planters said. That was the Texas senator's name. "A few more like him and Preston Brooks and we'd have this hooraw hushed."

But Isaac, who had fought under Andrew Jackson at New Orleans and followed his politics ever since, believed in the Union in much the same way as Jackson had believed in it. He thought sectional differences could be solved better within the Union than outside it. At first he would say so, with the others watching him hot-eyed over the frosted rims of goblets. Later he saw that it was no use. Like much of the rest of the nation, they were determined to have violence as the answer to some deep-seated need, as actual as thirst.

Clive took little or no part in these discussions which went on all around him. He had come home from the Institute with a soldier's training, but now he was busy learning the life of a planter; the slate-gray uniforms and the tactics texts had been folded away in a trunk with the unblooded sword. He was closer to his mother than he was to Isaac, and closer now to his wife than he had ever been to either of his parents.

He was quiet, indeed somewhat vague in his manner, with gentle eyes; his way now was very little different, in fact, from the way in which he had moved among the Bristol matrons and fanned their hopes with his almost casual attentiveness. It was as if, here too, he knew his worth, and what was more it was as if he knew that this state, too, was temporary. He loved horses and spent much of his time in the stables. Behind the softness of his eyes and voice there was something wild that matched the wildness of horses, and this was where he most resembled his father.

Then Lincoln was elected — the planters had said it would never happen; "Never in all this world," they said — and South Carolina seceded, followed within two weeks by Mississippi and then the others among the Deep South fire-eater states. That was in January; again there was a speed-up of events. Moderation was gone now, what little had remained. Clive even heard from the Institute that the chalkdusty Professor Jackson, a Mexican War veteran himself, had stood up in chapel and made a speech; "Draw the sword and throw away the scabbard!" he had cried. It did not sound at all like him, but anything was believable in these times. Two months later, a month before Sumter was fired on, Clive rode off as captain of a cavalry troop formed by the lake planters and their sons. With their wagons, their spare mounts and body servants, they made a long column; their ornaments flashed in the sunlight.

Nearly all of them returned within four months, not as a unit but in straggling twos and threes. It was the common end of all such 'elite' organizations; they had not expected war to be like that. The excitement lasted not even as long as the glitter of their collar ornaments. Once it was gone they thought they might as well come home. They had seen no fighting anyhow. It was mostly drill and guard mount, patrolling encampments while the infantry slept, moving from place to place, then back again. The glory had departed, and so did they. Some of them stayed at home through the next two years, under the twenty-Negro clause of the Conscription Act, which provided that any man who owned as many as twenty slaves would be needed at home to work them, producing goods and feedstuffs for the armies. One or two went to Europe, expanding their horizons through the war years; you saw them in Heidelburg and Paris, wearing the garb of students, bitter and dangerous, quick to engage in duels — or anyhow fist-fights — defending the honor of the Confederacy in sidewalk café arguments. Most of them, however, after the original sally (which had been mainly social, so to speak) returned to the army with sobered judgments. They fought hard and well and came to manhood, those who survived.

So it was with Clive. He came home, his uniform and saber sash a bit faded from the weather. Isaac came out to meet him in the yard, looking somehow more military in broadcloth than his son looked in uniform. They stood looking at each other. "How did it go?" Isaac asked him.

"It went all right, considering. There just wasnt anything to do."

"You wanted it another way. Was that it?"

"I didnt want it the way it was. We disbanded piecemeal, man by man. They would come and say they were leaving. Then theyd leave. Finally there were less than a dozen of us; so we left too. We made it official."

They stood facing each other in the hot summer sunlight; First Manassas had been fought two weeks ago. Clive was smiling. Isaac did not smile. "And what are you going to do now?" he asked. "Stay here and farm the place?"

"I might."

"So?"

"I might. . . ."

"So?"

"No, papa. I'll go back. But different."

"So," Isaac said.

He stayed ten days, and then he left again. This time he went alone. Within two years Clive Jameson was one of the sainted names of the Confederacy. It began when he came out of Donelson with Forrest, escaping through icy backwater saddle-skirt deep. Then he distinguished himself at Shiloh, leading a cavalry charge against the Peach Orchard and another at Fallen Timbers after the battle; Beauregard cited him as one of the heroes of that field. By the time of Vicksburg, in the summer of '63, newspapers were beginning to print the story of his life. Southern accounts always mentioned his having been born the year the stars fell; Starborn, one called him, and the others took it up. Poetesses laureate in a hundred backwoods counties submitted verse in which they told how he had streamed down to earth like a meteor to save the South; they made much of the flaming wake. Northern accounts, on the other hand — like the Bristol matrons at the time when his engagement to the lawyer's daughter was announced — made much of the fact that his mother had tended bar in her father's taproom.

He never wrote. Though for the first two years he would drop back occasionally to glean corn for his horses and men, once the Vicksburg Campaign was underway they heard of him only as everyone was doing, by word of mouth and in the papers and in the cheap, laudatory books that were beginning to pour from presses all over the country. They did not see him again until late in '63 when he was wounded at Chickamauga, his fifth but his first really serious wound, and was brought home in an ambulance to recover. He was still a young man, just past his thirtieth birthday, but he looked older than his years. It was as if the furnace of war had baked the flesh of his hard, handsome face, which by now was tacked in replica on cabin walls, badly reproduced pen-and-ink sketches clipped from newspapers, and mooned over by girls in attic bedrooms. The softness had gone from his eyes and voice. He did not resemble himself; he resembled his pictures. Having him at Solitaire was like having a segment of some actual blasted battlefield at hand. His mother, after an hour with him, came away shaking her head. "What have they done to my boy?" she asked.

"He's a hero," Isaac said. He had seen and known heroes before. "What did you expect?"

Clive mended fast, however, and soon after the first of the year he rode away. They heard of his raid into Kentucky that spring — 'brilliant' was the word that appeared most frequently in the newspaper accounts; the columns bristled with it, alongside 'gallant' — and in June he led his brigade in the attack that crumpled Grierson's flank at Brice's Crossroads and sent the invaders stumbling back to Memphis. The papers were full of it, prose and verse. His wife had left Solitaire by then, taking the three sons with her to the coastal resort where they spent the final year of the war being spoiled by guests and casual visitors. "What! these the gallant Jameson's heirs? Stand up, boys, and let us look at you!"

Isaac and Mrs Jameson did not leave; they stayed on. When Clive's wife left, and then all but a handful of the servants, Mrs Jameson closed the big house completely, boarding the windows, and sealed off the upper story of her own house. She and Isaac lived downstairs. She was fifty-six, an active, bustling woman who got things done. She still had the yellow hair and even the beautifully rounded arms, but she was subject to dizzy spells, which she called the Vapors, and during such an attack her mind would wander. She would imagine the war was over and her son was dead. A moment later, though, she would sigh and say, "I'm glad he's doing well, but I wish they would let him come home for a while. I really do."

She never thought of him the way he had been when he was there with his Chickamauga wound. In her mind she saw him as he had been when he rode away that first time, in the spring of '61, with the soft voice and gentle eyes, or as he was in the daguerreotype which she kept on the night table beside her bed. It had been taken when he was a child; he wore button shoes and ribbed stockings and a jacket of watered silk, and there was a small-boy sweetness in his face. Sometimes in the night Isaac would wake to find the candle burning at the bedside and Mrs Jameson sitting bolt-upright, propped on three pillows, with the picture in her hands. There would be tears in her eyes, like the ones that followed the death of their first child, and if he spoke to her at such a time she would turn and look at him with the face of a stranger.

On a hot July morning she was waxing the dining room table — a task she had always reserved for herself because it gave her a particular pleasure; the table had been her first purchase on the Memphis wedding trip — when suddenly she paused and a peculiar expression came over her face, the expression of someone about to sneeze. Then she did; she sneezed loudly. "God bless me," she said, automatically, and went on with her work, applying the wax in long, even strokes. Presently she raised one hand to her forehead, palm outward, fingers relaxed. "I feel so dizzy," she said. She looked frightened. Isaac reached her just as she fell. He carried her to a couch in the living room and knelt beside her, patting her wrists. Her breath came in harsh stertorous groans.

"Katy!" Isaac kept saying. "Katy, dont you know me?"

She did not know him; she did not know anything. Foam kept forming on her lips and Isaac wiped it away with his handkerchief. Two Negroes stood in the background. There was nothing they could do. All the doctors were off to war, but that was just as well since there was nothing they could have done either. It was a cerebral hemorrhage and she died within four hours.

Next day they buried her in the cedar grove, at the near end of the row of small, weathered crosses, beside the one she had cried hardest over. Isaac was dry-eyed at the burial; he did not seem to understand what had happened. He was bewildered at last by mortality, by a world in which a person could sneeze and say, "God bless me: I feel dizzy," and then be dead. He was eighty-six years old.

All but three of the slaves had left by then, gone on their own or as dish-washers and ditch-diggers with the Union armies which had roamed the district at will and without real opposition since early '64. There was Edward, the butler, who was almost seventy, the last of the original ten who had come with Isaac in the Conestoga north from Natchez. He was stone deaf, a tall, straight-backed Negro, part Choctaw — his full name was Edward Postoak — mute and inscrutable behind his wall of dignity and deafness. The other two were women; both were old, one lame (she did the cooking, what there was to cook) and the other half-witted. These three lived in one of the cabins that formed a double row, called the Quarters, half a mile behind the house. The other cabins were empty, beginning to dry rot from disuse, and the street between the rows, formerly grassless, polished by generations of bare feet until it was almost as smooth and shiny as a ballroom floor, was beginning to spring up in weeds. When Mrs Jameson died Edward moved into the house with Isaac. Five weeks later the two women joined them because a Federal platoon, out on patrol, burned the Quarters.

That was in August. Near sundown the platoon made bivouac in a pasture near the house. The cooks set up their kitchen and sent out a three-man detail for firewood. They were tearing up the floorboards in one of the cabins, the planks making sudden, ripping sounds like musketry, when one of the soldiers happened to glance up and see a tall yellow woman, her face pitted with old smallpox scars, standing in the doorway watching them. She clasped her wrists over her stomach and watched them gravely. It gave him a start, finding her there like that without having heard her approach.

"Yawl bed not be doing that," she said when the soldier looked at her.

The others paused too, now. They stood leaning forward with half-ripped planks in their hands. Their uniforms were dusty, still sweaty from marching all that afternoon. "Why not, aunty?" the first said. His speech was Southern, though obviously from north of Mississippi.

"I'll tell Mars Ike and he'll tell his boy: thats why. And the genril he'll come back and git you, too, what time he hears you messing with his belongings like you doing."

They resumed their work, tearing up the floorboards with a splintering, ripping sound, and the sunlight slanting through the western window was filled with dust-motes. Then one of them said casually, "What general would that be, aunty?"

"Genril Cli Jameson, Mars Ike's boy. You see if I dont."

Again they paused, once more with the ends of half-ripped planks in their hands. But this time it was different. They looked at her, all three together, and something like joy was registered on their faces. "Does this belong to him, that house and all these shanties?"

"Does indeed, and you best quit or I'll tell him. I'm a mind to tell him anyhow, the way yawl acting."

"Well," the first said, still not moving, still bent forward. "Well, well. What do you know."

Then he moved. He finished prizing up the plank he had hold of, took a jackknife from his pocket, one of the big horn-handled ones the suttlers sold in such volume every payday, and began to peel shavings from the edge of the plank. It was cypress, long since cured, and the shavings came off straight and clean, a rich pink almost red. The other two watched him for a moment, puzzled. Then they understood and began to do the same, taking out their knives and peeling shavings from other planks. They worked in silence, all three together. They were from a Tennessee Union regiment — what their enemies called home-made Yankees. All three had week-old beards.

"That damned butcher," the third said. He had not spoken until now. "Aint it funny what luck will sometimes throw your way?"

The woman watched them without understanding, still with her hands crossed on the bulge of her stomach, while one of the soldiers scraped the shavings into a small pile in one corner of the room. He laid planks across it, first the split ones and then whole ones, building a tepee of lumber. When he had finished this he took a tinder box from the pocket of his blouse, then bent and struck it so that a shower of sparks fell into the heart of the little heaped-up pile of cypress shavings. At first it merely smoked and glowed. Suddenly a flame leaped up, bright yellow, then orange, then rose-colored, licking the wall of the cabin.

"Yawl bed not be doing that," the woman said again, her voice as flat, as inflectionless as at the start.

The soldiers stood watching the fire. When it was burning nicely they gathered up the remainder of their ripped-up floorboards and started for the pasture where by now the cook had begun to beat with a big spoon against the bottom of a dishpan to hurry them along. One paused at the foot of the steps, turning with the bundle of planks on his shoulder. The others stopped beyond him, looking back and smiling as he spoke. "Tell him thats for Fort Pillow, aunty. Tell him it's from the friend of a man who was there."

Fifteen minutes later Isaac and Edward and the lame cook, and presently the half-witted woman too, stood on the back gallery and watched the Quarters burn. "I told um not to, plain as I'm standing here talking to you right now," the woman said. There was no wind, not a breath; the flames went straight up with a sucking, roaring sound like the rush of something passing at great speed. Even deaf Edward, though he could not hear it, felt its deep murmuring whoosh against his face. He turned his head this way and that, as if he had recovered his hearing after all those years of silence.

The Federal platoon, the men in collarless fatigue blouses and galluses, many of them smoking pipes while they waited for supper, gathered at the back of the pasture to watch the progress of the fire. They leaned their elbows on the top rail of the fence, and as the dusk came on and the flames spread from cabin to cabin along the double row, flickering brighter and brighter on their faces, they made jokes at one another up and down the line. Soon the cook beat again on the dishpan with the spoon and they lined up with messkits in their hands. The fire burned on. It burned steadily into the night,

its red glow reflected against the underside of the pall of
smoke hanging over the plantation. From time to time a roof
fell in, occasionally two together, and a bright rush of sparks
flew upward in a fiery column that stood steadily upright for
a long moment, substantial as a glittering pillar of jeweled
brass supporting the black overhang of smoke, before it paled
and faded and was gone.

Next morning when Isaac came out of the house he found
the pasture empty, the soldiers gone, with only an unclosed
latrine and a few charred sticks of the cookfire to show they
had been there at all. He walked down to where the quarters
had been, and there were only the foundation stones and the
toppled chimneys, the bricks still hot among the cooling ashes.
The cabins had been built during the ten-year bachelor period
between his arrival and his marriage (Memzy, who butted
heads with bulls, had been chief carpenter; he was gone now,
one of the first to leave) — sixteen cabins, two rows of eight,
put up during the ten-year span by a five-man building team
who snaked the big cypress out of a slough, split them with
axes and crosscut saws for timbers and planks and shingles
and even pegs to save the cost of nails. They had been good
cabins, snug in winter, cool in summer, built to last; they had
seen forty years of living and dying, laughing and weeping,
arrival and departure. Now they were gone, burned overnight,
casualties of the war.

As he turned at the end of the double row, starting back,
a great weariness came over him. He stood there for a moment,
arms loose at his sides, then returned to the house. He went
up the steps and across the gallery. In the kitchen a strange
thing happened to him.

The cook was boiling something on the stove, stirring it
with a long-handled spoon, and as he came past he intended
to ask her, 'Is breakfast ready?' But that was not what he said.
He said, "Is breck us riding?"

"Sir?"

He tried again. "Has bread abiding?"

"Sir?" The cook looked at him. She had turned sideways, still bent forward over the pot, and the spoon dripped a thin white liquid. It was cornmeal mush; she would boil it to a thicker consistence, then cook it into cakes to be served with sorghum. With her crooked leg, bowed back, and lips collapsed about her toothless mouth so that her nose and chin were brought into near conjunction, she resembled a witch. "Sir?" she said.

Isaac made a gesture of impatience and went on toward the front of the house. His arms and legs were trembling; there was a pulsing sensation in his head, immediately behind his eyes, a throbbing produced by pressure. Something is happening to me! he thought. He could think the words clearly: 'Is breakfast ready?' but when he tried to say them they came out wrong. Words came out that were not even in his mind as he spoke. Something has happened to me! he thought.

These were the first signs of motor aphasia, the words coming wrong from his tongue. They were not always wrong; sometimes he could speak with no trouble at all. But sooner or later a word or a phrase, unconnected with what he intended to say, would substitute itself. Then the lame cook or the half-witted woman, who was supposed to be the housemaid but who actually did nothing, would look at him with puzzled eyes. "Sir?" they would say, feeling awkward. They did not know whether it was a mishap or a joke; they did not know whether to worry or to laugh. So Isaac avoided them, preferring the company of Edward, who did not hear him anyhow, whether the words were correct or wrong, accurate or garbled.

Mostly, though, he kept to himself, avoiding any need for speech. His favorite pastime now was to walk eastward beyond the burnt-out quarters and on to where the Choctaw village had been, the pottery center with its clay deposit which he in his turn had used for making bricks. He remembered the Indians from fifty years ago, going north in their filthy blankets, braves and squaws, dispossessed by a race of men who were not only more cunning but who backed their cunning with gunpowder and whiskey. They were gone now, casualties not of war but of progress, obsolete, and had left no sign of their passing except the shards of pottery and arrowheads turned up by plowmen, the Indian mounds scattered at random about the land for archeologists to guess at, and an occasional lift to the cheekbones in a Negro face and a cocoa tint to the skin.

Isaac had never been one for abstract thinking; but now, reft of his vocation by the war, of his wife by death, and of speech by whatever had gripped his brain and tongue, he asked himself certain questions. It was as if, now that he could no longer voice them, the words came to him with great clarity of mind. Remembering the Indian days, the exodus, he applied what he remembered to the present, to himself. Was it all for nothing, the distances, the ambition, and the labor? He and his kind, the pioneers, the land-grabbing hungry rough-shod men who had had, like the flatboat river bullies before them, that curious combination of bravado and deadly earnestness, loving a fight for the sake of the fight itself and not the outcome — were they to disappear, having served their purpose, and leave no more trace than the Choctaws? If so, where was the dignity of man, to be thrown aside like this, a worn-out tool? He remembered the land as it was when he first came, a great endless green expanse of trees, motionless under the press of summer or tossing and groaning in the winds of spring and fall. He ringed them, felled them, dragged them out; he fired the stumps so that the air was hazed with the blue smoke of their burning, and then he had made his lakeside dream a reality; the plowmen came, the cotton sprouted, and he prospered; until now. The earth, he thought, the earth endures. He groped for the answer, dealing with such abstract simplicities for the first time since childhood, back before memory. The earth, he thought, and the earth goes back to the sun; that was where it began. There is no law, no reason except the sun, and the sun doesnt care. Its only concern is its brightness; we feed that brightness like straws dropped into its flame. Fire! he thought suddenly. It all goes back to fire!

At last he gave up the walks and spent his days in a big armchair in the parlor, keeping the curtains drawn. He had nothing to do with anyone but the deaf butler, with whom speech was not only unnecessary but impossible. Edward brought him food on a tray, such as it was—mostly the cakes of boiled-down gruel, with sorghum and an occasional piece of sidemeat — but Isaac scarcely touched it. He lost weight; the flesh hung loose on his big frame; his temples were concave, his eyes far back in their sockets. Sometimes, alone in the darkened parlor, he tried to form words aloud, listening to what came out when he spoke. But it was worse than ever. Often, now, the sounds were not even words. I'm talking in the tongues, he thought, remembering the revivals and sanctifyings he had attended around Natchez as a young man, a scoffer on the lookout for excitement. He had seen and heard whole creekbanks full of people writhing and speaking gibberish — 'the tongues' they called it; they claimed to understand each other in such fits. God had touched them, they said.

Maybe God had touched him too, he thought. He had never been religious, never having felt the need for it — not even now, when a general revival was spreading through the armies and the civilian population of the South — yet he knew nothing of aphasia, either by name or contact, and it seemed to him there must be some reason why he had been stricken like the fanatics on the creekbank; there must be some connection. But if it was God it was punishment, since it had not come through faith. He must be under judgment, just as maybe the whole nation was, having to suffer for the double sin of slavery and mistreatment of the land. Presently, however, this passed and he let it go; he stopped considering it at all, and he stopped trying to talk. He went back to his previous conviction. No, no, he thought, alone in the parlor with the curtains drawn. It's the sun and we go back there, back to fire.

In late October, a time of heat — the long hot summer of

'64 had held; dust was everywhere over the empty fields — he was sitting in the armchair and he heard footsteps on the driveway. There was a chink of spurs, then boot-heels coming hard up the front steps. They crossed the veranda. For a moment there was silence, then a rapping of knuckles against the door jamb. A voice: "Hello!" Another silence, somehow more pregnant than the one before. And then: "Hello in there!"

To Isaac all this seemed so loud that even Edward must have heard it. But when he turned and looked at him he saw that the butler was still locked behind his wall of deafness; he stood beside Isaac's chair, looking morosely at nothing at all. He had a toothache and the cook had put a wad of cotton soaked in camphor inside his cheek, binding the bulged jaw with a dinner napkin tied at the crown of his head. It was one of Mrs Jameson's best pieces of linen, big and heavy, and the two corners of the folded napkin stood up stiffly from the knot.

While Isaac watched, the Negro turned his face toward the door, his eyes coming suddenly wide with surprise. Then Isaac heard the voice again, the crisp Northern accent: "Didnt you hear me out there?" Footsteps approached and the voice began again, repeating the question, but was cut off by a surprised intake of breath. Then Isaac saw him. A Federal officer, complete with sword and sash and buttons stamped US, stood on the hearth. They looked at one another.

Isaac saw that the officer was a young man — rather hard-looking, however, as if the face had been baked in the same crucible that had hardened and glazed the face of his son Clive — and he thought: It's something the war does to them; North and South, they get this way after a time because now-days the wars go on too long. Then as they looked at each other, one on the hearth and the other in the chair, Isaac knew why the officer was there. He steadied himself to speak, intending to say, 'Have you come to burn my house?' But it did not come out that way; he spoke again in the tongues.

The lieutenant, whose rank Isaac saw when he bent forward, listened to Edward's explanation of the garbled language, then said carefully: "I have come to give you notice, notification." He paused, cleared his throat, and continued. He spoke carefully, not as if he were choosing his words, however, but as if from a memorized speech. "In reprisal for sniping, by a party or parties unknown, against the gunboat *Starlight* at sundown yesterday, I inform you now, by order of Colonel Nathan Frisbie, United States Army, that this house has been selected to be burned. You have exactly twenty minutes."

Isaac sat watching the hard young face, the moving lips, the bars on the shoulders. The lips stopped, stern-set, but he still watched. "Fire," he said or intended to say. "It all began and ends in fire."

Full in our faces the big low blood-red disk of the sun rested its rim on the levee, like a coin balanced lengthwise on a knife edge. We marched westward through a wilderness of briers and canebrakes, along a road that had been cleared by the planters in their palmy days to haul cotton to the steamboat landing for shipment to New Orleans. The column had rounded the head of the lake and turned toward the river where the gunboat waited. Four miles in our rear, beyond the lake, the reflection of the burning house was a rose-and-violet glow to match the sunset in our front.

I rode beside the colonel at the head and the troops plodded behind in a column of fours. They marched at ease, their boots stirring the dust so that those in the center were hidden from the waist down and those at the tail showed only their heads and shoulders. Their rifle barrels, canted in all directions, caught the ruddy, almost level rays of the sun; the bayonets, fixed, appeared to have been blooded. They kept their heads lowered, their mouths tight shut, breathing through their noses. The only sounds were the more or less steady clank of equipment, the soft clop clop of horses' hoofs, and the shuffle of shoes in the dust. It somehow had an air of unreality in the failing light.

While the upper half of the sun still showed above the dark knife edge of the levee we approached a live-oak spreading its limbs above a grassy space beside the road. Colonel Frisbie drew rein and raised one arm to signal a halt. The troops came to a jumbled stop, like freight cars. Then the sergeant advanced and stood beside the colonel's horse, waiting. He was short and muscular, thick-chested and very black, with so little neck that his head seemed to rest directly on his shoulders. "Ten minutes," the colonel told him.

The sergeant saluted, holding it stiffly until the colonel returned it, then faced about. The troops stood in the dust of the road. He drew himself up, taking a deep breath. "De-tail: ten *shut!*" He glared. "Ground — harms!" The rifle butts came down in a drawn-out series of thuds. The sergeant glared still harder, put his fists on his hips, then took them down again. "Now see can you do it right for a change. Right shoulder: shift! Make it pretty, now. Ground — *harms!*" The rifle butts came down in unison, sliding silently into the dust. "Yair," the sergeant said quietly. Then, raising his voice once more, he said to the troops still standing at attention, ankle deep in the thick dust of the road: "When I say fall-out, keep ready to fall back in. Fall out!"

Dismounting, the colonel smiled. "Good man," he said. "That comes of having trained him myself."

"Yes sir," I said.

The platoon fell out, coming apart almost unwillingly, like something coming unglued. Colonel Frisbie often declared that, properly trained and led, Negro troops made "the finest soldiers on the planet, bar none," and when he was given command of the *Starlight* he set out to prove his contention by supplying the proper training and leadership. Now he was satisfied; it was no longer a theory, it was a fact. The corporal-orderly took our horses and we crossed the grass and sat with our backs against the trunk of the live-oak. I was glad to rest my knee.

High in the branches a blue jay shrilled and chattered. The colonel looked up, searching, and finally found him. "Isnt today Friday?"

"Yes sir," I said.

"Thought so. Then here's another case of these people not knowing what theyre talking about. They say you never see a jay on a Friday because thats the day theyre all in hell getting instructions from the devil. And they believe it, too — I dont exaggerate." He nodded. Ever since he had heard the fable he had been spending a good part of every Friday watching for a blue jay. It bothered him for a while that he could not find one. But now he had, and he felt better; he could move on to something else, some other old wives' tale to disprove. "I suppose while we're whipping the rebelliousness out of them we'd do well to take out some of the superstition along with it. Hey?"

"Yes sir," I said.

He went on talking and I went on saying Yes Sir every time I heard his voice rise to a question. But I was not listening; I could not have repeated a word he said just then. My mind was back on the other side of the lake, where the reflection of the burning house grew brighter against the darkling sky — remembering, then and now:

When I had finished my recitation — "selected to be burned. You have exactly twenty minutes" — the old man looked up at me out of a face that was older than time. He sank back into the chair. "Far," he said; "It goes back far," and gave no other sign that he had understood or even heard what I said. I left the house, went back down the driveway to where the troops crouched in loose circles, preparing to eat the bread and meat, the midday meal they had brought in their haversacks.

Colonel Frisbie was waiting. "What did they say in there?" he asked.

"It was an old man. . . ."

"Well?"

"Sir?"

"What did he say?"

"He didnt say anything. He just sat there."

"Oh?" the colonel said, turning to accept a packet of sand-wiches from the orderly. This was officers' food. "Well. Maybe for once we've found one who admits he deserves what he's going to get. Or maybe it's not his." He opened the packet, selected a sandwich, and extended the rest toward me. "Here." I shook my head but he insisted. "Go on. Take one." I took one — it was mutton — then sat with it untasted in my hand.

The colonel ate rapidly and efficiently, moving his jaw with a steady sidewise thrust and taking sips from his canteen between bites. When he had eaten a second sandwich he took out his watch, opened the heavy silver case, and laid it face-up on his knee. Soon afterwards he picked it up again; he rose, brushed crumbs from the breast of his uniform, looked hard at the watch for a few more seconds, then snapped it shut with a sharp, decisive click.

"All right, Mr Lundy," he said. "Time's up."

I reentered the house with the sergeant and ten of the men. From the hall I saw the butler still standing in the parlor beside the fanback chair where the old man sat. At a sign from the sergeant, two of the soldiers took position on opposite sides of the chair, then lifted the old man, chair and all, and carried him through the hall, out of the door and across the porch, and set him down at the foot of the lawn, near the road and facing the front of the house. The butler walked alongside, his pink-palmed hands fluttering in time with the tails of his clawhammer coat, making gestures of caution. "Keerful, yawl," he kept saying in the cracked, off-key voice of the deaf. "Be keerful, now." The napkin-end rabbit ears had broken. One fell sideways, along his jaw, and the other down over his face. He slapped at it from time to time to get it out of his eyes as he stood watching the soldiers set the chair down.

What followed was familiar enough; we had done this at many points along the river between Vicksburg and Memphis, the Walnut Hills and the Lower Chickasaw Bluff, better than two dozen times in the course of a year. The soldiers went from room to room, ripping curtains from the windows and splintering furniture and bed-slats for kindling. When the sergeant reported the preparations complete, I made a tour of inspection, upstairs and down — the upstairs had been closed off for some time now; dust was everywhere, except in one room which apparently was used by one of the servants. At his shouted command, soldiers in half a dozen rooms struck matches simultaneously. (A match was still a rarity but we received a special issue for our work, big sulphur ones that sputtered at first with a great deal of smoke and stench till they burned past the chemical tip.) Then one by one they returned and reported to the sergeant. The sergeant in turn reported to me, and I gave the order to retire. It was like combat, and all quite military; Colonel Frisbie had worked out the procedure in a company order a year ago, with subparagraphs under paragraphs and a time-schedule running down the margin.

From the lawn, where we turned to watch, the house appeared as peaceful, as undisturbed as it had been before we entered. But soon, one after another, wisps of smoke began to laze out, and presently a lick of flame darted and curled from one of the downstairs windows. As I stood watching the flames begin to catch, I let my eye wander over the front of the house and I saw at an upper window the head and shoulders of a Negro woman. I could see her plainly, even the smallpox scars on her face. She did not seem excited. In fact she seemed quite calm, even decorous, sitting there looking out over the lawn where the soldiers by now were beginning to shout and point: "Look yonder! Look up yonder!"

I ran toward the house. The smoke and flames were mostly from the draperies and splintered furniture, I saw as I entered the hall again, but the smoke was thick enough to send me into a fit of coughing and I saw the staircase through a haze of tears. Climbing at a stumbling run I reached the upper hall. The smoke was less dense here; I managed to choose the door to the proper bedroom. It was not locked, as I had feared it might be. I was about to kick it in, but then I tried the knob and it came open.

The woman sat in a rocking chair beside the window. She had hidden behind some clothes in a closet while we searched and set fire to the house; then she had taken her seat by the window, and from time to time — the gesture was almost coy, coquettish — she raised one hand to wave at all the soldiers on the lawn. "Look yonder! Look up yonder!" they still shouted, pointing, and she waved back, flirtatious. When I stumbled into the room, half blinded by smoke, she turned and looked at me without surprise; I even had the impression that she had been waiting for me to join her.

"Shame," she said solemnly. She wagged a finger at me. "Shame on you, captain, for trying to burn Mars Ike's fine house. *I* seen you."

The tears cleared and I found myself looking into the woman's eyes. They were dark brown, almost black, the yellowed whites flecked with little points of red, and completely mad. Trapped in a burning house with a raving lunatic: it was something out of a nightmare. I was wondering how to get her to leave, whether to use force or try to persuade her, when she solved everything by saying in a hoarse whisper, as if in fear of being overheard: "Sh. Less us git out of here, fo they burns it." I nodded, afraid to speak because whatever I said might cause her to change her mind. I even bent forward, adopting her air of conspiracy. "Wait," she said. "I'll git my things."

While the flames crackled in an adjoining room, really catching now, she got what she called her 'things' — a big, brass-hinged family Bible and a cracked porcelain chamberpot with a design of overlapping rose leaves about its rim — and we went downstairs together through the smoke, which was considerably thicker now. "Look to me like they done already started to burn it," she said. As we came out onto the lawn the soldiers gave a cheer.

But I did not feel heroic. For one thing, there had been small

risk involved; and for another, even that small risk had
frightened me badly. The house continued to smoulder and
smoke, though little tongues of flame licked murmurous at
the sills. This went on for what seemed a very long time,
myself thinking as I watched: Go on, burn! Get it over; burn!
And then, as if in answer, a great billow of flame rushed from
a downstairs window, then another from another and another,
rushing, soaring, crackling like laughter, until the whole front
of the house was swathed in flames. It did not murmur now. It
roared.

Those nearest the house, myself among them, gave back from
the press of heat. It came in a rolling wave; our ears were
filled with the roaring until we got far enough back to hear a
commotion in progress at the opposite end of the lawn, near
the road. Turning, we saw what had happened.

The old man in the chair was making some sort of dis-
turbance, jerking his arms and legs and wagging his head. He
had been quiet up to this time, but now he appeared to be
making a violent speech. The soldiers had crowded around,
nudging each other and craning over one another's shoulders
for a better view. Then I got there and I saw what it was.
He was having a stroke, perhaps a heart attack. The butler,
still wearing the absurd napkin bandage about his jaws, stood
on one side of the chair; he bent over the old man, his hands out
toward him. On the other side were two women. One was
lame and witchlike except that now her eyes were round with
fright, the way no witch's ever were; I had not seen her before.
The other was the mad woman I had brought out of the burning house. She still clutched the brass-hinged Bible under one
arm, and with the other she had drawn back the chamberpot,
holding it by the wire handle and threatening the soldier on-
lookers with it. It was heavy and substantial looking, despite
the crack down its curved flank — a formidable weapon.
Brandishing it, she shouted at the soldiers.

"Shame!" she cried, not at all in the playful tone she had
used when she said the word to me in the house a few minutes

before. She was really angry now. Her smallpox-pitted face was distorted by rage, and her eyes were wilder than ever. "Whynt you bluebelly hellions let him be? Wicked! Calling yourself soldiers. Burners is all you is. Aint you hurt him enough aready? Shame on you!"

By the time I got there, however, the old man was past being hurt by anyone. The frenzy was finished, whether it came from the heart or the brain. He slumped in the chair, his legs thrust forward, knees stiff, and his arms dropped limp at his flanks, inside the chair arms. The only sign of life was the harsh breathing and the wide, staring eyes; he was going. Soon the breathing stopped, too, and I saw in the dead eyes a stereo-scopic reflection of the burning house repeated in double miniature. Behind me the flames soared higher, roaring, crack-ling. The lame woman dropped to her knees and began to wail.

These were things I knew would stay with me always, the sound of that scream, the twin reflection in those eyes. They were with me now as Colonel Frisbie stood over me, repeating my name: "Lundy. Mr Lundy!" I looked up, like a man brought suddenly out of sleep, and saw him standing straddle-legged in high dusty boots.

"Sir?"

"Come on, Lieutenant. Time to go." He turned and then looked back. "Whats the matter with you?"

"Yes sir," I said, not having heard the words themselves, only the questioning tone.

He turned back, and now for the first time in all the months I had known him, the pretense was gone; he was a man alone. "Whats the matter?" he said. "Dont you like me?"

It was out, and as soon as he had said it I could see that he had surprised himself even more than he had surprised me. He wished he could call the question back. But he stood there, still naked to the elements.

"Yes sir," I said. "I have come to feel very close to you through these past fourteen months."

I got up and walked to where the orderly held our horses.

Colonel Frisbie came on behind me; for a moment I had almost liked him; God knows he had his problems; but now he was himself again. The troops had already fallen into column on the road. We marched, and the sun was completely gone. Behind us the glow of burning had spread along the eastern sky. As we marched westward through a blue dusk the glow receded, drawing in upon itself. The colonel lit another cigar; its smoke had a strong, tarry smell as its ruby tip shone and paled, on and off and on and off, like a signal lamp. When he turned in the saddle, looking back, leather creaked above the muffled clopping of hoofs in the cooling dust.

"Looks lower," he said. He smoked, still looking back. The cigar glowed. I knew he was watching me, thinking about my answer to his question; he hadnt quite understood it yet. Then he turned to the front again. "Catch quick, burn slow. Thats the way those old ones always go."

I did not answer. I did not look back.

As we went up the levee, having crossed the swampy, cane-brake region that lay between the river and the lake — a wilderness belonging less to men than to bears and deer, alligators and moccasins, weird-screaming birds and insects that ticked like clocks in the brush — the colonel drew rein and turned his horse aside for the troops to pass. I took position alongside him on the crest, facing east toward where the reflection had shrunk to a low dome of red. Then suddenly, as we looked across the wilderness and the lake, the house collapsed and loosed a fountain of sparks, a tall column of fire that stood upright for a long minute, solid as a pillar outlined clearly against the backdrop of the night. It rose and held and faded, and the glow was less than before, no more than a gleam.

"Roof fell in," the colonel said. "Thats all, hey?"

I did not answer. I was seeing in my mind the dead face, the eyes with their twin reflection; I was hearing the lame woman scream; I was trying to remember something out of the Book of Job: *Yet man is born unto trouble, as the sparks fly upward.* And: *Man that is born of woman is of few days, and full of trouble. He cometh forth like a flower, and is cut down: he fleeth also as a shadow, and continueth not.* I was still trying to remember the words, but could not, when the last of the troops filed past. The words I remembered were those of the mad woman on the lawn. "Calling yourself soldiers," she said. "Burners is all you is." I twitched the reins, following Colonel Frisbie down the western slope of the levee, over the gangplank and onto the gunboat again.

THE SACRED MOUND

Province of Mississippi, A.D. 1797
Number 262: CRIMINAL

Against the Indian, Chisahahoma (John Postoak) *of the Choctaws, self-accused of the grisly murders of* Lancelot Fink *and*_____Tyree (*or* Tyree_____) *1796.*
Master Fiscal Judge, Mr John the Baptist of Elquezable, *Lieutenant Colonel and Governor.*

Scrivener,
Andrew Benito Courbiere.

DECLARATION: HEREIN SWORN & SUBSCRIBED. In the town of Natchez and garrison of St Iago, on the 23d day of September, 1797, I, Mr John the Baptist of Elquezable, Lieutenant Colonel of Cavalry and Provisional Governor of this said Province of Mississippi, proceeded to the house Royal of said town (accompanied from the first by Lieutenant Francisco Amangual and Ensign Joseph of Silva, both of the company of my office, as witnesses in the present procedure) where I found the prisoner Chisahahoma, a young man of the color of dusky copper, smallpox pitted, with hair cut straight along his forehead and falling lank to his shoulders at the back, who having been commanded to appear in my presence and in that of the said witnesses, before them had put to him by me the following interrogatories:

Question. What is he called, of what country is he a native, and what religion he professes? Answered that he is called Chisahahoma, that he is native to a region six sleeps north and also on the river, and that he is a Roman Catholic these nine months since the turning of the year. *Q.* Is he sufficiently acquainted with the Spanish language, or if he needs an interpreter to explain his declaration? Answered that he understood the language after a fashion and that if he doubted any question he would call for the advice of the interpreter. *Q.* If he would promise by our Lord God and the sign of the Cross to speak the truth concerning these interrogations? Answered that he would promise and swear, and did. And spoke as follows, making first the sign of the Cross and kissed his thumbnail:

Lo: truth attend his words, the love of God attend our understanding: all men are brothers. He has long wanted to cleanse his breast of the matter herein related, and has done so twice: first to the priest, as shall be told, then to the sergeant, answering his heart as advised by the priest, and now to myself makes thrice. His people and my people have lived in enmity since the time of the man Soto (so he called him, of glorious memory in the annals of Spain: Hernando de Soto) who came in his forefathers' time, appearing in May two sleeps to the north, he and his men wild-looking and hairy, wearing garments of straw and the skins of animals under their armor; who, having looked on the river, crossed westward and was gone twelve moons, and reappeared (in May again) three sleeps to the south, his face gray and wasted to the bone; and died there, and was buried in the river.

Desecration! his forefathers cried. Pollution!

So they fought: the strangers in armor, man and horse looking out through slits in the steel — of which he says rusty fragments survive in the long-house to commemorate the battle

where the Spaniards (he says) wore blisters on their palms with
excess of killing — swinging their swords and lances wearily
and standing in blood to the rowels of their spurs: and at last
retreated, marched away to the south, and were seen no more.

Then all was quiet; the young ones might have believed their
fathers dreamed it, except for the rusting bits of armor and
the horse skulls raised on poles in the long-house yard. Then
came other white men in canoes, wearing not steel but robes
of black with ropes about their waists, and bearing their slain
god on a cross of sticks, whose blood ran down from a gash in
his side: saying, Bow down; worship; your gods are false;
This is the true God! and sang strange songs, swinging utensils
that sprinkled and smoked, and partook of the wafer and a
thin blood-colored liquid hot to the throat; then went away.
But the Choctaws kept their gods, saying: How should we
forsake the one that made us of spit and straw and a dry handful of dust and sent us here out of Nanih Waiya? How should
we exchange Him for one who let himself be stretched on
sticks with nails through the palms of his hands and feet, a
headdress of thorns, pain in his face, and a spearpoint gash
in his side where the life ran out?

Q. Was he here to blaspheme? — for his eyes rolled back
showing only the whites and he chanted singsong fashion.
Answered nay, he but told it as it was in the dark time; he was
the Singer, as all his fathers had been. And continued:

Then came others down the years, also in boats — all came
by the river since Soto's time — but bearing neither the arque-
bus nor the Cross: bringing goods to trade, beads of colored
stuff and printed cloth and magic circles no bigger than the
inside of a hand, where sunlight flashed and a man could see
himself as in unspillable water; for which, all these, the traders
sought only the skins of animals in return. Now of all the
creatures of the field, only certain ones were worthy of being
hunted by a man: the bear, the deer, the broad-wing turkey —
the rest were left for boys. Yet the traders prized highest the
pelt of a creature not even a boy would hunt: the beaver: and
this caused his people to feel a certain contempt. Lo, too,

these strangers placed an undue value on women, for they
would force or woo a man's wife and lie with her, not asking
the husband's permission or agreeing beforehand on a price
or an exchange, and though they were liberal with their gifts
when the thing was done, there began to be not only contempt but also hard feelings in the breasts of his people.

So much was legend: he but told it as his father before
him told it, having it from the father before him, and so
on back. Yet what follows, he says, he saw with his own eyes
and heard with his ears; God be his witness. And continued,
no longer with his eyes rolled, speaking singsong, but as one
who saw and heard and now reported (making once more, in
attest of truth, the Cross upon his breastbone):

Two summers back, in the late heat of the year, spokesmen
arrived from many sleeps to the south, near the great salt river.
Three they were, the sons of chiefs, tall men sound of wind
and limb, sent forth by their fathers, saying: We have a thing
to impart. Will our brothers hear? That night they rested and
were feasted in the long-house, and runners went out to bring
in the chiefs. Next day as the sun went bleeding beyond the
river all assembled on the sacred mound, the leaders and the
singers (himself being one) and the three came forward, lean
with travel, clean-favored and handsome in feathers and paint,
upright as became the sons of chiefs, and the tallest spoke.
It is transcribed.

— Brothers: peace. We bring a message and a warning. May
you hear and heed and so be served. The white ones speak
with forked tongues, no matter what crown they claim their
great chief wears beyond the sea. We bring a warning of
calamity. It will be with you as it was with us, for they will do
as they have done. Thus. First they came boasting of their gods
and seeking a yellow metal in their various languages: Or,
they call it, or Oro. Then, in guile, they exchanged valuables
for the worthless pelts of animals, calling us Brother, and we
believed and answered likewise, Brother. And they lived among
us and shared our pipe and all was well between us. So we
thought.

— Then, lo, they began to ask a strange thing of us, seeking to buy the land. Sell us the land, they said: Sell us the land. And we told them, disguising our horror: No man owns the land; take and live on it; it is lent you for your lifetime; are we not brothers? And they appeared satisfied. They put up houses of plank and iron, like their ships, and sent back for their women. Soon they were many; the bear and the deer were gone (— they had seen and known in their hearts, without words; but we, being men with words, were blind) and the white men sent forth laws and set up courts, saying This shalt thou do and This shalt thou not do, and punishment followed hard upon offense, both the whip and the branding iron and often the rope. And we said, Can this be? Are we not brothers, to dwell in one land? And they answered, Yea: but this is Law.

— Nor was it long till the decree came forth, in signs on paper nailed to the walls of houses and even on trees, and the chiefs were called into the courts to hear it read. Go forth, the judges read: Go forth from the land, you and your people, into the north or beyond the river; for this land now is ours. And our fathers spoke, no longer trying to disguise the horror: How can this be? Are we not brothers? How can we leave this land, who were sent here out of Nanih Waiya to dwell in it forever down through time? And they answered, Howsomever.

— So it was and is with us, for our people are collecting their goods and preparing for the journey out. So too will it be with you. And soon; for this was all in our own time, and we are young.

I have spoken, the tallest said, and rejoined the circle. The chiefs sat smoking. Then another of the young men spoke, asking permission to retire to the long-house to sleep, for they had far to go tomorrow. And it was granted; they left, all three; and still the chiefs sat smoking.

The moon rose late, red and full to the rear of where the chiefs sat passing the pipe from hand to hand. But no one spoke, neither the chiefs on the mound nor the people below,

their faces back-tilted, looking up. Then one did speak —
Loshumitubbe, the oldest chief, with the hawk beak and thin
gray hair that his ears showed through, a great killer in his
day, and lines in his face like earth where rain has run: saying, Yea, the moon be my witness; we have offended, we have
strayed. This is not the cunning of the white man. This is
anger from the gods. They want it as it was in the old time.

So saying, he made a quick, downward motion with the pipe;
it might have been a hatchet or a knife. Some among them
understood, the older chiefs and the singers — he being one —
and nodded their heads, saying Yea, or smoked in silence. And
down at the base of the mound the people waited, faces pale
in the moonlight, looking up. After a term the chiefs spoke in
turn, grave-faced, drawing out the words, some for and some
against. By morning it was decided; they came down off the
mound with their minds made up.

Runners were sent one sleep to the north: five they were,
strung out along the river bank, a hard run apart. Three weeks
the people waited. It was cold and then it faired, the air hazy,
leaves bright red and yellow though not yet brown; it was
nearing the time of the corn dance, when a man's heart should
rejoice for the fruits of the earth. And the people said to one
another behind their hands, Can this thing be? (for such had
not been done since far before the time of the man Soto; not
even in that hard time, he says, was such a thing considered)
but others answered, not behind their hands but openly, proud
to have gone back: Yea, can and shall: Loshumitubbe says it.

Then came one running, the nearest of the five posted
along the river bank, running with his legs unstrung, and knelt
before Loshumitubbe, unable to speak but holding up two
fingers. Then he could speak, panting the words between
breaths: Two come by water. Trappers, O chief. In buckskin.

Here was a halt, the dinner hour being come. Next morning,
again at the house Royal, immediately I, the said Governor,

together with the aforesaid witnesses of my company, commanded to appear before me Chisahahoma, whom I found a prisoner in the care of the guard as before and still in bonds, who once more subscribed and swore the oath and resumed as follows, confronting the witnesses and Benito Courbiere, scrivener:

That night in the long-house they played the drum and painted, himself among them. Next morning they waited in the willows down at the river bank, again himself among them. For a long time, nothing. The sun went past the overhead; they waited. Then two together pointed, raising each an arm: Lo: for the trappers were rounding the bend in a canoe. Still they waited, knee-deep in the water, screened by willows, watching. The trappers held near to bank, seeking signs of game — one tall and slim; he sat in the stern, and the other short and fat; he was the older. They wondered if they could catch them, for his people had only dugouts: when suddenly the man in the bow stopped paddling. Lance! he shouted, and pointed directly at the willow clump. So he and his people bent their backs to launch out in pursuit. But the one in the stern changed sides with his paddle and the canoe swung crossways to the current, approaching. A sign from the gods, his people thought; their hearts grew big with elation. And when the two were within arm's length they took them so quickly they had not even time to reach for their rifles. Truly a sign from the gods! his people cried, and some began to leap and scream, squeezing their throats with their hands to make it shriller.

So the two were bound at the water's edge and brought up to the town, walking hunched for their wrists were strapped with rawhide at the crotch, one hand coming through from the rear and one from the front so they could not stand upright, though the tall one almost could; his arms were long. They were marched the length of the street, the smell of fear coming strong off the short one. Bent forward — his arms were short, his belly large — he turned his head this way and that, watch-

ing the gestures of the women hopping alongside, the pot-
bellied children staring round-eyed, and skipped to save his
ankles from the dogs; twice he fell and had to be lifted from
the dust. The tall one, however, kept his eyes to the front.
The dogs did not snap at him, for even bound he was half a
head taller than any Indian.

Hi! the women shouted: Hi! A brave! and made gestures of
obscenity, fanning their skirts. Hi! Hi!

The chiefs sat in the council room, wearing feathers and
paint in gaudy bars, and the two were brought before them.
Now they looked at each other, chiefs and trappers, and no
one spoke. Then Loshumitubbe made a gesture, the hand palm
down, pushing downward, and they were taken to the pit room
at the far end of the long-house. It was dark in there, no fire;
the only light was what fell through the paling disk of the
smoke hole. The cries of the women came shrill through the
roof, mixed with the yapping of dogs. The time wore on.
From outside, he says, they began to hear the short one
weeping, asking questions in his language, but the tall one
only cursed him, once then twice, and then ignored him.

So it was: they on the outside, waiting for the moon to fill,
knowing: the trappers on the inside, in the pit, waiting but not
knowing. Seven suns they were in there, feeding like hogs
on broken bits of food flung through the smole hole — for
they remained bound, the rawhide shrinking on their wrists,
and had to grovel for it. They fouled themselves and were gut-
sick on the scraps, he says, and the stench was so great that
the women approaching the hole to taunt them held their
noses and made sqealing sounds. From outside, listening, his
people heard words in the strange language: at first only the
short one, calling the other Fink or Lance and sometimes
Lancelot: then later, toward the close, the tall one too, calling
the short one Tyree, though which of his two names this was
no man could say, not even now, for they were Americans, a
people whose names are sometimes indistinguishable, the last
from the first, since they name not necessarily for the saints.

At the end, however, they called to one another not by name
but by growls, for the food was scant and hard to find on the
dark earth floor; they fought for it like dogs, snapping their
teeth, still being bound.

Then, lo, the moon would be full that night. Long before
sundown the people were painted and ready, dressed as for the
corn dance. The young ones wore only breech clouts and
feathers, fierce with red and yellow bars of paint, but the older
ones brought out blankets rancid with last year's grease and
sweat. The cold had returned; the leaves were brown now,
falling, and they crackled underfoot. It was yet above freezing,
he says, and there was no wind, but the cold was steady and
bitter and sharp and a thick mist came rolling off the river.

The trappers were taken from the pit as soon as the sun was
gone. Their clothes were cut from their bodies and they were
sluiced with hot water to cleanse them of their filth; they stood
in only their boots and bonds, their hands purple and puffy
because the rawhide had shrunk on their wrists, their skin first
pink from the heat of the water, then pale gray, goose-fleshed,
and their teeth chattered behind their bluing lips. Then was
when they saw that the short one was covered with what
appeared to be louse bites, small hard red welts like pimples.
The time in the pit had changed them indeed, and not only in
appearance. For now it was the tall one who kept glancing
about, shifting his eyes this way and that, while the short one
stood looking down over his belly at his boots; he did not
care. Just as the tall one had used up his courage, so had the
short one exhausted his cowardice. Then at a signal the guards
took hold of their arms and they went toward the mound,
stepping stiff-kneed. The old men with blankets over their
shoulders walked alongside. The young men, wearing only
feathers and breech clouts, leaped and shouted, their breaths
making steam.

Atop the mound the chiefs were waiting, seated in a half
circle with a bonfire burning behind them for light. They
faced the stakes. One was a single pole with a rawhide thong

up high; the other was two low poles with a third lashed as a crosspiece at the height of a man's waist. Then the trappers were brought. From the flat top of the mound, he says, they could see torches burning in the lower darkness, spangling the earth, countless as stars, for the people had come from three sleeps around; they stood holding torches, looking up to where the bonfire burned against the night. The tall trapper was tied to the single stake, arms overhead, hands crossed so high that only the toes of his boots touched the earth — the tallest man they had ever seen, taller than ever, now, with skin as pale in the firelight as the underbark of sycamores in spring. The short trapper stood between the two low stakes, his wrists lashed to the crossbar on each side of his waist. Both were breathing fast little jets of steam, partly from having climbed the mound but mostly from fear; for now, he says, they knew at least a part of what they had been wondering all that long time in the darkness of the pit.

The moon rose, swollen golden red, and now the dancing began, the young men stepping pigeon-toed, shuffling dust, and Otumatomba the rainmaker stood by the fire with his knife. When the dancing was done he came forward, extending the knife flat on the palms of both hands, and Loshumitubbe touched it. The drums began. Then Otumatomba came slowly toward the short one, who was held by four of the dancers, two at the knees and two at the shoulders, bent backward over the crosspole. He did not struggle or cry out; he looked down his chest, past the jut of his belly, watching the knife. What follows happened so fast, he says, that afterwards looking back it seemed to have been done in the flick of an eye.

Otumatomba placed the point of the knife, then suddenly leaned against the handle and drew it swiftly across, a long deep slash just under the last left rib. So quick the eye could barely follow, his hand went in. The knife fell and the hand came out with the heart. It was meaty and red, the size of a fist, with streaks of yellow fat showing through the skin-sack; vessels dangled, collapsed and dripping, except the one at the top, which was dingy white, the thickness of a thumb, leading back through the lips of the gash. Then (there was no signal, he says; they knew what to do, for Otumatomba had taught them) the men at the shoulders pushed forward, bringing the trapper upright off the bar, and for a moment he stood looking down at his heart, which Otumatomba held in front of his chest for him to see. It did not pulse; it flickered, the skin-sack catching highlights from the fire, and it smoked a bit in the night air. That was all. The short one fell, collapsing; he hung with his face just clear of the ground, his wrists still tied to the crosspole.

Hi! a brave, he heard one say among the chiefs.

But that was all; the rest were quiet as the rainmaker took up the knife again and turned toward the tall one, lashed on tiptoe to the stake. As he drew closer the trapper began to swing from side to side, bound overhead at the wrists and down at the ankles. When Otumatomba was very near, the tall white naked man began to shout at him in his language: No! No! swinging from side to side and shouting hoarsely, until the rainmaker, with a sudden, darting motion like the strike of a snake, shot out one hand and caught hold: where-upon the trapper stopped swinging and shouted still more shrilly, like women in the longhouse at the death of a chief, in the final moment before the cutting began. While Otumatomba sawed with the knife, which seemed duller now and slippery with the blood of the other, the tall one was screaming, hysteri-cal like a woman in labor, repeating a rising note: Ee! Eee! Then he stopped. He stopped quite suddenly. Otumatomba stepped back and tossed the trapper's manhood at his feet. The trapper looked down — more than pain, his face showed grief, bereavement — and now he began to whimper. Blood ran down his thighs, curving over the inward bulge of his knees, and filled his boots. He was a long time dying and he died badly, still crying for mercy when he was far beyond it.

Again the young men danced. The moon sailed higher, silver now, flooding the mound. In the distance the river glided slow, bright silver too, making its two great curves. Then it was over; the dead were left to the bone-pickers. The chiefs rose, filing down the mound, and he heard Loshumitubbe say to one beside him:

This will stop them. This will make an end.

Yea, the other told him. This will stop them.

But some there were — himself among them: so he says — who shook their heads, now it was done and they had seen, asking themselves in their hearts: Were they savages, barbarians, to come to this?

Here was a halt, the hour being noon, and after the midday meal and the siesta we returned to the house Royal: I the Governor, together with the aforesaid witnesses and scrivener: before whom the prisoner Chisahahoma, in care of the guard, swore and subscribed and continued, making an end:

Sudden and terrible then came the curse on his people, the wrath of God. The moon was barely on the wane and they felt pain in their heads, their backs, their loins; their skin was hot and dry to the touch; dark spots appeared on their foreheads and scalps, among the roots of hair. The spots became hard-cored blisters; the burning cooled for a day and then returned, far worse, and the blisters (so he called them: meaning *pustules*) softened and there was a terrible itching. Some scratched so hard with their nails and fishbone combs that their faces and bodies were raw. Many died. First went Otumatomba the rainmaker, then Loshumitubbe chief of chiefs, he who had given the signal; men and women and children, so fast they died the bone-pickers had not time to scaffold them. They lay in the houses and in the street, self-mutilated, begging the god for sudden death, release from the fever and itching.

He himself was sick with the sickest, and thought to have died and wished for it; he too lay and hoped for death, but was spared with only this (passing his hand across his face) to show the journey he had gone. Then he lay recovering, the moon swelling once more toward the full. And he remembered the short trapper, the marks on his face and body when they brought him out of the pit, and he knew.

Then he was up, recovered though still weak, and was called before Issatiwamba, chief of chiefs now Loshumitubbe was dead. He too had been the journey; he too remembered the marks on the short trapper. The people still lay dying, the dead unscaffolded.

O chief, he said, and made his bow, and Issatiwamba said:

I have called; are you not the singer? This is the curse of the white man's god, and you must go a journey.

He left next morning, taking the trappers' canoe. Cold it was, approaching the turning of the year, with ice among the willows and overhead a sky the color of a dove's breast. He wore a bearskin and paddled fast to keep from freezing. The second day he reached the Walnut Hills, where the white man had a town, and went ashore. But there was no house for the white man's god; he was in the canoe, continuing downriver, before sunset. The fifth day he reached this place and came ashore, and here was the house of the white man's god and, lo! the God himself as he had heard it told and sung, outstretched and sagging, nailed to the wall and wearing a crown of thorns and the wound in his side and pain in his face that distorted his mouth so you saw the edges of the teeth. And he stood looking, wrapped in the bearskin.

Then came one in a robe of cloth, a man who spoke with words he could not understand. He made a sign to show he would speak, and the priest beckoned: Come, and he followed to the back of the house and through a door, and — lo again, a thing he had never seen before — here was an Indian wearing trousers and a shirt, one of the flatheads of the South, who acted as interpreter.

The priest listened while he told it as Issatiwamba had instructed. The Indians had killed in the Indian way, incurring the wrath of the white man's god; now was he sent for the white men to kill in the white man's way, thus to appease the god and lay the plague. So he told it, as instructed. The flat-head interpreted, and when it was done the priest beckoned as before: *Come*, and led the way through another door. He followed, expecting this to be the pit where he would wait. But lo, the priest put food before him: *Eat*, and he ate. Then he followed through yet another door, thinking now surely this would be the pit. But lo again, it was a small room with a cot and blankets, and the priest put his hands together, palm to palm, and laid his cheek against the back of one: *Sleep*. And he slept, still expecting the pit.

When he woke it was morning; he knew not where he was. The pit! he thought. Then he remembered and turned on his side, and the flathead stood in the doorway with a bucket in one hand, steaming, and soap and a cloth in the other. First he declined; it was winter, he said, no time to scrape away the crust. But the other said thus it must be, and when he had washed he led him to the room where he had eaten. He ate again, then followed the other to still a third room where the priest was waiting, and there again on the wall the god was hung, this time in ivory with the blood in bright red droplets like fruit of the holly. The three sat at table; the priest talked and the flathead interpreted, and all this time the god watched from the wall. Here began his conversion, he says, making yet again the sign of the Cross upon his person.

He heard of the Trinity, the creation, the Garden, the loss of innocence, and much else which he could not follow. When the priest later questioned him of what he had heard he found that he had not heard aright, for the priest had said there were three gods and one god; did that not make four? And the priest at first was angry: then he smiled. They had best go slow, he said, and began again, telling now of the Man-God, the redeemer, who died on the cross of sticks but would return. There was where he began to understand, for just as the Garden had been like Nanih Waiya, this was like the Corn God, who laid him down to rise again; perhaps they were cousins, the two gods. But the priest said no, not cousins, not cousins at all; and began again, in soft tones and with patience, not in anger. In time they needed the interpreter no more, for he believed and the words came to him; he understood; Christ Jesus had reached him, Whose strength was in His gentleness, Whose beginning was in His end. Winter was past, and spring came on, and summer, and he was shrived and christened. His name was John; John Postoak, for Postoak was the translation of his name.

Then, being converted, he called to mind the instructions of Issatiwamba; a duty was a duty, whether to tribe or to church. So he asked the priest, kneeling at confession: must he go to the authorities? For a time the priest said nothing, sitting in the box with the odor of incense coming off him, the smell of holiness, and he who now was called Postoak watching through the panel. Then he said, calling him now as always My Son, that was a matter to be decided within himself, between his heart and his head. And he said as before, Bless me, father: knowing. And the priest put forth his hand and blessed him, making the sign of the Cross above his head, for the priest knew well what would follow when he went before the authorities and told what he had told the day when the priest first found him in the bearskin, outside the church where Christ hung on the wall.

He went then to the sergeant of the guard, Delgado, and standing there told it in Spanish, what had been done on the mound and how and his share in the thing, and offered himself this second time, as instructed by Issatiwamba, not to lay the plague, however, but rather to lay the guilt in his own breast. Delgado heard him through, listening with outrage in his face, and when it was done gave orders in a voice that rang like brass. Then was he in the pit indeed, with iron at his wrists and ankles. He dwelt in darkness, how many days he knew not; the year moved into September, the hottest weather; and then came forth under guard to face ourselves, Governor and witnesses, in the formalities which ensued and here have been transcribed even as he spoke, including whatever barbarisms, all his own. So it was and here he stands, having told it this third time: God be his witness.

Q. If he had anything to add or take from this deposition, it having been read to him. Answered that he has nothing to add or take, and that what he has said is the truth under the obligation of the oath he took at the outset, which he affirms and certifies and says he is twenty-four years old, and he subscribes with me and the witnesses over the citation I certify:

Witnessed:	*he signs this*	John the Baptist
Joseph of Silva	Chisa- **X** -hahoma	of Elquezable
Frsco Amangual	HIS MARK	Lt Col Governor

DISPOSITION: BY THE GOVERNOR. In the said Garrison this September 27th 1797 without delay I, Mr John the Baptist of Elquezable, Lieutenant Colonel of Cavalry of the Royal Army, Provisional Governor of the Province of Mississippi, in view of finding the conclusion of the present proceedings, commanded that the original fifteen useful leaves be directed to the Lord Commanding General, Marshal of the Country, Sir Peter de Narva, that they may serve to inform him in reviewing my disposition (tendered subject to his agreeing in the name of His Most Christian Majesty) to wit:

Free him.

First: in that he has renounced his former worship which led him to participate in these atrocities, and intends now therefore (I am assured by the priest, Friar Joseph Manuel Gaetan) to serve as a missionary among his heathen people. Second: in that we are even now preparing to depart this barbarous land, being under orders to leave it to them of the North. And third, lastly: in that the victims were neither of our Nation nor our Faith.

For which I sign with my present scrivener:

J the B
/ of El

A Benito
Courbiere.